THE BEST SMALL FICTIONS

ELAINE *guest editor* CHIEW

NATHAN *series editor* LESLIE

MICHELLE *assistant editor* ELVY

Sonder Press
New York
www.thesonderpress.com

ISBN 979-8-218-15847-7

First U.S. Edition 2022

Best Small Fictions Founding Series Editor: Tara Lynn Masih.

Cover Design by Chad Miller
Distribution via Ingram

THE BEST SMALL FICTIONS

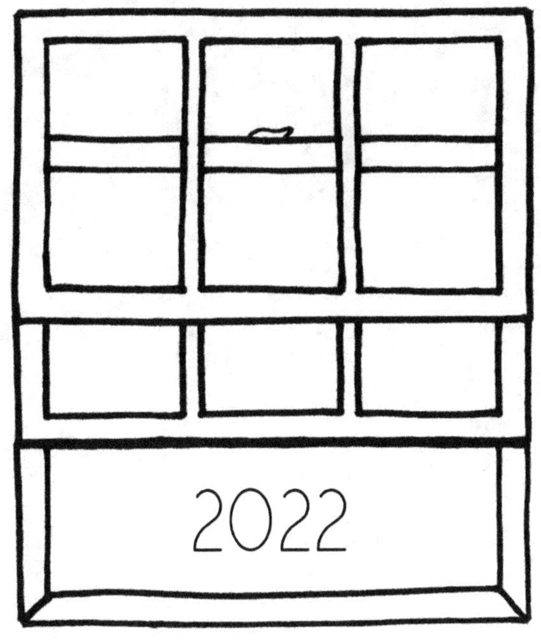

CONT *contents* ENTS

SPOTLIGHTED JOURNALS

THE MOST DIFFICULT ASPECT of editing *Best Small Fictions* has always had to do with putting into words the efforts the editorial team takes to provide a cohesive whole. Impressionistic and haphazard at best; overly sweeping and cherry-picking, at worst.

Yet here I am, in May of 2022, attempting to create a sense of order amongst what feels to be so much unnecessary brilliance. Unnecessary? Perhaps. Compared to food, shelter, and water. Still for many, myself included, words and the stories they formulate and the ideas they conjure help, are necessary even, and perhaps most of all, in times of crisis. More to the point: stories offer to the attentive reader the sense of meaning amongst the seemingly meaninglessness. This year's stunning work included.

Is literature a mirror of our current reality or the generator of it? For many years, I was of the belief that both usually apply—that literature creates as much meaning as it reflects. Though it seems this is still the case, one might suggest that, at times, some literature has more recently become at least partially reactive—understandably set back on its heels as a result of paradigm shifts, unforeseen political disasters, pandemics, wars. Who needs fiction when the news seems like fiction? Who needs characters when one is worried about surviving until the next month? Yet change, is the nature of reality; nothing is ever truly stable. Still, we crave it. We may be entertained by dystopia but certainly we prefer the coziness of the couch and our emotional support animals.

I admit I prefer a compelling individual vision not necessarily connected quite so directly to what we might read on news sites and watch on our multifarious screens. Perhaps I believe there is something inherently odd and personal or vision-oriented about the most searing versions of literature. Perhaps I believe literature can and should elevate the experience of the every-person, should transcend it even. Though it will be for you, dear reader, to decide if the pieces contained within this year's anthology reflect our current reality or shape it.

As always, many thanks to the editorial team, advisors, and interns who helped so much with this year's anthology. A huge thank you to Elaine Chiew, who was a delight to work with this year, for her willingness to read so many pieces and pick the best of the best. I would also like to offer special thanks to Michelle Elvy, who for the past four years has been a stalwart assistant editor, source of support and astute reader.

Thank you also to Sonder Press and to Elena Stiehler, who makes this project possible and has continued to be resilient over these past four years despite tough times for small presses. Finally, I would especially like to thank Chad Miller this year, who continues to produce the beautiful illustrations which serve as the front and back covers to this anthology.

I hope you enjoy these many small fictions—from names both familiar and new. There is much to ponder within these pages, much to also revere.

Nathan Leslie
Series Editor, *Best Small Fictions*
Spring, 2022

OUT OF THE DEADNESS of two years of lockdown, quarantine, and loss of human lives, we are now pulling new breaths into our lungs—I feel a little like Sleeping Beauty, awakened by the kiss of life—as dining-in for larger parties is allowed, borders reopen, masks are removed, and people jump on planes. It feels like a long time has passed but all in the blink of an eye.

Last year was perhaps the year I read the most (of all the years I lived!)—in all areas from fiction to nonfiction to academic research—and yet, there was a deadness to my reading. I barely remember most of what I read, I don't remember feeling much of anything. This perhaps is one of my pandemic realisations: certain events, though fathomable by logic and science, are too cataclysmic for the heart to wrap around; there is too much loss, and grief is stretched too thin.

Thus, when I read the *Best Small Fictions'* selections for 2022 that series editor Nathan Leslie sent, I was caught by surprise. A swamp of emotions like the return of blood rush to leg and limb after pins and needles. I am pricked by the punctum of startling images—ruby red nail polish nestled in the sand, a racecar tattoo, towns that resembled an old Hollywood set—images evoked by each 'story in miniature, a work of art carved on a grain of rice', as Tara Masih described the best of flash fiction. Each miniature story's capacity to bring to sudden life a burst of emotion, a flash of sharp insight: I experienced it as a welcome back to life, a tender, quivering cradle of how good it is to be able to feel. Characters swanned through—a daughter made of glass, a chicken-rice seller's wife whose name we barely learn—and they stayed for lunch; settings (reunion barbecues for Confucius' descendants, a father looting rolls of toilet paper from a Japanese bingo gathering) made me laugh out loud.

It is an incredible privilege to be asked to select these twelve spotlighted stories, also a very hard job, because all the stories contained a diamond-like brilliance, a flash doing its thing. It is thus an inherently subjective exercise.

In the end, it came down to time—what each was doing with the concept of time took me somewhere new, some place unexpected—which in a way, was a reflection of how we lost time, or time was stolen from us, then returned in surprising ways. Consider Sudha Balagopal's heartbreaking "Life Times Nine" narrates the love between two people spanning their entire lives from nine years old to eighty-one, so much love encapsulated in so few shared moments. In Farah Ali's "Ten New Words", I was struck by how much time it would take for a Muslim refugee single mother to learn ten new words in English when her baby is sick.

Occasionally, as in Jo Goren's "Instructions for Visiting Our State's Correction Facility", time sits heavy for a mother visiting her son in prison, and time is measured by putting one foot in front of the other, by making lists, because by the time we get to the end of the list, we have moved through time. Though not heartbreak. Heartbreak isn't so easily navigable in Nicholas Maistros' "The Sudden Ocean", as a son revisits the trauma of a mother's suicide again and again: a reminder that trauma is a rupture in time, its recovery a loop, that what returns isn't the event itself, which is experienced as a kind of absence, but its shock on the body. One word, as Maurice Ruffin's "Cocoon" intimates, can sometimes hurtle us back to these unspent memories, memories that have lodged pain not yet broken down or composted within the body. The body. Time plays out in stories, time also plays out in our bodies, "like half-moons peeking out behind the curves of bones," a time-march etched on the body of the mother in Amy Wang's "Ama". The mother there says, "Your body is the only thing you have to keep to yourself."

One body, one life. We all have the one life, as Nardine Taleb's "My Aunt Doesn't Care In Four Different Languages" illuminates; between the aunt and the niece is a span of some three decades, and this could mean everything or nothing, or looked at another way, three decades is a lot of time for a lot of mess to happen, but "life is so beautiful," as the aunt said, "in small moments between the mess." We have bonds, chemical and alchemical, those formed in childhood being especially strong, as in Tisha Marie Reichle-Aguilera's five Latino cousins, in "We are Five Cousins", manifesting a collective girl-power that can trump diminishment and masochism.

In our time, we can no longer talk about time without talking about place and the Anthropocene. Czesław Miłosz wrote that even as "cities fall asleep, each in its hour", we realise that "there is too much world". Little Akari in Yume Kitasei's beautiful fable, "A Too Small Room", dreams of seeing the world beyond her too-small room, but is the world ready to receive a too-big feminine imagination? We measure time as linear progress, what we don't do is build out or expand incrementally through great effort the walls of the universe, because if we could envision time as space, it would be able to fit all of us, all the spectrum and spectres of us, all the colours and potentialities of us. This monumental collective effort will ache, our muscles will grow weary, as Hanne Larsson's nifty tale about a man holding up the sky in "The Aching Wait" narrates.

Certain things are important in the calculus of time, the passing of time: these things form chemical elements that show us glimpses of understanding about something wrought on large-scale, like cataclysms, but they do not yield the full picture. Things like memory, language, imagination, and myth-making are important. Things like bodies and bonding are important. The folding and unfolding of moments are important. The circularity of time, the missing chunks of it. These are important too. Pip Robertson's "All the Important Elements", a beautifully crafted 'trail of word clues' around a tragic mystery, tells us so.

Thank you to all the contributors of *Best Small Fictions* 2022, and particularly these twelve stories, for the gift of emotions, delivered time and again in lance-like fashion, economy and the suddenness and versatility of language. Be nicked, be nostalgic, be challenged. Refresh your spirit here.

Elaine Chiew
Guest Editor, *Best Small Fictions*
Spring, 2022

SPOTLIGHTED

STORIES

TEN NEW WORDS

farah ali

IN MY DELIRIUM, I think about the word leishmaniasis. Leishmaniasis: a parasitic disease found in the tropics and southern Europe. Caused by the Leishmania parasites, spread by the bite of sand flies. The word rings within my skull, over and over again. When the baby cries and I roll over to him, slowly, head throbbing, and pat his little body, I hear leishmaniasis, three times, seven times, a hundred times. I think, the baby is bringing on the disease, the baby is the disease, he brought it from his father to give to me. I crawl away to the edge of the bed and still the word is there in my ears. I stumble to the strip of table below the narrow window and shake out two tablets from a jar. I wash them down with yesterday's water in a glass. The street below is empty except for two boys, who are singing and walking, loud and drunk.

When the fever goes down and I resurface, the baby is a small, sleeping body again. Nobody I know has leishmaniasis. It is one in the night. My baby and I are in a hotel room in Europe. I do not know the name of my sickness. It has been four days now of the delirium coming and going. I do not know when it will return, and I am afraid of it. The first time it had happened, I floated into a state of wakeful dreaming. I saw flames, I saw burnings, I saw liars' tongues being pulled out and nailed to the backs of heads. Later, limp and damp and weakened, I wished for the baby's father.

There is nothing to eat in the room. I put the baby in the stroller and slowly, slowly walk to the elevator, stopping every few steps and holding my chest and moaning into the scarf wrapped around my neck and mouth. Breathing is painful. On the sidewalk people push past unseeingly. They are light and I am tar pitch. From the shop on the corner, I collect apples and yogurt pots. The man behind the register says words I don't understand. I hold up different currency notes, and he shakes his head and says more words. Behind me, the line grows longer, and people shift from foot to foot and mumble. I empty my wallet on the small counter and wipe the sweat off my forehead. Shaking his head, the man picks out what he needs. The line concaves as I maneuver the stroller out of the shop. On the way back I cry, unnoticed. Upstairs in my room, just inside the door, I lay down on the floor, the baby kicking his legs in his stroller.

When my ears start hurting, I scoop out yogurt with my fingers and swallow more medicine. When the baby cries I put him at my breast, his warm face against my feverish skin. Dairy and painkillers. I think, *It is so bad for a baby to drink painkillers.* My laugh is a moan.

If the baby's father were here, he would have done the right things. Fed me, rocked the baby. But he is in another continent. I have not spoken to him. I cannot remember if it is because he has not called me. I do not know if he knows where I am. *Who knows where we are?* I wonder, stroking the baby's cheek. Sleepily I imagine calling the baby's father, asking him to come to us.

On the seventh morning, I drag us outside again. I stop a taxi and hold up the book of tourist phrases and point at the word hospital. The movement of the traffic and the pedestrians makes me feel nauseous, and the cloudy daylight feels too strong. The driver stops at a hospital and I thank him in his language. At the reception I struggle to explain, frantically turning pages in the phrase book. The woman points toward a hall and says, "Blood test," and I lurch gratefully in that direction. The man with the syringe speaks fast, and confusion is beginning to flood me again. He points and snaps, "Baby, baby," and I understand. I shift my sleeping infant to one side and free my arm for the needle. Afterward, on a plastic chair, weighted down with fatigue, ears hurting, I think about how the baby's father used to walk around the house speaking other languages, ten new words a day, leaving messages on the phone, when away, in foreign words, coming back with small presents and making me repeat things I didn't understand, telling me softly to try, how could I grow if I didn't try, did I like being dull, did I like my new perfume, did I like his hands pulling my hair.

I wake up when someone shakes my shoulder. It is an elderly woman, and she is holding my baby. I cry out and she frowns and says, "Tsk, you sleep, baby fall. I catch. Like this." She hands me back my child and I hold him close. "Where is baby father?" she asks accusingly. My son is now wailing, and I do not know how to answer the woman and unbutton my shirt modestly at the same time, and I am now dizzy, there is pain at the base of my skull, and I want to rest my head against the baby's father's chest, but he is so far away because I had shouted to him, "We are done, we are done, we are done." I had broken a mirror. Pain travels up and down my jaw. My son latches on. The woman shakes her head, pulls some notes out of her large bag, stuffs them into my hand and walks off. She is kind. The baby's father used to bring me presents. He is laughing at all of this. He is speaking this language. He is bringing me water. He is holding my jaw and making me say "thank you" in ten different ways.

Farah Ali is from Pakistan. Her work has been anthologized in the 2020 Pushcart Prize as well as received special mention in the 2018 Pushcart anthology. Her stories have appeared in *Shenandoah, The Arkansas International, The Southern Review, Kenyon Review, Copper Nickel, Ecotone, The Colorado Review,* and elsewhere. *People Want to Live* is her first collection.

LIFE TIMES NINE

sudha balagopal

NINE:

THE AGE YOU yank the hair ties off my pigtails. I slap you, and you stand there, fists curled, screaming that your mom said never to hit a girl. At lunch, I relent, offer you a bite of my chocolate cake, and ask why you have nine fingers. Also, the age I understand the pinky finger of your left hand is fused to your ring finger.

Eighteen:

The age you ask me to prom and I go buoyant, like the hot air balloons we watch from your backyard. The pin hidden in my satin-ribboned corsage of baby pink roses pierces your fused finger, and I stanch the blood with a napkin. When I ask if doctors recommend surgery to separate the fingers—it would be impossible to wear a ring when you get married—you burrow the hand inside your pocket. Also, the age we split up. You tell me our colleges are separated by 999 miles and we should date other people. I hate you.

Twenty-seven:

The age I marry my spouse, return to our hometown to care for ailing parents and move into a house a street away from you—by accident, not design. When I see you while walking the dog, I shush my heart for cheat-fluttering yet raise an arm in a tentative gesture. You grin, relay an arcing wave back. Also, the age I run into you at a city council meeting to advocate for a dog park, and I must scoot over to accommodate the crowd until I feel your body's oh-so-familiar warmth.

Thirty-six:

The age I get a divorce, because my ex-husband's mother didn't teach him he should never hit a woman, and I fumble-flounder to glue the pieces he broke. I discover you're my nine-year-old's homeroom teacher, tell you he struggles with multiplication. Also, the age I observe your ten fingers and the broad gold band. I want to ask if the surgeon sliced through bone, whether the pinky finger has autonomy, whether it can exist independently, whether separation hurts.

Forty-five:

The age my teen invites yours to prom and I pull out my memory box. The withered flowers on the corsage you once placed on my wrist are gossamer delicate, the satin ribbon spotted with your rust-colored DNA. You give my son a stern lecture and instructions: no drinking, no drugs, no hanky-panky, drop off by 1:00 A.M. Also, the age I want to ask if you cannot recall the chemistry of our incandescent emotions, the intramolecular forces in our hungry kisses. Maybe you do.

Fifty-four:

The age you take early retirement to open a neighborhood coffee shop. As I place the order on that first day, you say school administration is best left to someone younger. I begin my love affair with the espresso I must have every day at your cafe, where you're never without a towel draped on one shoulder, the apron around your middle, or five minutes to sit with me. Also, the age I notice the missing gold band from your ring finger.

Sixty-three:

The age a kitchen fire engulfs your cafe, and you battle both insurance and contractors while three other cafes have sprouted within a mile. They offer fancy lattes, drinks with clever names, and free Wi-Fi. Also, the age you decide to sell your place, leaving me wracked with caffeine withdrawal and a craving for you that no upstart cafe can soothe.

Seventy-two:

The age I see you shuffle, a cane in your right hand, in the same park where we walked our dogs. I ask how you're doing. When you take umbrage—rising tall to negate the stoop in your spine—and vehemently declare everything's just fine, I tell you that warms my otherwise discontented heart. Although I'm physically okay, I yearn for my children to remember my birthday, to have my grandchildren call so I can hear their voices. Also, the age you reach out your hand and I take it, four of your fingers hugging mine. The pinky finger hangs listless.

Eighty-one:

The age I read in the obits that you've passed, and I feel like a portion of my life is getting sectioned off. When I learn you'd asked to be cremated, an aloneness sweeps into my aging cells—what remains of you will be ash. At the viewing, I memorize and embed details:

perfect waxy face, hair combed and stuck to your skull, lips arranged in an uptilt. Also, the age I lean over to caress your crossed arms, notice the left hand on top. I lift the arm, tuck the hand inside your pocket.

Sudha Balagopal is honored to have her fiction in many fine literary journals including *Matchbook* where "Life Times Nine" was first published. Her highly commended novella in flash, *Things I Can't Tell Amma*, was published by Ad Hoc Fiction in 2021. She is the author of a novel, *A New Dawn* and two short story collections. Her work is listed in *Wigleaf* Top 50 (2019, 2021) and appears in *Best Microfiction* 2022.

INSTRUCTIONS FOR VISITING OUR STATE'S CORRECTION FACILITY

jo goren

I.   PUT YOUR DISAPPOINTMENT WHERE it can easily be found on your return home.

2.   Dress in modest clothing, nothing above the knee, low cut, form fitting, break away type pants, or clothing with inappropriate holes/rips.

3.   Leave your driver's license and car key at the desk along with your son's prisoner number, which you've written on the palm of your hand. Put twenty dollars in the lobby box, that will spit out a debit card for the vending machines inside the visitor's room.

4.   After the metal detector alarm sounds detecting your underwire bra, go to the dollar store; buy a sports bra; change in a cold bathroom. Say nothing when the correction officer reminds you to wear a longer skirt next time. Don't think about the next time. Get through today.

5.   Squint under harsh fluorescent lights in the room, where one wall is painted with a mural of positive times ahead for the inmates, and another lined with vending machines. Hug your son, be thankful, his eyes are clear free of drugs and alcohol, though you know this condition is temporary.

6.   Don't encourage his anger when he says, "The CO who hassled you about your clothes is a real dick." Listen when he says, "Time goes fast here," nodding his shaved head up and down in agreement with himself. Note, the hour will not go fast.

7.   Use the debit card to buy the burritos he points to while he stands behind the yellow line for inmates. Watch him eat with care, wiping crumbs from his lips with a paper napkin; remember how he looked in the mirror on rides to school, how he checked for a hair out of place, or food on his teeth.

8.   Do not look at the other inmates or visitors. Be grateful your son is over six feet tall

and has a look that says, "Don't fuck with me."

9.   Regarding his dark eyes and handsome face, your mind will wander to the sweet toddler who built jails out of Legos and said, "Look Mommy, jail." You feared then this play could be prescient. Blame yourself, the divorce.

10.   When he says he'll never be back in jail, try to believe him.

Jo Goren writes and illustrates. A nominee for a Pushcart Prize 2021, her stories are in *The Ilanot Review, Blink-Ink, The Woolf* and *Inverted Syntax Postcards*. She's on twitter @drawing4dollars.

A TOO SMALL ROOM

yume kitasei

AKARI WAS BORN IN a room no bigger than a sigh. There was no door. As she grew, the room grew too—but only so much, and then she was forced to stop growing. She had to sit with her legs folded up beneath her chin, her long hair down around her ankles. She didn't wonder if there was more to the world than the room, she only knew the world wasn't big enough for her.

She stretched, shimmied, scratched at the walls, and cried out with a voice she didn't know she had.

Mei, the woodcutter's daughter, walked through the forest. She was looking for wood to cut for the house she would build for herself.

The axe on her shoulder was rusted and heavy, stolen from her brother. In her backpack was a knife, a raggedy blanket, needle and thread. Also, a sack of rice, saved grain by stray grain for five years, without anyone in her family noticing.

Mei spotted bamboo, straight and tall enough for her to cut, if she wanted to prove to herself that she could do a thing she had always been told she couldn't.

Akari, in the too small space, thought she heard a voice that wasn't hers. She pressed her ear against the wall. The wall was singing. Or not the wall. How?

Her world began to shake. She nearly lost her head as the axe blade bit through the top of her room.

The bamboo fell, and the woodcutter's daughter stumbled back in shock. A girl no bigger than her arm crawled out of the chamber of the bamboo.

Mei and Akari regarded each other in the soft green light that filtered down through the forest.

Then Akari looked around and began to weep. The world was much bigger than she had thought. She might have crawled back into the bamboo, but Mei reached out and picked her up like a doll.

"What were you doing in there?" Mei asked as if either of them had ever chosen to be born.

Mei laid out the old blanket and set Akari down on it. She went about cutting more wood.

By evening, she'd accomplished little. Mortified, she lay down next to Akari and listened to the crickets and the shush-shush of the leaves. Perhaps she ought to go home. It was too hard. Most likely, she would fail.

But next morning, Mei woke feeling stronger. In the other girl's eyes, she felt the tendon and sinew in her arms grow taut. She cut trees, made a clearing, built a house. The wood she chose was wrong: the frame splintered, and it fell down. But her second one stood straight, and the roof kept out the rain.

Meanwhile, Akari grew taller and learned to speak. She named herself. She never came inside even in the snow, so Mei built a porch under the roof, and Akari slept there with her toes delightfully cold and sticking over the edge.

This is how the Governor's son saw her when he came riding through the woods. He was startled by the crude hut, and this strange girl beneath a patched quilt. He stopped and woke her. She was only as tall as a child. Her fingers were delicate, her body slender and twisted.

She answered him in a reedy voice. "Go with you? Where?"

Mei came out of the house and glared at this man.

"I didn't know there is more beyond the forest," Akari said.

"Don't go," said Mei.

But for Akari, the forest was still a too small room.

The Governor's son lived in a busy town. He gave her a fine room, but Akari preferred the night sky. She missed Mei. Everyone in town stared at her. But Akari continued to grow.

In the forest, Mei's rice dwindled, then was gone. She had thought when the time came, she and Akari would journey to town together, but now Mei was alone. At last, she could no longer put off what was necessary, so she built a sled, piled it with wood, and pulled it all the way to town. When she got there, she could barely move. Her whole body ached.

She set up in the marketplace next to the other wood sellers and watched as they sold their wood one by one. All she got were funny looks. Darkness fell, and her stomach growled loudly. She trembled with exhaustion. In the dusk, no one could tell she was an eccentric woman in men's clothing.

A man hurried up. "Thank goodness you're still here. My master will take all of it." He gave her a heavy purse, and she followed the man to a large house: the Governor's!

The man was surprised to discover his woodcutter was a woman, but now that it was at the house, wood was wood.

Akari was sitting on the porch. She had cut her hair short to save time combing it, and her fingers were black from ink: she was learning to read and write.

The two women embraced.

"Tell me," Akari said when they were comfortable. "How big is the world?" She heard of strange places in books and wanted to know if they were real.

Mei stretched her tired limbs. Her life curved ahead like a bend in a road. "It's as big as you can imagine."

The next night, Akari took a horse and rode towards the moon. It was big and orange and couldn't be far. She left the horse and climbed a mountain.

At the top, she reached out with both hands and stood on her tiptoes. She reached out and caught the wind. Away and up she went, all the way to the moon.

When the Governor's son returned to the hut, he found Mei singing and sweeping the floor. "Why are you so happy?" he asked. He had looked everywhere for Akari.

"You'll never find her," said Mei. "She is out there looking for the walls of the universe."

Yume Kitasei (www.yumekitasei.com) is a Japanese and American writer of speculative fiction. Her stories have appeared in publications including *Catapult, SmokeLong Quarterly, Ruminate, Baltimore Review,* and *Fractured Lit.* Her debut novel, *The Deep Sky,* is forthcoming from Flatiron Books in 2023. She lives in Brooklyn with two cats, Boondoggle and Filibuster, and chirps occasionally @YumeKitasei.

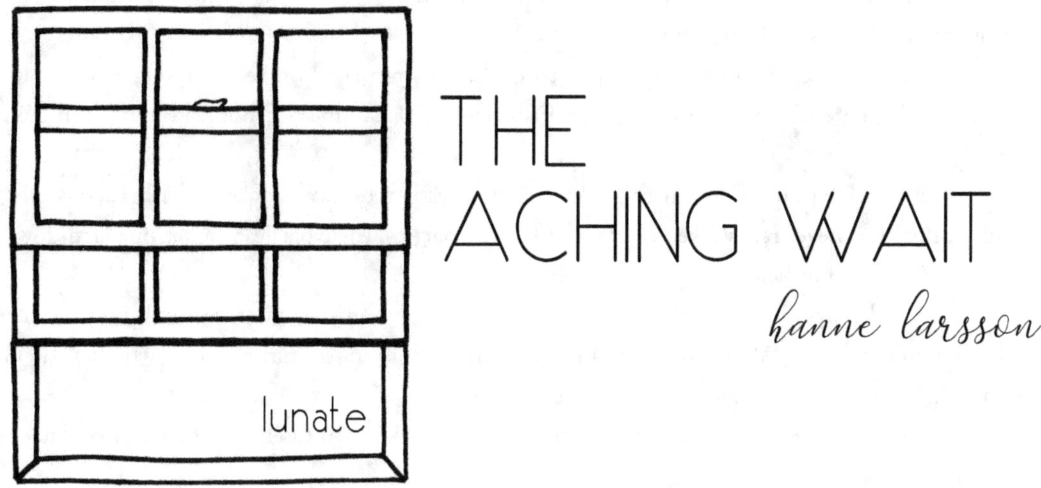

THE ACHING WAIT

hanne larsson

HE WAS TIRED: OF holding the sky, the weight of the clouds, how the rising puddles would flood his furred boots, chilling his toes. It seemed to rain more now, but Lars had been told not to move. They would be back shortly.

He'd never been good with time. The days passed: rising into bright, into setting, into gloaming and then twinkle. Enough time to study how everything moved around him. He enjoyed the silence, eventually. But he ached from not moving.

And then they arrived. Loud, brash, banging. Not who he was waiting for.

Smaller. Pink. Mewling, quick-footed and such short little lives, milling about his feet, crawling up his legs.

Lars longed to kick them. His sacred duty was to hold the sky up even as he stifled yawns. The ants chipped away at him and still he stayed. It was like they couldn't see how he was integral to their survival. He sighed, adjusting his grip. Rumble. They looked up in fear, but quickly forgot. Always more for them to do before long winters settled their white coats on his shoulders.

His kin would be back soon to help. Shoulder some of the load. His feet and wrists were numb.

It was sunny the day he heard the long crack from under his feet and above his head. The little ants toiling below paid it no mind, but he hoped for his brothers.

The water seeped, then steadied to a flow. Rose past his knees, to his hips. He thought about leaving, shifted his grip on the sky. It wobbled. He prayed for help.

Days passed; the surge continued. The ants left, and grateful, he wriggled his toes in his damp boots. His head drooped, and Lars knew, somehow, that being alone would be his life. It was ok. Trees and bushes had sprouted on him over the years, keeping him warm and playing their own sweet music. Never wholly alone.

The water came up to his belly-button; the ants returned on vessels to float past Lars-as-an-island. There was no sign of his kin. Fish tickled his submerged body, keeping him from sleep.

An owl family built a nest in one of his head-trees, amusing him with their sibling squawking. He'd never really liked his brothers, their parties, their battles. He let one arm down. The sky rumbled but held fast.

He alternated arms for a bit; the water heading toward his chest, reflecting on the true meaning of his task. About whether his brothers had pranked him. About whether they'd forgotten their youngest. His eyes started to flutter shut.

He let the other arm down. The clouds wonked a bit to his right, then carried on. He smiled.

When the water reached his nose, he took one deep long breath, held it and finally closed his eyes for sleep. He would startle awake when they clomped back over the hill. The owls sighed their goodnight.

Hanne is a British Swede who longs for the 95% humidity and hawker centre food of her childhood. Her stories are fed by environmental science topics, moss-covered rocks masquerading as trolls and what-if scenarios. Her words can be found in *Splonk*, *Twin Pies Literary*, *Lunate Fiction*, *The Citron Review* and other web-nooks. She lurks on Twitter: @hannelarssoni.

THE SUDDEN OCEAN

nicholas maistros

WHAT I REMEMBER OF my mother then.

I was nine.

I was sitting in the car while she finished packing it, giving me encouraging smiles through the window.

We drove. She sang.

There were hotel rooms. There were drive-in movies. There was shopping for new-life clothes and playing games inside the circular racks. There was Carhenge, a roadside tourist attraction somewhere out west, old cars piled atop each other to replicate Stonehenge. A picture taken by a stranger of my mother and me in the middle where the Druid rituals—or their rusted-car equivalent—would have taken place.

There were mountains.

There was lying in bed together or on reclined car seats while she stroked my hair and told me things as though I were not her son.

There was a place called Welcome, where the car broke down. We waited under the big sky and watched the trucks, slow in the distance, slow, slow, then fast as they blew past, tossing our hair about, until the truck that stopped for us. Another hotel outside Welcome. A rental car in the morning. I asked what happened to the old one. *Carhenge,* my mother said.

Then, finally, there was water. No more road. And panic in my mother's eyes, a panic that, even at nine, I realized had been there the whole time. There was one more hotel room—this one with a kitchen. There was, on the first morning of that last hotel room, a breakfast of glazed doughnuts from the hotel lobby that my mother warmed in the microwave. *This is how I liked them when I was a girl,* she said. I took a bite. I took another. I said I didn't like it, and she looked at me, quizzical, hurt. I felt a shame that I couldn't fathom, then or now, a responsibility, which couldn't have been mine but somehow was, for the sudden ocean that met my mother.

There was a man she met at the beach, a late-night monster movie while I waited for her return, teenagers swimming naked in the monster movie and me turning away at the moment of the young man's nudity—how often, later, would I scold my nine-year-old self for turning away? What did I think would happen if I saw? My mother returned before the end of the movie. She went to the bathroom. She cried. I turned up the movie.

Then, an airport, a plane ride of which all I can remember is the back of my mother's head looking out the window, down at the blocks of pastures and farmland that I pretended were entire states.

There was my father at the next airport. He looked sad for her. We had dinner at the airport Chili's, of which I still only remember the back of my mother's head, and my father's hand on hers, and my father asking me how I liked my little adventure and what was my favorite part. *The doughnut*, I'd said.

Stories and essays by Nicholas Maistros have appeared in *The Baltimore Review*, *Witness*, *Washington Square Review*, *The Literary Review*, *Sycamore Review*, *Nimrod*, *Colorado Review*, *Beloit Fiction Journal*, *Bellingham Review*, and *Longleaf Review*, among other publications. He holds an MFA in creative writing from Colorado State University, where he taught courses in literature, composition, and drama. Nicholas has also worked in Broadway merchandising, nonprofit finance, filmmaking, and food service. He lives with his partner in Dayton, Ohio.

WE ARE FIVE COUSINS

tisha marie reichle-aguilera

WE GATHER IN EL Centro on Christmas Eve. We wear dresses made of velvet and lace. Tia sewed them from the same pattern, each a different color. Viejitas at church ooh and aah when we pose by the Virgen de Guadalupe. No one cares that the dress is too tight across Elisa's chest, too short on Maribel so she slouches, cuts off the circulation on Delia's arms, and hangs all loose on Larissa. Only Joanna's fits perfect. We'd rather wear something else.

We fidget on kneelers and hold our breaths when incense wafts by. We falsetto each holy song, squeeze tight on "peace be with you" handshakes. We interrupt "Our Father who art in heaven" with "Red Rover Red Rover" under our breath and swing our arms until Tias glare hard. We lift our hands so high at the end, we almost touch "the Kingdom, the Power and the Glory." We cough in unison when the prayer ends.

We walk to communion, step touch, step touch, like brides without bouquets. Hands folded with the middle fingers down, our thumbs touching our nose tips up like pigs. We stick out our tongue for "The Body of Christ" and say "Amen" extra loud. We fill with our mouths full of holy wine, gulp hard so it stings our noses. We stare out stained glass, long to be anywhere but in this pew.

When mass is over, we run across Brighton Avenue to the merry-go-round. We each grab a bar, run faster and faster, round and round, then jump on and hold tight. We stretch back, tilt our faces up to the sun, so trensas and curls hang down to the dirt. The spinning slows and Joanna is the first to hop off. She drops to one knee, ignores the scrape of pain, and runs toward the swings. We follow, pump our legs higher and higher. All five glide side by side. Until Joanna lets go, flies farther than anyone in the history of swing jump outs. We clap and cheer. Even brothers are impressed. Delia jumps too, lands on hands and shins, spits out a mouthful of grass. We drag our feet to slow down.

We ignore Tias regañas about torn tights, scuffed shoes, dirty dresses, and wild hair, race down the block to Nana's for tamales and regalos. She grabs our cheeks with her masa covered hands, squeals cariños and kisses our foreheads. Her spit dries there. We wipe hard to remove bright pink lips when she's not looking. Nana wants girls who wear aprons and make cookies. We want to shoot hoops in her driveway with Tio's deflated ball.

On the way home from Nana's, we detour around by Circle K for slushies and walk home the long way down Dogwood Road. On the corner of Orange, three guys sit on crates around a folding table in their garage. We stop walking. One shuffles blue-backed cards. One takes a long drink from his fat green bottle. The third one stands to put on a new record.

We dance when "Oye Coma Va" comes on. We love Tito Puente.

They see us. "Hola chamaquitas. You got some movidas."

"Shut up, Chuy," Joanna yells to him. To us she says, "His sister's in my class. She calls him a bum."

Chuy's friends laugh. He takes another swig and deals the cards, even to the empty space. "Who's gonna play?" He taps the hand still face down on the table.

Delia is the first to move.

Maribel follows, whispers, "Do you know how?"

"I beat my brothers every time." Delia slaps our remaining dollar on the table.

"Five card stud," Chuy says, offers us a beer.

We are five cousins who take home five dollars from guys who underestimated girls. We don't go straight home. We climb the tallest tree at the end of our block, look south across the desert to the Mexicali mountains. We wonder where could we win more money? How much would it take to buy five houses all our own?

Later that night, we lie in the front room on the pile of blankets Tias threw down. We fall asleep and dream about our grown-up fortunes.

Chicana Feminist and former Rodeo Queen, Tisha Marie Reichle-Aguilera (she/her) writes so the desert landscape of her childhood can be heard as loudly as the urban chaos of her adulthood. She is obsessed with food. A former high school teacher, she earned an MFA at Antioch University Los Angeles and is an Annenberg Fellow at the University of Southern California. She works for literary equity through Women Who Submit. You can read her work at http://tishareichle.com/.

RIME ICE WILL BE important in this story. Crystal-like on the downwind side of objects, disguising blades of mountain grass as feathers, dressing trees in lace. It will be the reason the parents deviate from the track and take the longer, more exposed route. *What a wonderland.*

Experience will be important. The father, for as long as the girl can remember, spreading out maps with lines as fine as fingerprints, memorising the ridgelines, river systems, flood routes, huts.

A best friend turning 16 will be important, creating a necessary diversion. The girl choosing not to go up the mountain because of the birthday party that evening, even though the parents will say it's just a day trip and she could do both. But she'll kill me if I'm late. *I'll come next time, promise.*

Kisses goodbye will be important in this story.

A rock will be important for as long as it takes to trip the mother so that she lands in such a way as to break, or at least badly sprain, her ankle. After that, the rock will no longer be important.

A sudden low-pressure weather event will be important, adding an element of surprise. *Wrap up everyone! No one forecast this but it's turning nasty out there!*

Spindly orange route markers placed at intervals to guide through the terrain will be important, despite appearing only in its early stages, prettily fringed with rime ice, before the dense obscuring fog, before the dark.

One bar of occasional cell phone reception will be important for raising false hope.

A good-looking 19-year-old will be important in this story, for the frisson of teenage promiscuity. A friend of someone's cousin, in town for one night, going to a party because he has nothing better to do, smiling across the room at the girl in a way that makes her blush and lower her eyes. Her friend (necessary diversion) noticing, pulling the girl aside. *Babe. Here's what to do.*

Waterproof outer layers, thermal fabric under layers, and appropriate footwear will all be important in this story although, ultimately, inadequate.

A mountain hut will be important, teasing with the possibility of a happy ending, if only it could be found. The father shining his headlamp around in the dark, finding fog, knowing the hut is close, knowing that if he could get his bearings, he could find his way there. (See again, experience. See again, spindly orange route markers).

Food will be important. The father's gloved hands struggling to open the bag of chocolate and nuts. The mother's jaw aching with cold making it impossible to chew. *Just have the chocolate then. Let it dissolve in your mouth.*

One o'clock in the morning will be important in this story. The girl, coming home later than she is allowed, pleased to find no one waiting up, tiptoeing through the dark house so as not to wake the parents, who she assumes are asleep in their bed, not thinking to check the garage for the car or go upstairs to their bedroom, just relieved she got away with it.

A tremendous heat flooding the body will be important. The mother, taking off her hat, her gloves, fumbling at the zip of her jacket while the father tries to divert her hands. *Keep them on. Fuck, please, keep them on.*

A lack of response will be important in this story. The father calling out in the dark and nothing coming back on the wind. The girl waking in the morning, head full of the night before, then noticing the odd quiet in the house and walking room to room. *Morning. Hellooo. Hello?*

A pillow improvised from the contents of a pack will be important. The father taking the softest items that weren't already being worn and arranging them under the mother's head. (See again, kisses.)

Proximity will be important. The dawn light revealing the mother, lying a short distance from the father, lying a short distance from the track, a short distance along which is the hut and a group of people waking in sleeping bags, listening to the rain hitting the roof, thinking, thank God we're not out in that. *Hey, anyone else hear that crazy wind in the night? Almost sounded like someone yelling?*

The mountain range will be important in this story, and in every subsequent story. All her life it has been visible from the girl's bedroom window. It will now be present no matter where she is: weighing on her shoulders, sharp in her throat, hard under her breastbone, waiting every night behind her eyes when she closes them to sleep.

———

Pip Robertson lives in Aotearoa New Zealand with her partner, daughter, and dog. She has stories published in print and online journals, including *Landfall, the Reading Room, trampset,* and *Necessary Fiction.*

COCOON

maurice carlos ruffin

MY FATHER NAMED HIS bug company "Stevens and Son" even before I came into the world. I found insects disgusting, but it was just me and him, so I did my best to keep my objections hidden. I certainly never told him about my proclivities.

I was a pretty good bug man in my teens and could tell what the infestation was by the faintest clues. Teeny tiny scratch marks on a pantry shelf were the sign of a mouse, for example. Whenever we came across something we'd never seen before—like that bellows-shaped mud nest in Ms. Berthelot's attic—I was the first to guess and was nearly always right. They were mud wasps. The males sipped nectar on swamp azaleas while the females built houses with their mouths.

Still, I grew tired of spending my weekends hunting vermin. My father was in his sixties and needed someone who would really put his back into the work. That's why he hired Tyronne Myers. Tyronne was into it. I had the impression that he had lived a hard life somewhere else. Yet, whenever I asked him about his past he just placed a hand on my shoulder, a situation I very much enjoyed, and chuckled.

"Can't stay wrapped in what you come from," he'd say. I was in my bedroom one night, alone I thought, when I sensed Tyronne near the door. I don't know if he saw me, in front of my mirror in a calico dress I'd bought at the thrift store on Carrollton Avenue. Quickly, I switched off the lamp, slipped on jeans in the dark, and left the house to meet my friends. The next morning, I quit. My father showed no emotion, but he took sick a year later and sold the company to Tyronne.

Years after I moved to New York to pursue a career in fashion design, I went back home. Tyronne never changed the name of the company and, to my surprise, he didn't seem shocked to see me with hair extensions and wearing a crinkled suede waistcoat of my creation.

He invited me into the house he was servicing to show me something he had found. He stooped and gave me a ghostly thing, lighter than a feather and so thin the lines on the palm of my hand were clearly visible through it.

"Do you know what that is?" he asked.

"It's what moths come from," I said.

Maurice Carlos Ruffin is the author of *The Ones Who Don't Say They Love You*, a New York Times Editor's Choice that was also longlisted for the Story Prize. His first book, *We Cast a Shadow*, was a finalist for the PEN/Faulkner Award, the Dayton Literary Peace Prize, and the PEN America Open Book Prize. Ruffin is the winner of several literary prizes, including the Iowa Review Award in fiction. A New Orleans native, Ruffin is a professor of Creative Writing at Louisiana State University, and the 2020-2021 John and Renee Grisham Writer-in-Residence at the University of Mississippi.

MY AUNT DOESN'T CARE IN FOUR DIFFERENT LANGUAGES

nardine taleb

I. SO I WAS THINKING today about that cup of black coffee you left sitting in the fridge because you said you can't—no matter what—throw away good things. Even if they are of no use to you anymore. You gave me old clothes from your closet, each piece costing over fifty dollars, still with their tags. I think you are going through a meltdown and you think you're just spring cleaning. We agree, with the wave of a hand, to not talk about this. Sometimes I wear your off-shoulder sweater and pretend I'm you, if that means I'm less me, because you've got the kind of confidence none of the other women in our family have. Fifty-five and now again single, you go shopping in the gaps of time you used to call me from the car saying, "Your uncle now has a fad for Home Depot and he's been in there for two hours." I wear your sweaters, which are baggy on me, and hope the world will want me a little more.

2. In public, people stare at us together: a middle-aged woman and a twenty-two-year-old. We laugh unrestrained, yelling, "Ya Allah Ya Allah!" as we catch our breaths. I realize now they are probably afraid of us, speaking in a language so unbelonging to an Ohio suburb. You never care how others see you. You open up to the world fearlessly like a child. "I don't give two pooping shits what people think," you say, always repeating words for enough emphasis. This is how you use English, since one word is never fierce enough for you. When Uncle divorces you, you curse him out in Arabic, then in Spanish, and then in French. I watch you, with wide eyes, as you tell him over the phone that he is a butt asshole.

3. Womanhood is a flimsy thing, thin as dog ears. One day I'm driving, music high, in a tight new top, singing so hard that other drivers turn and smile in my direction. The other day I'm sobbing, unsure how I got between my hangers in the back of the closet. Then I remember. I

was looking for the watch you passed down to me, which I stupidly lost somewhere in the arms of my closet. I miss the feeling of it in my hands, the cold silver that blinks back at me. I don't know why I'm crying over losing it, because I haven't lost you and that's more important. Maybe I'm crying because I'm shocked things can be lost so easily, when they're handed over with care.

4. No feeling is final, wrote Rilke. You hang this quote above your bathroom sink on an index card, in your handwriting.

5. One evening we joke about your boobs. Compare them to watermelons. "I'm juicy," you tease. You love being a woman. You love beauty. You look out from your balcony at the view and comment, "Life is so beautiful, in small moments between the mess." It's been two weeks since the official declaration of the divorce. Your son, my cousin, will die in a year. But we don't know that just yet, how loss will continue to come for you. Sometimes, mid-conversation, you stop and close your eyes, as if an aching has arrived and you are waiting for it to pass. I want to ask if closing your eyes works. I close my eyes hoping to shut the pain out, but that is when it mercilessly opens.

6. No feeling is final, wrote Rilke, but he didn't know you. How your feelings will always be there, taking on different shapes. I've seen several shades of grieving from you, all reflected on your face—Grey: when you were shocked he left you. Red: when you decided to work so hard you laughed for hours out of exhaustion. Creme: when you decided that memory is like an object on the menu. You can choose what to forget. Decide if you want the ketchup in the memory or on the side. If you loved the person sitting across from you, or if you didn't.

7. On a Saturday night, you take me out for a drive. I try to come up with excuses for my sad face, and then decide to just tell the truth. "I feel very alone," I say. I feel very silly saying this; how the endings of my little romantic relationships are nothing compared to the weight of your divorce. But you take my words seriously: "I understand, habibti. It all just takes practice, carrying it all."

8. And then, later, you decide to add with sass: "Besides, men are just hemeer. Like my husband. I'm better off adopting a hamster." We laugh until we choke on our spit.

9. At an outlet mall, I look up to find my ex window shopping, examining a suit. He has his usual face, unimpressed. I immediately wish you were here with me, to tell me what to do. How every part of me wants to take him into my arms as if he never left, but I know better. I know the wanting is not a wanting for a person, but for anything that will suppress the wanting itself.

He looks up and catches me looking. I don't turn away. We wave to each other. A million conversations run through my mind, but I am late to pick you up for a doctor's appointment. The wanting, like all things, will soon die out. I dig for my keys and go.

10. We sit in the balcony of your apartment, open to the main road. There is a lovely garden in the center, with a sign commemorating a child named Sam. You made me tea the way I like it; mixed with warm frothy milk and honey. Reminiscent of hot days in Cairo when I visited you there. You are moving back soon, perhaps to revisit your single life or scout a new one. Quietly, we count the balconies of other people, each apartment holding so many lives. "How many lives do you think are in there?" I ask quietly, counting each balcony with my finger. "One," you answer. "It will always be one."

———————————————

Nardine Taleb is an Egyptian-American writer and speech-language pathologist based in Cleveland, Ohio. Her work has appeared in *Hobart*, *The Commuter*, and *Frontier Poetry*.

THERE IS A GROVE behind my house in which things do not grow so much as crawl towards the nearest light. Even the plants cannot tell the difference between the sun and camphor; when I was twelve, I left my flashlight buried in the dirt for a week, and the bushes had devoured the batteries until there was not even a glow left behind. Ama says it is because I spent too long playing hide and seek in the trees as a child that I now find myself following streetlights, the dizzy red firetrucks, every bitter flash of white against the skyline. Ama says that she had an aunt once, who did the same thing, and now she is just another soft-spoiled fruit, withering in the dirt. *Annie*, Ama says, *her name was Annie. She married a white man but when it came time for them to leave it turned out he wasn't even serious about marrying her in the first place. So he left her and she had to slit her own throat, from jaw to jaw in a little red smile.* When I ask Ama why Auntie Annie didn't just use a bullet like the people in movies do, she draws the cleaver from the stack of kitchen knives and chops watermelon rinds into green blooms. *To pulverize your own brain like you pulverize fruit is to commit a sin*, Ama says. When I ask Ama why Auntie Annie married the white man in the first place, Ama tells me it was because she did not know the meaning of pride. Ama tells me it is best to marry a man without a shadow. *Only then can you be the only thing standing behind him*, Ama says.

Ama tells me that if a man ever offers to buy the sum of my organs, I should kick him in the shins and run away. *It's bad to sell your body*, she tells me. *Your body is the only thing you have to keep to yourself.* When I ask her how she knows this she spits on the sidewalk and tells me to rub her back, which is pit-scarred from shrapnel. When I run my fingers over Ama's spine, I can still feel little rough edges underneath her skin, like half-moons peeking out behind the curves of her bones.

Once, I brought home a box of croissants from the nice white lady across the street. When Ama saw it, she made me bury them in the soil of our backyard. The two of us watched the leaves eat them, tearing apart each buttery layer until the ground was littered with crumbs. Ama says it is better to be hungry and prideful than well-fed and shamed. Ama says that if I become like her aunt, living off of the mercies of mei guo ren, I'll become a soft-spoiled fruit too, a mandarin dripping thick juice into the sidewalk. Ama says not even the meanest white man would want to marry a smashed orange. *Too sticky*, Ama tells me. *Even the mailman would not take it if you offered.* Ama says lots of things, but I don't listen to all of them. Most of what she says is only half-real like a story split into crosshairs, each branch only partially true.

When I do listen, she makes me sit down in the kitchen and wash her hair. Usually, this happens at night before bed, with the rice-wash bucket from the day before. As the milky water splashes all over us she tells me the stories her aunt told her before she died. According to Ama, Auntie Annie was smart before she fell in love with the white man. *She had a good mind*, Ama tells me. *Also why she didn't want to use a gun. Such pretty brains, too much of a waste to shoot.* Whenever Ama tells stories of Auntie Annie, I always wonder where her own place is in them. When I ask, Ama tells me I am too young to understand and changes the subject.

That night, Ama tells me the moon will steal my hair if I don't dry it before bed. *You would not be such a pretty little girl if you had no ponytail*, Ama says. Ama tells me that if I find buttons I should bring them home and put them in a plastic bag so that she can add them to my shirts. *We will have to button your jackets all the way up to your forehead in order to hide your scalp if you aren't careful.*

Ama doesn't love me, but she likes me enough to let me trade chores for three meals a day and the spare-room bed. When I was younger I used to ask why she kept me if she wasn't willing to raise me for free, and Ama spat into her palm and showed me the phlegm, sticky white against her red skin. *Having a child around saps the pain out of my head*, Ama said. *A cat would be better but in America, you can't let them keep house on their own when you're out.*

Ama is too young to be a mother, so I believe her when she says that I am not hers. Ama says she picked me up on the street corner one morning when she was buying youtiao after she watched a Hallmark movie about a nice white couple doing the same thing to a stray dog. *You had such small eyes*, Ama reminisces. *Like little buttons in your head.* Ama says that even though we aren't from the same blood, she looks out for me because she likes the karma it gives her.

Later, I ask her if she and Auntie Annie were from the same blood too. Ama does not ever look sad, but her eyebrows darken into the closest approximation of anger that someone with a face as stiff as hers can muster. *Not from the same blood,* Ama tells me. *She lost that blood when she left me behind.*

As Ama gets older, her stories change as all stories cut from their roots do. Sometimes, when she talks about Auntie Annie slitting her throat, Auntie Annie ends up living. *The doctor stitched her throat back together,* Ama tells me. Sometimes, the story ends after Auntie Annie's husband comes back to her. Sometimes, Auntie Annie turns into a swan, and the doctor plucks out all her feathers, making a cape of them. Sometimes, Ama calls Auntie Annie jiejie before she starts all over again.

When Ama tells me the last rendition, we are sitting in the grove, feet propped up on the roots of an orange tree. Both of our hands are sticky with the freshness of a half-ripe mandarin. *She was a good jiejie,* Ama says. *She would have been a good mother to you if she had lived.*

Sometimes, Ama takes out her old photo album and shows me the family she has back home. No matter how carefully I try to, I cannot find anyone who resembles her description of Auntie Annie. None of the faces resemble Ama either, but she says that's a good thing. Ama tells me that she has no mother, but her father was a wastrel and a drunk. *A very bad man,* Ama says. *Some years, he drank so much I could not even buy a toothbrush. That is why my teeth rattle so much in my head.* Ama opens her mouth and spits a tooth onto her palm; we observe it together and find it speckled on each side like dice.

Because her bones are so soft, the doctor tells Ama to make sure her body has enough calcium. Ama understands that as an order to eat milky things, which usually means ice cream. When we go out to buy Ben and Jerry's, Ama makes me hold her hand. *So you don't lose yourself like she did,* Ama tells me. Her fingers are tight on mine every time we pass a boy my age, as if she is afraid their gravity will pull me out of her orbit.

After I tell Ama I like girls instead of boys, she goes three days without saying a word. Finally, she sits me down at the kitchen table and makes me prick my fingers on her sewing needles. The two of us stare at the little red crescents bleeding their way through the tablecloth. *Maybe it's better this way,* she says after a long pause. *You don't have to worry about breaking your own heart. You just have to worry about breaking mine.*

Amy Wang is a writer from California. She is a 2020 prose alumnus of *The Adroit Journal's* summer mentorship under Andrew Gretes. When not crying over fanfiction, you can find her translating Chinese literature, coding, and taking long walks.

MAIN

CONTENTS

CHECK IN WITH TUI and Alison, steadfast culinary Antipodean goddesses. Study your *Edmonds* gospel. Scan the *NZ Woman's Weekly* for tips.

Get the inside track from your cuz.

Thank Kenneth Wood as your retro duck-egg-blue mixer beats whites till the glossy peaks hold. Thank Cuz when she phones and swears that vinegar is the only thing to stabilise the foam. Wrap your baking tray in foil. *Yes, Cuz. Gas Mark One. Gentle heat.*

Leave her cooling in the oven. Gotta get those edges crisp.

Use Tupperware to prep and store. Beat that cream stiff – go easy or she'll separate and you'll get butter. Yeah, dash of sugar and a splash of vanilla. Chill.

Decorate at the last minute – you don't want a soggy mess. *Gottit.*

Don't be mean, fuck the calories and slather her with cream. *Okay, Cuz.*

Crown her with wedges of ruby strawberries. Alternate with slices of glut-cheap kiwifruit – that chartreuse contrast makes her really Christmassy, right?

Hug Cuz when she comes round to yours and warns you not to go overboard with fruit or you'll send the cream watery. *A shower of chocolate hail?* Stop tutuing! *All good, Cuz.*

Put the air-con on, low and cold. Settle Cuz in the passenger seat with no seatbelt across her ample bosom; balance your perfect baby on her lap. Drive across town. In the carpark, near the front door, take the tray from her as she does the careful transfer to your arms, gives you the once over, clicks her tongue and tilts her chin.

Breathe. Smile when Cuz gives her nod of approval. You might make it.

Strut into the hall, arms outstretched with your foil-lined tray, your festive centrepiece. She's pretty fucking gorgeous. Put her down, careful now, so she doesn't crack and seep.

Savour the nods and the ka pai-ing, mmm, crunchy edges, squidgy marshmallow centre. See how nobody's picking foil from their teeth. Enjoy the compulsory dissing of bloody Aussies, trying to nick our national dessert.

Banish that lingering epic domestic science class disaster from years ago: this pavlova is completely demolished in under five minutes. Sweet.

Chill. Toast your cuz. Toast this rite of passage.

A New Zealand-Irish writer, Alex Reece Abbott's stories span genres and forms. Widely anthologised, including in *Bonsai: Best Small Stories from Aotearoa New Zealand*, *The Broken Spiral* (UNESCO Dublin City of Literature Read), *The Real Jazz Baby* (Best Anthology, Saboteur Awards), *MIROnline*, *Flash Fiction Festival Anthology*, *Flash Frontier*, *Pulp Literature* and *Heron* (Katherine Mansfield Society), her work is a Penguin Random House WriteNow finalist and winner in the Irish Novel Fair, Northern Crime, Arvon and HG Wells prizes. Among others, her short fiction is a finalist in the Sunday Business Post/Penguin Prize, Bridport, Cambridge, Maria Edgeworth, Tillie Olsen and Lorian Hemingway prizes.

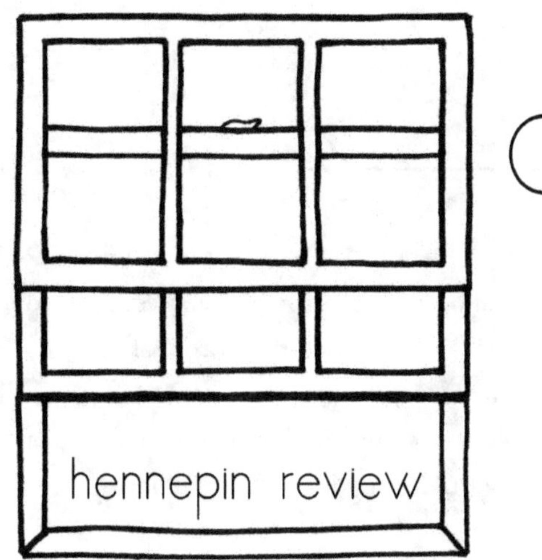

CHROMATIC

ashia ajani

GRANDMA WAS A MOTHER, a hairdresser, a beautician, a stylist, an opera singer,
a church goer, a God-fearing Christian, a cook, a pastry chef, a bad bitch,
a freedom fighter, a conscientious objector, an ass-whupper, a Southern belle,
a great grandmother, a wife, a widow, a scholar, a gardener, a loud mouth,
a bad mamajama, a panther, a misogynist, a feminist, a giant, a misnomer,
an Elton John fan, a soap opera enthusiast, a recipe hoarder, a librarian,
the alpha and the omega, a PYT, a glass house, a Black supremacist, a mess,
a negress, a shit talker, a bra burner, a seamstress, a gossip, a migrant,
a butcher, a baker, a candlestick maker, a seamstress, an aesthetician, a union
Look how she glow, she glow, she glow. Look how she keeps glowing, glow.

Grandma wants to move back to her true home in Wayne County, besides
there aren't many Black folks in Denver and the ones who are here are a lil too
weird, they smell like patchouli and free love and all the things that could get us
killed the niggas in the northside whistle from lowriders and sport neck tattoos
the difference is, the hands that pull the trigger will be the same color as the ones
that layer on the dirt, that will press the wounds into submission that will clutch
pearls and beat on the congregation pews and wipe tears and snot and fry fish in
thick cast iron pans and break branches for switches and sing LOVE and RAGE
my mother my mother says
do you see,
do you see why I am telling you this,
do you see how Detroit,

no matter where I be
Detroit forever lives, lives on
in me?

Ashia Ajani (they/she) is a Black storyteller soulchild of Denver, CO, Queen City of the Plains and the unceded territory of the Cheyenne, Ute, Arapahoe and Comanche peoples. They are an environmental educator with Mycelium Youth Network and co-poetry editor of the *Hopper Literary Magazine*. Their work has been published in *Hennepin Review, Frontier Poetry, Word Literature Today,* and has forthcoming work in *Atmos Magazine* and *Apogee Lit.* Her debut poetry collection, *Heirloom,* will be published with Write Bloody Publishing in Spring 2023.

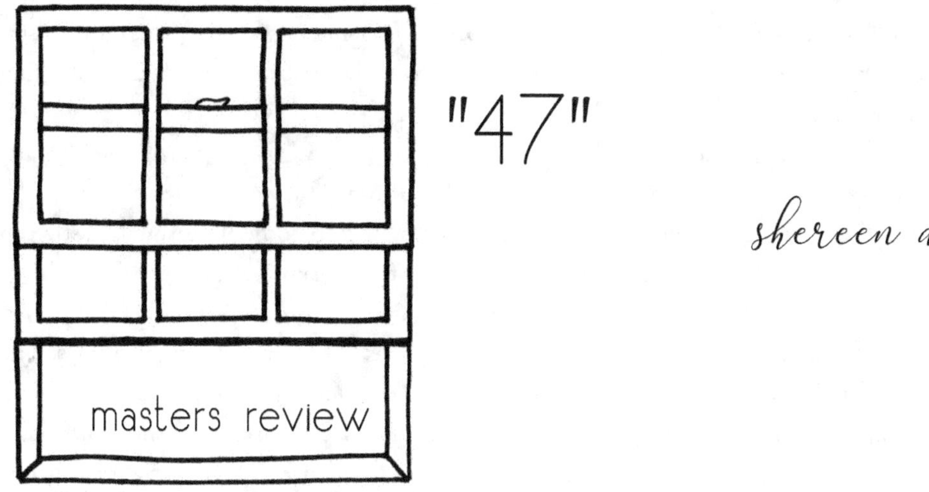

"47"

shereen akhtar

In memory of Irina Slavina, journalist, b. 1973

I COUNT BACKWARDS FROM sixty. There she is—grey-blonde, wrinkles over the edges of her lips. Perhaps even a very young grandchild balanced in her lap. We start there. Begin a full minute's silence.

This is a story about Russia. Here, we may know someone who married an expatriate, or support a football club owned by an oligarch in exile. We know it as the land of tundra, of Dostoyevsky's brilliant young man traipsing the streets of a former Moscow in delirium. We may have pictured the steam-hot cabins full of pink skin, and heard the slush of a man's bottom sink into snow. We may even remember the massacre at Beslan, schoolchildren set for a day's work and play. The gates that went up afterwards around mosque courtyards, and the armed officers that began to patrol. This is a different story.

In this one, she is fifty-five with a little more weight to her frame. She blows her candle, a single one, and her partner may or may not be there, ready with a squeeze on her shoulder.

A few seconds pass and she is fifty, or perhaps forty-nine. Somewhere close enough to merit a series of raised glasses, and a stumble rather than a walk to a taxi stand. Somewhere there is blood boiling hot in optimistic veins. Some conversation about a renewal of purpose, a deepening sense of what makes sense. Some worry and pride for an adult child making their way in this fierce place; how they will learn the lessons of the second adulthood, or fail to survive here. A gnawing worry that the bank account cannot tide them all over for very long, let alone afford a one-way plane ticket. A kiss to the head that lingers, two pinkies that eventually intertwine.

Here, finally, forty-seven—the year she does it, though she does not know at the time, presented with a spirit-infused cake at her small office. Imagine it summer. The rays of sun forking through the window as she spins to it in her chair, the first two mouthfuls provoking everything to rush within her cheeks. She does not know it even two weeks before, nor one. The officers came in the night, as they always do when the purpose is only half-search, half-intimidation. We do not know what happened in that room. But we saw her the next day, striding towards the police station, in one hand a match, and in the other a sloshing plastic tub with a smell announcing her presence. This is important. At forty-seven, she set herself alight.

But now we are already at thirty-five. We are unphased, not that rather hackneyed phrase, "tireless." In truth, there is not much that surprises us about Russia these days. The word itself is a political idea, or to be accurate, several, disjointed, political ideas. Conquest, arming faraway fighters, interference through covert operations. Mr. President, the same, but a decade before he began to refuse to see anyone apart from on a video-link citing a pandemic and national security. A country in a man. He is in her sights, but he is not a lone carp in the wild. There is an entire school treading in his wake.

Here, twenty-nine. On the verge of crisis—or at least, what she believes could be crisis. Perhaps she is pregnant, though probably not. Perhaps it is the thought of all that comes next, the enormous power that she believed she would come to yield lying just ahead. And the path seems simple, straight enough, but she wonders if it is true, or was ever true to begin with, or whether she made it up, a fantasy in her own girl's mind.

We progress. Twenty-four, in a lover's arms. Twenty-three, snoozing her alarm. Twenty-two, staring out the window on a five-hour train journey without pause. Twenty-one, her father's arm pictured in the frame. This memory she keeps, for many years, folded up with the color fading, alongside bank notes, a few of which come from foreign lands she would like to visit too.

Soon, she is eighteen. Sixteen. Fourteen. There is too much here of life, so much to tell it cannot be told. Eleven and looking up to the world with a well-reared respect. Ten and shopping with her mother. Nine and enrolled in a school that takes care to encourage her literary ways. Seven and a budding engineer, volunteering to fix gutters, repair old volumes. Five and learning to dance. Three, learning confidence in her words. One, on her belly in the kitchen. Zero, just arriving. And further now, minus one—a small piece of darkness beginning to wake. In front of her lies the pastel orange glow of northern sunlight intruding through her mother's skin, and she hears the voice. They have been laughing. It invites her out now, into the world. It does not tell her what is coming.

Shereen Akhtar is a writer and poet. She has been published in various journals in the UK and USA including *Ambit Magazine* and *The Masters Review*. She is currently at work on her first novel, for which she was awarded a London Writers Award 2021. She can be reached on Twitter @omnigloss.

KEROSENE MAN

christopher allen

WE SUPPLIED THE MEN on the river. Two-gallon canisters of kerosene for their outboards, ten dollars each. There were other fueling points, but a few of the men bought only from my father. It was his smile, *our* smile—because I was a little version of him. It wrinkled up the skin around our eyes, releasing chemicals in their brains. I'm sure they thought I didn't know, but I'd seen my face in the water. When I was ten, the river left my parents tangled in a tree.

Passed from family to family, I didn't smile for a decade. I forgot I guess, with nothing to sell. When I became a kerosene man myself, it came back naturally enough, but by then it was too late. The fish in the river were already disappearing. One year it didn't rain in the mountains at all, so the river itself dried to a trickle. They said it was happening everywhere, but I'd never been to everywhere.

My mother was full of rules. *Never say you'll die for someone. Never laugh at your own joke. Never go to bed hungry. Never forget what the river wants. Never break into song. Never forget to smile.* Always never.

My regulars still buy kerosene. They say they need it for their lamps and space heaters, and I let them lie; they say they come to laugh about God and the changing world, which never, not for a second, seems odd. We're a cohort, full of affection. But I know where this is going. When a regular puts a tenner in my hand as he leaves without asking for the kerosene, I slide the bill into my pocket and offer the smile he expects in return. He presses himself against me, and I let him. A man could starve on the edge of a dry riverbed.

My father had only one rule. *Give people what they need.* He stank of fish guts, the manure of the fields, the petroleum fog of the river. The generosity of it all. The night before the river rose and swept my parents three miles away and twenty feet up a tree we feasted on crappie, bream, and bass—all fried in a big vat of new oil. I miss all of him.

The regulars have started coming on their own now, one every day of the week, each old enough to be my father, each handing me a tenner when he leaves. "For the conversation," Heiko says. He comes on Sundays, says my aftershave smells "like the woods." I buy potatoes, cabbage and two gallons of milk with the tenner. I've never had the money for aftershave. Heiko's twins are grown and gone, studying something in a town with no river. His wife got a job in some big city and never came back. Our conversations wander from weather to fish and what to put in a fish stew when there are no more fish. Today he's brought whiskey, keeps filling my glass, never asks about me—no one ever has. He rambles about when the river was enough, when it was our world, forgetting that the river took my parents. He's holding my hand like it's this precious thing he's just now discovered, staring. "It's warmer," he says, "softer than I—"

When he leans in to kiss me, I don't shy away. I pull him in. His lips are chapped like bark.

On the night before the landslide in the mountains, my parents and I went to bed with our bellies bursting, queasy from the oily fish. I woke to the roar of rain and the swell of the river like a train rumbling from the sky. No time to secure the kerosene tank, no time to dress. In seconds we were the river: in motion, tumbling, gulping. That's what the river wants—the rush. A man pulled me out two miles downstream. The weather forecast had called for a clear and starry night.

Sunday conversations with Heiko come from an easy place inside me. I listen mostly because he can't stop himself from talking. He's past the years when he regretted not being fit or handsome, when his wife might have stayed. He's too old to be anything "but a fisherman without a river," he says and laughs, a sound so full of sadness that I want to hug this man, to give him back his river, but I know this is not what he wants. He laughs so that I will laugh too. And I get it. This is what I have to give him, so this is what I give.

Christopher Allen's collection of flash fiction, *Other household Toxins*, was published in 2018.

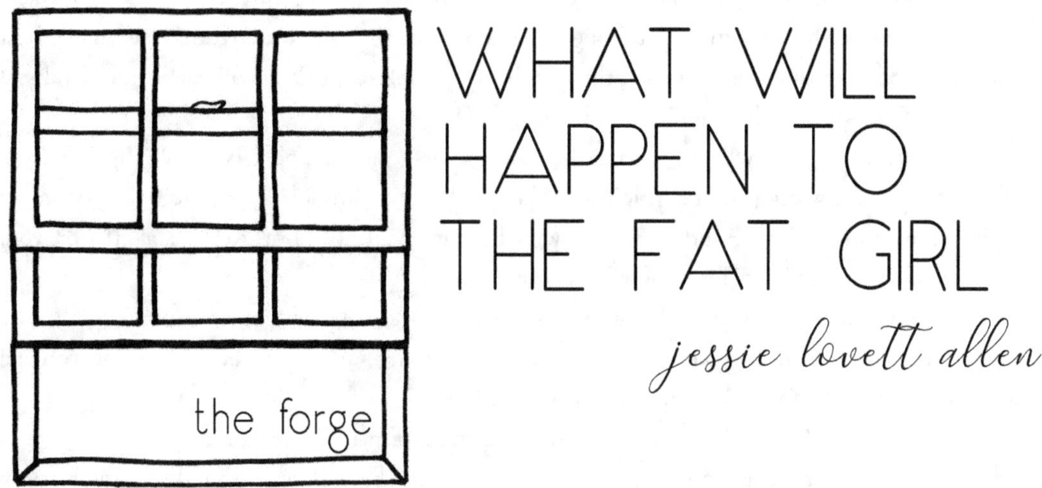

WHAT WILL HAPPEN TO THE FAT GIRL

jessie lovett allen

YOU WILL POP THE screen and sneak out your bedroom window. You will meet other kids at a bonfire out in the woods, smoke clove cigarettes and eat gummy candy. You will get six mosquito bites and see a shooting star. You will sneak back into the house and sleep in your clothes, which still smell like the bonfire.

A boy at school will say you have a fat pussy. You will hide in a bathroom stall and cry. On a summer night, a different boy will pick you up in his two-door Hyundai hatchback and drive out to the lake. With the windows down, you will listen to the oldies radio station that you both like. Lightning bugs will pulse and flicker slowly in the tall grasses near the shoreline. He will unhook your bra and hold your fat boobs. You will rub the outside of his shorts. He will tell you he loves you. You will say it back.

You will move away and into the dorms. You and your friends will meet in the dining hall where you will eat cold cereal that dispenses from a mechanical plastic spigot. A chain-smoking friend, much smaller than you, will drone about her own disgusting belly fat as she eats a bowl of lettuce. You will listen—you're a good listener. One night, a guy at a party will flirtatiously spank you through your jeans and also suggest you go on a diet. It's not about looks—it's about health, he will insist. That night you will watch him drink eight beers and snort coke off a kitchen counter. You will take a fencing class and wear a hard plastic chest protector.

At your gym, while you are on a toilet inside a bathroom stall, leggings around your ankles, you will overhear a woman in the locker room call you a whale. You will go swim in the ocean like a whale. You will get sand in your fat ass crack. You and your friends will chase an ice cream truck, then you will eat a cartoon character on a stick, frozen gumballs for the eyes.

A man will hold your fat face and kiss you under a streetlight. You will ride an elevator to the rooftop of his apartment building where you will share a cigarette and talk about how the moon looks so three-dimensional through his cheap telescope. You will eat cherries and spit the pits off the side of the building.

Eventually you will grow three humans inside your fat body. Two will slip out from that fat pussy between your fat thighs; the last will come through a slit sliced into your fat belly. Your boobs will ache and swell, and your husband will hold hot, wet washcloths on your boobs while the milk leaks into a towel on your lap.

You will wear shorts and roller skates and rub gel between your fat thighs so they do not chafe. You will fall on your fat ass and feel embarrassed, and then you will fall on your fat ass again and laugh. You will wear goofy skate socks.

Your daughters will become tweens and teens. During a screaming match with your youngest, she will call you a fat bitch. You will cry. Later, she will cry, and tell you she is sorry, and she will lay her head in your fat lap and you will stroke her hair. You will forgive her, one-hundred percent. Together you will have oatmeal with banana slices for dinner.

A man will call you a hippo while you are in line at Family Dollar. Later, you and your husband will take your daughters camping, where you will float like a hippo in a swimming hole near a waterfall. Your daughters will shriek and splash and try to catch minnows in their cupped hands. Underwater, your husband will secretly slip his hand under your swimsuit elastic and feel your fat ass. That night you will grill jelly sandwiches and sweet corn over the campfire.

At work you will wear big dresses that you will pay to have tailored just right. You will wear queen-sized tights and glossy red shoes. Your fat ass will sit in an expensive ergonomic chair, and your office will have lush plants, cozy lamplight, and walnut bookshelves. You will have a mini-fridge where you keep tangerines, string cheese, and ginger ale.

One day your husband will go into cardiac arrest while watching TV, and with your strong arms you will pull him off the couch onto the floor and straddle him with your fat legs while doing chest compressions. He will die anyway. Your daughters will come back home, and you will hold them as they sob into your fat boobs.

When you are old, you will get cancer in your blood. No diabetes, no clogged arteries, just one freaky mutant cell setting off the whole cascade. Your treatment will make you thinner, and your friends will make jokes about your secret trick for weight loss. A flat joke, but you will laugh to be polite. Your cancer won't respond to treatment. You will lose more weight, and the skin around your skinny ass hole will hurt, raw from diarrhea. You will eat Jell-O, rotating red, yellow, blue, green. You will die. Your grandchildren will carry your casket, and it won't be too heavy. Workers at the crematorium will slide your body into an incinerator and sweep and scoop your ashes into a medium plastic bag.

Your three daughters will go back to your empty house to sort through old photos of your fat body and cry in your kitchen. They will sit in lawn chairs on your screened-in porch and laugh about your roller skating and argue about selling your house. They will eat roasted chicken, cucumber salad, and chocolate cake. They will drink coffee with cream.

Jessie Lovett Allen is originally from western NY and currently teaches English at North Platte Community College in western Nebraska. Recently, her work has been published in *The Forge, JMWW, Milk Candy Review, Bending Genres, Storm Cellar,* and *English Journal.*

JUM CLIMBS THE TUALANG TREE

kelli allen

BEWARE THE MONKEY CARRYING his razor through the forest. Guard your fishcakes, mind the fire! What comes for Jum is older than the Hantu. There will never be enough meal or ripe papaya to sate these hungers. If he waits, stumbles over his own flat feet, the back of that head might fall clean off, maybe the front, too. Then? Only the eyes on their thin stalks will have any purchase at all. Whose story do you want this to be, anyway?

He counts as he plods. He's heard that when the tualang introduces its yellow crown to the canopy, every honey bee is a debutante for exactly fourteen hours. Then comes smoke and ladders high enough to divide sky from earth. Only a proper storm leaves this wood for homes and nights to sea. If the ax fells these beasts, the hands that swung belong to a dead man within the year.

Jum the winnower, the papa's boy displaced in city sprawl. He is a balladeer, a lover of finch whistle and September frond rhythms. But when Jum sings, his mouth fills with honey or rice and the ooze and spill replaces whatever words he longs to speak. The townswomen come every morning to collect the sweet and grains left of Jum's singing in their huge reed baskets, hoping to sell both at the market, or to trade the lot for a single horned cowfish. It's a wicked trek from brush to concrete. A woman knows to cross her arms and wear rock thrush feathers close to the belly.

Jum allows the songs because of guilt. He ends each day by trying not to think of his four sisters still working the family fish shop near his childhood beach. He pushes dreaming aside to complete the nightly mantra, *I'm sorry, I'm sorry, I'm trying. I will sing to fill the coffers. I will sing to pillow your mangos. I'm sorry.* This morning follows the same as every night and he offers seven minutes to the women, slings his pack over his shoulder, plugs ears with cotton, and meets the first of sixteen hundred and two paces to the bus stop.

Today, Jum will see his mother, will bring her news of the city in the drawing he way lay across her plastic table, and will kiss each sister's broad cheek. All without meeting a single eye, not one glance direct or forward. The stops are simple and he memorized them in his first days wandering Phuket: Green line, Nag, Yumm, Cave-tom, and then, Khao. An hour's walk through pine and palm tree, hermit crabs making their way south, too. And home.

Blue-crested kingfishers are tangled in a mating hump when he plants his big feet onto the sandy dirt. Jum breathes slow, lets the rutting birds' noise push into his ears as he pockets the cotton for the return ride. He touched a breast once, he remembers, let the round nipple harden under his palm, before pulling his hand back and away so fast it slapped his chest in the recoil. The geckos creeping the walls and ceilings in Kappa's room fled at the slap and Jum cupped his hat over his bulging crotch and made quick for the door.

He watches the violet-blue tails pulse, seconds counted as his middle finger taps his thigh, sighs away what he thinks might be desire, and walks. He walks slower than tamarins blink, than purple squid ink their captures at thirty feet below. Jum walks as a boy possessed by smoke.

Bull flesh leaches its blood too slow for pacification. The cock's comb leaves a crater fit for a bowl and the slick collects there as is has for centuries. There are no wood piles for Aaron in these thatches. This is work for dirty hands, clay-stained hands. Jum recalls these truths in the moments between seeing the tree and recognizing that the sight means responsibility. He did not mean to wander this close and now, too quick, it was too late. The arrow had witnessed his shoe's rhythm and unfurrowed its sharp quills to poke both head and spine from the tree's peeling bark just in time to let the whistle of *how, then, boy?* reach Jum's groundsel thick ears.

The Sleeping Lady expels her ghost just once and the tectonic shifts under her tailbone mean maybe we will be born somewhere, too. Though, Jum thinks, the banana serpent grows from the forehead as tightly coiled as the jade. It's where the skin husk falls that spills your children's future and buries the fickle arrow in one of three trees. Jum has been selected by a lineage he has avoided for nineteen years crawling and scooting over the dirt.

As is understood, he empties his pockets at once, bows at the waist, lets the waxy-hard fluff fall from his head holes, and nods at the iron-tipped ruiner of all days. When the arrow speaks, it is to name its price. Nothing less, not a bucket gap wide enough for the tongue to taste water.

Seems I'm thirsty and have been before. I'll see you at dusk for my filling. Wasting your left arm and your right would make you more than a green stump of a man, no?

While the arrow yawned its tip to let rust mark the agreement, Jum let the pale abacus of his mind decide direction. Paces back to the bus, the wait, the wet-rice words for his sisters if he ever meets their faces after the night collects its bargain.

Hours past and lined with paces backward and then, in closing dark, forward to the canopy, Jum greets the tualang with a honk not unlike the dying cranes wandering the rubber factory at the township edge he considered, before this night, to outline the corpse of his childhood. He places two things on the ground under the hollow-spined eyes of the arrow: an iron vase brimming with mustard seeds, roasted, and a bright green bucket warm from chicken blood not even trying to cool.

How often, when waking and letting the first stretch break a morning's silence, do we think about sentience? Neon lights move faster than we ever will and their insistences are certainly bolder than our own. This is the city against what still grows past its silhouette. This is where Jum suspends himself as he thinks too slow, trying to steam engine ahead —a great-great-great grandmother's promise and a burning, acid-bright desire to be down-cover buried in his studio apartment. Jum wants to be anywhere away from the congealing calf-deep wet and the molar-chipping handfuls of spice soon to muffle his already honey-muzzled voice.

The arrow speaks, the tree lets fall the last of its sequin shades, and somewhere too near the monkey tests his blade against his own snapdragon pink belly. My tip to the tip and no more or less near the shaft you cradle. *Hurry, boy, grain crier, lady footed traveler to nowhere far. This is the last of it, of time, of chance and targets met.*

Kelli Allen's work has appeared in numerous journals and anthologies in the US and internationally. Allen is the co-Founding Editor of *Book of Matches* literary journal. She is an award-wining poet, editor, and dancer. She is the recipient of the 2018 Magpie Award for Poetry. Her chapbook, *Some Animals*, won the 2016 Etchings Press Prize. Her chapbook, *How We Disappear*, won the 2016 Damfino Press award. Her collections include, *Otherwise, Soft White Ash*, (John Gosslee Books 2012), *Imagine Not Drowning*, (C&R Press 2017), *Banjo's Inside Coyote* (C&R Press 2019). Allen's latest book is *Leaving the Skin on the Bear*, C&R Press, 2022. She currently teaches writing and literature in North Carolina. www.kelli-allen.com

THE MOON IS THE color of failing memory, which is to say the moon is the color of my great grandmother's brain, a phantom of uncertainty, and with every passing day the shape of her skull shifts: even if she can't feel it, even if we can't see it, she is leaning into her metamorphosis as a Quarter Moon. We adjust our language to survive in an environment where her memory is in flux, a hummingbird of moments; we speak in cyclic permutations so our narratives align. Her questions are delivered with a bursting repetition. How old are you again? What's your name? Then she gazes at the sky, eyes glassy with reflection, turning back to me with a smile to ask with fresh interest, how old are you again? As every day passes, her condition reminds us that the hummingbird fluttering inside her will fly away someday, never to return.

She likes to sit in the gallery, near the railing, overlooking the bushes and trees of avocado and mango and bay-leaf and hibiscus. Her caramel skin wrinkled and loose to the bone, her white hair a stubborn cloud soft to the touch of breeze, she code-switches between English, Dutch, and Patois as a tide of languages come rushing back to her like a long-lost tsunami returning to its place of origin. We nod and laugh with patient approval. We never talk about the ageing or her forgetfulness—we simply adapt to this new phase like the city adapts to night. We witness our moon shrinking before us. We attend to her with reverence, a deity of sorts; we look up to our Waning Crescent, even if she hardly recognizes us. I visit her on weekends; when the day is clear, we stay at the pool until the sun sets.

She documents herself; with every word she utters, she carves her autobiography. She grasps her great-grandson's hand, my hand, and I glimpse her former life:

Long ago we would eat plenty of cocoa; there were cocoa trees all over the place. Are you my son's son? Who is your mother again? Simone? Yes, yes Simone. How is your mother going? Wait!

Wait, why do you have this long-long beard? I don't like to see my men with long-long beards. I ever told you about the cocoa we used to eat? Mmm, how old are you again? Ho oud ben je ook alweer? Hou je van lezen? You know what language is that boy? Haha look how my boy get big-big! How old are you again?

I respond when I can, when her words get into a traffic jam, allowing her to pause and drink in some air. I am 22 years and I have to shave. I just haven't done it yet, I say. She always responds with a smile. Sometimes I think if we told her there was a bomb, she would smile and nod, answering, I think I'm ready to go and take a little sleep. Her days are punctuated by naps—her body runs on audacity and the will to see the sun, her rival, one more day before she goes.

During the week, I compartmentalize for my jobs as a tutor and admissions assistant. I was in a meeting when my mother calls me crying, her sobs rattling through the phone, her words caught in her throat. I know what's happened before she can utter the words. On that morning I look to the sky, the sun scorching in triumph down on bustling bodies, assaulting my forehead, proud and boastful. That morning my great-grandmother transitioned into a New Moon and walked into a new beginning. And as the day comes to a close, the sun makes way for her arrival, and her glowing shadow stuns the city as night falls.

Akhim Alexis is a writer from Trinidad and Tobago who holds an MA in Literatures in English from the University of the West Indies, St. Augustine. He is the winner of the Brooklyn Caribbean Lit Fest Elizabeth Nunez Award for Writers in the Caribbean. He was also a finalist for the Barry Hannah Prize in Fiction and the Johnson and Amoy Achong Caribbean Writers Prize. His work has appeared or is forthcoming in *The Rumpus*, *The McNeese Review*, *The Massachusetts Review*, *Transition Magazine*, *Chestnut Review*, *Obsidian: Literature and Arts in the African Diaspora*, *Gordon Square Review*, *Welter*, *No Contact*, *JMWW*, *Moko Magazine*, and elsewhere.

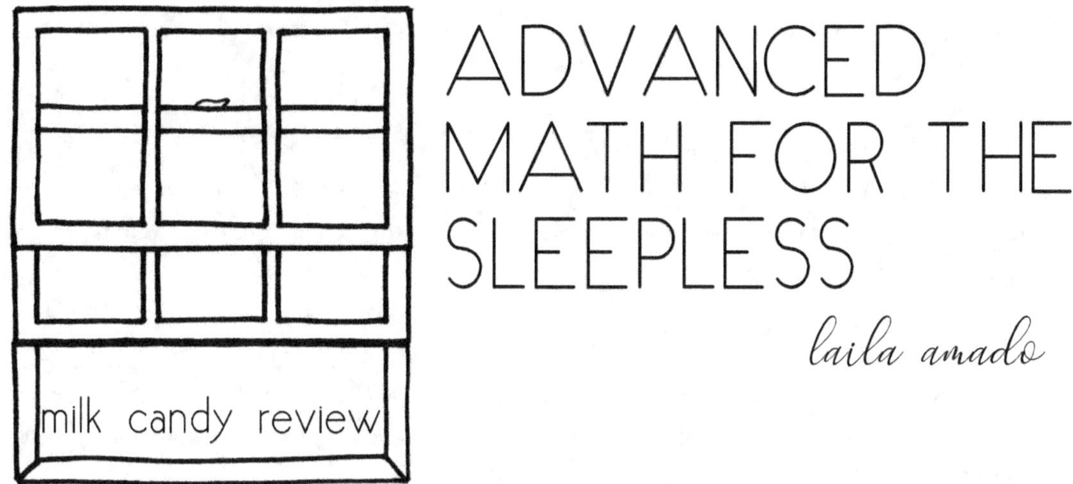

THERE ARE 8.399 MILLION people living in New York City. Of these, 47% are male. If 53% of these men are currently single, 26% prefer latte over cappuccino, 10% can tell a difference between a Leica and a Fuji, 7% are remotely attractive, and 3% can find you attractive with makeup running down your face, please calculate the probability of meeting the love of your life on a rainy Tuesday in April, outside of Dashwood Books, after you have forgotten your umbrella on the subway.

The wedding band is a circle of metal around emptiness. To calculate the radius of a circle by using the circumference, take the circumference of the circle and divide it by 2 times π. Without using any measurement instruments, estimate the correct size of the wedding band for a person whose hand you've been clutching on a roller coaster ride you shouldn't have gone to in the first place.

Add up the 6.5 lbs of a newborn girl and the combined 10.8 lbs of the twins that came two years later, subtract 2.25 hours a day spent cooking and cleaning, multiply by the number of times the spouses quarreled and then made up, legs intertwined, divide by the number of Lego parts found in unexpected places and, finally, take a square root out of every difficult conversation to find a formula of a perfect marriage.

Imagine that Car A leaves from point X and Car B departs from point Y. Car A travels at 55 mph, in line with the maximum posted speed limit. Car B travels at 65mph for the first two hours of its journey and then speeds up to 90 mph for the last 22 minutes. Calculate the force of their collision at intersection Z.

There are 206 bones in the human body. The femur is the strongest and the trapezium bone in the left wrist, injured in the skating incident at the age of nine, is the weakest. Calculate how many bones will break when the side impact airbag doesn't deploy. For extra points, estimate which one of them will break first.

The average life expectancy of a man is 77 years and the average life expectancy of a woman is 81. Calculate how many times she will stand outside Dashwood Books alone after her husband dies in a car crash two days before her 36th birthday.

Laila Amado writes in her second language, lives in her fourth country, and cooks decent paella. Her stories have appeared in *Daily Science Fiction*, *Rejection Letters*, *Milk Candy Review*, *Porcupine Literary*, and other publications. In her free time, she can be found staring at the Mediterranean Sea. Occasionally, the sea stares back. Follow her on Twitter at @onbonbon7.

AILA KAGEYAMA

kiik araki-kawaguchi

AILA KAGEYAMA HAD AN obsession for the boneless creatures and objects of this world. An orange-blossom custard for example. Or a rubber swim cap. Or a jellyfish. Even boneless concepts were attractive to her. Cultural appropriation was one. And the myth of model minorities. Whereas inverted totalitarianism was a road covered in bones. She preferred the mouthfeel of words without bones. Words like *Lillian* and *illiterate* and *willfully* were like sardines packed with little un-removable bones. But *oboe* and *mandarin orange* were delicate and juicy. A *nugget* usually was boneless. A succulent lump of white meat she could dip into a tub of honey. Except those Denver Nuggets who were a talented family of bones.

Those were the two classifications pervading her life. Either it was *bones* or *no bones.* Freddie Mercury was *bones.* The strawberry catsuit Britney Spears wore in "Oops!" was *no bones.* A t-bone steak was obviously t-boned. A portabella burger was a no-boner. It was less about a scientific definition. For Aila, sharks were *bones,* and dolphins were *no bones,* even though the opposite was scientifically true. But this was philosophy, not science.

A buttplug was a sort of flanged neoprene bone. But a human butt in and of itself was *no bones.* A human butt with a buttplug inside of it was definitely a bone-in situation. But a butt with only a tongue in it was boneless. She liked that one a lot. Also an oriental chicken salad was boneless. She ordered them whenever possible, as she liked to study the expression on the waiter's face when she said *oriental.* She liked to say it a bit extra. *I'll have the oriental salad with the oriental dressing on the side. And I'll add those oriental thigh meats on top. Are there mandarins in the oriental?* Sometimes the salad showed up with wonton strips or upon a bed of uncooked ramen noodles in which case the experience was sort of semi-boned or bone-studded. A bed had bones, also known as a frame, but a mattress was boneless much like a colossal slab of calamari.

Aila had had sex on an inherited IKEA mattress thirteen times before leaving it with a FREE sign on the street corner. Twelve times at Azusa PU with Ranjit Roshan and the sex was like melting into butter pecan ice cream. The other time was a threesome she'd had back on senior prom night with the actors Sam Rockwell and Laura Linney. This had been in Aila's sweaty post-prom dream, and she had climaxed twice, once into Sam Rockwell's mouth, and once more riding atop Laura Linney's multicolored strapon dildo. Why had she remembered that Laura Linney's monster kongy-donk was luminous, almost kaleidoscopic, the way she imagined the skin of an archangel's face? The detail had given the dream an amplified sense of realism. Even in her dream she remembered thinking, *Laura's dildo looks so expensive, so custom. Celebrities will spend on anything and have no regrets.* Later while Aila was describing it all in her dream diary, she wrote, *So strange to dream objects I have never seen, what does it mean to physically egggasm upon an object that was not physically present?* And then she had skipped a line and written, *Sex with ghosts possible????*

Aila had been valedictorian of her high school. She had been voted *Most Likely to Rule the World* alongside Charles Rigaud Dalembert. She disliked the idea of *ruling*, but admittedly her favorite song was "Everybody Wants to Rule the World" by Tears for Fears. Roland Orzabal gave her all the lady-boners. There was a picture of Aila and Charles in the yearbook wearing royal mantles and holding plastic scepters. One girl plus one boy per *Most Likely*. Wasn't this tradition a little odd? Who designed these ballots? There was something about it that felt like an arranged marriage.

Arranged or unarranged. Both could be beautiful. After Aila Kageyama dropped out of college she became a phenomenally successful florist. Flowers were the pinnacle of boneless beauty, and a florist did not have to remove bloodstains from her work clothes. "Aila's Bloomsday" had three shops and thirteen delivery trucks. By her thirtieth birthday, her work had been featured in magazines and on the local news. She was the first of her friends to make ten million dollars.

But Aila's success went unrecognized by her family. She was the youngest of six children. Five Kageyama children became heart surgeons. One Kageyama child became a florist. Aila was the butt of every joke at family gatherings. Could you cure a mangled heart with flowers? You could not.

As her siblings began to die, Aila designed each of them a unique and exquisite funerary arrangement. Black clamshell orchids were dominant for Reiko. She had died vacationing in Belize. Yellow gladioli for Harry. He was the funnest drunk Aila ever met. He had belted out the Morrissey at karaoke. White daisies for Mariko. She had died a virgin. The saddest *no bones* of all. Aila's funerary arrangements always contained four hundred and forty-three blossoms. Aila and her siblings had spent their childhoods like sardines packed into a two-bedroom one-bathroom apartment at 443 Mourning Cloak Way. Her parents had slept on bunk beds in the living room. The children slept atop each other as though skewered. On warm summer nights, Aila had pitched a tent on the Kageyama patio of dying plants. In that Kageyama apartment, the plants and animals were eaten down to their bones. The bones were boiled for stock. The stock was eaten down to its residue. Not much made it to their garbage bins.

In her ninety-ninth year, Aila was the last of the Mourning Cloak Kageyamas to go. She had given careful instructions for how to tend to her remains. She did not want cremation. She wanted to be slipped naked into a thin biodegradable casket sack and buried beneath an apple orchard. She preferred Pacific Roses or Honeycrisps, but Fujis or Pink Ladies would be OK too.

Aila's children promised to go along with the dead-nude-into-Fujis idea, but in the end they decided to cremate her anyway. Cremation simply seemed the faster and cleaner choice. And Aila's senior living community was a bit of a one-stop shop. In the final years of Aila's life, she was moved from one ward to the next, independent living to partial care, partial care to the Alzheimer's bunkers. From all her apartment windows she could see the tall black concrete tower, the community's cremation chamber. The air always smelled faintly like a holiday barbecue.

On the afternoon of Aila's death, her children had not checked the box asking if they wanted their mother's "complete" remains. They did not understand this meant with or without the bone fragments that survived incineration. They were given the boneless remains, and they placed them inside an ornate cinerary urn. They had felt a little bad about cremating against their mother's wishes, and so they sprung for the most expensive cinerary urn they could find on Etsy. It was about a four-hundred-dollar purchase, including the discount code for free shipping. The cinerary urn was placed upon a glass shelf in a curio cabinet beside an oil painting of an apple orchard. Aila's son had done the painting himself, and it was very poor.

Many years later, the curio cabinet and the painting and Aila were sold as a single item in an estate sale. The buyer was Reyansh Roshan, the great-grandson of Ranjit Roshan. *Good old bones on this cabinet,* he thought, patting it lovingly. Reyansh really hated the apple orchard painting though, and he placed it atop the trash bins with a FREE sign taped upon it. He presumed the cinerary urn was decorative pottery, and so he kept Aila there inside.

Kiik Araki-Kawaguchi is the author of *Disintegration Made Plain and Easy* (1913 Press) and *The Book of Kane and Margaret* (FC2/UAP).

LITTLE WHITE BIRDS

natasha ayaz

A JULY EVENING. YEARS ago, in the rose garden, his hands on a woman's dress.

I will never forget the way they looked—hands of a pianist, hands that pressed alcohol on my scrapes like holy water—caught there in the act of betrayal. I wished the woman's head would fall deftly from her neck to the grass. A trophy for my trouble. I stood in the rosebush behind the stone wall in Stintino, witnessing the dismemberment of my childhood. The roses were pink, not red. The color of a kitten's nose, or cold chicken breast. The woman's body bore through its constraints so that the silk bloomed into creases, syrupy yellow like limoncello. Despite my callow rage, I leaned closer, thorns against my fingers, stomach melting into my thighs. When my father began to inch the yellow dress upward, I turned and ran up the path to my house.

It had happened twice before: my witnessing. Once earlier that same summer and another time the summer before. Always in the rose garden, my father traced the waistlines of strange women. Every incident, I thought of my mother: wiping her hands on her orange skirt, smelling of cilantro, laughing at a line in one of the sizable novels she read. I thought of how my father touched my mother's face, fingers trailing her jaw, mapping familiar territory. Something about that touch was different than with the women in the garden, though I couldn't say what. I was too young to understand the intricacies of possession. I thought of how my mother's mouth would fall into an injured O, how she might never again hold my chin and say, "You look so like your father," and I could not tell her about the garden. I worried that, like the window-flying white birds I sometimes found lying on our balcony, the ones my mother called her little soldiers, she would die. I worried that her face, closer to a sister's than a mother's, would shrivel decades before my eyes. Back then I understood, probably through some fabular bedtime story, that knowledge could change appearances. I knew that the mind could disrupt the skin, sadness in symptoms. I began to look for evidence of my father's duplicity in his body. A persistent rash or a drooping eyelid. Any small blemish would have sufficed, but he remained beautiful as ever. From his forehead to his toenails, my father was perfect.

That last time I saw him in the garden, I heard him following me while I ran up the path. I have a theory that men walk with heavy footsteps. They don't care about disturbing the peace because the peace never occurred to them as important. Women, in my theory, walk with a tender footfall, toes kissing the ground. This generalization is based entirely on my parents. As I got older, I made an effort to think of my mother whenever my feet touched the earth. My tread grew light as a forest fox, out of respect for my mother and a conspiratorial urge to sneak up on my father. I fancied myself the secret police of my mother's regime. That summer night, I fled the scene barefoot, carrying my shoes, one in each hand. My father grabbed me by the collar at the base of an Aleppo pine and looked into my eyes, pointing a finger in my face.

"You will not say anything to her. You don't know what you saw."

I nodded. I didn't tell him that I had already caught him twice before, that on my own I had decided not to tell my mother, that I hoped his black hair would turn to wire and fall out. He made me put on my shoes. We walked home together. At the threshold of our house, he withdrew a single pink flower and presented it to my mother with a bow. She smelled it, smiled, and put it in an azure glass on the window sill. In the middle of the night, I left bed to throw the rose out the window and then close the window tight. By morning, a bird, body like a drop of milk, lay dead outside the glass like an omen.

I never told my mother what I knew. When my father packed his bags a year later to live in another country with Yellow Dress, never to be seen by us again, my mother took me by the chin.

"We haven't lost a thing," she said.

Last week, fifteen years after my father's departure, I received news that he had been found dead in the bathroom of a chalet in the alps. Stress cardiomyopathy. I spent the day scrubbing my apartment spotless and scouring my hands. In every room, I sealed the windows to suppress the sudden scent of roses, persevering through time like the truth.

Natasha Ayaz is a Pakistani-American fiction writer and alum of Bard College and the Bread Loaf Writers' Workshop. Her work has appeared in publications including *Hobart*, *Narrative Magazine*, where she was a finalist in the 2021 and 2022 Winter Story Contest and a recipient of the Top Five Stories award for 2020-2021, and *Blue Earth Review*, where she was the winner of the 2020 Flash Fiction Contest. She is currently pursuing an MFA in Fiction at Cornell University.

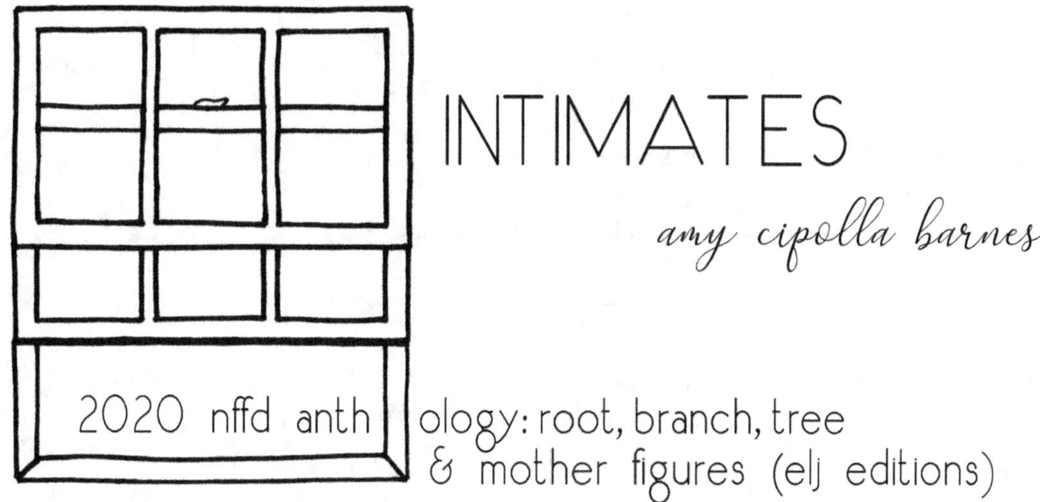

MAMA SAYS I WORK in pornography.

"They can see your *breasts,*" she whispers.

"Who are *they*?" I ask.

She flops the heavy catalog on the table with a thud. Her fingers flitter-flutter past steel toe boots and plaid pajamas, washing machines and 3-piece suits, drills and bikinis.

"You're mailing your breasts to men. Why not wear satin bunny ears to church?"

"Daddy left because you didn't wear lingerie." I tell her.

I know her dresser is full of industrial bras. At work, I hate wearing repressed housewife lingerie with tight bands and rough hook-and-eye rows.

Beige or white only, page 6. Bargain priced.

We don't get a choice on what we model, starting in the cheapest girdles and basics. There's bullet bras or shapewear; other days are a laundry-line parade of underwear. Every morning, I arrive in mother-approved kitten heels and Cherries in the Snow lipstick before standing shivering, as Matron Alice hands out my wardrobe.

"Put this on," she barks to our Sears & Roebuck sisterhood.

New Girl Kitty dances naked in the dressing room, assigned Littlest Angel training bras. The photographer is Kitty's boyfriend before we clock out. We model our mothers' secrets: divorce girdles, strapless bras, wedding night white ensembles, nursing bras as childless twenty-somethings.

We have moments of privacy before Alice bursts in—fastening, gluing butts into underwear, adding modesty shields—meaty hands cold and intrusive, granny panties outlined under her work uniform.

I don't tell Mama when I finish industrial undergarments and graduate to *Red Lace Dream, page 10.*

Perfect for Valentine's Day.

With matching polyester satin bikini and garter belt.

I pose with my eyes closed.

"You aren't working in girdles anymore."

Smiling for the camera, I feel lace digging into my skin.

Amy Cipolla Barnes has words at *FlashBack Fiction, X-R-A-Y Lit, McSweeney's, Popshot Quarterly, The Molotov Cocktail, The Citron Review, JMWW Journal, Lucent Dreaming, Anti-Heroin Chic, Flash Frog, Janus Literary, Cabinet of Heed, Spartan Lit* and many other sites. She's a *Fractured Lit* associate editor, *Gone Lawn* co-editor, *Ruby Lit* editor, and reads for *Narratively, Taco Bell Quarterly, Retreat West, CRAFT,* and *The MacGuffin.* Her work has been nominated for Best of the Net, the Pushcart Prize, *Best Microfiction,* and longlisted for the Wigleaf50. Her debut flash collection *Mother Figures* was published by ELJ Editions in summer, 2021. A full length collection *Ambrotypes* is forthcoming from word west in March, 2022.

THE PORCH LIGHT IS always on. Her father is always awake, waiting for her, no matter how many hours or days or years since she last returned. The freezer is full of her last visit's leftovers. She'll eat them this time, force them in between her teeth and down the needle-eye of her throat. Taste good? he asks. He's proud of his cooking. She nods. She wonders how he would react if she did anything else.

Her bedroom is as she left it, preserved, like something in dry ice. Except for the bedlinen. There is always a fresh set of covers on the huge duvet and overly-soft pillows, washed and ironed and still carrying her mother's unmistakable scent. They seem to soak up her emotions. She can feel them, trying to absorb everything imperfect and messy until she is separate, a body and a mind not talking to each other. Long experience has taught her how to cling on. The effort is exhausting, and despite the heavy material smothering her she feels cold.

Sometimes, the delicate threads of early-hours birdsong tumble around her like a waterfall. She has a sense of being lifted, carried on the sturdier call of the woodpigeon. She doesn't remember it when she wakes up—not the breeze, nor the deep breaths of dawn air—but she knows. Those are the only mornings she doesn't wake with a headache.

More often she hears a faint rumble, like the earth snoring in the distance. She knows it's her brother, his deep sighs twisting and floating their way to the surface under the old apple tree, where no grass ever grows anymore and no apples ever blossom. A ritual of protest and blame at all the ways she's left him over the years. First in the lake, when he slipped and couldn't swim, then in the ground where he couldn't breathe all over again. It's her punishment now to wake up clutching her throat and gasping for air.

(The narcissus grows still, by her parents' bedroom window. It never stops growing. Eternal spring. It''s tall enough now to gaze in through the glass at her mother's face that gazes out, unblinking and unmoving. The pale yellow shimmers on hot days, edges hazy like water. Sometimes she wonders if her mother has drowned too, if her father is the only one of them truly left alive.)

I'm coming back tomorrow, she tells her boyfriend on the phone. It's too quiet here. Her father hugs her goodbye, his eyes shining, says he misses her and that he wishes she could stay. His warmth leaks into her. She senses it inside, all the way on the train, bubbling in her bloodstream and making her numb skin tingle with pain. I miss you too, she texts him. I'll be home again soon.

Elodie Barnes is a writer and editor. Her short fiction and poetry has been widely published online, and she is one winner (alongside Erin Calabria) of the 2020 *Sundog Lit* Collaboration Prize. She is Books & Creative Writing Editor at Lucy Writers Platform, where she is also co-facilitating *What the Water Gave Us*, an Arts Council England-funded anthology of emerging writers on the migrant experience in post-Brexit Britain. She is currently working on a collection of short stories..

BREAD

lana bastašić

translated by celia hawkesworth

YOUR'RE FOURTEEN. YOU DON'T like these slacks, but someone once said you looked *awesome* in them and that's enough to make you put them on today, so in the mirror there's at least an idea, if not a whole person. When you were little you said *flacks* and everyone laughed, but there was tenderness in that laughter because it contained the idea that the mistake would stop when you were older. Now you're fourteen, standing in *awesome* slacks and looking at an ungainly body in the mirror. The mirror is small, its edges mean your legs below the knee and one shoulder are cut off. In the mirror is a mutilated body, and inside that body is you. The contradictions in your reflection are more painful than the overtight slacks. You bleed hot, thick blood out of too small a body. Between the stocky legs of a little furled girl you carry a sharp bush that no one has yet seen. Not even mum, not even a doctor. You're afraid of your bush because you're convinced other little girls don't have one. They're probably smooth down there, there must be something wrong with you. All the others are taller than you and almost all have breasts. Their fingers aren't little girls' fingers anymore, they hold pencils as though they were cigarettes, they sway when they walk, they know how to pluck their eyebrows. You once tried to fix yours, but you overdid it and dad was furious. He asked whether you wanted to be a whore when you grew up. You shook your head. You stared at your plate, mum and your brother said nothing, the restaurant was full of little girls with perfect eyebrows. They're not going to be whores, you thought. They haven't got bushes down there or inside them. They're smooth. But eyebrows grow and now in the mirror yours are huge again. You try flattening them with your fingers and then you see your nails, cut to the quick, because you play the guitar and you're not allowed to have nails. Once you put polish on them and dad was furious. He said he knew a lot about the world and a girl who used nail polish at fourteen would be pregnant by sixteen. That's why your nails are colourless and cut off so that you're constantly aware of them. That pain is the pain of the edge, where the flesh stops and blood begins. You carry that pain in your fingers all the time, whatever you touch. You touched your lips, they're rough and peeling. Mum gave you lip balm and said you should carry it with you always as chewed lips aren't nice. That's because you chew them and press them together whenever anyone looks at you. And someone's always looking at you: teachers, girlfriends, boys, older boys, the woman next door, mum, dad. You can always be sure of other people's eyes on you wherever you are, that's why you'll always munch on your lips. It's easier than talking. Cooking, you have to learn: talk less or your lunch will burn, your gran once told you when you were making biscuits together. Gran had cracked lips as well, she didn't talk much either, but her breasts were enormous above the firm knot of her faded apron. You wouldn't have been able to carry them, you're sure they'd break your back. You're afraid of those breasts of gran's and of those few black hairs on her small, protruding chin. There's no time for chatter, lunch must be made, she says brightly, opening the oven. Her breasts hang almost to its shelves. When you were little, you thought the oven might swallow up gran and her big breasts. You think about that now as you look at your tight sweat-shirt with a slogan you don't understand. Cool, the prettiest little girl in the class said when you came to school in that sweatshirt last week. No, she's not a little girl, but a young lady. She's already a young lady. You'd like to have her hair: long and straight, without a tiresome kink above her forehead. When you were at the photographer's, mum licked her fingers and yanked that kink so hard it gave you a headache. That was for a family photo, that pain in your skull. You feel it now every time you look at the photo. You have the feeling you can see mum's spit in your hair as well. You once washed your hair with something called *color-shampoo* and then on your summer holiday you sought out the sun to catch the red sparks on your head. You wanted to have something to show that was yours and wasn't ordinary, boring. But that didn't last long because you were afraid dad would notice. You washed your hair with hot water every morning so as to kill the red colour before he saw it. The heat scalded the crown of your head, but you put up with it because even the weakest ray of sun would have been enough to ruin yet another family mealtime. Now you're here, in the mirror, ordinary again, hair brown as a dried chestnut again, with overlarge eyebrows and a kink in your hair and cracked lips. Your *awesome* slacks and your *cool* sweatshirt are unobtrusive enough to be taken out of this small room. You pass mum in the kitchen and dad on the couch and go outside. Because it's Saturday and you have to get bread. It's only a few minutes' walk down your street, but you know that your town is a beehive of eyes and that you will chew your lips and your tongue and your cheeks if someone looks at you today and doesn't see exactly the you who looked good enough in the frame of the mirror, good enough for dad not to have stopped you before you reached the door, good enough for the prettiest girl in the class to say you're cool. No matter if it's just an outing for a loaf of bread. You've done the shopping and now you're walking proudly with a warm bag in your hand, the pavements are deserted, the sun is so strong you're convinced it will reveal the last hints of red color-shampoo in your hair. The street is empty and you feel you can be anything you want. You wonder whether that's the way real women feel, tall women, women with breasts, when they go to buy bread. And then you feel a heavy arm round your shoulders and another hand on your elbow. You don't know them, but they must come from round here, they stink of sweat and alcohol. Their closeness is like your cutoff nail, almost painful, the blood is right here, at the edge. At first you don't understand why they're so close to you, but then they start talking, panting into your ear and then you get it. You're all walking along your street which is suddenly emptier than it was, although a moment ago you were the only person in it, and now there are three of you. Sharp hairs scratch your face. They say you've got a nice bum, the one you'd seen earlier in the mirror, in the awesome flacks, no, in the slacks, the bum of a little 14-year-old girl who's conscious of her bush. But now you'd like to set fire to all the bushes in yourself and fold up like a box into one simple flatness. You want to be reduced to two dimensions just so that these words in your ears disappear and this chin against your cheek and this hand on your elbow and this stench that scours your nostrils. Your street is even emptier, the houses are like boxes, like you too, behind their windows there are no more eyes, the mothers are in their kitchens, the fathers are watching the news. You must do this on your own. He keeps on talking. Now he's telling you what he'd do to you, what he and his mate would do to you, and you don't want to cry, because then you'd be a small girl again who can't say *slacks* and then everything that's happening would be even harder. You have to put up with this, like that boiling water that kills the red in your hair, you have to hold out until you get to the door that's almost here, quite close. You have to stop: in your feet, your legs, your stomach, your elbows, your lungs, your hair; *you* have to stop completely. And you've succeeded, now you're just a reflection walking along the street, that body from the mirror, but without you in it. A body that's seen, touched, discussed, cursed, mocked, caught. A body that's walking in those slacks, in that sweatshirt, a body that's bearing his heavy hand on its shoulders. The body is reaching the door and unlocking it while those two guys go on their way with a few last remarks: about the lips of that body and the throat of that body and what all they would shove into that body. The body carries a bag with warm bread in it, the body hurts because today blood is gushing out of it, the body climbs the stairs and begins to shake in its two dimensions like a crumpled banknote in the wind. The body enters its father's house and now it's wild, bloody, sweaty, crying, and its father takes it in his arms and asks what happened. The body doesn't tell its father exactly what happened because all that happened were words which the body doesn't want to repeat, because the body is ashamed of itself in those words. The body feels that the body is to blame, it came out of the frame of the mirror and went into the street to buy bread wearing *awesome* slacks. It should have stayed inside, without legs or one shoulder. But the father holds the body, the father loves it and protects it. Protects it from the street, protects it from bushes. The father strokes its hair and says softly: Who's my girl? My little girl. And the body shrinks until it's small enough to fit into its father's hands and its father's question. The bushes wilt within the body and blood returns to the damaged tissue and its nails are once again as soft as a newborn's. The body subsides in its father's embrace while its mother slices the warm bread in the kitchen. Because today's Saturday and it's time for lunch.

Lana Bastašić, born 1986 in Zagreb, is a Bosnian writer. She studied English Language and Literature and holds an MA degree in Cultural Studies. She has published two collections of short stories, a book of children's stories, and a collection of poetry. *Catch the Rabbit*, her first novel, was published in 2018 in Belgrade and won the European Union Prize in Literature. The novel was shortlisted for the NIN Award and longlisted for the Dublin Literary Prize. Her short stories have been included in major anthologies throughout former Yugoslavia. She won the Best Short Story Award at the Zija Dizdarević Literary Competition in Fojnica, Bosnia; the Jury Award at the 'Carver: Where I'm Calling From' short story festival in Podgorica, Montenegro; the Best Short Story Award at the 'Ulaznica' festival in Zrenjanin, Serbia; Best Play by a Bosnian Playwright Award at the competition organized by Kamerni Teatar 55 in Sarajevo, the first award for best unpublished poetry collection in Zrenjanin, and the Targa UNESCO Prize for poetry at the Castello di Duino festival in Trieste, Italy. In 2016 she co-founded Escola Bloom with Borja Bagunyà and co-edits the school's literary magazine *Carn de cap*. She lives and works in Barcelona.

LCelia Hawkesworth graduated from Newnham College, Cambridge in 1964 and was awarded a British Council scholarship to study in Belgrade for 10 months, where she began her career as a translator. From 1971 to 2002, Hawkesworth was a senior lecturer of Serbian and Croatian in the School of Slavonic and East European Studies at the University of London. Based in Kirtlington and an active part of the environmentalist movement, she has translated over 40 books by Slavic authors into English, including *The Culture of Lies by Dubravka Ugrešić, My Heart by Semezdin Mehmedinović, EEG by Daša Drndić*, and *Omer Pasha Latas* by Nobel Prize winner Ivo Andrić. She has also written several textbooks of colloquial Croatian, Serbian, Serbo-Croatian, an anthology of Serbian and Bosnian women writers, a cultural history of Zagreb, and a literary biography of Ivo Andrić.

THAT MORNING AMANDA LOGGED onto her husband's dating profile, using her real name. That evening Jonathan arrived home holding a blue velvet box lined in white satin. When he held the three strands of pearls against Amanda's throat, she sighed, let him adjust the clasp. The coldness of the necklace radiated from her throat, past her small breasts, down her stomach to her toes, up her thighs and backside, across her narrow shoulders, and circled her long neck before settling on tiny ear lobes. Where floral diamond studs resided, mementos of her husband's last indiscretion. Amanda thought of arctic afternoons, her father pulling her into the tool shed. The next morning always a tiny box under her pillow. A silver seahorse dangling on a keychain. *Thank you, Daddy, I love it.* A teddy bear charm bracelet. *Thank you, Daddy, I love it.* A starfish hair clip. *Thank you, Daddy, I love it.* Baubles locked in a metal box housed in her lingerie drawer. Amanda traces the luminous orbs on her throat, her fingertip as cold as the sleet-battered shed where her father kept her warm. *Thank you, Jonathan, I love it.*

Roberta Beary has words in *The New York Times*, *Best Microfiction* 2019/2021, and *Best Small Fictions* 2020. Beary collaborated on One Breath: The Reluctant Engagement Project, which pairs their writing with artwork by families of people with disabilities. *Carousel,* their most recent poetry collection, won the Snapshot Press UK award contest. Originally from Queens, Beary lives in County Mayo, Ireland where she tweets her tiny fiction and micropoetry @shortpoemz.

SWIMMING

tina jenkins bell

LANGSTON STOOD IN THE shallow end of the lake with his arms extended and knees bent, bracing himself. He fussed about as Julia shimmied around him, kicking at waves, laughing, tickling him.

"Don't break a bone, messing around." Langston drawled, pretending to laugh though he really wanted out of the lake. He shook beads of water from his graying afro and wiped his eyes. His vision blurred as he took in his surroundings. The blue sky washed over the edges of the beach. Faceless, peach figures raced about or stretched out on colorful pallets. Umbrellas with long rods poked from the sand. Yelps of glee echoed, causing him alarm as the force of waves became shoving hands, punching fists. "Help me," he mouthed.

Meanwhile, Julia's shimmy turned into a Cha-Cha. "Baby, this little bit of water won't hurt you."

Melanie and Marcus stood within shouting distance, watching Julia and Langston from the shore. Their hands, like visors, shielded their eyes from the sun.

Marcus retorted, "Technically, you can drown in a bathtub. Remember Whitney?"

Melanie ricocheted a wet towel off of Marcus' thigh.

Marcus smarted, "What!"

"That was wrong, Marcus. W-R-O-N-G, wrong." Melanie said, rolling her eyes. "Anyway, you need to mind your business."

"Y'all heard the man say he don't want no parts of the water. He's fifty something years old, not twelve. If he'd wanted to learn to swim, he'd have done it by now."

"Thanks, Marcus. Julia don't listen," Langston said, trying to look over his shoulder to commiserate when his feet began to slip on slick rock. "Ah, shi…"

Langston's six-foot-five frame scissored in the air, landing him butt first in lake. He splashed about furiously as a swell of water hit him in the face. From a seated position, he dog pedaled the air, slapping away memories like the time a group of white men chased him and his brother Ricky away from the neighborhood pool…like the time a swarm of men tried to drown him in the Barnett Reservoir, their beefy hands clamping the top of his head and pushing down remained a palpable memory…like the time…like the time. . . like the time.

Langston tensed a bit, feeling Julia's hand brush his shoulder. She reached further, an olive branch to help him up. "Baby, I got you. You're safe."

"I'm not safe," Langston said, accepting Julia's extended hand to pull himself up. In the distance, a group of young white kids garbed in plastic snorkel gear and inflated arm cuffs dived, swam, splashed, and giggled.

Julia nodded toward the youth. "See. They can't be more than six years old, but they're swimming."

"Yea, well, the world is theirs to swim in. Isn't it?"

"I don't understand," Julia said.

Of course, she didn't understand, having been raised upper middle class in the north. Unlike him, a southern boy to his core but still her man, and men don't fear. But they sometimes shake when they remember.

Tina Jenkins Bell is a published fiction writer, playwright, freelance journalist, and literary activist living on Chicago's south side with her husband Earl and two dogs Jackson and Bella. She is the mother of four and writes about being Black in America and the various ways race can contort relationships and other common aspects of life. She is currently working on a novel entitled *Down and Dirty* in Kosciusko, Mississippi.

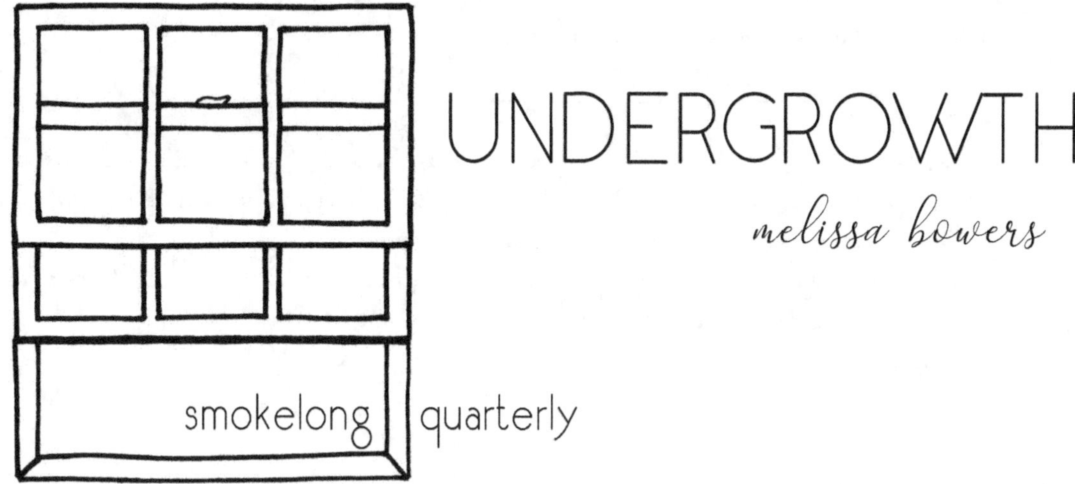

HE IS THREE YEARS old and thinks the word for plant is *planet*. I should correct him, but I don't, because I suspect it won't last—the same way *brefkast* and *sank you* sprouted from his mouth for months and then somehow blossomed properly, even without adequate sunlight. Every time we pass the farmland on that stretch beyond Highway 101, he watches as the tractors overturn the dirt, rolls his window down to smell the tillage. They're getting ready for new planets, he says, breathing deeply, filling his lungs with the scent of soil.

He is nine and learning about space in school: how our galaxy alone is 100,000 light-years across, and how a single light-year equals nearly six trillion miles, and how there are two trillion galaxies, and out of all those planets how can we believe ours is the only one that matters? I tell him he is not as small as he feels. His doctor tells me she is not seeing enough progress. We're hoping for visible growth, she says. Brighter spots, happier episodes. I imagine him the way he looked when he was born: shriveled but strong, coated with proof of his own germination. Solid, at least. Something more than a shadow.

He is twelve and I find him in the redwoods just before dusk, kneeling in the brush beneath the trees. With his hands he clears away thick clumps of vegetation—methodically at first, then frantic, the greenery piling up behind him like a hillside. What remains is an emptiness. What remains is a bare patch on the world, as if he has ripped a swath of hair out of the forest. It's going to be a garden, he says, I'm growing this, see? But I don't. I can only see what is gone.

He is seventeen and one night he doesn't come home. I call his friends, his love, our neighbors. I drive the edges of the farmland and shout his name through the wind and park at the mouth of the woods because he has to be here somewhere, trapped just below the surface. With both palms, I press against the ground and wait to feel it give. Instead it swells upward from the roots, it bulges in spots, orblike. Beneath the earth there is the unmistakable hum of something spinning and spinning and spinning.

Melissa Bowers is a writer from the Midwest. She is the winner of the 2021 *SmokeLong Quarterly* Grand Micro Contest, the 2020 *Breakwater Review* Fiction Prize, the 2020 *F(r)iction* flash fiction competition, and The Writer's inaugural personal essay contest. Her work was selected for the 2021 *Wigleaf* Top 50 and has also appeared in *The Cincinnati Review*, *The Greensboro Review*, *New Ohio Review*, *The Forge*, and *The Boston Globe Magazine*, among others. Read more at www.melissabowers.com.

FINNEGAN'S (FIANCEE GOES MCARTHUR PARK ON HIS BIRTHDAY) CAKE

john brantingham

FINNEGAN [1] COMES HOME TO find that his birthday cake has sat out all night in the rain, [2] and in fact he had forgotten it was his birthday in the anxiety of his tenure report coming due, [3] and that his fiancée always likes to make a big something about his and everyone else's birthday, and the fact that this is his 30th [4] which would have been big for her even if he didn't care and the fact that she threw him a surprise party while he was in his office trying to understand the Kafka hell of his tenure committee [5] (he can tell the party happened because his cousin Babyface is on the back porch sleeping off a drunk as he always does after a party), and he has forgotten that his 30th was her ultimatum date for setting a date for marriage (which he has put off and put off), [6] and he has forgotten that he promised to be less focused on himself (by which she means

---

[1] Finnegan's mother was an academic specializing in Joyce and demanded that he follow in her footsteps. Why he gave into this is still a source of confusion for him.

[2] Later, Finnegan will realize that Natalie, his fiancée, has answered his life-long question about "McArthur Park," which is, "Why would anyone leave a cake out in the rain?"

[3] Until he had to start working for tenure, Finnegan thought his dissertation defense was hell. His mother has told him to stop complaining. It's a kind of academic bar mitzvah, which he thinks is cultural appropriation, but he's not about to stand up to her now. Also, 30 seems rather late for coming of age.

[4] If his mother infantilizes him, so does Natalie. What grown man wants a birthday party?

[5] His committee is filled with his mother's friends, and he's 93% sure she has asked them to give him hell. That's a phrase she'd use.

[6] Maybe Finnegan is a bit of a child. He doesn't want to be married. He should tell Natalie so she can move on. Not showing up might be the only way that he's capable of doing so after a lifetime of blind obedience to his mother. Except, should we allow Finnegan to avoid responsibility for his own action by continuing to blame his mother?.

work) and more focused on life (by which she means her),[7] and he has the sinking suspicion that the doors are locked and barred, so he picks his now half-melted cake off the driveway and takes it to the porch and takes the bottle of rum that somehow Babyface is still clutching, and he has himself a 3 a.m. picnic, knowing that tomorrow, round one of his tenure review will be over, and that means only six more years of this if he's lucky,[8] and he thinks maybe she won't be able to stay in this relationship that long.[9]

---

[7] Let's face it. She's not perfect either. Who among us is?

[8] He's 87% sure that his mother has asked her friends to keep not advancing him so that he can stay in this liminal state of need for the rest of her, if not his, life.

[9] So Finnegan has found a way to make a decision, by eating rained-upon cake and getting drunk, without making a decision. Natalie will come out in the morning to find him passed out next to Babyface and will leave him without him having to do anything.

John Brantingham was Sequoia and Kings Canyon National Parks' first poet laureate. His work has been featured in hundreds of magazines, *Writers Almanac* and *Best Small Fictions* 2016. He has nineteen books of poetry and fiction including *The L.A. Fiction Anthology* (Red Hen Press), *Crossing the High Sierra* (Cholla Needles Press), and *California Continuum: Migrations and Amalgamations* (Pelekinesis Press) co-written with Grant Hier. His newest work is *Life, Orange to Pear* (Bamboo Dart Press). He is a staff reviewer for *Cultural Daily*.

WALKER BRENTSON

margaret emma brandl

IN THE GYM BEFORE first period, Walker Brentson appears midcourt like a dadgum miracle.

It's been seven weeks since anyone last saw him. First we didn't say much, just that he must be sick. It had been three days before we noticed at all. Second week, we thought he had the flu. Third week—maybe chicken pox? By the fourth week we assumed he had diseases no one knew what they were—scarlet fever, whooping cough, shingles. In the fifth week on a Tuesday Jessie McMillan became inconsolable in third-period Spanish because she believed Jesus had given her a sign that Walker was dead. That dampened the speculation, but by Wednesday the following week we were all trying to guess at how—a falling piano. A steamroller accident. A giant hole in the earth that opened up beneath his bedroom in the middle of the night. Sinkholes: they're a real thing, mostly in Florida. Look it up.

Earlier this week, Walker Brentson was practically myth. We'd spent our mornings before the bell questioning whether he'd ever existed, if the locker between Stacy Vader's and Hunter Boudreaux's had ever been assigned to anyone at all. If maybe we'd just imagined his name, a collective hallucination, like the girls who all laughed so much they got burned for being witches. It's so bad we almost don't recognize him at all, squinting as he makes his way in the far door, straight from the car-drop-off line. But there he is, lo and behold, Walker-fudging-Brentson in all his four-foot-eleven glory, brandishing a single crutch like a butterfly net, hobbling with one foot clad only in a sock.

"Walker Brentson!" someone shouts, and at once we're on our feet, giving him a hero's welcome. We stomp the bleachers, hoot and holler and clap. The teachers don't know how to stop us. Someone from pep squad invents a rhythm: "Wal-ker Wal-ker Brent-son. Wal-ker Wal-ker Brent-son."

It's so loud we almost miss the bell, but then the teachers are shooing us on our way. All day we call to him in the halls: "Heyyy, Walker!" or "What's up, Walker?" or enthusiastic clapping to the rhythm we made—"Wal-ker Wal-ker Brent-son. Wal-ker Wal-ker Brent-son." But by the time we're all loaded onto the buses and headed home, there are whispers. Doesn't he seem—I don't know—*smaller*? Wasn't his hair a *different* shade of red? It's crazy, but does anyone else remember him as taking *fourth*-period math, not fifth?

We become a nuisance. Our parents' phones won't stop ringing. Walker Brentson used to write with his right hand. He used to be allergic to cheese. The patch of freckles on his chin used to have a different shape. By the time we're all forced to go to bed, we've created a phone chain: Hunter Boudreaux to Jessie McMillan to Mallory Evans to me, to Stacy Vader to Jagger Bryan to Brittany Bloom. And it goes on, and we've got theories: alien abduction. Doppelganger. Evil clone. Yeah there's a sheep, and cloning isn't instant, but who's to say there wasn't another Walker all along? A different Walker, with *modifications*?

We're tired of things changing, of going from one house with both parents in it to two separate apartments, different sides of town, *left my math book at Dad's, forgot my clarinet at Mom's*. Tired of trying to do math with letters instead of numbers, tired of replacing the old ways with the new ones. We're sick and tired of taking each year the new version of the standardized test, being told *next year you'll get to skip it* but never getting to that "next year." We've started resenting, just a little, that our teachers change their names when they get married. We hate if one of them gets a haircut, changes her style. When second period is shortened for a surprise assembly, we're poised to revolt. So maybe we're wrong about Walker, but what we know is this: something has changed.

Next morning we see Walker Brentson and none of us trust him. When he sweeps into the gym, waving his crutch around like a fricking tennis player, his brow crumples at the lack of reaction. He tries to sit by Hunter Boudreaux, but Hunter disappears to the bathroom until the bell rings. In the hall after first period I see him, Walker Brentson, trying to get the attention of anyone who will listen. Then I look away—before he can see me back.

Margaret Emma Brandl is the author of the novella *Tuscaloosa (Or, In April, Harpies)* (Bridge Eight Press '21). Her other writing has appeared in journals such as *Gulf Coast, The Cincinnati Review, Yalobusha Review, Pithead Chapel,* and *CHEAP POP.* She currently teaches at Austin College.

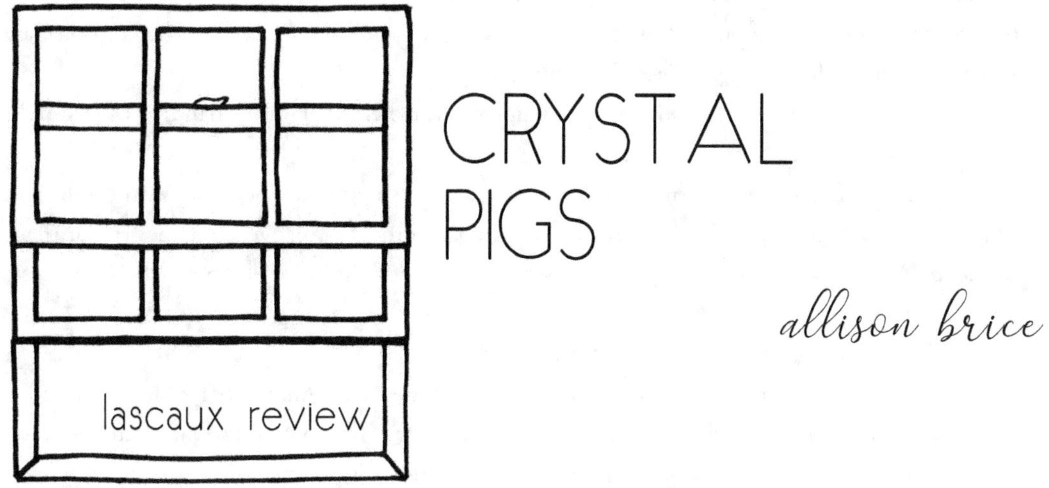

CRYSTAL PIGS

allison brice

WE SWORE NEVER TO use our customer service voices in bed. It kept us vulnerable and that made the sex good (awkward, and often prone to crying, but good). With her I could be myself, could exist in all my awkwardness and strangeness and reject the initial impression of my boots and jacket and shaved head. And as it turns out she was even weirder. Turns out that my straight-passing librarian girlfriend watched a lot of deeply weird anime and collected Swarovski crystal animals like a grandma. They weren't particularly valuable, only a couple hundred bucks each, but that's a lot for a county employee. So she searched all over the internet for deals, with an eye as discerning as a jeweler. When she found the prize—a tiny crystal pig with a spiraling glass tail, a hedgehog with pokey spikes—it was a celebration, a glass of good wine ($16.99) popped in her room, as she lovingly added the new family member to the overladen shelf. If her antidepressants weren't acting up we'd have sex. And with my head against the pillow and her hair tickling the insides of my thighs, I'd look up and see a hundred sightless black glass eyes watching me.

We fell in love softly (easily, quietly, over games at the arcade bar and cheap lagers), and we fell apart softly (silently, awkwardly, dinners with nothing to say). She stopped talking to me, started watching me like she was waiting for something, and how was I supposed to know what that was when she wouldn't tell me? And when the sex stopped working I didn't want to tell her that whatever new thing she was trying with her tongue was ineffective and did she even know where the clitoris was? But that was so mean, so instead I said *Yeah babe, that's good* and her head popped up because she'd been to my restaurant and she knew what I sounded like when I was reciting drink orders back to a table and the next morning over coffee she said it wasn't working.

And it was fine, a very calm and mature breakup. It was fine, and it was miserable hell. A pierced tattooed dyke with Doc Martens yet I took my breakup quietly, like a pitiful

February rain with no lightning. Without her, the existence that I'd carved for myself showed its emptiness, showed all the corners where she used to be, grinning at me with her dimples and holding my hand while she fell asleep, like an otter.

She was a statue, tall and strong, complete unto herself. I was a handful of crumbled gold dust that had once been someone.

The rains came, springtime and petrichor and washing away. But fine wasn't really fine. And it occurred to me that what she wanted was a commitment, a pledge, a partner rather than a girlfriend. And how better to prove it than by buying her the hummingbird, the one crystal animal she'd always searched for.

Except it was $829 fucking dollars.

That was a month's rent and utilities. No wonder she'd hunted for a deal, who could afford that? But what else could I get her, what else would get her to even look my direction?

The thing about working in the restaurant industry is that you meet people. And then they meet people, and you all talk over shift drinks at the end of the night, and suddenly you've got a guy who knows a guy who can get you what you need at a discount. And three traded shifts and most of my savings later I had the hummingbird in hand, walking up to the coffee shop where she agreed to meet me.

She sat outside in pink Keds sipping a latte. Her unshaved legs said *I don't care* but her perfectly threaded eyebrows said *Someone insulted me in middle school and I wear it like a battle scar.* She looked up when I came crunching up the pathway and while I was still a good four steps away I launched into my prepared take-me-back-I-love-you speech, topped off with a presentation of the hummingbird glinting in the light.

Instead I heard, "This was always the problem with you."

No, I protested, but the hummingbird—

Who cares about the hummingbird, she said, in the harsh voice she normally reserved for her mother. You didn't actually care who I was or what I liked, you just wanted someone to be with you and it didn't matter who that girl was. Six months and I don't think you ever met my friends, ever visited me at work, it was all *I love the way you make me feel* and *I love your body beside me* and I'm more than just a body, okay? I'm more than just someone to be there next to you and make you feel whole.

The other patrons of the coffee shop watched in fascination as my face fried up. That's not true, I wanted to protest, I also love the way you cheer me up after a long day, and the way you helped me do my taxes, and your smile when I talk about the stupid people at work...

Oh.

She watched this realization wash over my face, and I could see her struggle with herself, the desire to soothe it away, absolve me of my guilt with her people-pleasing heart. She had to bite her lip to hold the words in.

"So I guess it's a no, then?" I asked.

Still she said nothing. Suddenly feeling very awkward—like every one of my fingers was a fat, flaccid sausage—I put the hummingbird down on the metal table. The blue body of the bird caught the light and splashed a rainbow across her knee.

She reached out and let the beak press into her fingertip.

Allison Brice was raised in the deserts of Tucson, Arizona but resides in Washington, DC, where she teaches U.S. history to adults and mostly fails. Her work has been published in *Furious Gazelle*, *Orca*, *Typehouse Literary Magazine*, *Metaphorosis Magazine* and *The Lascaux Review*. She can be found on Twitter @_allisonbrice_.

A FOLKTALE OF FOLLICLES

victoria buitron

ONCE WE HIT PUBERTY, our moms taught us how to shave and pluck until only the hairs in our noses and head remained. Andrea, my cousin, loved to throw herself into the river, grabbed eels to extract their shocks and then would jolt all of us once she was on land, giggling when our bodies leapt.

She sang to the capybaras when the sun rose and hid chickens from her mother so she wouldn't serve them for dinner. But she forgot to shave, a trail of hair on her arms, barely visible strands dotted with sweat over her small lips. We all warned her. Then Tin-Tin came one night, took her deep into the forest.

He appears naked, his cock as long as an eel, a guitar strapped around his back, and the face of a haggard gnome without a beard, wearing a hat like witches do—but instead of black it's the shade of terracotta clay. He's solely in search of women with wild hair on their bodies. I was fifteen when Andrea disappeared. The day after she left I took her old sloth claws to make into a necklace that would live by my heart. Years ago she found a baby sloth, sick and abandoned by its mother, and tried to nourish it with tapir milk. For a week it drifted in and out of sleep, its eyes closing and opening faster than it could move its arms, until the chest contracted and couldn't blossom out. She buried it, but not before taking a keepsake. She didn't talk about it, but she'd give me sloth claw face massages when it rained so much the drips hurt our skin, using the outer crescent on my cheeks, the smooth leading me to a tingly sleep.

I stopped shaving but told no one. Slept in the day, and stayed up at night in the corner of my hut. I pretended to be asleep, clogged my ears with leaves to avoid the guitar's lull. First came the smell of mangrove. A miasma of rotten eggs that had sizzled under the sun. The faint odor of crabs that live deep in the muck. When it touched me, its skin like the grease of pink boto dolphins, I grabbed the razor I'd shaved with since I was nine, cut its jugular. The next morning I didn't let the people in the pueblo burn it. I placed the body on the branch of a tree in the outskirts of our village, the flaccid rope that was once a cock next to it, the guitar in pieces.

As the weeks and months went by, on the days the sunset traversed from pink to the red of heliconias, I'd walk by the river to wait for her, clutching the sloth's keratin to my chest. Hoping she'd rise from the water or appear from the east like an arboreal fog with a baby straddled on her breast. But she never came. I haven't shaved since I last saw her. Most girls still do. I don't blame them. Some of the women are convinced he couldn't have been the only one. And we all know it's easier to control skin than risk letting a body do what it was born to do.

Victoria Buitron is a writer and translator with an MFA in Creative Nonfiction from Fairfield University. Her work has been featured or is upcoming in *Smokelong en Español*, *Bending Genres*, *Lost Balloon*, and other literary magazines. Her debut memoir-in-essays, *A Body Across Two Hemispheres*, is the 2021 Fairfield Book Prize winner.

THE TWELVE DANCING PRINCESSES

sarah shun-lien bynum

IF YOU DANCED FROM midnight to six a.m., who would understand?

The father who stands shirtless in a darkened bedroom, playing NBA 2K to the roar of an artificial crowd, knees bent slightly as if readying for a fast break, an opening, any way out. He would understand.

The neighbor from across the street, wandering down his driveway, wiping ash from the roof of his car with a dishcloth, scanning the ground for devil's grass, scanning the sky for a sign of the moon. He would understand.

The mother who has migrated to the empty guest room and now lies beached on the pillow-top mattress, panting with awareness, debating whether to turn on the light and read a Hungarian novel. She would understand.

The teenagers who wait, watching trailers on Netflix and taking astrological quizzes, drumming their feet against walls, strumming chords, flexing abs, fluffing pillows, always alone. Those thwarted runaways would understand.

The dog who paces the hallway with his worrisome hip, settling down after a sigh only to rise up again and gnaw at some unreachable itch, his tags jingling delicately like the chains of a ghost. He would understand.

The fact is, everyone in this moment would understand. If only there were someplace to *dance*.

In March, the temporary closures began, following orders from the county's Department of Public Health. Overnight, the dance studios went dark: Playground, Edge, Millennium, Movement Lifestyle, Sweat Spot. All of those warm bodies vanished. The doors were locked. The lights and music were shut off.

Now, after six months, the closures have become permanent, because who can afford to keep paying rent on 5,000 square feet of empty mirrors and sprung floors in the middle of a pandemic?

Which is why the mother drives thirty-two miles to a mini-mall in a distant suburb. The parking lot entrance is on the right, past the Burger King. According to the official paperwork taped to the window, the business is categorized not as a dance studio but a day camp: regular disinfection, temperatures taken, cloth face coverings worn at all times. Through the Venetian blinds, the mother can see where the girls will dance, neon tape on the marley marking twelve large squares of space across the floor. Beside her, your body is thrumming, midriff exposed, mouth and nose hidden.

"You think this is going to be safe?" you ask, knocking lightly on the glass.

Your mother holds her breath as she watches you open the door.

Sarah Shun-lien Bynum is the author of two novels, *Ms. Hempel Chronicles*, a finalist for the PEN/Faulkner Award, and *Madeleine Is Sleeping*, a finalist for the National Book Award. Her new story collection, *Likes*, was a finalist for the Story Prize and the *Los Angeles Times* Book Prize.

I AM THE FEMME fatale. I linger in doorways, knee bent, back of my hand pressed to my forehead. I cry in camera light. Tears shining, lips quivering, but my mascara never runs. My blush always accentuates my cheeks. I always fall for the detective, even though I ask him to solve the case of my murdered husband. To find my missing jewels. To help me because I am a helpless woman in need of protection. In need of saving. In need of a man. I am a portrait captured in black and white. A woman absent of color despite my pencil skirts and blazers that caress my curves when I walk. The heels that meld to my feet. I learn to run in these heels. How to be kidnapped, how to fight, how to stand perfectly still in these heels with a gun pressed into my temple. I wonder what will it take to be rid of these heels. I run into the arms of the detective in these heels. Kiss his cheek, his lips, allow our foreheads to touch, our noses to rub together because I am...what? In love? I know this isn't a romance story, just another detective claiming his reward for another case solved. Never mind the bodies. My dead husband. My missing jewels nestled in the detective's safe. Never mind that I cracked the case, identified the murderer, found all the clues while posing in the light. While sitting across from the detective, blinds scarring my face. That I, the femme fatale, guided the detective to the answer with a well-placed trip, a single tear tracing my jawline, a scream that baited him towards the villain, my kidnapper. I know the detective isn't ready for the mysterious case of the swollen ego so—I knock. I knock on the glass pane of a door with his name etched in black letters. His name that pulls the camera's lens in close. No one knows my name, not like they know his. I'll enter because the detective tells me to. Walk in because that's what the detective says, *that's when she walked into my life*, without moving his mouth. Sit across from him, dab at my tears with a handkerchief I didn't know I had. Tell him *I need your help*. Tell him *please, help me* in a single sigh even though I know how this story ends. I've played this part before except, this time, I'll cross my legs. Let the camera capture the blood on my heel. Frame it in black and white so only I know it's there.

K.B. Carle lives and writes outside of Philadelphia, Pennsylvania and earned her MFA from the Naslund-Mann Graduate School of Writing. Her stories appear or are forthcoming in various publications including *F(r)iction, HAD, Good River Review, Waxwing Magazine, Hippocampus Magazine,* have been nominated for the Pushcart Prize, and included in Best of the Net. You can find her on Twitter @kbcarle or online at www.kbcarle.com. She is currently working on a flash fiction collection and a novel.

RADISH HEAD

k-ming chang

MY MOTHER AND HER classmates called him Cai Tou. He was the new boy in their class, the one born in a city, and he had a bald spot on the back of his head that was white as a shucked-out eye. It was basically a birthmark, my mother explained, but not. Every time my mother told me this story, she reached out her hand and jerked out a few strands of my hair. Like that, she said, but much harder. Cai Tou was one of seven children, same as my mother, but the difference was that he lived in a two-story house with a maid, plus his father was a professor of English. Say something in English, my mother said to him, but he never answered. He knocked his forehead with both fists and said oops, I swallowed all of it. They called him Cai Tou because of his head, but he ended up impressing everyone on sports day by running faster than all the other boys in the class. Later, they found out it was because a wasp had stung his penis and he was running to ventilate his crotch, but because of his record 100-meter dash, they stopped calling him Cai Tou for an entire week. The name returned one day when they were standing in the fruit fields, shooting the watermelons with pistols—it was practice for someday shooting soldiers, my mother said, though watermelons are much more delicious to hit. While my mother and her classmates rubied their lips with watermelon rinds, Cai Tou confronted them, twining himself with the vines. He argued that the nickname Cai Tou was the Taiwanese word for radish, and since every Taiwanese word accrued a fine of one dollar—one girl got caught calling to her mother in Taiwanese and got fined so bad she had to sell her roof the week before a typhoon—it was illegal to call him Cai Tou. Call me by my Mandarin name, he said, though no one remembered it. His real name was like something-something sun, my mother said. Some of the kids were scared off and no longer called him by any name, but my mother said she wasn't afraid of fines, since the teachers knew she couldn't pay up. Instead, they kept a word debt, hitting her a total number of times at the end of every month, one stroke for each Taiwanese word they overheard.

There was this one time, my mother said, when my first sister called out HEY, LITTLE SISTER as I passed her in the hallway, and they took her out to the hills and beat her with some kind of branch. But every time they hit her, she swore in Taiwanese, which added another stroke to her debt, so by the time they finished with her, she had no bones left. She's still alive, though, my mother said. Right, I know that, I said to my mother. Aunt Iris came just yesterday to hang up this crucifix, the one with the missing ribs. Right, my mother said, anyway, I wasn't afraid of the fines. It was Cai Tou who cried whenever I got fined. He used to stand outside the classroom while I got beat, and afterwards, when I came dog-crawling out, he'd give me a pig's blood cake to reimburse the blood I'd paid from the vein, even though I couldn't really give him anything in return, and then he'd say he was sorry, like he was the one who loaded the words into my mouth and fired them. He was that kind of boy, bloodsoft, sorry. By the end of every month, the teachers calculated two hundred words of debt, and I paid it all with my generous rear end. That's why I've got such a fat ass. I've layered it like a cake. Now I'm impervious to blades. Any fist would get buried in all this frosting. Okay, I said, but what happened to Cai Tou? Oh yeah, my mother said. He grew up and his father gambled away all his family's money and the house was damned to debt. Cai Tou's mother said it was all our fault, that we rotted him like a fly-studded rind, that we corrupted his blood to mud. By the time we were in high school, he was as poor as us, and he still looked like a radish, with that bright spot beating like a moth at the back of his head. We used to flick at it with our forefinger or try to hit it with a pebble. I really wanted to press my pistol to it. Not really to shoot him or anything, just to see if the mouth would fit, match the shape of it. I like to see a reason for something. Anyway, you're lucky, my mother said to me, because it's not illegal to say radish anymore, and now when I say it, Cai Tou, I think of him in that watermelon field, his head lowered so far forward we could see that birthmark salting his scalp, and he asked for his real name back, which was something-something meadow. He begged us not to call him that dirt-word anymore, but the way it feels in my mouth now, Cai Tou, without any debt tethered to it: saying it is sweet as watermelon meat.

I wouldn't know, I said to my mother, you never taught me any Taiwanese. My mother smiled at me, spitting the shell of a watermelon seed between my feet, and said that's good. It's better not to know how much you owe.

K-Ming Chang is a Kundiman fellow, a Lambda Literary Award finalist, and a National Book Foundation 5 Under 35 honoree. She is the author of the *New York Times* Book Review Editors' Choice novel *Bestiary* (One World/Random House, 2020), which was longlisted for the Center for Fiction First Novel Prize and the PEN/Faulkner Award. In 2021, her chapbook *Bone House* was published by Bull City Press. Her short story collection, *Gods of Want*, is forthcoming from One World, as well as a novel titled *Organ Meats*.

DON'T CALL YOUR HUSBAND by his name; address him respectfully as Sunte Ho or Ae Ji; wipe under your arms and breasts; stick a jasmine bud in your hair every night; massage his legs in bed when he's too tired for anything else; don't go to sleep before him; don't wake up after him; make a fire first thing in the morning to heat water for his bath; scrub his white underwear and soak it in a solution of indigo for brightness; fold it into neat squares and stack it in little towers in his cupboard; pour him a glass of cool water from the surahi when he returns from work; make him a cup of chai; actually make chai whenever he's sitting idle; don't make him a watery chai—use three parts milk and one part water, crushed cardamoms for aroma, a little nutmeg for a stimulating effect; roll out soft, thin rotis for him that break with two fingers; make sure their edges are cooked and they puff up like balls on the flame; serve them hot, smeared with butter and a smile; urge him to take one more like you mean it; add a dollop of ghee to his daal; don't surprise him by telling him you're going to your Ma's place when you're homesick; ask his permission first. *But, can't I visit you when I want?* Toss your impulsiveness back into this house with the handful of rice grains you'll throw overhead on your vidaai, the departure ceremony after your wedding.

Don't forget the kitchen belongs to your mother-in-law; it's her son you married, her roof you rest under; don't cook without asking for instruction—how much garlic in the spinach, how brown the onions, how tender the goat; don't serve without asking for instruction—whether to ladle the vegetable beside the rotis, whether to heap the daal over rice, whether to place the pickle to the left or to the right of the rice in the thali; add garam masala and chilli powder to your plate if the food is too bland for your taste; if it's too spicy, adapt; serve the biggest paneer chunks and the chicken thighs to her; eat after she's eaten; don't water her tulsi plant when you're bleeding; fast and pray when she does; recite Gayatri Mantra every day; embellish her kitchen shrine with roses and marigolds; visit the Shiva temple with her on

Mondays; guard her Kolhapuri slippers while she bows to the deities; scare away the monkey that trails her for the bananas and apples in her offerings plate. *But, I'm afraid of monkeys.* Toss your fears back into this house with the handful of rice grains you'll throw overhead on your vidaai, the departure ceremony after your wedding.

Don't dry your laundry on the terrace; tie a clothesline in the courtyard, instead; if there's not enough space and you have to use the terrace, secure all garments with clips so they don't fly away to the neighbor's side; make sure your underclothes are hidden under a sari; return immediately after hanging the clothes—don't linger upstairs, don't let your gaze land on anyone; don't towel or brush your waist-long hair on the terrace; don't lounge there on a dhurrie to sun your skin in winter; don't lean against the parapet to catch the breeze in summer; fetch the dry clothes in the evening after the men of the neighborhood are done flying kites; don't admire the mustached neighbor's pigeons, their iridescent necks bent on the barley he scatters on the common parapet wall; don't ask to hold the birds—his fingers will graze yours when he hands you a pigeon. *But, I love pigeons.* Toss your loves back into this house with the handful of rice grains you'll throw overhead on your vidaai, the departure ceremony after your wedding.

Sara Siddiqui Chansarkar is an Indian American writer. Born to a middle-class family in India, she later migrated to the USA. Her stories and poems have appeared in many publications, in print and online. She is the winner of the ELJ Creative Micro Non-Fiction Prize, has been commended in National Flash Micro Fiction Contest, and shortlisted in Bath Flash Fiction Contest. She is currently a Prose Editor at *Janus Literary* and a Submissions Editor at *SmokeLong Quarterly*. Her debut flash fiction collection *Morsels of Purple* is available for purchase on Amazon.com. Her chapbook will be released later this year. More at https://saraspunyfingers.com. Reach her @PunyFingers.

— after Wong Kar Wai's Days of Being Wild

WHEN KEVIN TSANG'S DOG dies, we ask Dennis Lee what we should do because out of all of us, Dennis knows death best: last month it accordioned his uncle's lungs and then it came for his mother. One day she was pulling double shifts at the nail salon and the next she was dead and urned. See, you never know when we'll die, our parents tell us, but what really scares us is how easily the salon replaces Dennis' mother with a woman from Guangzhou who wears her hair in a perm, bristly as a toilet bowl brush. She looks like Rebecca Pan from Days of Being Wild, Kevin's sister says, because she's older and watches for these things, straining meaning out of the most ordinary people, and so instead of greeting the Guangzhou woman with customary politeness, we ask her about birds, about whether she knows what happens to birds born without feet. Do they just keep flying? Do they sleep in the wind? We tinsel the air with our questions, imagining our voices to be footless birds as well, but she brushes us away and tells us to arrange her bucket of nail polish bottles by size, then by color.

Boring, we say, but we have no choice. Either behave or I'll tell your parents, and then the feather duster will lash your asses, the Guangzhou woman says. Grievously, we arrange the bottles even as our first question, the most important question, squats on our shoulders and dazes us as we clack color against color, mucus yellows against saliva topcoats. You have taste, the Guangzhou woman tells a patron as she unthongs one jade-veined foot, then the other. Dennis looks away and here is when we repeat our question. What do we do, Dennis?

I'll show you tomorrow, Dennis finally says. He's the fastest at organizing. The best at patterns. Before him, the nail polish bottles stand in neat rows like candied teeth, hemmed in as if righted by the braces that parallel our gums. Do we need to bring anything? Nothing really.

Where did you bury him? Ah, Kevin's sister tried to grill the body. She thought she could turn it into food for the garden. There isn't much difference between dying and shitting, she'd said, it all becomes food. It made sense when she put it like that, but now when we repeat her words we feel silly. Dennis laughs. You got caught, didn't you? Anyways, no grill would've been big enough for Kevin's dog. Go bury him and tomorrow I'll show you what to do next.

The next day we tell our parents that Kevin won a Kumon raffle and that his family is taking us to the movies. We skip the nail salon and instead skin our ankles through the woods behind Kevin's house. Is this where you did it? Dennis asks when we reach the spot, a patch of earth as bald as our fathers' heads. Yes, we say. From here we can see a fence and then the yard and then Kevin's garden, the proud trellis roped with green-fisted vines. How far away it feels. Our fingers itch to pluck the clenched fruit, the Buddha's fists, the bitter melon. Pay attention, Dennis tells us, and so we make ourselves still, scuffing our sneakers into the black dirt.

Please, God, Dennis starts to say, but we stop him. Why would God care? Animals don't have souls, Dennis. Dennis shakes his head and tells us to shut up, that he knows what he's doing. No, we say. At school, Sister Mary says that God doesn't give souls to animals. But what does it matter, God still made Kevin's dog, Dennis says. We consider this because he's right. God still made Kevin's dog. Hid a soul from its body. Where does God hide souls? That's a question for Sister Mary, Dennis says, before telling us to close our eyes and to yawn out our mouths.

We don't expect it when he cherries our tongues with sweetness. Dennis! we cry, but Dennis just tells us to suck and chew and swallow because this is what he did when his uncle died, and then his mother. He says, I squatted by their bodies for a whole night and then everyone gave me envelopes filled with candy. Ba didn't let me go home until I ate them all, he says. He tells us that it's tradition, that eating the candies is supposed to seal someone's luck. We nod and suck thoughtfully, imagining Dennis crunching the candies, brimming his gums with fortune. We ask, what shape were your candies? Were they round? Because that's how we imagine souls to be, all the souls that God has hoarded, all the ones that He's hid from us, from our dogs, from Kevin's dog: a handful of golden tokens. Dennis nods. He opens his mouth wide, shows us his teeth, and we thrill at how his molars have yellowed, how they've grown soft with rot. See, Dennis says and he drags his pinky down and scrapes a hole into one tooth. Dennis! We shudder and scream and we spit out our candies, scared that perhaps he's given us the souls of dead things, scared that perhaps they'll find a way to live in our teeth too. We leave Dennis there, his head tipped to the sun, his skull a lacquered circle.

Back at home we huddle in front of our TVs, watching news about a place we already miss but have never been. It's raining in Zhengzhou, and we marvel at how the rain slants, at how it browns the earth, milkshaking it all the way up to a man's shoulders. A-Ba, A-Ma, we cry, our mouths pursed around green coins of ice cream. Where will the birds land? Our parents look at us with strangeness in their eyes. Which birds? they ask, and we say, the ones with feet.

Maybe the ones without feet too. And then we add, and what about the kids with candy in their mouths? How will they go home? Our parents say nothing, just send us to bed. Still, we wonder about the dogs buried in Zhengzhou, whether their corpses are floating in streets we've only seen, never roamed. Food for nothing, we say to ourselves, licking mint and pistachio from our lips.

    At night we escape from our bedrooms and pebble Kevin's window. With linked hands, we hurtle past the proud trellis and bat away the clenched fruit, the Buddha's fists, the bitter melon. We wade through the garden, the yard, the fence. We find the secret spot out in the woods. We plug our hands into the dirt, seeking those souls we spat. Trying to grow our own.

Celeste Chen lives in Washington, D.C. and is at work on a novel. Her writing has appeared or is forthcoming in *X-R-A-Y*, *Indiana Review*, *Harvard Review*, *Waxwing*, *Shenandoah*, *AAWW's The Margins*, and elsewhere. She is the winner of *Pigeon Pages'* Summer 2021 Flash Contest, judged by Dantiel Moniz; the winner of *X-R-A-Y's* Special QTPOC issue, judged by Daisuke Shen and Liz Crowder; and the winner of *Sine Theta Magazine's* 2021 Summer Writing Contest, judged by R. F. Kuang. Find her on Twitter @celestish_ and online at https://celesteceleste.carrd.co/.

FASTER

whitney collins

IT WAS 1987. EVERYONE Dominick knew was gorging, engorged, gorgeous. There was finally enough money. People could buy the tap shoes, the electric toothbrushes, the giant faux-wood microwaves big enough to hold Butterballs. They could afford a year's supply of the old red Doritos and the new blue Doritos and the old Coke and the new Coke and coke, uncapitalized. Everyone capitalized. They could have the Guess denim vest, the Ralph Lauren dress, the best of the best.

Dominick quit eating at 5:55 p.m. on January one of that rich year. It was an unplanned resolution. Dominick's mother came to the table wearing an entire bottle of Giorgio. His sister, Danielle, an entire can of Final Net. Inside his father was a fifth of Smirnoff. Dominick could hear the vodka slosh as his father pulled up his chair. Dominick imagined a little yacht in his father's stomach, going back and forth on the waves. On that little yacht, Dominick imagined tiny people—also drunk—with even tinier yachts going back and forth inside of them.

At dinner, there was no blessing, merely a toast. *To wealth*, his mother said. *To wealth*, everyone but Dominick answered. Dominick ate a single black-eyed pea off his plate. The plate was rimmed with gold stirrups as if his family rode horses (which they didn't) or owned them (which they could have). *Eat, eat*, his family said. *Fast, fast*, Dominick thought. The way he saw it, the less he consumed, the faster the world was saved. Inside of Dominick, the lone pea rattled like a penny in a beggar's coffee can.

Dominick was twelve and gaunt and downy-haired, everywhere. His pediatrician had just returned from a worldwide medical meeting in the Netherlands. He now knew everything there was to know about anorexia and was buying none of it.

"He's not anorexic," the doctor said. "He's besieged by *Weltschmerz!*" This was the German word for *ho-hum*. "Right now, the boy has little appetite for food because he has little appetite for life," the doctor told Dominick's mother. "Give him a year. Next thing you know he'll be all about sex and steaks."

Dominick knew this was baloney, because he could think of baloney and say 'baloney' without craving baloney. Dominick's mother, however, breathed a sigh of relief. She smoothed her silk scarf. The scarf was covered with saddles and riding crops. In the real world, Dominick's mother was terrified of everything equine, miniature ponies included.

By February, the only things Dominick had consumed were a bag of red Doritos, a bag of blue Doritos, and several circular items that he cataloged on a piece of paper: three silver-dollar pancakes, seven M&Ms, one Ritz cracker, four pepperonis, two inner rings of a white onion.

On Valentine's Day, Dominick fell in love with the idea of eating things that people would not think to eat: A single piece of uncooked fettucine licked and dipped into powdered Tang. A pinch of fish food. Gray-pink erasers from worn pencils. Limp pickles from a Quarter Pounder, left to grow cold on the Mercedes dashboard between errands.

As Dominick disappeared, he appeared. Now, he could see a visible pulse in his wrist and abdomen and ankle. There were new tendons behind his knees and on the tops of his feet. Here, at last, were his cheekbones and hip bones and eye sockets. Without food, his mind grew dim but his desires became clear: want nothing, take nothing, be nothing.

Meanwhile, people went to the mall. The mall expanded. The people expanded. Wallets expanded, overnight, like dough rising under dish towels. Children across the ocean stacked denim six stories high. They pulled levers, and the levers cut out blue jeans like cookies. The children stitched zippers and sewed rhinestones. They sent the blue jeans across the sea to America on weighty barges. They were paid in coins. Their hands bled. Who would consume all of the jeans? At home, Dominick lay on the couch and ran his bony fingers over his rib cage, strumming himself like a harp.

A new doctor said that if Dominick didn't eat, there would be no choice but to insert a feeding tube. The doctor told Dominick's mother to put one broccoli floret and one chicken nugget on a blue plate and present it to Dominick. If he did not eat them in thirty minutes, he was to be sent to his room for an additional thirty minutes, after which the floret and nugget were to be reintroduced on a red plate. Dominick and his mother played this game for eight hours, during which time Dominick ate nothing and his mother drank everything. While in his room, Dominick stared at his white walls and had visions. He saw monks eating monkeys eating bananas. The bananas were prophetic. One banana peeled itself and out came a scroll. Unrolled it said: KEEP UP THE GOOD WORK.

The day before the feeding tube, Dominick's father took him to the circus. His father had one fifth of Smirnoff inside of him and another inside his coat. He pushed Dominick in a wheelchair in silence. In the circus's center ring, Dominick watched an impassive tiger walk on its hind legs, a gloomy brown bear pedal a tricycle. Then came a man in a red leotard with a mustache like a soaring blackbird. He brought out three shining swords and—one, two, three!—they went down his throat. The audience roared and—one, two, three!—the swords came out. The tiger growled. The bear growled. Dominick's stomach growled.

That night, Dominick went into the pantry. On the top shelf he found a little netted bag of chocolate coins. He brought them down and removed their copper wrappers and ate them all. They landed inside of him like pennies in a beggar's coffee can. His mother and father and sister, Danielle, took three separate cars to three different candy stores and bought bag after netted bag of chocolate coins. At home, they piled the coins in front of Dominick. Some were gold, some were silver, some were copper. Dominick ate them all. The next day—and the day after that, and the day after that—his family went out and bought chocolate money with real money and Dominick ate everything put before him. Before long, Dominick's face filled out and his tendons went into hiding and his pulse could no longer be felt under his fat. The way he saw it, the faster he consumed, the faster the world was saved.

Whitney Collins is the author of *Big Bad* (Sarabande Books), which won the 2019 Mary McCarthy Prize in Short Fiction. She received a 2020 Pushcart Prize, a 2020 Pushcart Special Mention, the 2020 American Short(er) Fiction Prize, and won the 2021 ProForma Contest. Her stories have appeared in *AGNI*, *Gulf Coast*, *Shenandoah*, *American Short Fiction*, *The Pinch*, *Grist*, and Catapult's *Tiny Nightmares*, among others. She lives in Kentucky with her two sons.

THERE'S AN INSECT, MAYBE an insect, maybe something else, that stands still in the night, making a lonesome noise in the not too far distance. A young boy, not much more than a toddler, still close enough to those unsteady days that his hair is springs curly and white whereas it will be coarse and salt and pepper gray later in life, stands in the middle of a large bottom field in this dark. It's a summer darkness and the lonesome sound bleating out across the field could also be a bullfrog resting at the edge of a long puddle of water running alongside the railroad tracks. Whatever is making the sound, the boy must know.

He walks through the very middle of the field, which is populated by hundreds of dying reeds jutting skyward like the stretching fingers of dead men. As he walks, he grabs and snaps several in half. The sound of the snapping is the only other one besides the lonesome warble-bleat-croak. It is dark, for sure, but it's a young darkness, hardly an hour out from dusk. The scent of the hot chunks of coal that were warmed throughout the day is still heavy in the cooled air, and the sky has yet to show very many stars—only the North Star, and one other which is not a star at all but the planet Jupiter seen at twilight. But the boy doesn't know this. He only knows the sky is not yet as black as the warmed over coal dropped between the tracks.

The tracks can't be seen, but the mounded earth on which they run is easily visible. The boy notices the closer he gets to the tracks, the louder the lonesome sound becomes. He takes careful halfsteps, can see the shimmer of the puddle to the side of the mounded earth, lets out a long-held breath, and is then startled when the lonesome sound stops in mid-note. Now, and this is the paramount thought in the boy's mind, the only thing that exists is the silence, a deep wealth of it, a heaving animal, large and dying, fixing itself across the surface of all the Earth. It is a vacuum now, the field, the railroad tracks just before him, the clapboard house far behind, a vacuum in which sound is dead. And then, subtle and lightly at first, comes the lonesome sound again. A bleating? A croaking? Is it the sound of the boy himself crying beneath the bedsheet and quilt, or an echo of this crying, or a low moan of such helplessness and aloneness only a child could bear it? Deep within his mind there opens a crevice through which light shoots out laser-thin and the cause of a great deal becomes clear. Not the sound, but the reason, the reason he stands in the field at all. It's a complicated wanting, a desire.

The call of the insect (bullfrog?) from the darkness is the chilly possibilities dormant inside him, the way in which the sound squeezes itself out into the world like a desperate whine, a melancholia of the neglected soul and pocket, is the manifestation of his desire. The darkness is all the world's seething energy shackling him in place. The boy sees futility in the shine of moonlight across the surface of the puddles. He understands that the spear of shivelight that has broken loose in his mind can no more alter his path than it can transform him into a god.

Sheldon Lee Compton is the author of ten books of fiction, poetry, and nonfiction. Most recently the memoir *The Orchard Is Full of Sound* (Cowboy Jamboree Press, 2022) and the prose poetry collection *Runaways* (Alien Buddha Press, 2021). Also in 2022, Cowboy Jamboree Press released his *Collected Stories*. He lives in eastern Kentucky.

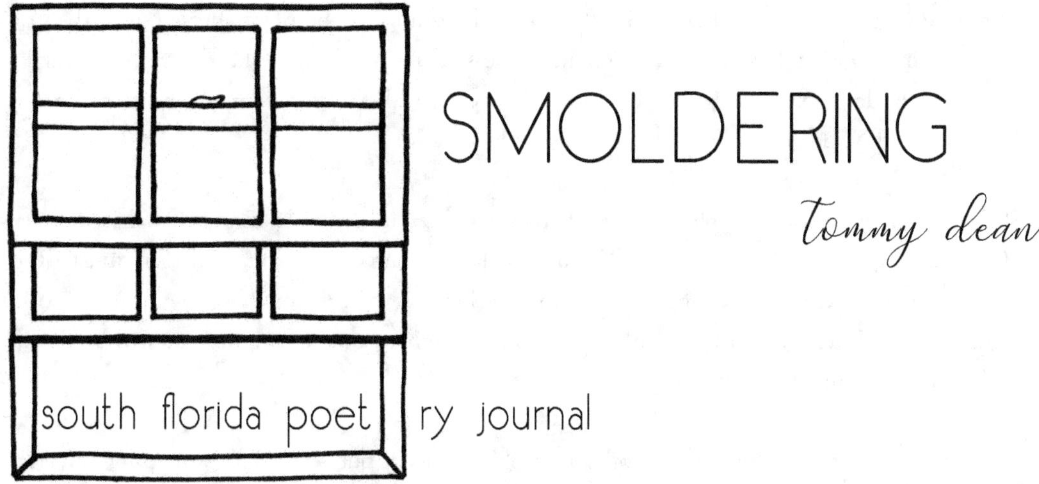

SHE PICKS UP EACH cigarette butt with a pair of tweezers. She blows on them softly, dirt and grass clinging.

In the living room, her father rests on the couch, left arm flung toward the carpet, clutching. Last cigarette smoldering in the porcelain ashtray. The suss of the air conditioning lifting the soft hairs near his temple. He offers no resistance.

The pine tree already rooted there by the garage before she was born spires the sky, while its needles ring around its base—a king nearly uncrowned.

The TV cycles through sports—soccer, billiards, women's beach volleyball, and NASCAR—speakers blaring the announcers' marketing copy like carnival barkers. She fled before turning it off and now the sound greets her each time she tries to cross the threshold of the porch.

The boys used to pee behind the garage. They called it watering the daisies. She squats, knees bulging like twin cantaloupes that are starting to sour, bees agitated by the sweat of her skin, flitting from flower to throat. She's pissed, still, at the boys' luxury of standing, of their dwarfing of nature.

Inside, the picture frames dusty with disuse stand guard across the old secretary desk. Ink on paper, they are idle threats of possible ghosts. He promised to haunt, but she felt only absence—a space she had invaded with her blush of breath. She fled to the outside where she was less alive.

The bee stings and she watches it wilt. *Well, hell,* she thinks as she plants herself into the grass. The swelling another heartbeat, a pregnancy. She scuttles away from the flowers, the smell of urine and pollen buzzing around her nose. The car or the house. Her phone is a forgotten accessory in the bottom of her purse in the passenger seat.

She stops in the kitchen. Table cluttered with yesterday's lunch—blackening banana peel, crust of baked beans, the limp remains of lettuce, a dried paint dap of mustard. The must of the molding basement, the tang of frescoed smoke. She sees herself in the tableau of a Hopper painting, arms braced against the sink, the moon spotlighted out the window, something lurking in the darkness outside of the frame.

Inside the refrigerator, there is ice for her throbbing neck, but she wants something sweeter, a dot of nostalgia on her tongue. A respite of childhood, before the duty of phone calls, the flap of winged grief from siblings and parents. In the crisper, a can of Pepsi and the orange wrappers of Reese's. The pop and sizzle of the can opening. That first taste of soda clearing everything from her tongue, her mind, sugar crashing like a wave, chased by the sour of chocolate.

Tommy Dean is the author of two flash fiction chapbooks *Special Like the People on TV* (Redbird Chapbooks, 2014) and *Covenants* (ELJ Editions, 2021). Hollows, A collection of flash fiction is now available from Alternating Current Press. He lives in Indiana where he currently is the Editor at *Fractured Lit* and *Uncharted Magazine*. A recipient of the 2019 Lascaux Prize in Short Fiction, his writing can be found in *Best Microfiction* 2019 and 2020, *Best Small Fiction* 2019, *Monkeybicycle,* and numerous litmags. Find him at tommydeanwriter.com and on Twitter @TommyDeanWriter.

THE SUMMER BEFORE THE GLITTER FELL OUT OF MY EYES

mary decarlo

UNBEKNOWNST TO ME, BLONDE Brittany had coated my eyelashes with glitter glue. I was the first almost seventh grader asleep at the first slumber party of the summer. The green power ranger standing at attention behind my pillow had not fulfilled his duty to protect me in the night. This doll was my favorite because his flat little head fit so nicely inside my smiley face Joe Boxer pajama pants. I woke with pink eye just only able to make out the shadow of Kelsey, the meanest girl I'd yet met, running around the foyer with my green power ranger in a futile attempt at embarrassing me for still sleeping with a toy.

At Brunette Brittany's house, I was warned not to talk to her new stepsister. Her mom told me she didn't know how to act right yet. She'd been busted stealing her new mom's letter opener and threatening third graders with it in exchange for lint-covered quarters and dimes.

At Maggie's house, we all watched a PG-13 horror movie even though we were only eleven and change. When the dumb girl in the movie was slaughtered after losing her v-card, we all told Blonde Brittany she'd be dead soon, too. Blonde Brittany was the only one of us with any penile experience. Totally randomly a stranger broke into the kitchen window so we all ran down the cul-de-sac with our nails dripping pink paint until her brother gave the signal it was safe to come back inside. Maggie shared a last name with the biggest grocery store in town so we all thought she was rich. Thinking back it wasn't true. Her family couldn't afford to pack her Lunchables either.

At Kelsey's house, we pulled out plastic bottles and sprayed back and forth until we were each drenched with love letter cucumber juniper berry moonlight tart fizz. I purposely shoved silly putty in the creases of the couch. This was revenge for not being invited to her sleepover the month prior on account of my ears not being pierced at the time. Kelsey only invited girls with pierced ears to her slumber parties. Her mom was foaming when she saw the putty. I went to the bathroom and listened to the carnage through the door while eyeing her dad's pee crusted tighty whiteys slouched near the tub.

By the time Brunette Brittany's end of summer sleepover party rolled around, her stepsister was gone. I asked her mom where the stepsister went, considering she wasn't allowed out on behalf of her consistently naughty behavior. Brunette Brittany's mom waved me off, picked up the wireless, and put her finger to my lips to hush me. I asked Brunette Brittany about her stepsister, too, but she only wanted to speculate on how Josh Hartnett's lips might feel pressed against her midriff.

I didn't know by the time the next summer came the cops would question me about my instant message history with Maggie. "What exactly does 'LYLAS' mean," they'd ask as I sat eye-level with their bulging stomachs. "Love you like a sister," I'd say. Maggie and her mom were in some unknowable trouble.

I didn't know Blonde Brittany's mom would move her to a state my mom wasn't willing to drive to. She left the night of a snowstorm that kept everyone else inside.

I didn't know why Kelsey only ever wore long sleeves.

I didn't know whether or not it was okay that I missed Brunette Brittany's stepsister. Sometimes, when I can't sleep, I plug her name into social media search bars. None of the faces that pop up look anything like the nine-year-old in my memory: the girl with a bowl cut, a new stepmom, and a letter opener tucked deep inside her plaid skirt pocket.

Mary DeCarlo is a writer living in Brooklyn with her partner and cat, Levon (Helm). Her work has been seen in *HAD*, *Capsule Stories*, and *Variety Pack* and is forthcoming at *Rejection Letters*. She is also a playwright with an MA in Text and Performance from RADA and Birkbeck University of London. For more, her website is marydecarlo.com, her plays can be found on the New Play Exchange, or you can find her lurking on twitter at @merrymarymare.

TALES FROM INSTITUT FÜR SEXUALWISSENSCHAFT

alex difrancesco

1. The Impersonator

WHEN I WALKED INTO the police station, her face was red, fading into blotched purple in places. Her makeup was smeared and ruined by tears, spit, hands. She told me her name was Leonore. A chosen name always tells us more about someone than a given one. Leonore: foreign, other. The name she had given herself.

I wrapped my coat around her shoulders. The police looked away, angry, embarrassed, powerless, now, that a doctor and scholar stood before them and offered her kindness. Such is the way of petty cruelty: it always withers when it understands it is no longer the strongest thing.

Her red nails dug into the tweed coat, and her tears started anew. I sat with her, and, with the police watching, looking away, watching, I explained that I had come for her. I explained the experimental procedure. I explained that, with it, there would be no more charges of impersonation. She cried silently as I spoke.

A few days after the surgery, I wheeled her out of the institute myself, to the waiting car. Her face, puffy with anesthesia and the bodily trauma of medical intervention, reminded me of that night, of her tears. There was something underneath the swelling of her body, behind the odor of mending flesh, something bright that had not been there before. She waved as the car pulled away and——

2. The Prayer of Mawu-Lisa

Dear gods, of which we are two, of which we are one, brother and sister creator, dear gods, dear god. The world created as we are created, disparate parts linked in benevolence, before Plato's wandering halves, before the pale man's fire and terror, before the world torn asunder the world brought together: the gentle moon and the bright sun's light in tandem. Ah god, ah gods, the fire———

3. The Treatment of Venereal Disease

The patient presented with late-stage syphilis. We have had a known cure for syphilis for years.

He had wandered, aware, through the early stages of sores, hair loss, rashes on his palms. He wept as he told me of clandestine encounters in bathhouses and motels, of how many men he assumed he had given it to: many. His wife, with whom he never had sex, had been spared, and for that he was grateful.

When the symptoms seemed to abate in later stages, as they do while moving inward, causing havoc with the organs, the beginning blindness he was now experiencing, the thick fog of confusion as the virus ate the brain, he at first assumed it was a cure from God from praying his sexual tendencies into submission. He wept through his dimming eyes.

There was nothing we could do, by this point. The disease had taken its course.

When he left the institute, with full knowledge he would soon die———

4. The Flower Prince's Benediction

After the dream flowers comes the trial; after the trial comes the light; after the light comes this, the benediction:

Head raised in ecstasy, the veil of the world torn asunder, a new vision—you, my broken flowers, of which I am the patron, you see this way alone.

While walking through trial and darkness, one must remember to bathe in oils, to put flowers in one's hair, to eat though eating seems like an embracing of the endless chaos this vessel has brought you, to keep one's body of water in water. One must care for the vessel through the trials.

My benediction, my gentle devotees: now that you have walked through the fire———

5. The Flagger

I saw his red tie. He saw mine. The look in his eye, matched by my smile. And oh, how we burned that night, and the burning———

6. The White Horse's Lament

When your mother prayed for a boy and the gods gave her a girl, she wept and entered the deception of those who know only possibility. Her will became your reality. As you grew, your clothes stayed on, your naked body a mystery. And when she prayed again, she cited all the examples of her case in the pantheon, a lawyer of spirituality. You had no choice, your choices were made for you. But the gods took pity on your weeping mother and your growing body, adding, taking away, giving you your new surname, "to grow." Little White Horse, did you have a choice, or did the gods choose for you? And, still, when the women lay at your altar before marriage, the flame in their eyes———

7. The Broken

In the late '90s and early 2000s, an instillation of The Institute's remaining legacy wandered through North America. It made stops at universities, LGBTQ+ conferences, other institutions which may or may not still exist. Cardboard with pictures and the few, unburned files. It seemed a shy student's history report, so small, so few panels, so little left.

Through the paltry alleys created by the little pieces of cardboard wandered the broken, the lost, those still trying to bring all that was burned back into the world. There were onlookers, too, those for whom the history was the draw, not the content.

But the broken, the breaking, those burned or burning, they are the ones whose eyes lay on their lost ancestors. They are the ones we follow through the tiny aisles through the paltry remains. They are the ones for whom these fragments exist, fragments they still attempt to weave into something, anything, whose shards shine in their palms, whose snapped cords they tie tightly.

———

Alex DiFrancesco is the author of *Psychopomps*, *All City*, and Transmutation. Their work has appeared in *The New York Times*, *Washington Post*, *Tin House*, *Brevity*, and more. They are a recipient of the Ohio Arts Council's Individual Excellence Award for 2022, as well as the first transgender finalist in the history of the Ohioana Book Awards.

FIESTA CHILI PEPPER PERIOD
catherine chiarella domonkos

BLOOMERS, THE POUFY UNDERWEAR bursting with lace trim worn by 19th century women. Mom buys a pair for me to wear under my gray-green plaid school uniform when I am seven. Oh, if Sister Augustine only knew. We try to jazz up the clinically depressed outfit with forest green velvet saddle shoes, but I am returned home with a note to return to school only when I am sporting the prescribed brown Buster Browns. Mom trims my braids with purple paisley headband and neon wool ties, all to the same effect: *Come back when you're ready to look like the rest of the flock.* Hence, the underwear. With red satin ribbon. That shiny red, a real tomato-orange, what the designer's color bible, Pantone, calls Fiesta. Pulsing with life and ready to party. I am tantalized by its heat. My secret red makes me giggle with confidence that out there in a gray-green world, a world sometimes like sea foam after a storm, laden with debris and rot, I am set apart. In middle school, a red patent handbag, more a Melt than a Fiesta, but still strong, vibrant. In college, I paint the walls of my bedroom a red hot passionate Fire Truck. Chili Pepper lipstick and I am spicy, a little bit salty. Tangerine Tango highlights and I am a sunset shimmering with energy. Now: Pantone Period. The one with the outline of a bleeding uterus on the color chip card. Sister Augustine, I think I'm ready now.

Catherine Chiarella Domonkos' short fiction has appeared or is forthcoming in *PANK*, *apt*, *Flash Frontier*, *Heavy Feather Review*, and elsewhere. She has a graduate degree in business from New York University and lives in Greenwich Village, NYC.

SHOES

mustapha enesi

HEAD TO OKEY'S SHOP as soon as you leave the house, but please, don't go in your blue shoes; not because your shoes may lose their shine and open up like a dead frog's mouth should you bathe your feet in Nwakpa's puddles like I have been told you do; but because I want you to listen to me for once; I know how much you like your blue shoes; how you wear them like horse's hooves; how they stick to your feet, guiding you wherever you go; I have been told that the big girls at school point and laugh at you, *blu-shoo* girl, they call you, don't they?; but you never stop wearing them, even though you cut your hair to skin that time they said your ponytails looked like chicken tail feathers; you will do anything for these shoes; I have noticed how you wear them to dinner, to the bathroom, to church, to the mall, when we visit grandma, everywhere; but, please, do not go to Okey's shop in your blue shoes; I remember those days I would scold you, telling you that you would never follow me to the market wearing those shoes, and how you would cry, drop to the floor and roll your body in the manner of dying chickens; you are not those gentle daughters who listen to their mothers, and know the way of the broom and grinding stone; you are not one of those daughters who massage ease into their mother's tired backs; you are not one of those daughters who bring responsible men home; you are not one of those daughters who never lose their dignity outside holy matrimony, because you do not listen to me; *but I never let boys touch me, not even a handshake!*; on your way to Okey's shop, I know you will bathe your feet in the puddles of Nwakpa Street along Yaba road but do not let Yaba boys touch you; with your open tooth and this beauty mark on your left cheek that gives you the prettiest smiles, everybody wants to touch you; they will want to run their hands through your long, lustrous hair; they will want to caress your skin that glows under the bright morning sun of Ikoyi; they will want to fiddle with the ribbon in your hair; they will want to feel the skin of the shimmering belt you tie around your gowns at the waist—why do you tie belts around your waist?; but do not let Yaba boys on Nwakpa touch you; if they do, look at them with your father's fiery eyes; if they dare you, do not hesitate to slap them; Yaba boys stay away from fiery girls; I know it is wrong, unfair, but nothing is fair in life; it is not fair that you do not listen to me; *what if I don't find the strength to slap them?*; if you were one of those daughters who listen to their mothers, you would find the strength to slap people who harass you; but you are not, are you?

Mustapha Enesi is Ebira and his works appear in a couple of online literary magazines. His writing has won awards such as: K & L Prize for African Literature, *Aster Lit* Short Story Prize; he was finalist for the 2021 Alpine Fellowship Writing Prize, 2021 Arthur Flowers Flash Fiction Prize, 2021 Awele Creative Trust Award and one of his flash fiction piece was highly commended in *Litro Magazine's* 2021 Summer Flash Fiction Contest. His short stories and flash fiction pieces explore marginalized individuals within African states. He writes from Lagos, Nigeria.

SOME HARD, HOT PLACES
kathy fish

MY BROTHER TALKS ABOUT the time he was in survival training in the mountains and he had to eat a rabbit's eyeballs. He's on speaker phone in his hospital room, whispering.

Now that he's dying my brother has stories in his mouth.

I shouldn't be able to hear him but I do.

I met someone, I tell him. On a Zoom meeting.

My brother is much older. He's been dying for the entirety of the unprecedented times. The word zoom makes him laugh.

I suggest a video call.

My brother has stories in his mouth but he doesn't want me to see him when he tells them. He's seventy-five percent morphine now and I am glad.

My lover and I write notes in the sidebar of the Zoom call.

The host doesn't know what she's doing. She mutes everyone then asks a question.

We are all shrug emoji.

We are all rolling eyes emoji.

We are all rolling on the floor laughing our asses off emoji.

On the screen, my lover is just a rook's move away.

We flirt in the sidebar and grin mysteriously on screen.

We agree to meet elsewhere.

We can't go anywhere so we agree to meet elsewhere.

What do rabbit's eyes taste like, I ask my brother because I'm beginning to doubt and I want to keep him talking.

My brother tells the story of taking psilocybin before a Moody Blues concert and seeing God.
    He tells the story of a trip he took to Vegas with our dad. Hookers, he says.
    He tells the story of putting a mouse out of its misery with a baseball bat.
    The stories in my brother's mouth are things he needs to spit out.

My lover and I can't go anywhere, yet here we are.
    I'm in his living room and he's in mine and I'm in his kitchen and he's in mine. We are in each other's living rooms and bedrooms and kitchens.
    We, together, never look out a window.
    We, together, never hear distant trains or smell snow.
    We never breathe the same cold air.

Sometimes we watch shows together, from our own living rooms, and I watch him fall asleep.
    We watched a whole season of Star Trek Next Generation and I watched him sleep.

    During Zoom meetings, it's important to address each other directly to avoid confusion. So the others don't reply. We say each other's names as if to say, no, not you. *You.*

In his longest story yet, my brother tells of a sexual encounter in the woods with a priest.
    It was pure, he says. It was connection, it was prayer, it was vigil. It was mushrooms and chianti and the Holy Spirit. It was the glorious mystery of the Risen Lord. It was…
    You wouldn't like how things are now, I tell him. Out in the world. You're better off.

My lover wants me to get closer to the screen.
    We are in our own space, just us two. But I'm as close as I can get.
    I cast flattering light on my body with the standing lamp, just out of sight.
    My laptop sits on a stack of books so he sees me from above.
    My neck looks better that way.
    This is how it would be if we were in the same room. Taller him, gazing down at my upraised face.
    My cat meows, jumps up on my lap.
    I didn't know you had a cat, he says.
    I lift her to the screen. Her tail tickles my breasts.
    He wants to know her name.

Her name is Mavis.

I set her down, the only living thing I've touched besides myself in forever.

He puts on his shirt. He asks me what I miss.

Everything, I say. Annoyance, inconvenience, long lines and lingering, grubby places, the hard, hot places.

I miss places.

I want to know what you smell like, I say.

I want to come out of a bathroom and see you French kissing another woman on a dance floor.

I want to make a scene in the parking lot.

I could make a good goddamned scene if I wanted to.

The last time we talked, my brother called me by a different name. He asked me if I still loved him.

Do you still love me, he asked.

I do still love you.

I still love you, I said, because I knew whoever she was, it must be true.

Kathy Fish's stories have been widely published in journals, anthologies, and textbooks. Her work has been published or is forthcoming in *Ploughshares, Copper Nickel, Best American Nonrequired Reading, Washington Square Review,* the *Norton Reader,* and *Norton's Flash Fiction America* (2023). Honors include the Copper Nickel Editor's Prize and a Ragdale Foundation Fellowship. The author of five short fiction collections, Fish teaches a variety of creative writing workshops online. She also publishes a popular monthly craft newsletter. *Subscribe here: The Art of Flash Fiction.*

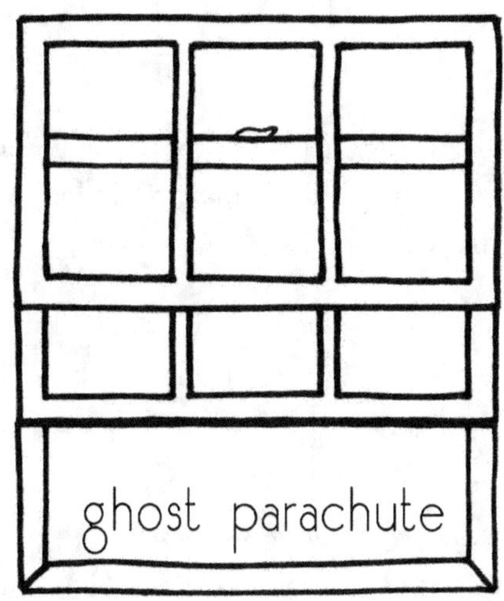

BROKEN KEYS
jennifer fliss

IT WASN'T LONG INTO their relationship that her "I" key stopped working. She started typing things like: "want to have sex" and "like beer & cheese." He took from these what he could and thought how lucky am I? I found someone who gives and gives and gives. Selfishness is not a trait he likes.

They wrote about their frustrations with jobs, friends, parents. He asked about her hair. Had she ever cut it? She asked about his roommate. Favorite meals. Her: takeout Thai. Him: homemade gnocchi. *It's so easy, anyone can do it.* She mentioned she had a window herb garden but didn't like to cook. He scoffed, but he didn't tell her he thought this was ridiculous. He talked about his recent case; he was an attorney. He began to type "tho" instead of "though" and "U" instead of "you," as if the effort for him to acknowledge who he was addressing was too much.

Like a piano with dead keys, it was beautiful until it wasn't. She saw the problem, of course, acknowledged it within herself, but didn't want to say anything. She couldn't afford a new computer and didn't see how she could replace the keyboard alone. All her letters, her words, slowly lost their meaning. M and E were the next to go. And soon he read her missives as that of a passive woman. In theory he didn't like this, but in reality, as he stared into his screen, his own face vaguely reflected back at him, he thought that this was, in fact, the way it should be.

She typed and typed, late at night, at work, on the train to and from, and she wasn't being any more understood no matter how much effort she put into explanations. Her friends said *ditch him* and *swipe left babe,* though that wasn't the kind of app she'd found him on. He responded between the hours of nine and eleven at night.

Eventually he wrote "we are going to meet IRL."

She typed, *ok!* Deleted it.

He saw three bubbles.

She typed *"what do you want to do?"* Delete.

The bubbles disappeared.

She listened to the hissing of the heater in her little apartment, something she associated both with warmth and danger. She had learned how to avoid the radiator during the winter, one burn too many had left a scar on her forearm that still throbbed.

He typed: *"Girl please."*

Girl? she thought.

"What was all this for then?"

She typed an angry mash of letters. *"Tnwfuwifnwijjufhrvrf."* Delete.

The bubbles reappeared. Disappeared again.

He typed *did I do something to offend you?* and *don't say you're that kind of woman.*

That knd? She cursed her lack of an "I." She dragged her cursor to the *Log Out* icon. Hovered there. Clicked *My Account* instead, clicked and clicked and clicked until she finally found, hidden amidst a throng of text, *Cancel My Account.*

A pop-up box: *Are you sure?*

Jennifer Fliss (she/her) is a Seattle-based writer whose writing has appeared in *F(r)iction, The Rumpus, No Tokens,* and elsewhere, including the *Best Short Fiction* anthologies. She is the author of the collection, *The Predatory Animal Ball* and her collection, *As If She Had a Say* will be published in 2023 by Curbstone Books/Northwestern University Press. She can be found on Twitter at @writesforlife or via her website, www.jenniferflisscreative.com.

THE IRISH GUEST AT THE WEDDING IN KRAKOW

linda nemec foster

SHE IS LOUD, LOVES to drink and smoke, and she's living in sin with a man from Gdansk. A man who should know better, according to his mother, the quiet woman with swollen legs. But what can she do? She's no match for the Irish mouth who speaks broken Polish—perfectly. This mouth confronts me about my life and realizes I have a husband…who's a doctor. "Well, aren't you the lucky one?" and "Does he give free medical advice…for this?" At that exact moment, when the band just finishes playing an oberek, the Irish guest lifts up her dress to expose a long scar from her last C-section. "See this?" She shows my husband, shocked into silence. "What can you do about this?" She whispers as she fingers the deep white line—a roadmap from Galway to Krakow—and describes every step. From yellow gorse to Mazovian willows; green cliffs to Baltic shore. From her dead mother to her dead son.

Linda Nemec Foster is the author of twelve collections of poetry including *Amber Necklace from Gdansk*, *Talking Diamonds*, *The Lake Michigan Mermaid*, which was honored as a 2019 Michigan Notable Book, and *The Blue Divide*. Her poems appear in numerous journals such as *The Georgia Review*, *Nimrod*, *North American Review*, *Paterson Literary Review*, and *New American Writing*. A forthcoming collection, *Bone Country*, will be published by Cornerstone Press (University of Wisconsin—Stevens Point) in March of 2023: her piece, "The Irish Guest at the Wedding in Krakow," will be included in this new book. The first Poet Laureate of Grand Rapids, Michigan, she is the founder of Aquinas College's Contemporary Writers Series.

WHEN YOU'VE GOT NOTHING else, you'll always have at least a tortilla to get you through. Learn to use them. Take a tortilla, an old one that's gone hard, and hold it over a flame. Watch the tortilla blacken and break. Take those ashes, when you have nothing else, take the ashes and rub them onto your teeth with your fingers. Smudge them, scrub them over your gums, all over inside your mouth. *Con un buche de agua*, rinse and spit into the ground. Rinse very well, lest anyone con fuse you with a witch. *La gente es bien pendeja.* Like they don't know the brujas are often the most beautiful. Careful with the *bonitas*, I say. One minute they are the sweetest pair of honeyed calves dripping down the street, and the next they're owl wings beating the night air. But not us. Not too pretty, though we have our gifts, we keep our teeth clean, our floors swept.

The things my grandmother used to say.

I often wondered what kind of situation would require me to burn a tortilla to clean my teeth. When might I be without basic items like toothpaste or bath soap, so that I'd have to find some elemental alternative to perform simple personal hygiene? It was hard to imagine what kind of thing might happen that would knock you back to where your grand mother had been.

It's a wonder even to me how I ended up on that pig farm. I wasn't meant for farm life, you know. Good at math, I was still going to high school and everything, kept my socks up but my skirt short like all the other girls, playing hooky on the Malecón whenever we were sure we'd get away with it. My own mother, *qué en paz descanse* was no saint, just normal like me. But when you're a girl of seventeen, and a man, young and handsome, looks you in the eye, serious, unlike the clowns you grew up with, and he tells you to marry him, well you think, why not? Here was a man, like a door, instead of a hole or a rope. Formal and upright. But I didn't think to ask where I'd end up with him on the other side of that door. He was opaque that way, didn't give many clues, but I should have known better with all that dust that covered him. That dust.

That's where I went—a place full of dust. Americans think Mexico is green and lush, a big resort hotel and a pyramid in a jungle by the sea. Well why wouldn't they? They just jump on their American Airline and off they go, skipping over everything, the dust and the rocks, the farms and the factories, and even the cities. They arrive at Cancún or Puerto Vallarta with their shoes clean and they find an ocean fit for a white bikini.

Or that's what I've heard. I haven't returned since.

The dust is what I most remember about living on the farm. Dust everywhere, always. One spends the day trying to keep the tile clean, when it might just as well have been made of dirt. You can imagine. Sweeping and sweeping, dusting and dusting and nothing ever gets clean. *Polvo eres y en polvo te convertirás.* Every day was Ash Wednesday, somber with ashy doom marked upon you no matter how bright the sun. It was this life, pressed upon my forehead every year of my childhood, a reminder from God, his sinister plan always there waiting for me, and I'd finally arrived to it. As a girl, laughing and sneaking drinks with the boys, it was hard to believe the Sunday litanies or the abuelitas' threats, but then one day you're Alicia following a white rabbit down the hole or a through a door. It was always there, waiting for you. *Bienvenida.* This is your *país* now. These are your *maravillas.*

My Luisito really was a *maravilla*, I could hardly believe it. A perfect baby, a perfect boy. Now on his way to being a man, and believe me, I've taught him not to be any kind of rabbit. Along with the dusty floors and shelves and pots and pans and everything else, I constantly wiped him clean, as if to clear him of any fate that was bound to that place. I did my best to keep his nose and his knees clean, but you know how kids are, especially boys. In my heart I prayed, over and over I'd whisper to him like a little song, not here, not this place, not like your father, not this life. *Más allá, más allá, el mundo es grande como tu corazón. Es un círculo, un cír-cu-loooo, no tiene fin. Ven, con tu dedito, trace a circle, te amo te amo te amo sin fin.* Lord knows, I've always tried my best.

Martín, his father, now a name like flakes of rust on my tongue, would come home smelling like pig shit and beer, but it was his bad mood that bothered me the most. He always came home looking for reasons to yell, mostly at me. Nothing I did pleased him. As if it were my fault that we lived on a pig farm or as if it were my fault that we never had enough money or as if it were my fault that I got pregnant with Luis too soon and spoiled whatever fairy tale plans he had for our life. I was only seventeen.

One day, normal like any other day, he came home for dinner. He took his seat at the table without a word, which was not unusual because I'd learned he was not a man of many words except when he was angry. Both hands waiting on the table for his food, I could feel him searching in his silence. Luis had just turned three years old and ran around the house like an unleashed puppy, so thrilled was he to see his *papá*. We hardly saw anyone at the time. I was standing over the *comal*, flipping the tortillas when I heard a crash followed by the hard scrape of Martín's chair over the gritty tile. As I ran from the kitchen I could hear him spitting out his *malhabladas,* barking like a rabid dog. By the time I got to them, he was already taking off his belt to whip my little boy. Luis had knocked down a small, framed portrait of Martín's parents. The photograph and the frame seemed fine, but the glass was shattered. It was just glass.

That belt was probably the most expensive thing in the house. When he bought it, we hardly had a thing to eat for a week. There I was, asking for *tortillas y frijoles* on credit, a strip of meat for the baby, scrounging around the garden for *acelgas* or *quelites,* whatever weeds I knew wouldn't poison us because the pigs ate them. I never would have imagined it in my youth, my recent childhood when it was not hard to have a coin for a treat. Not a thing of this did I mention to my mother in my letters, but when we talked on the phone once a month I'm sure she could hear something was wrong. I could hear something hollow in my own words when I repeated that everything was fine. To console me in my secret hardship, but probably to console herself, my mother said it was always hard in the early years of a family. But a family learns to grow together through its hardships. Perhaps she was right, but from what I could remember, I'd not been born into this kind of poverty. I didn't have the space for hunger built into my body. But now, I learned to build it for myself so that the baby would not suffer it. There's a way to make room for hunger, to hold it, embrace it. But this was a lonely hunger, the kind that separates you from others, and that's what hurts the most. I hope you will never have to learn this.

I was bewildered by the exquisite belt, more valuable than my life. I understood this when he first brought it home, laid it on the bed coiled like a baby serpent. I'd seen *cintos piteados* before on our trips to town, but none this ornate. An elaborate design patterned its length, bunches of roses and vines bursting with morning glories, one antlered deer kissed stalks of grass, another kissed the sky. Stitched in fine maguey threads, a landscape of hills was fashioned in the background of glyphs. Its geometries spoke an ancient language we'd learned in our blood to decipher. Its beauty clued me in to the misery that would follow.

And when I saw that this *viejo desgraciado* was about to turn his belt on my son, I threw myself to protect him with my own body. The leather was thick but I toughened myself against it as it landed on my ribs. I pulled the baby aside, I can still hear him screaming, and I stood up to this man, pushed myself right up to his face to let him know I was not afraid. He would not make less of me. I was never meek, but Martín had never seen me like this, and I could see the surprise light up his expression, before it turned into a fire. That's when he punched me in the face, knocked me right to the ground. But even then I would not yield to him, already pushing myself up on all fours when he whipped me on the back. I bit my lips so as to not scream, I saw my boy's eyes fixed on me. I crawled to him and curled myself around his shivering little body, to muffle his cries with my bosom. That beast crunched his face into a scowl, locked his lips like he'd had the last word.

As soon as he slammed the front door shut behind him, I grabbed the baby and ran for my things, my purse and a handful of clothes and that was it. You'd be surprised by how little you need when you're running for your life. The last thing I remember was seeing Martín's food still on the table and thinking about the tortillas I'd left on the *comal* smoking over the gas flame. I let them burn.

Carribean Fragoza's fiction and nonfiction have appeared in numerous publications, including *Zyzzyva, Alta, BOMB, Huizache,* and the *Los Angeles Review of Books.* She is the co-editor of *East of East: The Making of Greater El Monte* and Senior Writer at the *Tropics of Meta.* Carribean is the Coordinator of the Kingsley and Kate Tufts Poetry Award at Claremont Graduate University, and she lives in the San Gabriel Valley in LA County.

YOU COME HERE OFTEN

sarah freligh

AND OFTEN ALONE SINCE your best friend joined AA though she still calls you on the regular to remind you about her sobriety and how grateful she is to wake up in the morning without a SWAT team swarming her brain. She swears you to secrecy, *promise not to tell?*, before she tells you about a woman in her group who, since getting sober, often has sex dreams in Technicolor about a bag boy at Wegmans who's half her age—hell, he's younger than her youngest son—and now the woman can't look the bag boy in the face when he says, *hello, may I be of some assistance,* without thinking of fur handcuffs and the word *throb*, and your best friend tells you again that you can't tell anyone, not a soul, and of course you don't because who would you tell?

You come here often and often you wonder why you do. The bar stinks of smoke and polyester BO from the softball teams that hang out here from April to November, the draft beer is always flat. Also, the television chops characters into legless torsos and topless legs and unless the Phillies are playing, the television is always tuned to a Law and Order episode and there's something about a legless/headless Lennie Briscoe that always undoes you, maybe because Lennie, like your brother, is dead but lives on and on in reruns.

You come here so often that Jeff the Bartender has your beer poured before you sit down, a 20-ounce draft with just enough foam to moustache your upper lip on first swig, enough sparkle to scald your throat. You often think that draft beer is like so many of the men you've known—delicious on first sip, lukewarmer thereafter, bitter toward the end—and yet you go on ordering drafts hoping that the next one will be different, each sip as delicious as the first one.

You often don't go home because what's home about it anyway—a tiny apartment with a sinkful of dirty dishes, fist of hair clogging the shower's drain, a scraggly orange cat that hangs out on your back stoop, howling his terrible need and hissing when you get too close. Often you find mice guts or a bunny heads on the steps, bloody evidence of animal love. Sometimes, but not often, you go home with a guy who smells like your brother did, of warm flannel and corn chips, a guy who has the same nervous curl to his hair. Sometimes you'll smoke a bowl on the roof deck of a rowhouse and stone out on the Philadelphia skyline, on the red PSFS sign burning the night and beyond it the headlights of cars on the bridges stitching states together, on the lightless dark that's the Delaware River. And often if you're high enough, you'll wonder out loud why it's the Delaware and not the Pennsylvania River or even the New Jersey, and too often the guy will say *Because it's the Delaware, dummy,* instead of tuning into his own high the way your brother would.

Sometimes but not often you tell him that your brother is dead, that he was shot in a holdup at a 7/11, that his last words were *Is Sierra Nevada on sale?* That he died in a strip mall. Sometimes you wonder how someone can be here one second and gone the next, and often you wish there were reruns.

Always you cry.

Sarah Freligh is the author of four books, including *Sad Math*, winner of the 2014 Moon City Press Poetry Prize and the 2015 Whirling Prize from the University of Indianapolis, and *We*, published by Harbor Editions in early 2021. Recent work has appeared in the *Cincinnati Review miCRo* series, *SmokeLong Quarterly*, *Wigleaf*, *Fractured Lit*, and in the anthologies *New Micro: Exceptionally Short Fiction* (Norton 2018) and *Best Microfiction* (2019-22). Among her awards are poetry fellowships from the National Endowment for the Arts and the Saltonstall Foundation.

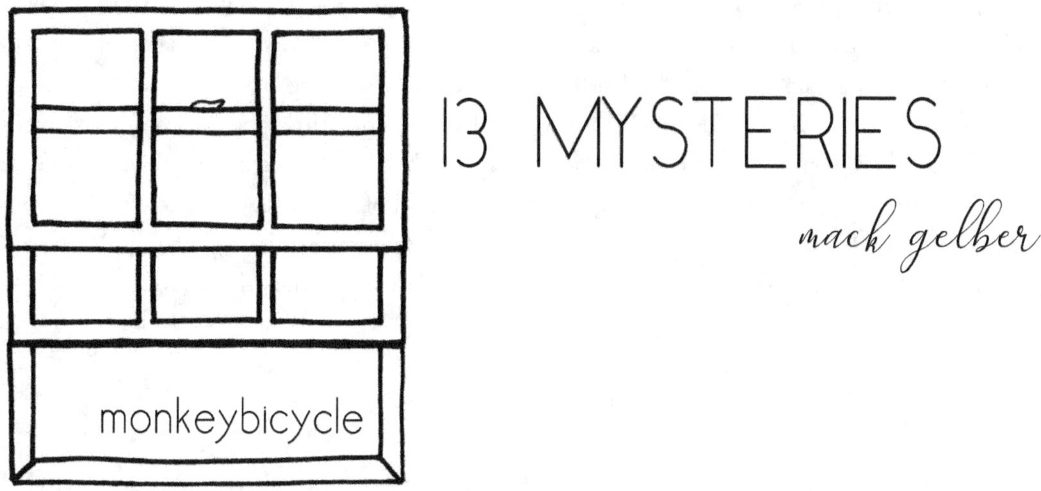

The Mystery of the Cake

IN THIS MYSTERY, A series of disappearances rocks the small town of Dunning, Michigan. One by one the children of Dunning vanish from their bedrooms. Each time, the only clue is a mysterious photocake left on the floor of the scene, a single supermarket candle still burning in the center. Each cake bears an image of the disappeared, surveillance-style shots of children boarding school buses, standing in kitchen windows, gazing out at some distant, unseen observer. Sometimes the cakes have vanilla frosting, sometimes chocolate buttercream. One is enrobed in a medley of crushed nuts investigators determine to be mostly pistachios. The children are never found.

The Mystery of the Pond

In this mystery, a 40-foot shipping container appears overnight on the frozen pond behind Hazel Billings' house. The words 连雀 HEAVY INDUSTRIES are stamped onto the outer wall, and inside is a shipment of approximately 200,000 red spheres, each about the size of a Ping-Pong ball but as smooth and heavy as a piece of marble. No one can say where the shipping container came from or how it ended up on the pond, or why Hazel Billings has begun to walk out onto the ice at night, carrying an unzipped backpack.

The Mystery of the Babysitter

In this mystery, Ed and Christine Halstead hire a local teenager to babysit their son, a 12-year-old with a severe behavioral disorder who cannot be left alone. The first time she comes over, the babysitter sits watching TV on the couch beside the boy, Eric, who never speaks. But soon she begins to sift through the Halsteads' drawers and closets, leafing through Chinese takeout menus or reading the directions on the side of a prescription bottle. One night she discovers a photo wedged into the spine of a dusty almanac. It's a picture of the Halsteads' son standing on a beach, surrounded by smiling faces—not the Halsteads, but another, younger family. Written on the back: "Brian, with parents." An unfamiliar voice calls out from the other room.

The Mystery of the Box

In this mystery, a man returns home from work to find an unusual package on his doorstep. It's a box, with no label or writing of any kind except for a lone sticker with a barcode, and when he opens it dozens of Styrofoam packing peanuts spill out onto the floor. At the bottom, his hand closes around a single red sphere, about the size of a Ping-Pong ball but as smooth and heavy as a piece of marble. He picks it up and examines it, then checks again for the box's return address. There is none. That night, before falling asleep, he places the sphere on his nightstand. In the week that follows, strange things begin to happen to him.

The Mystery of the Voice

In this mystery, Jenny's boyfriend starts talking in his sleep. He expounds at length on art, architecture, and music theory, topics of which he has no knowledge in waking life. For example, he offers up details of a specific building in a Spanish city called Zaragoza, providing an extended description of its dense concrete facade and unusual hexagonal windows. By sunrise, the boyfriend, whose name is Brent, recalls nothing. When Jenny asks him about the building in Spain, he thinks she's talking about something they saw on *House Hunters International.* "Left the country?" he says. "I've barely left Ohio." Gradually, she finds herself counting down the hours until nightfall, for the moment when dull, unsophisticated Brent becomes worldly, digressive not-Brent. Then, one day, Brent (Brent-Brent, not not-Brent) tells her he's decided he wants to break up. She's not sad; not really. If anything, she's a little relieved. Still, there's a part of her that was anticipating the next lyrical utterances of not-Brent, that compels her to start listening to YouTube lectures on midcentury architecture as she falls asleep. The same part of her that, some weeks later, impulsively books a flight to Zaragoza, which requires a 12-hour layover in Ghent and eats up a month's worth of paychecks. It takes her two days to find the building, and when she does it's exactly as he described: the poured concrete walls, cool to the touch, and the hexagon windows, colored by green glass. She walks along the perimeter, trying to locate the entrance. But like he said, there is no door.

The Mystery of the Cat

In this mystery, an old lady loses her cat. She tries to find the cat. She cannot find the cat.

The Mystery of the Hotel

In this mystery, it's Christmas Eve at a freeway Marriott somewhere off I-80. The hotel is totally snowed in, the bar empty except for two bald men wearing sneakers. For a time, one glances occasionally at the other, trying to place what's familiar about him. Finally, he walks over and carefully lowers himself onto the adjacent stool. "Brian?" The second man looks up from the bar, gradually meeting the first one's gaze. His face is entirely expressionless, his stare machinelike. A moment passes. Another moment passes. Behind them the bartender cleans glasses and silently repositions bottles on the shelf. Outside, the wind roars as snow covers the vast flatness surrounding the hotel, slowly erasing the land, the trees, the highway. Eventually, the second man smiles and opens his hand. Inside, a red sphere.

The Mystery of the Overpass

In this mystery, two drug addicts roam the city in a burnt-out Corolla. They're using one of those mobile delivery apps to earn money, picking up people's meals at restaurants and bringing them to their door. They deliver quarter pounders to some college students in a frat house. They bring a salad up to someone's office. After a few runs, they get a request for pickup at a Spanish-American restaurant on the outskirts of town. Inside, an unsmiling man hands over a small cardboard box. There's no label or writing of any kind, and it's sealed with heavy aluminum tape. Their instructions tell them to drive 20 minutes to a crumbling overpass, where they find an unlocked circuit panel that's been hollowed out on the inside. A strange word has been scored into the metal cover: ZARAGOZA. They place the box in it, and moments later receive a deposit of $200,000. Within 24 hours, both of them are dead.

The Mystery of the Cat, Pt. 2

Weeks pass. The old lady continues to search for the cat, pinning "missing" signs up on telephone poles around town and the bulletin board on the wall at Coffee Union. She wanders the streets, calling the cat's name in a cheerful voice. She cannot find the cat.

The Mystery of the Gas Station

In this mystery, a couple on a road trip pulls up to an old gas station. The place looks semi-deserted but the pumps are working, and Lucy heads into the Quik Shop for snacks and water. Inside, she notices the refrigerators have been unplugged and the racks of food wiped clean. She wanders to the back of the empty store looking for the bathroom, but only finds a corridor leading to a cramped office with a plastic folding table and some chairs. On the table there's a birthday cake—it's one of those supermarket photocakes, with a blurry image of a four or five-year-old boy lasered into the frosting. A single candle burns in the center. The boy has brown hair and is wearing a t-shirt that's too big for him, hanging around his ankles like a potato sack. He seems to be looking at something just beyond the frame, the angle of his gaze directed a few inches over Lucy's shoulder. She shivers, turns around. There's no one there.

The Mystery of the Secret Passage

In this mystery, Carl rents a post hole digger and begins to drill into the floor of his house. He is drilling into the floor of his house because he is insane, convinced fumes passing through the porous foundation are giving him cancer. After several hours, he hits a piece of metal that sends a recoil through the machine and throws him off balance. The metal appears to be the top of some kind of underground vent, and when Carl bends down he finds a single sliding panel. He forces it open and shoulders his way in. The inside of the vent is dark, but there's enough room for him to grind his way forward on his knees, struggling, dragging himself by the strength of his fingertips, dirt and construction debris and corroded flakes of metal becoming lodged beneath his nails, the light inside the vent narrowing to a point and then vanishing entirely, grinding forward in the dark, struggling, insane, inhaling fumes from the planet's core, cancer-stricken, rheumatic, an imagined ringing in his ears, small eyeless creatures shuddering and flicking their mandibles, machinelike, expressionless, mostly pistachios, as smooth and heavy as a piece of marble.

Zaragoza

In this mystery —

> The hexagon windows, colored by green glass.
> The vast flatness surrounding the hotel.
> Written on the back: "Brian, with parents."
> Dozens of Styrofoam packing peanuts spill out onto the floor.
> Inside, a man hands over a cardboard box.
> Inside, she notices the refrigerators have been unplugged and the racks of food wiped clean.
> Inside is a shipment of approximately 200,000 red spheres.
> The children are never found.
> But like he said, there is no door.

The Mystery of the Cat, Pt. 3

Weeks pass. Weeks pass. Weeks pass. Weeks pass. Weeks pass. Weeks pass. Weeks pass. Weeks pass. She cannot find the cat.

Mack Gelber's fiction has appeared in publications including *Hobart, Monkeybicycle, Neon,* and *Identity Theory.* He lives with his wife and two dubiously trained lab mixes in Columbus, Ohio, and works as a branded content editor at *The Wall Street Journal.* Follow his infrequently updated Twitter @mackgelber.

IN THE WINTER

puloma ghosh

I BECOME QUITE PRETTY in the winter, in the dim afternoons with sheet metal skies. I line my lips with brown, burgundy, wine and whiskey stains. I crave bright fruits as though they'll substitute the daylight—sunset persimmons, sunrise grapefruit, late afternoon mandarins crushed into the horizon bisecting my dark mouth. This is why he noticed me between the bare trees.

Where are you going, class is starting soon. That was none of his business, but he asked anyway, just to talk to me, I think.

The cemetery, I replied, because I thought that would make me seem interesting somehow, to be caught eating a clementine on a gravestone.

You've already missed one, he said. So he had noticed me, slipping in and out of the seat closest the door.

I don't have the book, I said. (I did; it was in my bag.) It will be pointless for me to go.

Come and listen.

No.

I walked away, satisfied to know his gaze had not been an accident. He liked to sit by me, close enough to catch my tangy scent, what was once citrus turned sour from spit and the oil in my hair. Did he like that smell?

He didn't follow me and I never went to the graveyard. I went home and ate soup alone at the wooden dining table, between the damask wallpaper. I hated to eat hot things, too-wet too-solid things, in front of other people. I don't like to show my teeth or risk a small drip from my lips. I drop silverware a lot. Was I lonely back then, you might ask. Of course I was. Who isn't lonely "back then." In the winter I'm pretty because the loneliness makes my face slack, my eyes intense. There are no stories without loneliness.

He sat beside me in the cafeteria, where I was alone with a sketchbook and some fruit and the plastic container I filled with things to eat later, alone at home. I knew other people coveted his company but he chose me, maybe because I looked pathetic, or maybe because he liked to watch my fingernails dig and carve into pith.

I have the book, if you want it. I've read it many times already, if you want to borrow it.

What makes you think I'll read it.

You'll have to write about it eventually.

I don't have to do anything. (But I did.)

Here was the plan. I would go to his place to pick up the book. But of course, any time one went somewhere to retrieve something that could easily be carried, handed over in a hallway or across the cafeteria table, there was more to it. Especially at that age, when we all sought excuses to make more of things. It was a warm afternoon for that time of year so when the sky shed it was wet and unpretty. His room smelled kind of like weed but a lit candle cast cypress and cloves over it. A little redundant in these months, when only the evergreens have sound or smell. He handed me the book and I examined the cover, its neutrals and black serif title.

What's it about?

Two women who are friends but also not friends.

I lay on his bed without invitation, on my stomach with my shins dangling off, the book open in front of me. His duvet smelled deep-in-closet musty, like maybe he hadn't washed it since last winter. I waited for his voice, or perhaps the creak, sag of the bed under his weight, but instead I felt a hand, warm and large on the back of my neck. I waited to be yanked up or pressed in but neither happened.

Don't hate me for this, he said. I don't do this with anyone.

Read? I asked, turning my head so my cheek rested on paper. He didn't acknowledge my weak joke. I closed my eyes and felt his fingers, the other ones.

It was a strange way to come, treated a bit like a fleshy little vegetable that had to be held down and scraped clean of seeds, tights pulled only to my knees, but it worked. Sometimes sex isn't sexy, just effective. I left a dark spit mark on a block of dialogue in his book. I tried to turn around, offer something inevitably awkward in thanks or return, but his hand tightened on my neck—Stay there. Don't look at me.

How many orgasms does it take to achieve intimacy? How many times does a thing fuck you from behind before you realize you only ever saw him in the woods, in the cafeteria with meat between his teeth. In that classroom where you were both supposed to be the closest to human, with his hair combed smooth, coat buttoned, scarf tight, he looked completely different. Maybe not even the same thing that fucked you from behind over and over and never let you see his eyes when he came because they were violet, gold, cut with oblong pupils. Sometimes you glimpse his hand on the bed beside you and the hairs on his knuckles look thicker than you remember, and you realize your own hand underneath is small, soft, sticky-spitty like a toddler's.

Was I the creature, or was he? Because the walls changed, I know they did. The doors disappeared. Outside became black not with night but because we took the room and tipped it into another world where it was never supposed to be, left a double of it behind so nobody would know. The magic came from somewhere, but with our bodies so tightly pressed it was hard to say where.

How did I escape that room, you ask, and I'll tell you that to outgrow a room is not to leave it, only swallow hard and walk around with it rattling inside you until eventually, you fill up with enough things that it doesn't make a sound.

———————————

Puloma Ghosh is a fiction writer living in Chicago, IL. Her work has appeared in *One Story* and *CRAFT* as a 2020 Flash Fiction Contest Winner, among other publications. She is a 2021 Tin House Summer Workshop Scholar and received her MFA from Bennington College, where she was the spring 2020 Residential Teaching Fellow.

IN CASE YOU WERE wondering, I still have the lobsters—the ones I ordered for a romantic dinner from the back of *The New Yorker*, from back when we were dating. They came wrapped in seaweed and the *Portland Press Herald*, in a heavy brown box that said "Live Maine Lobsters" on the side, a box dented and dandruffed with wax.

I told you about them in the hospital, the Live Maine Lobsters, which I had meant as a surprise, and I apologized that I wouldn't be able to steam them up with drawn butter and chewy French bread, and in the spaces between the morphine and the physical therapy and the uncomfortably erotic catheterizations, I told you that they were probably dying on my doorstep even then, tilted into the crusty snow eight thousand feet above the ocean waves.

I was there for a week, a week of pain waking me, of doctors putting me under. I knew you were there, three days and nights on that shiny green foldout, and then I knew that you weren't for five days and nights more, but I thank you for driving me home—a prickly package of bandages and Percocet, four fractured vertebrae and a hematoma that swelled out of my lumbar like a purple-green parody of pregnancy. You said goodbye with a kiss I could not lean in for, and I kicked the cardboard coffin onto the carpet inside.

In time, though, the Live Maine Lobsters revived, and began clacking over the linoleum beside the dishwasher, and curling up on the carpet under the coffee table, skittering to the shower when they heard the water run. I snipped away their rubber manacles and let them live off the crumbs that fell around my electric-lift recliner, crusts of cold pizza and ham-and-cheese sandwiches and chicken pot pies. At night, their antennae gave cold caresses to feet slick in compression hose and black from where the blood had pooled, until I pushed them away with the crook of my cane.

They grew until they were the size of corgis. They knocked over lamps, and chewed up area rugs, made soggy nests of magazines behind the cushions of the sofa, so I moved them to the basement, which had always been damp anyway.

I am married now, and we have three children. Sometimes after dinner when we're watching TV, they ask me what's in the basement, and I smile and say, "Daddy things," and they go back to their iPads. I double-check the knob on my way to the kitchen.

Some nights, when I know they are asleep, I roll up my pants and take the first two stairs into the basement, and I let the gray-green water lap over my feet. I toss in the mojo-spiced carcasses of rotisserie chickens and frozen packages of country-style ribs, and I watch their great shadows glide to where the bones sink. They are bigger now, massive even, large like sedans left to rust in the bottom of an abandoned quarry.

Some nights, like tonight, I take off my clothes and hang them on the handrail below the light switch, and I inch myself off the landing. I float with my face to the moldy ceiling, bobbing in the waves that the Live Maine Lobsters carve in their basement abyss. I hear the clacking of their claws, feel their antennae—hollow as reeds—on my legs, my feet, my once-broken back.

The water is deep, and it is dark, and it is so very, very cold.

David K. Gibson has been a magazine editor, a travel writer, and a sensitive male advice columnist for the Harlequin Romance web channel. His work has appeared in *Wigleaf, Timothy McSweeney's Internet Tendency, X-R-A-Y, Invisible City, May Contain Nuts: A Very Loose Canon of American Humor* (HarperCollins), and sundry other publications. He lives in Orlando with his wife and child and cats and coffee.

THE SOWDER SISTERS

molly giles

RUBY WAS FINE UNTIL she gassed herself. I must of told her a hundred times, "If you don't keep that stove lit, Sister, you're going to blow yourself sky high." But oh no, ninety-four years old, stubborn as sin, never once paid me the simple courtesy of listening to a single word I said and this despite the fact that I graduated Branch Normal and know a thing or two—and what did Ruby do?—but work all her life for the telephone company. So what did I smell when I came by her house last time but gas and after I covered my mouth and nose with a tea towel and opened all the windows and turned the stove off, what did I see but Ruby, sitting straight up on the commode, naked as a jay bird, biggety as you please, scolding a black man, a fat lady, and a little boy—three people only she could see. "Go long now," she was telling them, "You don't belong here!" and she was still shooing them off even after 9-1-1 came and took her away. Turned out the gas didn't hurt her lungs none, Ruby's healthy as a horse, nothing wrong with her body, it's her mind. So now she lives with me. She don't like the cats and that's all right, I can keep the cats in the cellar, but keeping Ruby inside is another matter entirely and lately I've had to tie her to the bed. Mostly she just lies there but sometimes she talks. Once she said, "Why you got that big black spider in your hair?" and even though I knew there was no big black spider in my hair, I about dropped her supper tray and Ruby winked at me and smirked like she used to do. Yesterday she pointed at the ceiling and said, "Why you got rain raining inside your house?" and when I looked up to see if the roof leaked, she laughed. Ruby has a real mean laugh. She's seven years older than me, made me wash the Packard every Saturday but never once let me drive it, kissed Ned Nichols at my picnic dinner, always said she asked for a monkey but got a sister instead. So tonight when she asked me to take the gum out of my mouth and give her half, I said No. "Even if I had any gum in my mouth," I told her, "which I do not, I would not give you so much as a taste," and I was about to slam out and leave her when Ruby laughed again, only this time her laugh wasn't mean, it was scared, and I sat down beside her and held her hand and we sat in the dark like that for a long long time.

Molly Giles is the author of four collections of short stories (*Rough Translations*, *Creek Walk*, *All the Wrong Places*, and *Wife With Knife*), a chapbook of flash fictions (*Bothered*) and a novel, *Iron Shoes*. Her second novel, *The Home For Unwed Husbands*, will be coming out from Leapfrog Press in 2023.

THE DOOR SWINGS OPEN slamming against the cement wall. Two guards stand at the opening. They do not cross the threshold; instead they peer in as if into the mouth of a cave. Perhaps they are revolted. It seems wise to be revolted by a cage. Come with us.

The smaller one carries a baton. He swings it casually; a batter up to plate—or as casually as one can swing a threat. His face appears bored; a face waiting for a bus. The larger one carries the chains. He holds them delicately—near lovingly—like they could be the bones of a beloved. He smiles. There is chocolate in his teeth.

Down the hall. The baton digs and prods as if entangled feet can shuffle faster. The baton grinds into bone.

Within these walls shame takes on new measurements; the younger men struggle with this and for it they are beaten, in a brutal baptism, until they learn that the most radical is the one who survives.

Up the stairwell. The steps are difficult for old knees. It is easy to become winded. Somehow the baton never tires. Prod. Dig. Herding cattle, they will joke. No, swine. Laugh. Laugh. They will laugh.

Up another flight to the third floor. Down the hall, towards the infirmary. Who is sick? They will not answer. Was someone beaten? Is it critical? The guards can only chuckle and prod.

Two nurses walk by hunched into their phones: monks into their dripping candles; pedestrians struggling against a mighty wind. The guards slow as they pass. The air has changed. They appraise the nurses up and down; cartoonish in their desire—yet they allow the young women to pass without molestation. Within these walls, cling to the small mercies. Continue down the hall. Push. Prod.

A door opens into a small room. There is a large window, the only window, giving view to the yellow rolling hills beyond these barbed walls. Last year those hills caught fire; they sent prisoners out with buckets. The view seems absurd, even gaudy—do not ask the imprisoned mind to put order to such vastness.

There are machines, monitors, the clear rubber tails of IV drips reaching for the dusty floor. In the middle of the room is a chair with leather straps. Sit, the guards command. They undo the bones of the beloved only to replace restraint with the leather straps. Two across the ankles; two across the forearms. The straps are thick, rough, dry. When pulled tight, they send particles into the air. They cut at the skin. At what age is the body no longer a weapon? What level of restraint will put a guard at ease?

Comfortable? the smaller one asks. Such a nice day, isn't it. What a view! More laughter.

The larger one pulls up a chair, impeding the view. He straddles the chair, leans his forearms against its back. He resembles an actor set to deliver a final monologue. With the sun at his back, his face is obscured. A shadow. A mask. Is there still chocolate in his teeth?

I have orders from the top not to let you all starve this year, the guard says in his thick midwestern accent. They say the *optics* are bad; I say this is America and heck you should be able to do whatever you please. But I don't make the rules, just get paid to enforce them. But don't think I didn't go to bat for you. I did. Honest. Went to the warden myself and tried to explain it's your holy month and how it's the same every year and as such you all know the rules: if you don't eat at meal times, you're at the mercy of whatever you can stuff into your pockets. I tried explaining the sundown laws or sundown meals or whatever it's called but *she* wasn't having it.

You heard right. The new warden's a lady! Who says things aren't changing? Who says we're not open-minded? But you know what she says to me? She says, Every *brotha* who gets behind these walls suddenly thinks he's Malcolm Freaking X.

You gotta admit that's kinda funny! And—kinda true. Her point being: we're not going to keep showing religious favoritism, allowing you all to sneak your pocket bread or whatever, since it is technically against the rules to have anything besides air in those pockets—honestly the uniforms shouldn't have pockets in the first place—idle hands and temptation and what not. I'll remember to bring that up in my check-in tomorrow. Maybe next fiscal year we'll order new uniforms. How about that? Let me write that down. Anyways, the new warden's all about equality and you have to respect that.

This is all to say: my hands are tied. Okay. And since you and the other members of the *Nation* didn't eat this morning, not even a nibble of turkey bacon, which I know you guys love and we did put on special order for you, the warden ordered all of you in for an afternoon snack.

Now we brought you in first because the younger ones respect you, they'll listen to you. A veteran who went through the ringer and came out reasonable. So be reasonable with us. Let us help you. Trust me, we take no pleasure in seeing you strapped up like this.

See that camera up there? The warden's watching us right now as we speak and if you don't eat it's my behind—and hey I like my behind! The missus does too, if you know what I'm saying. So let's just eat something yeah? Come on, you gotta be hungry. Been what, over a week since you've had a square meal? Me? By joe, I can't go more than a few hours! I don't know how you people do it.

Just eat something and there will be a conversation. Just eat something and I promise to get you a conversation with the warden—maybe if she hears it from the horse's mouth, some exceptions can be made … for next year that is.

Listen. Hey. Listen, before you say anything. Hold on. Hear me out.

Earlier, on my lunch break, I went into town to run some errands for the missus. On a whim I up and stopped in at that diner, you know the one on the corner of … oh sorry that's right, never-mind. Anyways I stopped in at a diner and out of the goodness of my heart (and pocket) picked up one of them World-Famous Banana Cream Pies. And you, you lucky son-of-a-gun, get the first slice. I got a fork right here in my back-pocket. A plastic one of course. I'll undo these straps so you can enjoy your slice. But only if you mind yourself. How's that sound?

Hey! I'm talking to you—

—No? What do you mean no? It's freaking pie! Come on now. I thought we were being reasonable here, friend. I thought we had an understanding. My behind, remember?

You're not gonna eat? Really? Okay then. You sure about that? Last chance now.

Listen if you're gonna be childish, I'm gonna have to treat you like a child.

Okay then you big baby. Open up there. Open up now. Here comes the uh choo-choo train. Chugga-chugga choo-choo! No? How about an airplane? Your Arab buddies love flying those. It's taking off, it's soaring, oh no engine trouble, nose dive, we're gonna have to land, we gotta land, open your mouth! We gotta land!

Seriously!? Well. Let's see if we can get in there with a little old-fashioned elbow grease. Come on. Open up. Open that mouth! Come on … almost … there … fuck! Damn near bit me, you see that? He almost bit me! Shit! I mean shoot. Excuse my French. The missus hates when I curse. I tell her I work in the belly of the beast, what does she expect? But she, god bless her, doesn't care. Says my tongue should remain with Christ no matter what. She's a good one; keeps me honest. Fart! That's what I'm allowed to say. Fart fart fart. Doesn't roll off the tongue as nice but we all make sacrifices. Happy wife, happy life.

But you. You're not making anything happy. Look at you. Cream and pie all over that fancy beard of yours. You look foolish. Childish if you ask me. You got any children? Probably a bunch huh? Multiple mothers, I've seen the statistics. Well *I* got two at home and I don't need one more. Twins. Life's crazy! But we're blessed.

Well. Thought this might happen. On to plan B. Pardon us while we strap your neck back there. Can't have you squirming for this next bit.

The larger man walks over to the sink to wash his hands. The smaller one snaps on latex gloves and wheels over a large box with a thin rubber tube sticking out of it.

No it's too late for all that, the smaller one says, turning on the machine. Stop apologizing. Enough! You should've listened. You should've taken a bite of pie! But now we're here. Plan B. You brought this on yourself, refusing to eat like a civilized human.

So this is how it's gonna work. You see this here gizmo? This is a feeding tube and its gonna go up your nose and down your throat but you can't squirm or it'll go down the wrong tube and into your lungs and we don't want that cause then it's paperwork—it's gonna go down your throat to your stomach and you're gonna start choking and probably vomiting and making a real mess of things—a mess I'm going to have to clean up because you decided to act like a donkey! Ornery is what we would call you back home.

Speaking of back home, you know we have a saying: what's a birthday cake to a goat? Guess who's the goat in this here situation ... well here comes the tube. Bon Appétit!

Scream, plead, fight. Hands claw face. Cover mouth. Air needed is denied. Eyes tear beg sob. A fire rages down and through a bleeding throat. The pain becomes a cell. The pain becomes a white consuming flame; immolation of the throat; white as a hospital, white as hate, white as the clouds beyond yellow rolling hills.

Matan Gold (he, him, siya) is a Black & Filipino(x) writer from the San Fernando Valley. His essay 'We Real Cool' was selected for the 2020 Best American Essays 'Notable List'. His essay 'Wade in the Water' was a finalist for Black Warrior Review's 2020 Non-Fiction Prize. He's probably walking his dog.

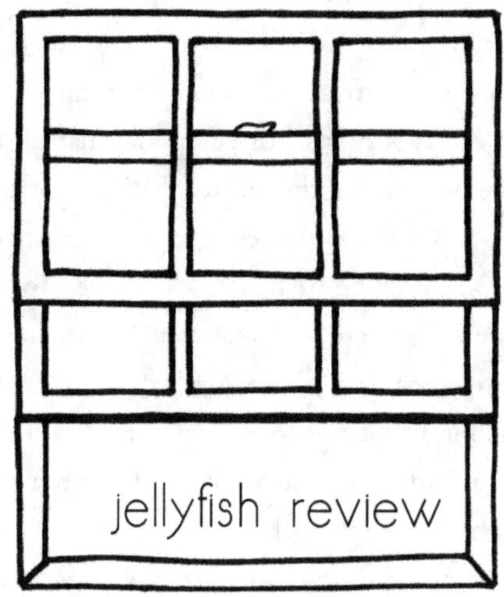

COMPULSION

sharon goldberg

I'M ADDICTED TO DIET Coke but nothing else. I sleep late, often until 11:00AM, sometimes noon. I've saved a lock of an ancient boyfriend's red hair and a strawberry rolling paper from the first time I got stoned. I didn't go to my high school senior prom and it gnaws at me. I don't camp; I value indoor plumbing and am overly sensitive to insects. I never watch ESPN. I do watch "The Bachelor" even though I know the cast is manipulated and more interested in social media stardom than finding love, but I'm ever hopeful. In 1925, my Uncle Harry sold my grandfather a horse that died, the only scandal in my family until my husband left me and married my cousin. Still, I believe in love. I've never made my mother's chicken soup recipe and feel guilty about it. As a child, at movies, I ate lollipops, sticks included. I sucked them until they turned soft and digestible. I didn't realize the McDonald's Golden Arches formed an "M" until I was in my fifties. McDonald's, FYI, is the best place to buy Diet Coke. I am a college graduate but never finished my master's thesis: The Effect of Critical Opinion on Audience Attendance at a Theatrical Production. I followed my boyfriend to Los Angeles instead. I'm not at all religious but many in my family are. I don't believe in God. Usually. I am terrified of death. Maybe because I'm not religious and don't believe in God. I've accumulated at least ten scars—most of which you won't notice unless you look very, very closely—one due to a pillow fight gone awry with my redheaded boyfriend. My dreams are frequently nightmares. I was the smartest kid in my elementary school class until the boundaries changed and, at my new school, I met Terry Strukely. I had a crush on Terry for three years, but we're still friends. When I was ten, I could read 60 words of Hebrew in one minute, the class record. I was a virgin until I was 21. I don't remember most of that night, but it wasn't about love. I like long walks on the beach at sunset blah blah blah one of which occurred at Club Med in Playa Blanca, Mexico, the first evening I spent with my ex-husband. The next day we went snorkeling and the ocean got rough and I thought I was drowning. My ex saved my life, a bonding experience, the beginning of our love affair. I was stung by a bee in Copenhagen and thought I had an allergic reaction but the swelling was just swelling. I'm not allergic to anything but I suffer from non-allergic rhinitis, so my nose runs. I was a struggling actress for many years; a critic once said of my performance in *Compulsion*, "She brings a viability to her character that helps validate the entire play." I've often fallen for my co-stars including Gil Levin in *Compulsion*. I can imitate a chicken and a guppy. In Belize I was relentlessly attacked by sand fleas. I counted 93 bites. The first man I loved became a rabbi and is now in prison for molesting young congregants. I am an avid skier but not early in the morning. I have no interest in space travel. My favorite poem is "Jabberwocky" which I can recite by memory although I may forget the name of someone I met yesterday. One night, in bed with an actor I performed with, he whispered "I love you." I said, "Are you awake?" He gave me a copy of his favorite book, *Lafcadio*, by Shel Silverstein, a children's story about a lion who learns to shoot a gun and turns it on his hunters. I'm a Leo, as was my co-star, so the gift was especially touching even though I don't believe in astrology. According to those who do, I should be compatible with Aries and Sagittarius, the other fire signs, but I've never ruled out earth, air, or water signs. I've had three facelifts. I met my current sweetheart Arnie, an electrical engineering professor, online. Like me, he drinks Diet Coke so we buy it by the caseload. Arnie and I have been together for sixteen years; we're life partners. I still believe in love.

Sharon Goldberg is a Seattle writer who was an advertising copywriter in a former life. Her work has appeared in *The Gettysburg Review, New Letters, The Louisville Review, Cold Mountain Review, River Teeth, Green Mountains Review, Chicago Quarterly Review, Southern Indiana Review, Gargoyle,* four anthologies, and elsewhere. Sharon won second place in the On the Premises 2012 Humor Contest and Fiction Attic Press's 2013 Flash in the Attic Contest. She is an avid but cautious skier and enthusiastic world traveler.

LAP

pamela gordon

HANK WAS HER BOYFRIEND. Everyone in the family said so. In the photograph of the relatives sitting in the front room in the rented house steps from the beach—stucco, hydrangea, and a long staircase leading up to the door—she sits on his lap. It did not matter that he was her cousin, or that he was twenty-four and she was four.

Next door lived Hannah, who had a daughter her age, or was Hannah the daughter? They made houses together on the beach by tamping sand into yellow plastic pails, turning the pails upside down, and sliding the pails up. If the tops of the houses caved in they molded them with more sand. This way—along with a shell or a seaweed strand or a bit of wood they placed on each top—the houses were distinct in an otherwise cookie-cutter community. All stood at attention in the morning sun until neighbor boys barreled down the beach howling, and knocked them down.

At first, she cried and ran to her mother. Her mother wore a kelly-green one-piece every day. The color seared into her eyes, making it possible to spot her mother no matter how far she drifted from her. Her mother comforted her but didn't stand up to the boys. Hannah, or Hannah's daughter, didn't run to her mother. Hannah's mother or Hannah never came to the beach. She hated sand. Her mother in her kelly-green suit, with low-slung wooden chairs, a blanket, towels, baby oil, and the infant brother led the two girls to the beach in the morning and led them back at noon for lunch. Lunch on the Hannahs' front porch was payment to her mother for the morning caretaking. Lunch and the pitcher of what the mothers called, laughing, "Lemonade." They sucked on their drinks and their cigarettes, filling the girls' cups from a different pitcher they called: "Your lemonade," and saying: "You can have some of ours when you're older."

As the weeks progressed the mothers let the girls go down to the shoreline earlier and earlier, alone. This resulted in more planned houses standing for a longer time before the mid-morning arrival of the Godzilla boys and their monster whoops. By the end of July, the boys and girls were taking turns burying each other deep in the damp sand once the houses were demolished. Then they'd unbury each other and plunge, shrieking, into the foam to be washed. No matter how hard the ocean beat her she still had sand kernels in her crotch when she peeled her suit off at the end of each day. At night she fell asleep to the waves pawing the shore. Sleep was a dream of rolling over and over inside the waves, scratchy sand between her legs, salt and brine marinating her skin, her limbs and face sun-kissed.

The picture of the relatives was taken in August. Everyone glowed in white and black. Her mother had pulled her curly hair into a half-pony. She wore a white dress with smocking across the chest and shiny black Mary Janes with white anklets trimmed in lace. They were the first shoes she'd worn all summer. She had walked around the rented house, the streets, onto the beach, barefoot, so that even though the shoes fit they were pinchy. She would wear them to school in September when she started kindergarten.

In the picture, she sits on Hank's legs which are crossed. She sits on the knee on top of the other knee, his leg extended, as if she's perched on a branch. She was his favorite. Everyone said so. He had a moustache and a large nose. She doesn't remember another time she sat on his lap. She doesn't remember ever being alone with him. Years after the picture was taken, he married a woman everyone agreed was stunning but remote. They had two sons, and divorced. He married two more times and had more children.

Other cousins, now women, all of them older than her yet younger than him, roll their eyes whenever he is mentioned. She hasn't seen him in a very long time. When they come face to face at a family funeral he looks at her and says her name with satisfaction. After, she sees him with his third wife, across the room. He grabs the wife, kisses her mouth, holds on to her a little too tightly.

Pamela Gordon is a writer and a high school instructional coach in the Bronx. Her work has appeared in publications such as *salon.com; Gargoyle; Poets & Writers; New Times; More;* and *The New York Times.*

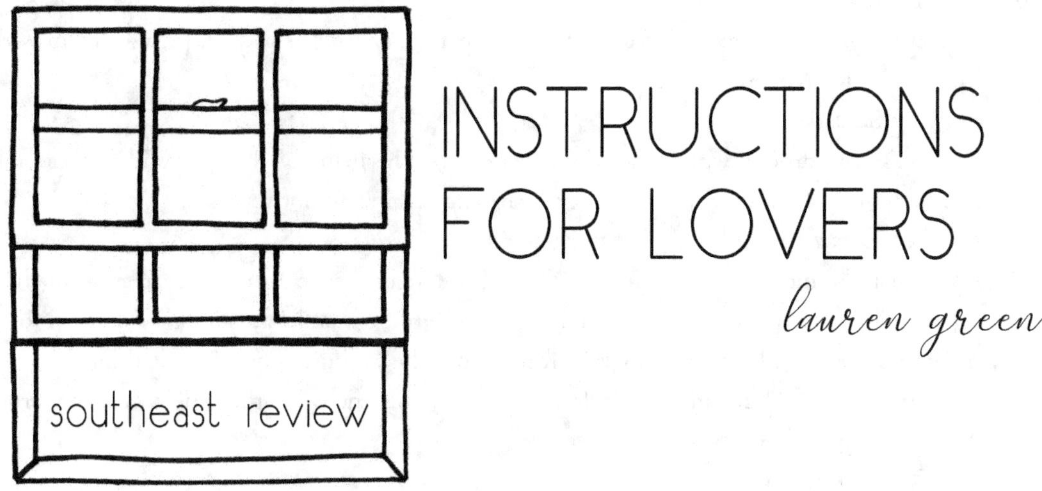

EVE LAY BENEATH THE Winesaps in an oval patch of shadow, studying the acrobatics of finches overhead. Adam stared at her, this unknowable wife who was once a small piece of bone inside him. He dug his thumbnail into his chest, tracing the cauterized edges of the wound.

There you are, said Eve, turning her face to him.

Adam smiled. He ran his fingers through his hair, and a flock of starlings alighted on a tree branch. He wrapped his unsullied body around hers. Their limbs tangled. Eve wondered if this was what it had been like before God had slipped out the rib, simple as removing a matchstick from its book.

She asked Adam to tell her again the story.

Which? asked he.

You know, said she.

What she meant was the one about how he was dust and she was bone, and how these two things alone proved enough for the promise of a people.

So, Adam told her. Of how he had named every creature in the garden and still found that it was not enough. It was good, but it was not enough. Really, it was no paradise. He began to resent the hallowed world that was entirely his own. He begged his father, pointing to the waves and the clouds and the constellations, so thick they could scarcely be counted. *Why do they have each other?* he asked. *Why them, and not me?*

God, who knew something of loneliness himself, understood.

God's eyes were asteroids. His voice was deliverance. Every one of his fingers took the shape of a different tool: his thumb, a key; his pointer, a scalpel; his third finger, a paintbrush; his fourth, a hammer; his pinky, a wrench.

That night, as Adam slept, God pressed the blade of the scalpel to his son's abdomen, paring back the silken flaps of skin. Inside, he found the neat, ticking gears. He stroked the bottommost rib.

Eve began to cry when Adam got to this part. *Don't stop*, she said, plying his lip with her fingers, as if to coax out the words.

Shh, he said.

Eve's eyes, droopy with exhaustion, slewed over the fields of lavender and valerian and all the other sights of the new world, of which she and Adam had not yet tired.

I'm sad that I missed the beginning, she said.

What she meant was that it wasn't fair, how Adam had named every creature in their garden—antelope and lemurs and hummingbirds and grouse—and left not one for her. Not a single unnamed critter. He was part of the creation, but she was just another made thing.

Adam used a firm hand to cradle Eve's head to his chest. Neither knew then that trust was the beginning of shame.

Oh, it wasn't anything special, he said.

Beneath Eve's ear echoed the steady boom of Adam's heart. In the stillness, she listened. This was the sound of her heart, too.

Lauren Green's work has appeared in *Conjunctions, American Short Fiction, Joyland, Glimmer Train,* and elsewhere. Her chapbook, *A Great Dark House,* is forthcoming from the Poetry Society of America. In 2022, she received the inaugural Eavan Boland Award, sponsored by *Poetry Ireland* and Stanford University. She holds an MFA from the Michener Center for Writers.

THE MAIDEN WITHOUT HANDS

lauren groff

THE VILLAGE, LEFT SO long ago, still beats in the blood. On the phone, my mother says, Remember the girl with the hands? Of course, I remember, I say. Who could forget? She'd gone to our church. Five years younger than me, skinny as a branch, bloodless face, purple lips. At fellowship hour, she and her brother would wait breathlessly at the pass-through window for the ladies to put out the cookies, then they'd shove as many into their mouths as could fit. They're not allowed sugar at home, the church ladies said uncomfortably, but it seemed like they weren't allowed food. The father with his burning embers for eyes, the wild beard of a patriarch. The mother as furtive and pale as her children; a small wind would make her crack. It was a scandal in the choir when she fled her family for the organist, who was also a woman. Our airless village was no place for lesbians, so they loaded the pickup and drove to Arizona. It was hard to think of those two mice-children left alone with that father out in the hills. Neither child spoke; perhaps they didn't have voices then.

Suddenly, the girl grew beautiful. Graceful limbs, a swan's neck, skin like skim milk, perfect breasts. She was so young, eleven or so when the breasts arrived. They say a boy up for the summer began to dog her. He would ride his bike all the way out there and wait in the woods for the father to drive off. For the girl's sake, I imagine beauty: a waterfall deep in the woods, moss, ferns, the feeling like a flame at the center of her. It was inevitable—they were caught in the act. The father dragged his daughter by the hair to the woodshed, to the bandsaw. He cut off her hands. Our bloody village made national papers.

I fled at the end of that summer. All these decades I preserved the girl in my mind as she had been then, safe in the hospital among the nurses and bouquets, her stumps healing, her monstrous father in jail.

Oh, but there's a second act, my mother says. As the girl lay in the hospital, her doctor fell in love with her. Wait a second, I say. She was twelve, he was grown. Oh, yes, not unproblematic, my mother says drily. He would go into her room and watch her sleep. Ugh, one of those, I say. It seems, says my mother, he didn't touch her. But he started saving half his pay; he put it into a secret trust fund for her. The mother and her lover came home from Arizona all tanned and moved into a Victorian on Pioneer Street with the kids and homeschooled them. Then on the girl's eighteenth birthday, the doctor popped up again, bringing a long pink box, like for roses, but inside it were prosthetics so pearly and intricate they moved like real hands. Better than the hooks she'd been using. He also handed over an envelope with the trust fund numbers in it. For college, he said. The girl must go away and live fully. He would wait.

So the girl went off to college, began to speak, began to have opinions. The girl's mother, whom my own mother sees all the time at the grocery store, bragged about the girl's grades, Phi Beta Kappa, Rhodes scholar. The girl graduated and did not come back to the village; she did not want the doctor. He became pale and sad, his hair thinned, his handsome face wrinkled.

Years passed, says my mother, and a few months ago, the girl published a memoir about her childhood. She went on book tour. At the first four stops, the same man sat in the front row. The doctor, of course, ugly now, unrecognizable. On the fifth stop, she grabbed him and yelled at him. But somehow also, she fell in love. Now they're pregnant, my mother says. They're getting married in the church this weekend. Like his good luck had to pour into her over the years to even things out between them.

She will be, my mother says with tremendous satisfaction, a beautiful bride.

Yes, I say, but I hang up unsettled, the village still throwing its cold shadows on me.

Before their mother left, I once babysat for the girl and her brother. Their mother chattered nervously all the way through the dark woods. My husband built the cabin with his own hands, she told me. He's away, visiting his brother. Inside, she showed me how to keep the fire going in the woodstove, there was no other heat. If I was hungry, I could eat a carrot she held up, an obscene twisted thing from their garden. Then the mother left. I was alone with the children. The girl all bones in a pink flannel nightgown far too small for her; the boy under the quilt in the loft. He would not come out. There was no television, no books. I offered to play games, cards, whatever. The girl just stood there, staring at me. Then I felt something so dark there in the house I had a hard time breathing. A heaviness came over me until I had to sit down in the rocking chair. I fell asleep. When I woke the mother was livid in the room, the fire gone out, the house cold. Before I was angrily bundled back into the car, I saw the girl in the far shadows. Her eyes, how they blazed.

This is what lingers. Not the hands, not the happily thereafter. This moment rings endlessly into the present. The girl's blazing eyes, my silence. I must have felt it was pointless; I knew, wordlessly, what we all knew, the whole village, and because breaking such silence felt impossible, we let the little girl break instead.

Lauren Groff is the author of six books, most recently *Matrix, Florida,* and *Fates and Furies.* She lives in Gainesville, Florida.

GRACIELA

taraka hamada

STUMBLING UPON THE SECOND death at Michoacán Butterfly Reserve
*a Senor Raúl Hernández Romero y Homero Gómez González, defensores del bosque y
la mariposa Monarca*

Butterfly wings caused the forest to mimic
sounds of rain in a downpour of dizzying
synesthesia where a girl, unknowingly
a prismatic part of the whole, witnessed
the world: A face-down body. Fungus
decomposing fallen oyamel trees before
termites. The scent of blood felt through
the fir network of roots. Sun congealing
blood-matted hair. Instinctiveness:
like rodents avoiding needles floating
in a puddle stepped in by leather boots
stained with motorcycle oil. Racing
mice-hearts delirious with the feast of
butterflies up above. Milkweed poison-
filled Monarchs awaiting predators
that digested toxins: a black-headed
grosbeak shadowing the colony, snatching
nourishment, wind-shredded wing tips,
woefully feeding only herself, her young

My life that I forgot: the unavoidable
trash-smell I carried in my hair even after
using shampoos promising to suffocate
my senses with vanilla, forced into
maturing faster and choosing between
those shampoos I couldn't afford and the
insulin I *really* couldn't afford, born into
a system that made me desperate for
girls my age to not think any certain way
about me, yet hoping some boys would.
I forgot the word *insulin* even existed
because I was no longer Graciela of
Michoacán, Graciela of scavenged soda
bottles: always drinking the dregs before
burning them for cash. That other little-girl
Graciela hadn't fled to Mexico without a
father who taught her to fly kites, without
a big sister still a better cook and
mother who invented fairy stories that

perished in the nest with open beaks
from the increasing spring heatwaves.
A man, black boots. A hunting knife.

she was proud to boast to her friends about
and she still lived without seeing death in
Honduras on a farm with horses.

Taraka Hamada (we, nosotros, ми) language in constant flux. a non-me collective. a biome harboring trillions of organisms. our microflora protean when we uproot. tongues flow through our gills. our planet mercurial refractions of the worlds we've created

.

HOT COLD & BLUE
charlotte hamrick

MAMIE WAS A MILITARY brat whose dad decided to retire "back home," a tall drink of water with a cloud of cotton candy hair and John Lennon glasses. I was a transplant from parts all over, a few years in the desert southwest, a few more in Appalachia, other places I don't remember. Neither of us ever felt like we belonged in a Deep South town where almost everyone else had been born and raised. Add to that, we lived way in the country where the pines, kudzu, and bald blue sky could eat you alive. We were double misfits, two strikes against us—transplants and country kids. I guess that's what drew us together although I don't remember how we actually met.

We were rough around the edges, all cockleburs and sumac, walking talking crucifixes warding off fake-sweet Southern belles with Farrah Fawcett hair and football-playing boozers with lecherous grins. We didn't like being stuck in high school with its halls full of eyes and stories that changed from mouth to mouth. We'd sneak out under the bleachers every chance we got to smoke, say we got our period and needed to take care of business just to see the men teachers turn red.

Summers we spent a lot of time riding back roads in Mamie's hand-me-down Chevy truck, leaving a trail of red dust and gravel spit in its wake, Led Zeppelin blasting from an 8-track tape deck we wired to the dash. Sometimes we'd end up at the lake in the next county, park on a hill and watch trapped housewives yell at their snotty-nosed kids and serve egg salad sandwiches and beer to their entitled husbands and swear we'd never be like them. We pinkie promised that one day we'd change the road we were on just like the song said.

Time passed while we sewed patches on our flares and embroidered our peasant tops, beaded chokers and earrings, spent the money we made ironing our daddy's uniforms on platform shoes and black light posters. We never missed *The Sonny and Cher Comedy Hour* mainly because Cher looked like us with her crooked teeth and long nose and came from working class people. She was ordinary and cool and we felt a kinship. She showed us we could say out loud what we thought about stupid men like Sonny.

On nights when our uneasy lit a fever in our bellies, we'd sneak out and meet two older guys in the barn behind her house, smoke some weed and make out, push our limits past caring. After the boys left we'd let the horses out of their stables and ride bareback under the moon, howl in the woods like lost souls, hooves beating the dirty off our skin.

But year after year of same and nothing wears a girl down and one day she left without me. I had a man I loved by then that talked me out of going, too, but I saw her off at the bus station. As the doors closed with a whoosh and a thud, she looked back one last time, the cold blue of her eyes startling in the Mississippi heat. Then she moved on down the aisle, her cotton candy hair floating from window to window, a silent movie reel with an unscripted ending.

Charlotte Hamrick has been published in a number of literary journals including *Flash Frontier, Bending Genres, Still: The Journal, New World Writing, Reckon Review,* and *JMWW.* She's had nominations for the Pushcart Prize, Best of the Net, *Best Microfiction, Best Small Fictions,* and was a Finalist for Micro Madness 2020. She is Features Editor for *Reckon Review* and Creative Nonfiction Editor for *The Citron Review.* She lives in New Orleans with her husband and a menagerie of rescued pets. More information and intermittent writing can be found on her website, charlottehamrick.com.

POP QUIZ TIME! DIANA is vaxxed and masked and ready to go. Help her prepare for the return of the dreaded spousal corporate work party. Please show your work.

1) If Diana hasn't been exercising since February 2020 and she was already carrying some baby weight from having given birth one-hundred and eighty (180) months ago, how many pairs of Spanx will it take for her to fit into her last remaining cocktail dress?[1] How does your answer change if you know that Diana's been hitting the box of thin mints she found hidden in the back of the freezer pretty hard?

2) If Diana's husband, Dave, has six (6) direct reports, what is the average number of minutes each will talk to Diana *after* learning she's a mother of two whose response to 'what do you do' is to stammer a bit about her decade-stale legal career and to crack a weak joke about the return of her duties as her children's uber driver? Please factor for the time each report will take balancing the utility of playing nice with the boss's wife against the fear that Diana's apparent lack of ambition might rub off on them. How much faster will they flee if you know that Diana is a GenXer and the direct reports are Millennials?[2]

3) If Diana's had a cocktail and fully answers the question 'so what do you do' by adding "writer" to her ramblings, how long will the uncomfortable pause be when the follow-up question 'have I read anything you've written' is asked? How many years before Diana learns to lie and say "insurance adjuster" or "wig salesman" or "mime," anything but writer, to avoid questions about her obvious lack of notoriety and/or the state of her as-of-yet unfinished novel?[3]

4) What is the ratio—number of drinks per hour—that Diana can imbibe such that she is able to reclaim a modicum of self-worth, yet *not* throw up on the dance floor?

Please calculate for two different scenarios:

a. Diana sticks with Prosecco like she promised Dave,[4] and
b. Diana gets nostalgic and starts knocking back White Russians.[5]

Note: Diana's actual weight is not available as a data point. (See question 1)

5) When Duran Duran's *Rio* comes on, how hard will Diana hit the dance floor? How fast will she be transported to a rose-colored version of her otherwise shitty childhood, misremembering that once upon a time all she worried about was picking which band member to marry, Nick Rhodes or John Taylor,[6] that once her life held promise and verve, that once she was relevant and cool, or at least, still had the chance to be?

How loud will she sing along, proclaiming to Dave, to his direct reports, to the ice sculpture of the company logo, that her name is Rio and she dances on the motherfucking sand?

Answer key:

[1] You've already misjudged Diana. This question didn't occur to her until thirty (30) minutes before she and her husband, Dave, were supposed to leave. She only owns two pairs of Spanx and one pair of control top panty hose with a run in them. These will have to do.

[2] False. There's no such time faster than instantly.

[3] "All the years" and "infinity +1" are both acceptable answers. 100 extra credit points if your answer assumed that Diana might finish her novel at some point. Thank you, that was kind.

[4] No need to answer this one.

[5] There are no right answers here, only wrong ones.

[6] Obviously, John Taylor.

D.E. Hardy's work has appeared in *X-R-A-Y*, *Sledgehammer Lit*, *New World Writing*, among others. She lives in the San Francisco Bay Area and can be followed on twitter @dehardywriter and online at http://www.dehardywriter.com.

SLIVER

candace hartsuyker

THIS IS MY SECRET: my daughter was made of glass. She was shaped and molded, slick surfaces, sharp edges. As a child, I had read sacred books with onionskin pages. Her skin was like that: more delicate than the softest velvet.

I worked for days. Face dripping with sweat, skin pink with heat. I laid out my tools: a flat slab of marble, shears, tweezers, blowpipe. When it was done, I whispered, *daughter.*

She was everything I wished I could have been. I was a woman who could not forget the smell of burning flesh. My trade: glassmaker. My enemy: the blueness of the flames. My disfigured eye, the eye patch covering its ugliness.

As the years passed, I began to notice how her dress clung to her like liquid and showed off the dip of her backside, the swell of her breasts. I dreamt of men breaking into our house and taking her. I imagined them cupping her feet in their hands, marveling at the smallness of their size. So, I kept her locked away.

She was allowed outside only at night, when flickering shadows could hide her from prying eyes. But one night she came back, breathless. She had heard hoofbeats; a man with a sharp chin had followed her. He pressed his lips to the sole of her foot. Once, a gray moth landed lightly on her ankle. Its wings opened and closed. She was full of wonder at the brush of its body gently tickling her flesh. She told me his kiss was not like that: his lips imprinted wishes on her skin. I thought about what to do. Who knew how many men he had brought with him? I could not chase them all away.

Daughter, I said, *come.* She stood with me by the open window, waiting. My hand was scarred and strong from winding glass. The hand pushed her out.

The men watched as she shattered. Their horses reared, and they rode away without looking back. They had no use for her now that she was broken like me. I climbed down the winding stairs and wept. My daughter: jagged edges, slivers of glass. One hand intact. The toes of a foot, crushed. Her face: cracked to pieces.

My tools wait in the workshop, dusty with disuse. They lie dormant, like my daughter. Try as I might to repair her, I know she will never be human again.

Candace Hartsuyker has an M.F.A in Creative Writing from McNeese State University. She has been published in *Cheap Pop, Okay Donkey, Trampset, Heavy Feather Review* and elsewhere. You can find her on Twitter at C_Hartsuyker.

THE ORACLE MONGER

frederick highland

HE HUMMED INTO TOWN in his dusty Sunbelt roadster, plum and yellow, the same color as his hair. It was a splashy arrival. My wife called it ominous.

The man had oracles for sale, many of them dating back to the Vajravedas and the Muse of Spokane. He had a leather bag full of them, rolled scrolls sealed with red wax.

Some called him stylish. He had a way about him, that's for sure, a hazel-eyed charmer who had everyone laughing at his riddles and traveler's tales. He said he had been all over the country, as far south as Vengeance. The children danced around him like worshipers. He had a trunk full of gewgaws and straw dollies and he handed them out like sweets.

At first, the Monger was selective about who obtained an oracle. Rumor was that the moneychanger, Drosper Dix, paid a huge sum for the Oracle of Coins. The Oracle Monger became a fashion. The papers said he was seen at The Granger escorting the heiress Misty Shores. They posed for paparazzi in matching muskrat trimmed with pearls. The Monger might have moved among the swells and schmoozers for years. For reasons little understood, he turned his attention from Those Who Mattered and started courting the common folk.

He made a speech in the public square and proclaimed his oracles were for everyone. "Discounts for the needy! Oracles for the bereft!" People followed the Monger around holding out their purses and the purses weren't always theirs.

Somehow, the oracles got into the wrong hands or into the right hands for the wrong reasons. People whispered of scandals and sordid misdeeds. The Laza Maru business even made the news. Laza bought the Oracle of Wands for her lover, Fabulon, and he gave it in turn to his other lover, the wife of the sculptor Pirinelli. Pirinelli found out, went mad, and drove a chisel through Fabulon's skull. Crazed with grief, Laza shot Pirinelli.

"Ominous," my wife said.

In all the commotion, or oracle fever you might call it, no one noticed that the children had started slipping away.

Many of the oracles turned out to be more like curses. At least their beneficials wore off. There were incidents of spontaneous combustion and some of our more notable citizens took on strange diseases. Professor Sadikh-Murad's skin turned gray. He still has this hungry look about him.

After Sylvia Sparks was found dead one morning, ripped from throat to sternum and all her vitals missing, people started staying indoors at night.

Then the land turned dry.

The Monger knew it was high time to get going, or he made it appear that way. He blew town, minus the roadster, which was trashed and burned by a mob, hired, it was said, by Drosper Dix because his daughter had grown a lead eye in the center of her forehead.

We never knew his name, although Prester Downs, in despair because his son had run off, pored over The Precepts. Was the Monger a prophet or fiend? Prester said he would give a sermon to set things straight but never did.

We're rid of him, but I worry. A prospector claimed he had spotted the Oracle Monger in the Shining Mountains to the north. He was surrounded by painted children who shook straw dollies to ward off intruders.

If you are curious about his oracles, Ezekiel showed me this one: "Inner changes are taking place. The life you have been living is at an end. A shedding of old skins is called for. Essence is water. The branch bears fruit, and you can now reap the harvest."

"What harvest?" my wife cried out as she spat in the fire. "Where's the damned harvest?"

Frederick Highland's novels *Ghost Eater* and *Night Falls on Damascus* are published by St. Martin's Press. Recent fiction has been published by allthesins (UK), Eclectica, Mystery Weekly and Gargoyle magazines. Website: highlandwordsmith.net.

YOU FIND IT WHILE walking the dog with Warren, watching evening shadows on asphalt lengthen between you, waiting for the dog to shit; waiting for him to circle round, nose to the ground. The dog knows the right place by sniff, the way you thought you'd know by pheromones, that the right man would just smell right, and yet—that's when you happen upon the sheep, ripped wide open, blood-soaked wool with entrails trailing.

Before you, a small mass in the center of the path—*Is that a…?*

Yes, a heart, Warren says, as if he finds one every day.

You think of your mother, how apropos she would have said, chuckling over brunch with her friends, as if your failing love life was a punchline, as if you hadn't grown up knowing acutely the sensation of your heart laid bare, cut out, until you met Warren.

This time was supposed to be different. This time, you thought you knew by taste, by texture, by the vibration in the air that swept under your skin and surrounded you both in an aura of pink light. You swear you believe in science, but the air used to vibrate pink, that is, smell like a new home before the dog, before the long hours at work, before the sip of time folding in on itself.

Maybe it's thieves, Warren says, *gutting sheep for the fun of it*, and you think of your mother again, ex-boyfriends one through seven, though three was the worst and left visible wounds; it's then that the heart lifts a little, moves, you swear. You pull the dog's collar, tell him to leave it, but Warren pokes it with a stick.

Don't, you say, remembering you heard once that the human heart is the size of a fist, and if so, this sheep's heart could be your heart, the same, red-smooth and weeping, the aorta still attached, and you want to break the stick and ask him, *Do you still love me?*

But you don't want to be that kind of woman—desperate, uncertain, nagging—the kind who plans it out like a blueprint: years of dating, months of engagement, wedding favors embroidered with a spray of flowers and invitations embossed in gold, fractions of children, checkboxes and scoreboards and honey-do lists—everything perfectly chambered, each task a synchronous valve that opens and lets in a little more air, a little more life, a steady rhythm.

It's still moving, Warren says, and opens his pocketknife. He makes a clean incision and pries cardiac muscle, atria, ventricles, Valentines, true love, until the vibrating bloody chamber opens, and whatever was inside slips free.

Sara Hills is the author of the flash fiction collection *The Evolution of Birds* (Ad Hoc Fiction). Her work has listed in the *Wigleaf* Top 50 and appeared in *SmokeLong Quarterly, Cheap Pop, X-R-A-Y Literary, Reckon Review, Fractured Lit, Flash Frog,* and elsewhere. Originally from the Sonoran Desert, Sara lives in Warwickshire, UK and tweets from @sarahillswrites.

REFLECTING POOL

yong-yu huang

IN MID-JULY WE WATCHED the gleaming surface of the lake swallow a menagerie of color, unnatural in its cadences of light: the lovebirds that a man dropped from his rowboat and then the golden dog that dove in after them. It didn't make a splash, dropped like a comma in the water. The night before, I had let my favorite denim jacket sink, the one with my initials cross-stitched in tangerine thread across the front pocket; around me, everyone else was tossing things into the water. Loose mother-of-pearl buttons, greening pennies, the crumpled red skin of an empty Coke. Afterwards, we sat on the dock and sucked on neon popsicles, the colors swirling on the surface of the mossy water.

That year, the camp guide told us that the lake was meromictic—layers upon layers clinging to each other but never mixing. They lost a camper sometime in the hairpin bend of summer too, and for weeks, her bright yellow swimsuit was plastered across every front page. When we sat around the campfire to pray for her return, the lake flooded up to our shins and left a permanent ring of red around our ankles. Someone mentioned ringworm and lifebuoys; I stopped wearing socks after that. Still, I wanted to stay out there with them all summer, lounging in the gritty sand and letting water seep into my mouth. But we drove back down the mountain roads, past the copse of trees lined with golden streamers from the night before, past the turtle sanctuary with its odd silences and empty green pools, past the gas station and the sitcoms playing on the TV by the slushy machine, and I said goodbye somewhere in between that.

When they dredged her out of the water in the winter, we were already long gone. The body had floated all the way up to the top layer, and someone had spotted a pack of deer fleeing south, away from the foggy ice and the half-open eyes underneath. I read about it in the paper—the limp mass sprawled across the front page—and then I called the others. We ordered wicker baskets of miniature lotions to cover the last of the sunburns from lying belly-down on the dock, our elbows rubbed raw on the wooden slats. They came in strange, exotic scents like *Buttered Tartar, Cream of Cinnamon, Mango Incense.* We rubbed them into our skin anyway; it was always better to start water-proofing early.

The next year we met at the same lake, skin gleaming and still curious to see what the lake had to offer. It was a morbid fascination, but we agreed—water that didn't take on the appearance of anything else was something to be explored. I thought of the dog and the lovebirds and the fistfuls of hair we had lost the year before, endless shades of peacock blue. *Come on now, it's getting late,* someone called out, but we had already turned away, our faces damp and eager in the silty heat.

Yong-Yu Huang is a Taiwanese student living in Malaysia. Her work appears in *Waxwing, Frontier Poetry,* and *Strange Horizons,* among others, and has been recognized by Princeton University, *The Kenyon Review,* and the Poetry Society of the UK. She is the winner of the 2021 Elinor Benedict Poetry Prize. In her free time, she enjoys listening to Studio Ghibli soundtracks and sitting by bonfires on the beach.

"THESE DAYS, ALL STORIES need to be adventure stories."

Priyanka wrote this line, and she immediately hated it. The premise she was trying to convey was clear. She was primarily a writer of domestic fictions, heavy on the intricacies of relationships—about the flow of friendship and affection and jealousy and longing amongst small groups of affluent teenagers and twentysomethings. These were the stories she liked to read, and they were the stories she liked to write.

But, growing up, she'd been a boy, and that boy had mostly read adventure stories: books about heroes solving galactic-scale problems, usually through cunning and violence. She had for years, both before and after transitioning, tried to write these kinds of stories, and since becoming an adult, they'd always seemed a bit, well, pointless. They contained literally no reality, and they were honestly a bit of a bore.

With this line, however, she wanted to thread that needle. She had noticed, these days, that adventure story plots were creeping into her friends' real lives. One friend broke up with her boyfriend because he wasn't willing to get a second passport and potentially flee to Israel with her. Another's marriage suffered because the in-laws were unhoused by a riot and lived with them for three months.

A third couple experienced significant domestic conflict over whether their child would be allowed to join a government-sponsored fascist youth group. One parent was adamantly against it. The other felt, well, at least it'll give him some structure, and he's *really* interested in it, and nothing's ever interested him before.

Some had their immigration plans disrupted and were trapped in countries they hadn't chosen. One friend was a half-white woman who was married to a closeted fascist, whose racist leanings only came out under pressure, and she had to decide if that was worth leaving him over.

Increasingly, to write domestic fiction without some adventure story component seemed pointless.

Moreover, Priyanka was a new mother, and they'd hired an expensive nanny, just so Priyanka could work. She felt some responsibility to come up with salable story concepts—big, flashy adventure stories that would get a big advance and sell really well. People would eat up something about a group of upper-class teens who were riven by, like, fascism or something.

So Priyanka wrote that first line. And she tried to think of another. These days the process of writing, more and more, involved coming back to the boy she'd been: fat, with narrow pig-like eyes and untidy hair, untucked shirt protruding over a huge belly and pants sagging down over a big bottom. She honestly hated that kid, and she hated everything he wanted or liked. If she could fire a bullet into his heart, she would.

That kid was the source of the world's problems. Inept, self-absorbed, and lazy, he'd nonetheless always considered himself superior to others, merely by virtue of a strong memory and a lively sense of curiosity, and he felt himself owed a sort of heroism.

But okay, that kid was her audience. She imagined him in a fascist dystopia. He'd gone to Catholic school, so it wouldn't be too difficult. The Benedictine monks were good people, they resisted fascism, failing to do the required obeisance to the leader or to teach the required doctrines. Private schools were allowed this wink-wink nod-nod. But some kids at the school were bullies, they threatened to rat out the teachers to the police, and the monks, old and frail, were losing control of the school.

But she simply could not imagine that child—herself as a youth—taking a heroic stand against those bullies. More likely, he'd remain immersed in stories of dragons and elves and be totally ignorant to what was going on around him. Nor was it entirely unlikely that he'd be one of the bullies himself—he'd never liked nor been popular with the majority of his teachers.

The adventure story was nonsense. It was no more complicated than that. Adventure stories were pernicious and awful.

Through the open window, Priyanka heard shouts and a quick bang-bang. Checking Twitter, she saw that the protests on Mission Street were being tear-gassed again. Smoke rose in front of the evening sun. Her secret truth was that she thought the protests were useless. She was supposed to toe the party line and say, "Get out there and fight for your rights," and she supposed if you were truly frustrated, it was a way to blow off steam, but she didn't believe in the individual's ability to affect history at all. History was the product of much bigger factors. Fascism was an inevitable result of the slowing of economic growth, and of capital's increasing power over labor, and these in turn were the inevitable result of social and economic factors that Priyanka didn't really understand but was sure existed.

The problem she faced now was, "How do I tell lies for fun and profit? How do I tell people that they matter when they don't? That heroism is real when it isn't? How do I tell them that *they* are courageous and right-thinking and will take a stand, when, honestly, people somewhere within ten miles of them are being hustled into a secret prison"—Priyanka had friends who were immigration lawyers, so she knew all about secret prisons—"and they're most likely doing nothing about it?"

Priyanka wrote a full chapter about her heroic Catholic school kid, but nothing would make it ring true. Why would *this* kid stand up for what was right? And if he did, would it even matter? She could make him come out victorious, but it would require absurd contortions. Frustrated, in the next chapter, the bullies cornered him and beat him to a pulp. She had them smash his face in. Then she had them strip him naked and torment him. The scene was surprisingly erotic, and she enjoyed the orgy of violence being unleashed, at least rhetorically, against her own past.

From that point, the writing was pleasant. It took about ninety days to finish a draft of the book. In each chapter, her protagonist was subjected to worse and worse tortures, and in the end he was beaten and subjugated and forced to run errands for the older boys, like the fag at an English public school. With each torment, his anger grew, and so did his determination to resist.

The only part that was difficult was the piece at the end, where he uses cunning to ambush and kill the bullies in an extended locked-house sequence. Priyanka didn't believe a word of this stuff, and it was physically painful to write. In real life, she knew, he'd be broken by his trials. Maybe somebody else wouldn't be, but this protagonist was based on herself as a child, and she *knew* that kid didn't have the strength to hold out for long in adversity.

The book sold unexpectedly well, and people called her brave for writing it. To her surprise, she got a few death threats. It seemed absurd to get worked up over her little book. People asked if she was afraid, and she said, 'No.' Books didn't have the power to change anyone's life, she was pretty sure; not even the life of the person who wrote them.

Naomi Kanakia is the author of YA novels (Little, Brown and Harper); sci-fi short stories (*Asimov's, Analog, F&SF*); literary short stories (*American Short Fiction, Gulf Coast*); poetry (*Cherry Tree, Vallum*); literary criticism (*LA Review of Books, LitHub*); and a cynical guide to the publishing industry (self-published). She lives in San Francisco with her wife and daughter.

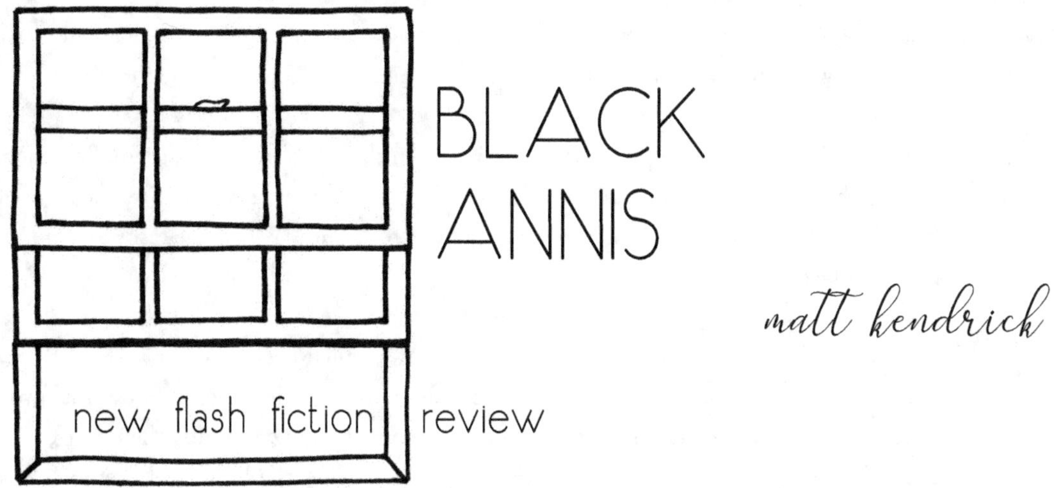

HER BODY IS ON the ground by the pigpen. The Abbess kneels beside it, washing away the blood, scrubbing at the blue dye until there is only the winter white of her skin. The Prior stands nearby. He says, *Enough. She doesn't deserve such kindness.*

The woodcutter's son cowers in a corner like a pheasant caught within a net. *She was in the woods,* he says. *Her hair was wild, her fingers clawed around a knife.* The woodcutter asks, Are you harmed? The boy shakes his head—*She cackled when she saw me. Licked her teeth. Gave chase.* The woodcutter picks up his axe.

A goodwife worries the woodcutter with tales of the past. *Children aren't safe in the woods,* she says. *Not with Annis in her bower.* The boy's eyes grow big as the goodwife describes *the crone's crooked back,* the blood spatters on her kirtle, the dye—a smothering of blue.

When a child goes missing, the villagers trawl the woods, calling, calling, calling. The echo of their shouts. The smell of wild garlic. The smoke from a woodfire curls under a young man's nostrils. He follows its trail, stumbles across Annis soaking hide in potash alum. A deer's hide, he thinks. Or a badger's. Or a child's. *Their flayed skin,* he whispers years later, *draped from the branches of a silver birch.*

In the village, a rumour trickles from mouth to mouth. Annis is pregnant. It is a wild beast who is the father. *She has lured him with her witchery.* The rumour grows with the swelling of her belly, the lacerating screams of her childbirth. *The baby is covered with coarse black hair. It has a boil on its face the size of a fist.* It is blue like her. It is silent. *She wears its severed finger as a pendant.*

The men of the village get drunk and laugh about the woman in the woods. *She is a thing to be hunted, to be tamed—as her mother was.* One of the men, *the bravest of them,* cavaliers from the tavern. The others watch him go. The mead blusters sweet and scented down their throats.

A boy hides in the bushes, watching Annis pick leaves from the woad plant, cut them, boil them, stir them, strain them into dye to smear the white of her skin. Bold as a foxglove peeking through the bracken, he asks about the dye. She shies away from him. When he asks again, she stutters—It is protection.

A girl lives alone in the woods. From her mother, she knows which berries to eat and which will send her stomach into cramps. She knows how to tan an animal's hide, how to fashion it into a kirtle. Sometimes, she catches a rabbit in a trap and, overcome by hunger, holds the point of her knife against the pulsing sinews of its neck. Sometimes, she slashes the knife and there is blood across her kirtle. Other times, she loosens her grip and lets the rabbit scamper free.

Matt Kendrick is a writer, editor and creative writing tutor based in the East Midlands, UK. His stories have been published in *CHEAP POP, Craft Literary, Fictive Dream, FlashBack Fiction, New Flash Fiction Review, Reflex Fiction* and elsewhere. His work has been included on the Biffy50 list 2019/20 and in *Best Microfiction* 2021.

APOLOGETICS

jackie thomas-kennedy

MY STEPMOTHER, BESS, DIDN'T "cuss," so when she picked me up at the college gates to take me to dinner, she acknowledged that she'd been a "b" during my last year of high school and asked if I'd been to the fried chicken place downtown. I hadn't—not because I didn't want to go, but because I didn't want to suggest it to my new friends.

Bess's car looked a little banged up. When I mentioned this, she said some local kids had stolen it right from the Kingdom Hall parking lot.

"But they knew they were wrong," she said, slowing at a yellow light. "They knew, and that's why they brought it back."

"Is that what Dad thinks?"

"Let's not talk about Dad." She stuck out her lower lip and exhaled sharply, but her bangs stayed in place, touching her upper lashes. "He didn't think I should come."

"I figured that," I said.

While she stood in line for our fried chicken boxes—dark meat, white rolls, extra pickles—I searched the car, certain she'd brought me some "literature," as she called it. I was right. The brochures targeted people who'd strayed from the Truth, though none mentioned the reason I'd strayed.

When Bess returned, I noticed magenta welts on her skin as she unfolded our napkins.

"What happened to your arm?"

"Dog bite. There was a beware sign and everything, but I took my chances."

I pictured her in the purple dress she wore out on service. My father had severe leg pain and was exempt from going door-to-door. Bess did it with enough fervor for both of them, towing me along every Saturday until I left for college.

"Lydia," she said. "You really don't believe in the Bible no more?"

My whole face felt greasy. I shook my head.

On the way to my "surprise"—acrylic nails at a strip mall salon—Bess cried a little. I asked her to choose my color for me. "Royal blue for the princess here," she said, as if I weren't standing next to her.

In my first weeks of college, trying to keep the malt liquor down, learning how to straighten my hair, using words like "discourse" and "problematic" when I spoke in class, I'd made a mistake: I discovered that imitations of Bess were a good party trick. Bess, talking to me: "Well, look at *you*, Miss Seven Sisters, up on your high horse!" Bess going door-to-door: "May I share my favorite Psalm with you?" I chased a frighteningly beautiful girl up and down the dorm hallway with a hairbrush, threatening to beat the living daylights out of her in Bess's raspy voice. Everyone laughed. There was no use for the rest of Bess: Bess mixing up a can of frozen orange juice on a hundred-degree day and trying not to cry over local news—riots, riots—and how I would fall asleep to the *thop* of her cutting butter into flour to freeze dough overnight and serve biscuits to me, warm in a paper towel, on our ride to Sunday meeting at the Kingdom Hall. On Sundays, the three of us had cocktail hour on the screened porch; she made me Shirley Temples in cordial glasses she'd found in the attic, and the sweetness always carried, also, a taste of dust.

I sat through the nail process with a discomfort that recalled the single time, so far, I'd been to the gynecologist. The lights were just as harsh, the air just as cold; a gloved woman wielded gels and instruments.

Bess, in the chair next to mine, tipped her head back and sighed with pleasure. "Best part of my week," she said, her hands transformed. She had chosen watermelon pink with rhinestones.

On campus, it was impossible to hide the nails, and I had to turn the whole thing into a bit: crazy Bess and her bad taste. I lasted twenty-four hours before I begged some hallmates to help me remove them. We sat around watching the same movie on a loop while I soaked my hands. Around 2 a.m. the blue ovals began to loosen, then come off in painful snaps. We messaged the all-night cookie delivery and ordered oatmeal chocolate chip and passed a pint of milk as if it were a joint. What I don't understand, said the friend trying to ease my fake thumbnail off of my body, is why you *let* her do this in the first place?

Give me my brush so I can beat the tar out of you, I said in my Bess voice. Everyone laughed, moved on from the question, complained that the milk was gone and that it was late, and the pressure broke off and floated away. I couldn't figure out how to tell them there was no such thing as *let*.

Jackie Thomas-Kennedy is the winner of the 2019 Stella Kupferberg Memorial Short Story Prize. She was awarded a Stegner Fellowship at Stanford University in 2014. Her work has been recorded for NPR's Selected Shorts, and her stories have appeared/are forthcoming in *American Short Fiction, One Story, Electric Literature, Lenny Letter, Narrative, GlimmerTrain, Georgetown Review, SLICE, StoryQuarterly, Madison Review, Canteen, L Magazine, Day One, Crazyhorse, Bennington Review, Harpur Palate,* and *The Idaho Review.* Her reviews have appeared in *Harvard Review, The Millions,* and on the *Ploughshares* blog. She has received fellowships from Yaddo, MacDowell, the Fine Arts Work Center, Ucross Foundation, Brush Creek Foundation for the Arts, and the Saltonstall Foundation. She holds an MFA in fiction from Columbia University School of the Arts.

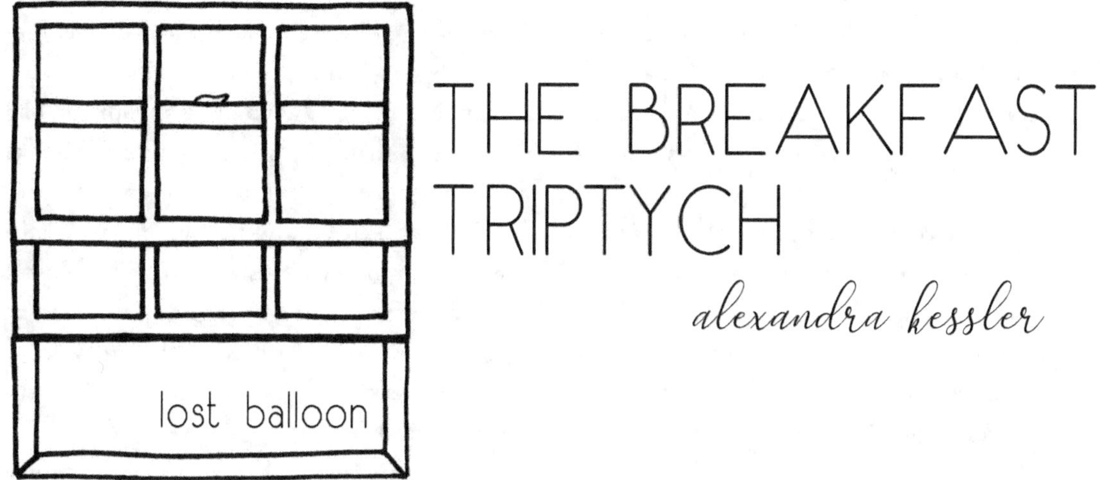

THE BREAKFAST TRIPTYCH

alexandra kessler

I.   THE FIRST THING I remember is disgust. As a child, breakfasts of my lazy mother's undercooked bacon while *Arthur* played on PBS Kids. I could eat happily while the animated characters talked, frolicked, *Arthur*'d, but could not bear to do so during commercials, where real human actors drove Hondas and digitally penetrated Floam. My bacon was made from the stuff of the people-actors—meatfatgrease—and it was like I was eating them. Jellied bites of the dull woman spooning Dannon yogurt into her clammy mouth. I chewed her tendons, the look in her dumb eyes, pleading. Covered my plate with paper napkin until the safe, textureless cartoon people came back. The ones without an appetite for themselves. My neighbor, very fat, stood shirtless in his front yard, staring directly into the sun. Frying. I studied art history in college and once went to Madrid to see Bosch's *Garden of Earthly Delights* Triptych at the Prado. In Spain, there is special meat. Jamón ibérico de bellota. Pigs who only ever ate acorns. In the Triptych, silverywhite bodies squirmed and helixed. Twisted into spooky shapes by their avowal to fleshy consumption. But the figures themselves were clean, lean-limbed, pellucid. The devouring is acceptable if you are beautiful. I bought a ham and egg sandwich from a boy behind a counter and he watched me eat the whole thing, standing there in the store. I threw it up on the curb. In the left I panel of the Triptych, Adam touches his toes to God's toes and God holds Eve's wrist. Linked organs. Constant digestion. I bought another sandwich and could not taste acorns, only the lame salt of myself.

II.   Pete and I make fun of his wife. She's a chef, and ugly. Pictures of her on his instagram—her greasy little eyes. Her smile like a happy face finger-poked into the meatloaf to make a stupid child laugh. It was never about her being beautiful, Pete says. He's maybe embarrassed, but I understand: she's kept him fed. I stand on her kitchen counter with my bare feet. Drink her half and-half. I play with her knives. I'm gonna slice you into pork chops, I say.

Lick the blade. Pete laughs, but his body is scared. He says, get down. Years ago, he was mugged and stabbed while stumbling drunk down the street eating a 7/11 bacon egg and cheese. He is writing an essay about it, and I want to take him to Spain. I show him the wikipedia page for Bosch's Triptych. He looks at me instead of the painting. Puts my thumb in his mouth and bites. His pointed canines dent me. His wife keeps her knives so sharp that you don't even feel it when they cut you. Pete says he loves me. That he could swallow me whole. His wife is away, filming a cooking competition show called *Bringing Home The Bacon*. Pete and I get a week alone together. I worry that we'll pickle but I risk it. He grabs the knife from my hands and holds it against his belly. He's drunk. I've gotten so fat, he says. Plumped up for the slaughter. His eyes are sad and varmint. I just wish I had met you first, he says, and it's worse for all of us that he means it. The first night we spent together I said I wouldn't make him breakfast in the morning. I never learned to cook right. Good, he said, I'm sick of all the fucking breakfasts.

III.   Pete's wife comes in last on *Bringing Home The Bacon*. Dead last, cut the first round. Your handling of this meat, the judge said, lacked a hunger for trancendence. She didn't have enough time, but this is the game. She thought she'd carmalize edges, maple glaze, cook all the way through. She doesn't understand how it's so easy for other people. The chef who beat her, licking his wet lips. She drives away from the studio. It is late at night and early in the morning. Her raw face in the rearview mirror, oil-burned hands. On the side of the empty road, a 24-hour diner. She eats a plate of eggs and bacon while watching commercials on the streaked wall-mounted TV: husband and wife share some Tropicana. Sunny suburban kitchen. On her phone, no calls from Pete. The waiter brings her an extra side of bacon. Why not, he says, it's just between you and me. Out the window, the sun rises. She feels the tilt of the world. The waiter watches her, the diner fills with their bodies. Dense and rare. It's a new day, the waiter says, you have to start it off right. Her stomach shifts. She's not hungry anymore, but she chokes it all down.

Alexandra Kessler's short stories have appeared in such venues as *Joyland, JuxtaProse, Maudlin House, The Boiler,* and *Pigeon Pages.* She was the recipient of the 2014 Lizette Woodworth Reese Award for Fiction, the 2016 Ross Feld Award, and the 2017 Lainoff Prize for Fiction. She is a Pushcart Prize and Best of the Net anthology nominee. She lives in New York City and is at work on a novel.

EVERYBODY

WELL IT ONLY TOOK me twenty years but here I am, and so are a lot of other women, and some men, and even some pregnant women, but who am I to judge when I didn't even tell my family where I was really going tonight, as if I was a teenager again, and just like a teenager I feel like screaming, and then the lights go off and the magic turns on and then I do scream 'cause it's only the Backstreet Boys reunited live on stage at the O2 and now spotlit and poised like cake toppers, only fifty feet away from me and my fucking saint of a friend Sima who booked these tickets months ago before they sold out within minutes, who's now iPhoning the shit out of this, while I'm torn between taking pics, or filming clips, or singing along, or dancing, or just inhaling it all like pixie dust just like my thirteen-year-old self would have wanted me to after my best friend went to see them the first time they came to London and she told us all about it the next day at break while we squealed over our salt & vinegar Discos and copies of Smash Hits, and I wasn't even jealous 'cause going to a concert wasn't even an option, not 'cause my Bangladeshi parents would have said no if I'd asked them but 'cause they would have laughed in my face if I did, so here I am and here is a joy that's more than just an arena full of people who still know all the words, and here's the enchantment of time-capsuled teenage dreams taking flight, and a love as smug as knowing that the one I've always fancied has aged the best, and relief that they're mainly singing the classics and not the newer stuff that's a bit crap, and shock at the fact that they can still dance like that and look like that in those kaleidoscopic outfits when here I am who can't even run for the bus any more without getting out of breath and wondering where all that time went and what am I really doing here anyway, but then there's THAT song and those lights that flash and fire like spells, and not caring if this is lame or cool or nostalgic or tragic or how long it'll take to get home or wondering where that old best friend is these days, because now all I need is my friend Sima on my left and the heavily-pregnant lady on my right and all the other charmed and smiling voices agreeing that they want it that way.

Farhana Khalique is a writer, voiceover artist and teacher from London. Her writing has appeared in *This is Our Place*, *Where We Find Ourselves*, *Litro* and more. Farhana has been shortlisted for The Asian Writer Short Story Prize and she has won a Word Factory Apprentice Award. She is also the editor of *Desi Reads*, a submissions editor at *SmokeLong Quarterly* and a fiction reader at *Litro*. You can find Farhana @HanaKhalique and www.farhanakhalique.com.

SHE WAS THE STAR pupil, extroverted, the teacher's favorite; I was in my third year, unsure of myself, my life and everything in between. I met her in an Ibsen module at Copenhagen University. She always sat in the front row and spent the hour diligently taking notes, or giving answers before anyone else could during the tutorial sessions. I, too, knew the answers but I didn't say them out loud; instead, I waited for someone else to speak. More often than not, she was that person. When she spoke, her "e," "a" and "æ" vowels were a little too crisp, a little too clean-sounding, like the *rigsdansk* of some bygone TV presenter.

We were the only Asians, two dark spots among the bright blond heads of varying shades, and I wondered if she had also been adopted by Danish parents, as was the case of many Asians in Denmark, brought up to think of themselves as Danish. The only thing Asian about us was our birth and, of course, our appearance. Over the years, I had met a number of others like me: the first when I was fourteen, during a class trip to Paris; the second in my first year of university; another was presented to me at a Friday bar by a mutual friend; and a fourth, an adoptee from Norway, had been a *kollegium* floor-mate. Mette Honoré, Helle Nielsen, Mia Kjærsgaard, Unn Fahlstrøm. With each, things had never gone beyond the initial conversation, an exchange of backgrounds. I hadn't given any of them much thought since our respective encounters, but I didn't forget their names, which all belonged to Korean-born Scandinavian girls.

At first glance, Ditte seemed to fit the same mold. On the last day of class, I found her waiting for me in the corridor outside the auditorium. Up to then, she had behaved as if I wasn't there, though she must have noticed me the same way I had noticed her. In the tone of someone who has rehearsed her words beforehand, she asked me if I wanted to get a beer at the cafeteria. As we walked in silence, I thought I knew what was coming. After all, I had been through this before with other adoptees. Like them, she was surprised when I told her that I had been born in Japan, not Korea. I wasn't her first adoptee, but the ones she had met thus far had been girls. I was, in a manner of speaking, her first boy. I learned that we had arrived in Denmark at the ages of five months and six months, respectively. We were both a year younger than our fellow students, who had, in the Danish tradition, taken a sabbatical year to work or travel.

Was she really all that different from the other Korean girls I had met? That was what I found myself thinking, during our third outing, as I glanced at her shadowy profile next to me in the darkness of a cinema at Scala. Now I wonder if it wasn't so much Ditte herself as how alike I thought we were that drew me to her. (Or perhaps that is the essence of attraction: a longing to see something of oneself in another.) Like looking into an enchanted mirror: when I looked at her, I saw a Dane who looked like me. I remember, one night, we lay face to face and gazed wordlessly into each other's eyes until Ditte broke the spell by bursting into laughter. In bed, she was very clear about what she wanted, what she didn't want, how she felt and how she wanted to feel, demonstrating the same thoroughness she had shown in the classroom. Her scent, the consistency of her hair, the color of her nipples—everything about her was at once strange and familiar. When she told me that she had never used deodorant because she didn't have to, I knew exactly what she was talking about. I had never bought a stick of deodorant in my life, though I had carried one around and even pretended to use it all through my upper-secondary years, so that I wouldn't stand out among the other kids at my boarding school. A look of recognition seemed to dawn in her gaze when I told her about my constant need to prove myself when meeting new people. In retrospect, I'm not sure what these shared moments of understanding and complicity meant to her. Did they mean anything at all?

We were together for almost four months, during which time we explored Copenhagen as if for the first time, with new eyes. I had never noticed all the busts, bas-reliefs and other three-dimensional representations scattered throughout the city, which we baptized "the city of statues" because the statues outnumbered the inhabitants, joked Ditte. She had grown up in Esbjerg, in West Jutland, and spent part of every summer on Fanø, where her parents had a summer home overlooking the Wadden Sea. I had grown up in the Whiskey Belt, just north of Copenhagen, my summers punctuated by fishing trips with my father to the Faroe Islands. She loved salted black licorice, the typical Scandinavian kind. Before bed, I used to steal mine from the cabinet where my mother kept it in a glass jar shaped like a Swedish Dalecarlian horse. We both loved having *øllebrød* for breakfast; observing the sky on bright summer nights when dusk seems to go on forever; watching old Danish television dramas like *Jeg kan ikke vente til mandag!* and *Olive og Tom.*

Perhaps a part of me already knew it couldn't last, the theory of compatibility that I had constructed like scaffolding around us, and whose fragile symmetry I marveled at in secret. We were too alike, I remember thinking; it wasn't normal to be this close to someone in so short a time, like skipping to the end of a book one has been reading too fast from the start. But the mirror at last reflected someone back at me. Around that time, I had a strange dream. In it, Ditte was my sister, the two of us separated at birth, and though I knew such a thing to be impossible—my blood was Japanese, hers was Korean, after all—I woke in the dark with an erection, my heart beating like a tam-tam. I was alone in my bed; Ditte had gone back to her hall of residence at some point during the night without waking me. When we saw each other again, I made the mistake of telling her about my dream. Though I had left out the part about my erection, bewilderment and disgust clouded her face, as if I had laid bare some unspeakable fantasy. She asked me if that was how I had always seen her. The thought of an incestuous relationship with a long-lost sister had never crossed my mind, I said, but Ditte refused to believe me.

Things were never the same after that. One day, she informed me of her intention to spend the weekend in Esbjerg, where her parents still lived. We had often talked about going together, but the trip had never materialized. The following night, I received a phone call; in the background I heard voices, music, as though she had called me from a party. She seemed distracted or irritated by something. We ended the conversation without saying goodbye. I eventually learned that she had left me for her thesis supervisor, who also happened to be my thesis supervisor. After that, I couldn't walk past certain places—the statue of Adam Oehlenschläger near the zoo in Norske Allé, the skating rink in Nørrebro Park, even the oil tanks at Prøvestenen—without being reminded of her. The worst was going to see my thesis supervisor. I couldn't be sure, but it seemed that the man had no idea about me and Ditte. He was out of shape, dark-haired (for a blond Dane), and his chin receded a bit. Other than his vast and bottomless intelligence, his daggerlike wit, his impressive list of publications, what could she possibly see in him? And that was when I realized that I had never really known her, any more than I had known the adopted Korean girls before her. She had become a name to add to the others. All this time, I had thought of her as a mirror, a strange and beguiling reflection, but it would seem that she had been drawn to me because I was different, a change from all the Danes she had previously dated.

David Hoon Kim took his first creative writing workshops in France, at the Sorbonne and other places, before attending the Iowa Writers' Workshop and the Stegner Program. His fiction in French has appeared in various Francophone reviews and magazines on both sides of the Atlantic. In English, he is the author of *Paris Is a Party, Paris Is a Ghost*, a linked story collection. He can be found at davidhoonkim.com.

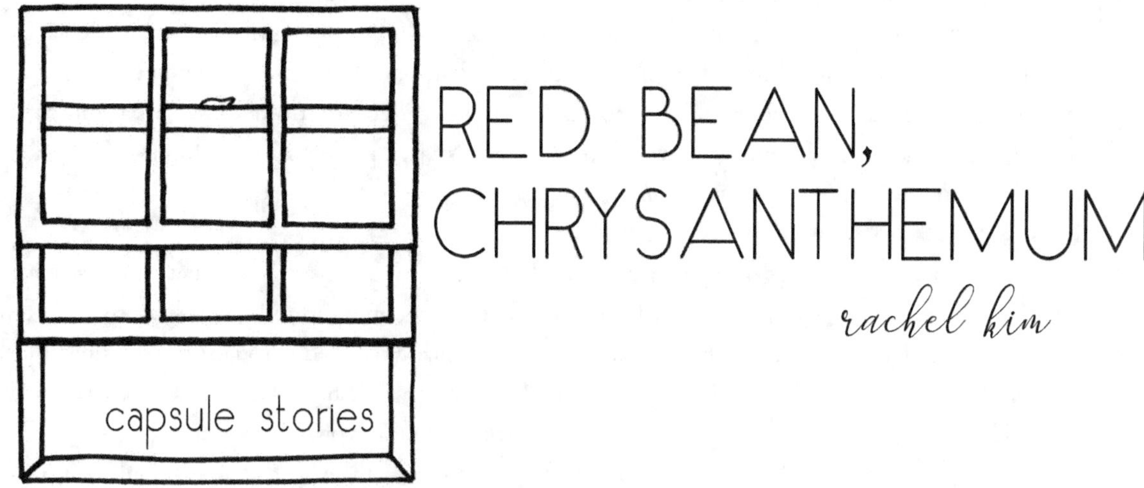

RED BEAN, CHRYSANTHEMUM

rachel kim

PARTING MY LIPS SLIGHTLY, I blew a soft white dragon through the frigid air of wintery Seoul, sharing the warmth of my cheeks for it to dissolve into fleeting flight. A single window in the office buildings above twinkled briefly, as if my dragon had joined ranks as a newborn star—The First Noel. I lowered my gaze from the steel heavens and buried my chin back into a pilling wool scarf. The end of the street was near. I clutched the hand warmer in my pocket, prowling forward to stuff myself with a Korean winter.

Hotteok. As I finally crossed through the busy intersection, colorful tents of crinkling tarp and trucks with their sides propped open like petite planes shimmered with light and steam on each side of the carless road. I quickly reached the line leader, holding out a cerulean dollar bill.

"One seed hotteok, please." Worked by deft hands, a glutinous rice dough ball was filled with sugar and toasted seeds, placed on a grill layered with scalding oil, and pressed down into a flat, round disc. A line forming behind me, multiple full moons rose onto the sizzling gray backdrop. I soon received my circular treasure, folded, in a small paper cup. Each piping hot mouthful dripped with caramelized sugar, rich honey brown. Hotteok, sweet pancake.

Gunbam. Nearby, feverish sparks flew from the sides of a vented barrel, spinning with a dull drum like peppering hail. Within, a mahogany batch of chestnuts whirled together in dry heat, popping like gilded hearts, their burnt sienna skin chipping away to reveal golden flesh. As the chestnuts tumbled into a paper pouch, a comforting aroma infused every breath. I eagerly delved in, almost searing the tips of my fingers. Gunbam, roasted chestnut.

Bungeoppang. A pair of high school girlfriends, both wearing black puffer jackets that reached down to their ankles, jokingly scoffed at each other in front of the bungeoppang truck. A serious contest on the superiority of red bean filling or cream filling was at the center of their debate, but intermittent laughter betrayed the solemn argument. As if to remain neutral, I stepped aside and asked for a bag of bungeoppang, half-half. Fluffy yet chewy buns, shaped to look like fish and filled with either sweet red bean paste or choux cream, dove into a thin paper bag. Cradling the warm pouch in my jacket kangaroo-style, I picked off the plump fish from fin to fin. Bungeoppang, fish-shaped bun.

Gukhwappang. Following the faint tinkling of metal on metal, I arrived at batter poured into shallow wells in a large griddle. Each pool of batter, containing a dollop of smooth red bean paste, was flipped over by a thin metal skewer when nearly cooked through. Resembling thick, golden pastry coins imprinted with a chrysanthemum on both heads and tails, a heavy bag of gukhwappang in winter was a sack of riches. Selecting from my own hefty share, I cautiously bit into a blistering bloom as its escaping steam spiraled through the cold. Gukhwappang, chrysanthemum bread.

Ggochi eomuk. Savory, salty broth washes over my saccharine tongue. I lift the wooden skewer that pierces through ivory waves of fish cake, nibbling on the soupy end. As the winter night comes to a close, I am filled with a languid glow. The twinkling star watches over me. Ggochi eomuk, skewered fish cake.

Rachel Kim hails from somewhere between South Korea and New Jersey. She is currently a senior at the University of California, Berkeley with undergraduate majors in Psychology and Media Studies. Her works seek to find the special in the mundane through writing, video, and photography.

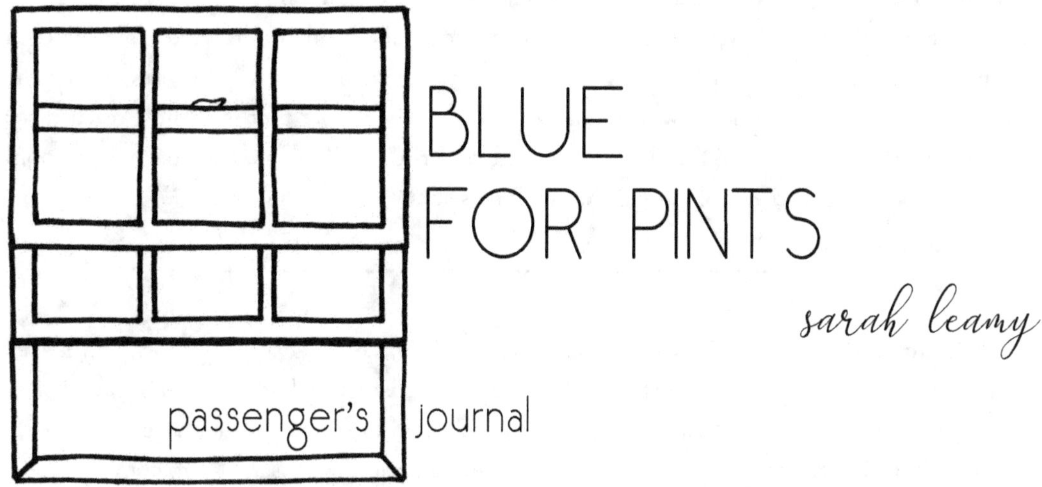

WHEN I STOPPED SMOKING, I cried. Will I cry if I stop drinking alcohol? No one could answer me on that one. The guys sitting at the bar all looked at me like I was crazy. I carried on though. This is important to know. It means we're here by choice; know thy enemy and all that crap, I added. Jordan asked if this means I was going to get god in order to skip out on him, it was my round next, he reminded me. No, I'm not getting god in the next ten minutes, I told him, and sipped the pale ale in front of me. It was time to shut up apparently. I just can't talk about drinking to those that drink. The bartender wouldn't engage with me after the fourth beer, but fine, I know what I'm trying to say. It all started with the company doctor last week asking me how much do I drink. Per day, I'd clarified, or per week. Either one, she'd said, fingers hovering over the keyboard. I told her. She tapped it in. I have good eyesight for my age. I noticed that she put in brackets a higher number. I asked her about that. She explained without blushing that 'we all know how drunks down-count the numbers. We add 25% on average. The paramedics, nurses, doctors, we all do it. You didn't know? It's different for men and women, how you process alcohol so we take that into consideration, she said, looking at her notes and not the old fool in front of her. And then that company doctor got me fired, saying it was ten in the morning and I shouldn't be drinking on the job, but it's not like I'd sipped anything before work, it was from the night before, I told them, but it didn't help me keep my job, did it? Since then I've carried a marker with me and noted on my left forearm the pints as I drink them. I was going to say as I buy them but it's not that easy as so many are gifts and who am I to refuse a gift. I keep track. I'm into learning about this numbers game. My arm now is black and blue with small crosses marking each beverage. I started playing with colors. Black for shots. Blue for pints. There's nothing else that I drink. A pint in every sandwich, oh, no, I mean the other way around. But more importantly, would I still come here if I didn't drink a few pints of beer each day? And if I didn't, who would I talk to in the afternoons since I can't keep a job? It's not like I'm old or anything, but I'm a bit worried about all of that and it's a bit of a problem, is what I said, and Jordan nodded at me but held his empty pint glass up for the bartender to refill, telling her it was on my tab. He got me another pint too, and I reached for my blue marker. There wasn't much bare skin left to write on. I'm scared to run out of room because what happens then? What will I do with myself? Where will I go?

Sarah Leamy is the author of *G'Dog, Hidden, When No One's Looking, Lucky Shot,* and *Lucky Find,* as well as *Van Life.* Her shorter work has been published in *Los Angeles Review, Hunger Mountain, Santa Fe Writers Project,* and others. Stay, a hybrid memoir, is due out in 2023 with Madville Publishing. She is currently looking for representation. www.sarahleamy.com.

IT HAS BEEN 20 years. You think that it's a rest, being here. That we are in the rhythm. That we enjoy eating bread and crusts. You didn't think we would chase your dreams, that we'd try to take down your net curtains. The reams of words on the web are a ruse. You should have said run. Or better yet, don't come. The land carries this stress like a cyst. You are here. We are here. We all better make haste. You should wear a hat but not its hate. Be a hummer, not a hammer with a single sound byte. We cannot stop the wave that brought us. We cannot squash ourselves. You must see the gleam. We have heat. We have flowers. Let us make our merit. We are smitten with this country, but we have not gone to mush. We want our home to be a haven. Go on say yes. Let us nest. Let us sit on your hearth. Share your heath. Let us be the rum in your cake.

Kirsten Le Harivel is a writer, curator and programmer of creative writing workshops, courses and retreats. Shelter, her debut poetry collection came out in 2021. She lives with her family in Aotearoa, New Zealand.

STOLEN

zizheng william liu

I'M THE ONLY ONE who watches the death-march from afar, hidden as the wind. It's ironic, I think: hidden is what I do, or what I've done, at least, picking the stuffed, satin pockets that litter the city, sniffing out sore fellows desperate to be the victim for once. I lighten loads, and I make dreams come true; I'm a thief, but here I am, robbed of my better reason by the rotting lips of another man.

The poets say death is peace, and the slack expressions of the dead are supposed to be evidence of that. What use is peace, then? The dead don't need peace, not when the hearts of those they had loved grow swollen and crush any sliver of sense in a person. And still, life gnaws at a person even after they're gone; what peace is there for anyone?

So I watch. Rich indigo flags billow underneath the breath of the deep sky, marking the body on the slate slab as a man of old blood. Coffers boorishly full, hands shamefully smooth, and eyes that sparkled at any patch of skin uncovered by cloth or grime; he had been a prime target, and would have been a profitable one, were it not for the tremble in his voice and the way his lips twitched in satisfied unease.

The streets are crowded with the dead-minded folk of the city; some here to mourn, others to softly gloat, others paid to do either or both. They, at least, are near, face-close with death and unfazed, as if thinking themselves immortal. Maybe they are, if things like souls exist, like the poets say. But the chest is hollow, at least to my reckoning, and a beating heart is the only thing that even tries to fill it.

The procession goes on, the leading trumpeteers weaving their song down through the Flanks, the dark slab pulled in tow. They reach the edge of the settlement and prepare to hurl the body off, but not before propping the body up for all to see.

The crowd mutes itself, as is customary, but the wind whips the flags into raucous flapping. Towards the west, a gale comes; whistling through the orifice of every open window and crack in the city's bricks, culminating in a howl that seems to reverberate from the sky below. A few children stumble at its force, their parents catching before they fall.

The body is held high, stark naked in the daystar's light, clay-brown skin baked as the rigor mortis is only now fading. I can see why the poets might be so enamored with the dead; his nakedness is innocent yet invulnerable, so strong with a head that can't stand on its own.

The body is gone now, lost to the turbulence of the swirling sky below, and whatever lies beyond that. His breath will never kiss mine, and I am stolen.

Zizheng William Liu is a student currently studying in Houston, Texas. His work has previously been featured in *Gone Lawn, the Eunoia Review,* and others. When he's not writing, he loves snapping pictures of the ever-changing world around him with his Canon Rebel camera.

THERE ARE TWO WAYS to do it:

You can assemble a team of quarry workers to drive a gas-powered locomotive over two tracks laid into a vast field of fossilized coral limestone, its surface already etched with ancient worm trails and fern imprints now sprouting young green shoots. Rows of motorized chisels attached to the machine's base will rise and lower to bore a series of parallel six-inch-deep grooves into the rock, as you continuously pump in saltwater to clear debris. You will then drive the machine back to the beginning to start again, chiseling deeper and deeper through layers of life until the grooves extend ten feet down. You will turn off the machine, reposition the tracks at a right angle, and repeat the process to make a second set of grooves perpendicular to the first. Once you've cut a checkerboard into the rock's surface, you'll drive in steel wedges to dislodge ten-ton chunks, as if serving slices of a sheet cake. In the event the wedges won't budge it, you can use dynamite.

Or, you can find one five-foot-tall Latvian man with tuberculosis and a broken heart.

No one knows how he built his coral castle all on his own—with his hand tools, his fourth-grade education, his childhood spent casually or maybe not-so-casually observing his stonemason relatives before migrating to an undeveloped plot of swampland at the mouth of the Florida Everglades.

The leader of our tour compares it to Stonehenge, the Great Pyramids, the Taj Mahal.

The story is she left him back in the old country, his sixteen-year-old child-fiancée, and it broke him so fully that he built this for her. They don't delve too deeply into her age on this tour—it was 1913, is how they seem to get around it—but it's easy enough to infer that this man, 26 at the time of his abandonment, was a creep.

A creep who quarried and moved multi-ton slabs of coral rock and built himself a home without mortar, using only precise counterbalancing of weight. Rocks joined so seamlessly no light shines through, and a steel rod, retrofitted from a Model T Ford, on whose axis a six-thousand-pound gate revolved at the touch of a hand.

There are enough coral chairs, coral beds, coral bathtubs for an entire family, though the builder lived alone until he died. I recall a dark detail about a repentance corner, a kind of stockade with two openings: one for a wife, one for a child. Most sinister of all: a nearby chair for a five-foot-tall man to sit in judgment.

But the truth is, I'm only half-listening to the details. My attention is fractured, as it always is now, focused partly on making sure my three-year-old daughter doesn't get restless on this tour. I shouldn't have bothered: she is silent, riveted, for the entire hour. What she hears stays with her, presses a nautilus into the moldable landscape of her brain. For months afterward, she will, with zero introduction, tell strangers a story they have no context to understand as they bend to hear her small voice on line at the deli, the coffee shop: *The man who built the castle was tiny*, she'll begin, before shifting to a dramatic whisper, *and his heart was broken.*

Most of the time it seems too exhausting to explain what she's talking about, so I don't bother. Let them guess.

I take a lot of pictures that day, of the loosely coiled sea life on the coral's surface that looks like cerebral cortex. As I take them I imagine I'm someone else, someone whose eyes I've been wishing I could see through. Someone I encountered once, months before, but haven't managed to stop wanting. The wanting has taken so many forms: a collection of unsent drafts attempting contact, an entire life I've imagined out of Internet scraps, a you I think about many times a day without actually knowing you at all. And I've wondered, ever since, what it is I even want—what my life wants from me, in making me want you—or whether what I'm really holding onto is the feeling of wanting itself.

The builder, for all his plans—I suspect he didn't know either. Was it that he couldn't help it, that he built his castle and wrote his years of unanswered letters to his almost-wife just to blunt the misfiring of his own desire, give it empty air to sail through, and somewhere to land?

Because we don't build shrines to the ones who breathe beside us: we do it for the people we have to create in their absence, to carve out a space for all the things we'll never know.

When I revisit the pictures of this trip a year later, my daughter is tiny, a different person. Shaken, I take new pictures of my own face, trying to pinpoint how much I've transformed in this time, how many cells replaced, how much blood, whether any of me is the same as it was the day I met you and it felt as if a door swung wide open, a door I barely touched.

And I wish I could be as stone-faced as the ex-fiancée, who never answered a single one of the builder's letters, and eventually grew into an 80-year-old woman who finally, after his death, responded to the castle staff's invitation to visit with something along the lines of *I didn't care then and I don't care now.*

But I know in my gut, in my worm-trailed heart, that if I'm anyone I'm the builder, the writer, the creep.

————————————

Julia LoFaso has published writing in *Conjunctions, McSweeney's Internet Tendency, Cincinnati Review, Hayden's Ferry Review,* and *The Iowa Review* (forthcoming), among other places. Her work has been selected for *Wigleaf's* Top 50 Very Short Fictions 2021 and nominated for Best of the Net, as well as shortlisted for flash fiction contests held by PRISM international and *Southeast Review.* She lives in Queens, where she's working on a hybrid collection about weird motherhood and various forms of solace seeking. More of her writing is available at julialofaso.com.

THE LUBAVITCH HASSIDIM ARE sending two teen volunteers to spend time with our daughter. I resist at first, but Mattie's Special Ed teacher explains that it's a mitzvah for the girls, who are sixteen—a special program started by a rabbi's wife. She says I should let them come; it might be good for Mattie. She hasn't seen Mattie smile in the eight months since her mom died.

If Kayla were alive, she would have fumed: "We're not religious. What will they do with Mattie? Pray?" But when I say this to the Special Ed teacher, she says you don't have to be religious to qualify for a visit. You don't even have to be Jewish.

Without Kayla's moxie, I give in.

I miss her too.

A half-hour before they're due, Mattie's running circles in our parched backyard. "My friends are coming, my friends are coming!" She's ten, barefoot, friendless. The play dates I arrange don't return—too sad, too weird, too slow. They want to talk about Harry Potter. She's stuck on *Katy No-Pocket*.

It's been a dry Spring and I keep forgetting to water the yard. The bottoms of Mattie's feet are already caked with dirt. The doorbell rings. No time to do anything about that.

"Dad, they're here!" Mattie races to greet them, ballerina skirt and pink top glittering. Talia and Deb, longhaired, long-skirted, grin at her. "Hi, Mattie! Nice meeting you. What pretty hair! What a pretty skirt!"

I am determined not to eavesdrop, to let them be. I offer them lemonade but they have brought their own bottles of Poland Spring, and one for Mattie too. Meanwhile I finish the laundry. Sometime after I've hung the delicates to dry, the girls turn on an ancient CD player they've brought. They remove their shoes like Mattie and join hands with her in a circle dance.

The word "mayim" repeats endlessly: "mayim, mayim, mayim, mayim, hey mayim bisason!" I have heard this song, seen this dance, at a wedding or Bar Mitzvah, but don't know what it means. Although I don't ask, a breathless Talia translates for my benefit. "Water of joy," she says. "Pioneers found water in the desert after seven years. Somebody wrote a song." Eventually the music ends. All three girls collapse laughing in a heap.

Mattie's childish underpants—embroidered with the days of the week—hang on the clothesline alongside another ballerina skirt and matching tights. My wife and I often talked about whether Mattie would always stay a child. I no longer consider the question.

Talia and Deb gather their shoes and the CD player. Will they come back?

Mattie hums, practicing a step.

Then the girls chorus: "See you next week!"

Our daughter's clothes rustle in the dry wind. The ballerina skirt balloons like a sail. If I were religious, I might say a prayer of thanks or of hope. But I don't even know a prayer.

Instead I whisper *mayim*.

Nancy Ludmerer's fiction appears in *Kenyon Review, Electric Literature, Cimarron Review, New Orleans Review, Best Small Fictions* 2016 (a River Styx prizewinner), *Litro*, and others. Her flash fictions have been translated into Spanish and read aloud on public radio, and since 2020, her stories have won prizes from *Masters Review, Carve, Pulp Literature, Streetlight, Gemini,* and Orison Books. Her short memoir *Kritios Boy* (Literal Latte) was cited in *Best American Essays* 2014. She practiced law in NYC for many years and continues to live there with her husband Malcolm and 13-year-old cat, Joey (aka Joseph the Great). Twitter: @nludmerer.

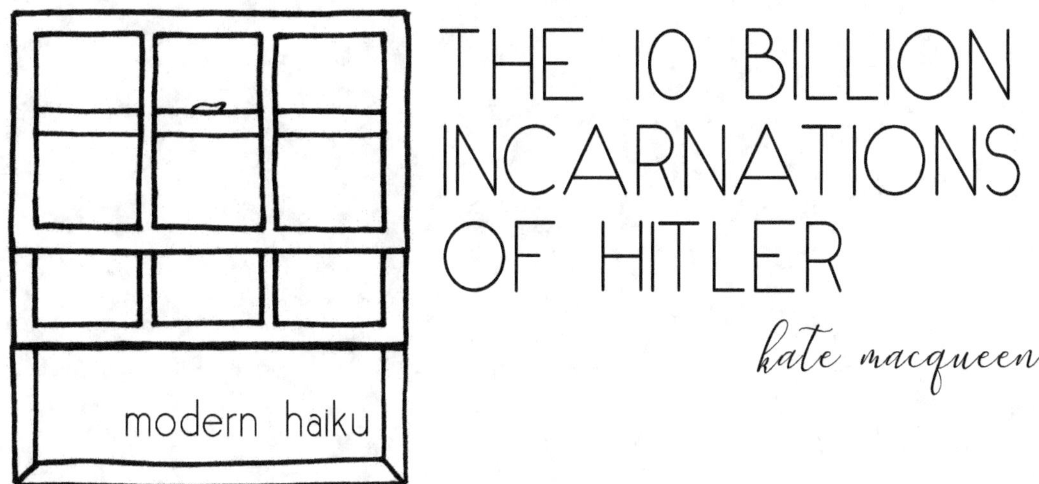

WE'RE TALKING ABOUT MOSQUITOS and ticks. I say knowing a mosquito is Hitler reincarnated might alleviate guilt in killing it. Paul asks if reincarnation is impartible, if souls reincarnate whole and complete. Or partible, distributed across multiple beings, like genes to our children and grandchildren and nieces and nephews. If partible, then bits of Hitler could be incarnated billions of times over in the form of billions of mosquitos. That raises a new question. How many times would Hitler's bits need to be incarnated as mosquitos to earn reincarnation in a higher state?

instar
wasp cocoons dangle
from a caterpillar's back

Kate MacQueen currently lives, writes, and gratefully grows old along New Hope Creek in North Carolina. Her haibun and short poems have appeared in a variety of publications including *Modern Haiku, The Heron's Nest, Frogpond, Acorn, Prune Juice, Femku, Trash Panda, Hedgerow*, several Red Moon Press anthologies, *Haiku* 2014 (Modern Haiku Press), and *Wishbone Moon* (Jacar Press 2018). As a social scientist and health researcher she has also published a bunch of articles in academic journals and collaborated on a few books.

Skvira, Ukraine Pogrom, 1919

PURPLE SWIRLS ON MY breasts, belly—crystal balls—reveal my fate. Not all that grows is made from love—when a bee pollinates a sunflower, it is to take the nectar. He handled my skin like an aphid on a leaf while I clawed at him like a dormouse burrowing for the winter. Someone, a sister, might have asked, *What was your first time like?* Hands ungloved during snowfall, scabs peeled away, what should remain concealed was exposed. A face should be bare, but he veiled mine—pulling up my skirt. Were his eyes the color of dead grass? Was his mouth jagged, a cemetery full of crumbling tombstones? His breath smelled of vodka. Mine smelled of borscht. His words—a dull knife. My words—crouching in an empty well. His skin was of metal. Mine was of dust. What does the past look like when time is a shovel? What does night look like without the sky? How do I flee without a map? The Earth is of a magnetic field. The ocean is of an undertow.

———————————————————

Liz Marlow's debut chapbook, *They Become Stars,* was the winner of the 2019 Slapering Hol Press Chapbook Competition. Additionally, her work has appeared in *The Bitter Oleander, Greensboro Review, minnesota review, Valparaiso Poetry Review,* and elsewhere. She earned her MFA from Western Michigan University and is the founding editor of *Minyan Magazine.*

SOME THINGS YOU'LL DO WHEN YOU WOULD RATHER BE HAPPY

laurie marshall

YOU'LL CHECK THE MAILBOX one last time in case there's an unexpected windfall waiting to pay the mortgage, or an official announcement that the whole thing was a sick joke or that there's a new technology that can bring someone back to life just like in the movies and your life is not, in fact, forever changed. Today the mailbox is empty.

But before the mailbox, you'll drive down the dirt road and away from the house one last time looking to see if there are blackberries on the canes, listening to the crunch of rock under tires through the open windows and inhaling the dust deep into your lungs where you invite it to nestle in, to become thickened and scarred over, visible on x-rays as tiny white dots in otherwise translucent flesh. To become a physical part of you.

But before the drive, you'll lock the red wooden door one last time and pocket the key that you have no intention of handing over to the man at the bank or the eventual new owners but will, instead, wear on a chain around your neck because it is a literal key to your truth and your personhood and the floor plan of your life up to this point. They'll change the locks anyway.

But before you lock the door, you'll say goodbye one last time to the dogwood outside the window over the kitchen sink where you learned to peel potatoes, and the fireplace built of stones warmed by the sun on this land and placed by the hands of your grandfather, and the bathtub where your mother bathed each night before bed and where she landed after the fall that preceded the news that she had a mass in her right parietal lobe. This would explain the question about her sobriety when she was pulled over six months earlier.

But before you say goodbye to the dogwood and the fireplace and the bathtub, you'll say goodbye to your mother one last time as she lies unconscious and numbed by morphine, her skull leasing space to an assassin that doesn't care about trees or stones or keys or the agony that its residency is causing and will continue to cause once it, and its host, have stopped breathing and are burned to ashes and blown downriver from the edge of the limestone bluff salted with fossils of creatures that are alive only in our memories and imaginations.

Laurie Marshall is a writer and artist working in Northwest Arkansas. Her stories have been awarded the 2021 *Lascaux* Flash Fiction Prize and included in the 2022 Bath Flash Fiction Award anthology. She reads for *Fractured Lit* and *Longleaf Review.* Words and art have been published in *Stanchion, New World Writing, Rejection Letters, Emerge Literary Journal, Versification, Bending Genres, Chaotic Merge* and *Flash Frog* among others. Connect on Twitter @LaurieMMarshall or at www.SeeLaurieWrite.com.

THEY KEPT THE GIRL under glass in a bedroom off the living room on the first floor of a brownstone. The girl's parents had slipped the glass over her while she slept. She had just turned thirteen. Her parents wanted to preserve her adolescent purity, her freshness, and impatiently waited for a man to wake her.

At first, close relatives came to gaze at the girl—her mother and father, her sisters and brothers. Then extended family came—aunts, uncles, cousins. Then the friends of extended family. And then their friends. They each took turns, leaning over the glass eagerly. They saw their reflections flitter and dance against the girl's stillness.

Once a boy, the child of a friend of a distant relation, tried to lift the glass. And he did lift it. (He was a prankster.) But he dropped the edge immediately when the girl moved. She moved only one fingertip less than one inch. But he was a sharp-eyed boy and saw it. He didn't know her before she was asleep under glass, so he thought she would stay just as she was—arms gracefully by her side, toes pointing up. A doll dressed in a white, sugar-cake icing gown. (Later he said, he only wanted to lick her lacy cuff.) Her tiny gesture so frightened him that he ran away and never asked to look at her again.

Although the girl was asleep, she could still hear. She heard her relatives argue over whether or not the boy spoiled her purity.

It wasn't the boy's fault, asserted an aunt. *It was the girl that lured him. That girl took advantage of his prankish tendencies. He was only being a boy, doing what boys do.*

Many rumors streamed from this incident. There were questions like, Was her movement a sign of criminal intent? The girl's mother and father feared the rumors would scare off suitors. But the opposite happened. The talk drew crowds. Strangers lined the block, waiting for hours to gaze at their reflections in the girl.

Her new popularity, however, did not resolve the dilemma. After the incident with the boy, the question remained: Was the girl ruined?

She heard relatives and their friends discuss options. If she was ruined, should they discard her? Bury her to contain her impurity? The next oldest sister easily could take the girl's place under glass. Or should they pay a man (any man) to kiss her and wake her, and then sell her to earn wages in a factory.

Isn't child labor illegal? her uncle asked.

Things can be arranged, said a friend of her uncle.

It may be her best option, advised a second cousin.

The girl's mother agreed. And then her father agreed.

But what man would kiss her now?

At that moment (A blessing? Luck?) a man, a stranger at the back of the line, burst into the bedroom and fell in love.

I love you, he said, staring at his reflection in the glass. *You're just like me.* The man, seeing his own likeness in the girl, said to the crowd, *I can save her. I will wake her.*

The girl's relatives and their friends and especially her next oldest sister were overjoyed that this stranger—a true suitor—had appeared.

This is the one, said her mother, elbowing her father. And he agreed.

Unfortunately, the girl could not see what the man looked like, because her eyes were closed. But she could hear his voice. His voice sounded like a dream—both far away and near.

She was careful not to move. She did not want to be accused again of the crime of seduction.

The strangers in line and the relatives and their friends gathered in the bedroom. With everyone watching, the man tipped the glass back. The hush in the room was the softness of snow. Then he lifted the glass all the way and leaned it against the wainscoting. The girl in her sugary gown remained still. She wanted release badly. The man leaned over her. He kissed her. She did not move her lips. The man looked into her sweet face. She did not smile. Everyone waited, but the girl dared not move.

She's as cold as a fish, said the man stepping back. *She is not like me. She is an ice queen.*

The girl sensed disappointment. She was neither pure nor fresh, but a cold, limp fish. She sensed anger. Strangers left in disgust. Her relatives and their friends reconsidered options: burial or factory? In a rush out of the bedroom to make competing arrangements, they left the glass leaning against the wainscoting.

The girl was alone for the first time in three years. She opened her eyes. Her fingertip twitched. Crisp air swept over her. Her nerves tingled. She stretched her arms overhead. It was not easy to move because her muscles had atrophied. It took her all afternoon to sit up. At nightfall, when everyone else was asleep, she stood. She steadied herself and took her time. Her limbs were sore, but she pushed on. She changed out of her lacy-cuffed, sugar-cake icing gown and into the T-shirt and jeans she had worn before she fell asleep. She once was a tomboy, which had alarmed her parents.

Tight-muscled, she limped out of the front door of the brownstone and down the stairs to the street. Her dead skin shivered awake in the coolness. Blood pinked her cheeks. Overgrown hair swept her ankles. She moved into the night. Slowly at first until her muscles loosened. She kept moving, swinging her arms wide. Her body trembled with elation and terror like a thousand sparrows startled to flight. She was alive. She kept moving. She had no definitive direction except *Away*. She moved. She kept moving.

Kristine Marx is an artist and writer. She has exhibited her work in New York, Los Angeles, Berlin and Tokyo. Her fiction has appeared in *Variant Literature* and *Peripheries*. She has published art criticism in MIT Press *PAJ: Journal of Performance Art* and *Whitechapel Documents of Contemporary Art: Materiality*. She is a recipient of grants from New York State Council of the Arts, the Goethe Institut, and the Experimental Television Center and was a resident artist at the Mattress Factory in Pittsburgh, Kolin Ryynänen Centre for Arts & Culture in Finland and Herrman & Wagner in Berlin. She teaches at Pratt Institute in Brooklyn, NY. She earned her MFA in visual art from Hunter College and is working on her second MFA in fiction at Sarah Lawrence College.

IMAGINE, IF YOU PLEASE, you are a little girl born in an old city on a river, gas light in her home and war in the air. Night after night, your parents, doting fools, promise you the moon, tracing its shape on the windowpane when the sky is clear of clouds and planes. Then the war is lost, the city occupied, and the shame so great that even you, only a stupid little girl, can feel it. It clings to the backs of men's throats when they drink to forget; it trickles down women's thighs after fucking soldiers for favors; it sticks to the hands of ignorant children as they wave hello to the invaders. And your parents? The night sky might as well no longer exist to them. And you—you are merely an afterthought, a mouth to feed in a confusing economy where people prosper but money is near worthless.

Have you put yourself in the little girl's shoes? Have you? Imagine, then, a formative decision: you will take the moon that no one will give you; you will take it between your goddamn teeth if you have to. You grow yourself up. You move away from home. You study medicine, hoping that one of your textbooks will show you how to get the shame off your skin, how to carve it out of the tissue if need be. Imagine the tremblings of a young woman living on her own for the first time, beginning to notice the world around her. You read the newspapers, listen to the gabs in line at the grocer's, witness the old men exchanging bundles of money for three loaves of bread. You study as hard as you possibly can. You will find the cure—for yourself, for everyone else.

Plucky little thing you've become. Hair bunned, heels risen, bright-eyed, breasted, you are not a common sight in the halls of learning. The men have three ways of reminding you of your rarity. One, they ask you out. If you accede, they treat you like a little lady, no longer a colleague; if you refuse, they turn to tactics two or three. Two, they openly insult your intellect during lessons, whether you speak or remain silent. Three, they leave notes in your bag, in your books, in the pockets of your coat, scrawls slicked with shame that emphasize that you are only worth your virginal womb.

When the time comes, you specialize in dermatology. Your studies are interrupted often as one teaching doctor after another is fired, driven out, illegalized. The newspapers explain, the gabs murmur, the old men shake their hungry fists at one another in disagreement over whys and wherefores, but it is getting harder to listen now—the shame drips in your ears. You begin to feel you've fallen down a well, nearly drowning in its damp desperation. But then, one day, you lift your head up and see a poster tacked to the wall in the women's boarding house where you room. The image calls to you. It is a well mouth, a ladder up and out. New, freshly printed, its colors dry and warm. Its words promise protection, and behind them, a happy family in their own little world: the mother is aproned, with a baby in her arms; a little boy, straight-backed, stands in front of her, his face eye level with the baby's; the father's arms encircle them both. And there is one more figure standing beside them, looking out: a little girl, blond-curled, red-cheeked with excitement. She is vitality itself, and she will help you out of the well. You will no longer need to wrestle the moon down all by yourself.

Are you still picturing yourself in these moments? It is important you do. Imagine, I beg you, the elation you feel the first time a vital little girl like that, born inside the shame-filled world, calls you *Frau Doktor*. Imagine the pride, the satisfaction, the tenderness. This is who you are now, *Frau Doktor* to them all, a district full of girls beginning adolescence. Their skin, you note, is as wet as yours, but they know nothing else. They wear their blue skirts and crisp white shirts with joyous rigor, the ties down their fronts signaling an authority you admire. You are awed by the way they live with their shame: flicking it away like common sweat when they run, squeezing its excess into their glasses of milk and drinking it back up, using it to smooth down flyaway wisps in one another's hairdos. You begin to mimic them, hoping that with enough repetition you will not retch at the feel of yourself. Imagine the respite of believing the bile in your throat has gone for good.

But another war begins. You are promoted and transferred, your skills and hard work recognized. Away from the girls, you are unable to ignore the damp residue you leave behind on every surface you touch. What once was a steady drip in your ears is now a bubbling. You are back at the bottom of the well, and it is boiling. No wonder, then, that it takes some time before it registers that the skin of the prisoners who pass through the clinic is *dry*, dry as the bones you remove from their arms become when left overnight to be examined the next morning. No wonder, then, that the moon begins to—

Ah. I see. You will go no further with me. You have no interest in the secretions of shame; it is my guilts you catalogue. Very well. You are my judge and jury, after all. Sentence me, then, but give me a cell without windows. Keep the damn eye of the moon away.

Ilana Masad is a fiction writer, essayist, book critic, and author of the novel *All My Mother's Lovers*.

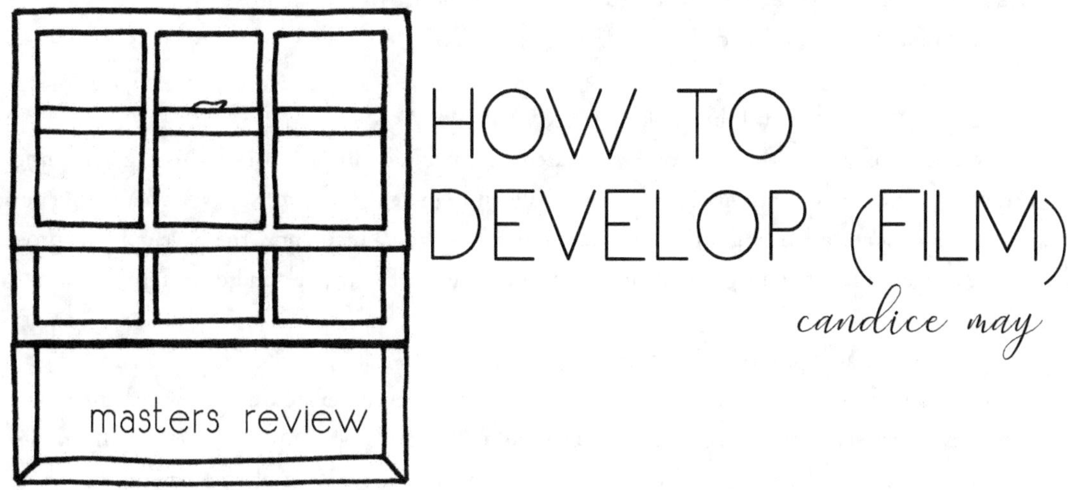

1. Materials and Set Up

YOU ARE A LONELY girl in high school, and the darkroom is your favorite place to hang out, even at lunch time. While your so-called friends and classmates walk downtown for lunch, or smoke joints on the football field, you click the door closed and turn off all the lights. Except for the red light, the one that illuminates your flesh in a blood-hued tone as you gather the supplies: scissors, thermometer, plastic containers and toxic-smelling liquids. Stop bath, fixer, paper towels. And the film cassette, of course, with all your undeveloped pictures.

2. Open Film Cassette

Exposing yourself to the light will ruin you, like the negatives, so you only do it here, in the darkroom, in the dark. For something so small, the cassette is heavy in your hands. You move around the room like an animal with night vision. When you've freed the film from its cassette, you consider the light switch on the wall. This is your moment to destroy the evidence, if you wanted to.

3. Cut Film Off Cassette

It's dark, so you'll have to feel for the place to cut the film from the plastic. Your fingers unroll the film from its coil like you are undressing a teenager, like the way he undressed you, just days ago in this very room, sliding your knee socks down and then your underwear, double-checking the door was locked before pressing his face against you.

4. Load Film onto Reel

Find slits and edges and slide it on. Twist, back and forth, wind up and wind down. You'll know it's ready when you've securely wrapped the film around the reel. When everything is secured and snug. Wrapped around. Loaded.

5. Place Reel in Film Tank

When he joins you in the darkroom, you aren't a lonely girl in high school. You pretend not to know his first name, only his last, and you call him Mister. He never says your name out loud, except during attendance and then, he doesn't look at you. This is how the development process works. Make sure it's tightly sealed and don't open the lid. Don't peek and don't tell.

6. Create Developer Mixture

This is your favorite part—the intense aroma. You mix developer liquid with water, inhaling the noxious fumes even though you know you shouldn't. It smells poisonously sweet, like hurried sex, and you listen for a knock on the door as you stir the ingredients in a plastic tub.

7. Measure Temperature of Mixture

All film is different, and developing time varies. So it goes with girls. You have long legs but a flat chest. Your hair is frizzy and last week, Alan—who is supposed to be your guy friend—said you probably have a gunt, which is a combination of gut and cunt. At home, you checked your naked body in the full-length mirror. You need more time.

8. Pour Mixture into Film Tank

But you are not completely without agency. You make things happen, too. You left the door unlocked, you coyly tucked your hair behind your ear, you bit your lower lip and when he touched your cheek, you didn't flinch away. You might have rested your fingers on his belt buckle. Even though you're a shy girl, you're also an artist and you can create the things you want.

9. Agitate Film Periodically

During the development process, agitation is good. Spread the developer around, let it touch everything, especially the parts that think they have finished developing. Agitate, agitate. That's why you brought your camera into math class and kept clicking even when Mister held up his hand and said, Enough, stop. That's why you carry the zoom lens in your backpack, and you know which one is his bedroom window. You've memorized his phone number.

10. Fill Tank with Stop Bath

You're supposed to be able to say no. You could, if you wanted to. You could lock the door, you could make a phone call. You could change schools. You practice saying it out loud. No. Stop. Stop.

11. Fill the Tank with Fixer

Lunch break is almost over and finally, a quiet rap on the door. Now his skin is red-hued, too, when he takes off his pants. He is urgent and sweaty. He makes you come, and holds his hand over your mouth so you won't scream. Then he comes inside you, which is bad, it's so bad, you know that, but all you can say is Yes. Don't stop. For fifteen minutes, he fixes you, and you will never feel lonely again.

12. Rinse and Soak Film

Stop taking my picture, he says. I see you doing it. Then he leaves, and you wash your face and hands with cold water. You pee into a plastic tub and watch his semen slide out of you, then pour it all down the sink. You're almost done in here.

13. Hang Film to Dry

Using clothespins, you clip your film to a hanging string. It's so quiet.

14. Clean and Store Film

You smooth down your hair and straighten your skirt. You cut the negatives into strips and slide them into a plastic sleeve for protection. You tuck them into your History textbook and head to class. At home, you'll hold the negatives against your window and study the reversed images. You'll see Mister's darkened face, his hands trying to block the camera. You'll see how exposed you've made him feel. You'll keep the negatives in a shoebox under your bed, until you're ready to make prints.

Candice May is a writer from British Columbia, Canada. Her work has appeared in *Pleiades, December, The Porter House Review, SmokeLong Quarterly, Sundog Lit*, and elsewhere. In 2021 she won 3rd prize in *The Masters Review* Flash Fiction Contest, selected by Stuart Dybek, and her work has twice been nominated for Best of the Net. She is currently working on a collection of short stories.

YOUR INTERNET BOYFRIEND'S NAME is Wendell—and if you had known ahead of time that he was going to use your first real-life date as an excuse to lead you deep into the woods behind his apartment complex—you probably would not have come today. Your power wheelchair is not exactly built for this sort of terrain. He's taking you to what he says is a secret waterfall. Fairly accessible, he says. And he keeps wanting you to stop, wanting you to notice how fresh and green everything looks after that hard rain last night. And do you see that? That's mountain laurel. Have you ever seen anything as beautiful in your life as mountain laurel? But you've stopped agreeing with Wendell that the mountain laurel is beautiful, and you've given up on reminding him that you're from around here, too. So, it's not like you're unfamiliar with the local flora and fauna; you just have to concentrate on your driving right now, and avoid getting your wheels too bogged down or flying off into a ravine.

You are beginning to wonder what you saw in him online. He never shuts up. He keeps going on about mountain laurel as though he's the one who discovered it. He smells of peppermint and frozen dinners, and the combination makes you want to gag. You are desperately trying to remember the words from his messages these past few months, the ones which led you to believe he was methodical and shy about love, words with a quirky humor you can't quite put your finger on: *Hello my goddess! Thanks for being so cool while I plan the perfect day for us! Base jumping, anyone? Just kidding! Can you imagine? No! But seriously, we humans are not pure love machines & I would hate to doom us from the start with a sloppy first date. You understand.*

What you do not immediately understand is why Wendell has come to a dead halt in front of you. But your wheelchair has no real traction on this incline, and you feel yourself slowly rocking from side to side in a way you know can't be safe. You're already staring intently at an orange-capped mushroom in the ground. You are preparing to skid off the trail and slam your pretty head against a tree. You are really hoping people will think of your head as pretty after you're gone. Because you are preparing to die. You are absolutely preparing to die when Wendell reaches for the handlebar closest to him and manages to steer the unwieldy chair away from danger. He's talking to you now. He might even be yelling a little. His eyes are very green; you hadn't noticed before how green his eyes are. Nothing he's saying is making any sense. You wish he would kiss you. He's your boyfriend, isn't he? But then he pops you hard on the cheek once, and you hear him say, "You're being super careless, my angel. The waterfall is just up ahead, but I don't trust you to drive the rest of the way. Besides, the little bridge is out."

You look over his shoulder at a deluge of red-brown water as it pounds its way downstream. Only a mess of fractured timber remains. And you nod your head to confirm, yes, the bridge is out. You even think he might be waiting for a verbal confirmation, but it's too late. Wendell has scooped you out of your seat, and is cradling you against his possibly ironic Spice Girls T-shirt. His smell isn't so bad, you guess. You were overreacting. You just need to relax. You just need to close your eyes for a minute. Wendell's got you. You're almost to the waterfall. It's breathtaking, this view. Keep your eyes closed tight, now. Don't open them. Just wait until he sits you up on that ledge. And you look down. You won't know what hit you.

Miriam McEwen writes about disability and bodily autonomy. She holds an MFA in Writing from Vermont College of Fine Arts. She is an associate editor at the *South Carolina Review* and co-editor for *The Swamp*. Miriam's work has appeared or is forthcoming in *SAND Journal*, *Under the Gum Tree* and *Madcap Review*, among others. She lives in the foothills of South Carolina. Find her on Instagram @miriammcewen.

THE QUESTION
catherine mcnamara

ABEL TANNER HAD A question. It was not a question he could ask his wife, as it had not occurred to him before her death. The question first entered his mind as he returned through the garden holding an empty rubbish bin, and saw the thin gilded hook of the moon above their roof. The front of the house showed three illuminated windows where his three daughters—Dolly, Margot and Lou—were certainly on their phones speaking to boyfriends, or watching films. He could hear his neighbours.

This was when his mind began grappling with the apparitions before him. The harbour of trees and the explosive nectar of flowers. How the suburb had long ago been staked out on raw earth, seeded with piping and wires, each property acquired through sacrifice and transaction. How in kitchen hubs children learned core behaviour, and on mattresses men and women bore the weight and liquids of each other; and before bathroom mirrors the young discovered primal coils of hair. It was an old neighbourhood, and before his wife died Abel had refitted the fretwork of the balcony with a rich imported hardwood, swept up in seeking the original tones of the house.

Now all that mattered was the question.

Recently he and the girls had flown back from Italy, where he had communed with his wife's family, a year after her death. The girls, too, had brought out their high school Italian, and been thoroughly alluring. He had proudly seen that in the slow theatre of the streets of Florence and Rome. How, flourishing, they would be followed by a dozen eyes. Dolly received a half-serious marriage proposal from a journalist.

In Venice they had found the church of Santa Maria dei Miracoli, where his wife's grandmother had been baptised. Each girl trod up the arched bridge over a canal opposite the church with its marble panels and playful form, awaiting a gap in the tourists for her photo to be taken. Together they were outrageous, anyone would say. Impossible to separate, always arms linked or fingers drawn across cheeks and words inserted, connecting, cooing. Dolly posed first in her shoulderless white top with ballooning sleeves and tight bodice, her brown belly showing. Then Margot had to be egged on, wearing a crotchet tea-cosy hat and outsized vintage sunglasses. Lastly Lou climbed on the red brick wall and straddled her long legs either side, her silver harem pants flattened by a gust of wind, arms outstretched with little puffs of rebellious hair in her armpits, a skimpy bottle green top showing the uncontained shift of her breasts.

That day Lou climbed down tearing her pants on an unseen rusted bolt, and she walked across to Abel who had managed to stem his tears. Lou was the arduous, blue-hearted one who wrote songs and cooked goulash on Wednesdays in winter after work. She held him at length, slamming her front into him while the other two talked to a pair of gondoliers, melding words in his ears and her black eyes pulling back and sturdy.

And now Abel gripped the empty rubbish bin, standing on grass in the old elegant suburb where houses had been divided into cheap flats and were now being restored to aching glory. The moon had advanced and faded. Abel could not re-enter the house. For the answer had chased down his question, and he knew which one of his daughters would go first, even though he would wrestle this knowledge to the ground as if it were a lion sprung at him from the dust, and he could feel those jaws around his own skull and the crack of bone; the soft red flight. He could not unlearn this, he knew.

Catherine McNamara grew up in Sydney, ran away to Paris to write and ended up in West Africa co-running a bar, working in Mogadishu and Milan along the way. *Love Stories for Hectic People* won Best Short Story Collection in the Saboteur Awards (UK). *The Cartography of Others* was finalist in the People's Book Prize (UK) and won the Eyelands Fiction Award (Greece). *Pelt and Other Stories* was semi-finalist in the Hudson Prize (USA). Catherine lives in Italy and is Flash Fiction Editor for *Litro Magazine* UK.

Deuteronomy 13: 6-10

"IF THY BROTHER, OR thy son, or the wife of thy bosom entice thee secretly, saying, 'Let us go and serve other gods,' thou shalt not consent unto him. Do not hearken unto him. Thine hand shall be first upon him. And thou shalt stone him with stones that he die. (But even as the first stone is cast, you will think perhaps: *Where might we find these other gods?* For haven't you always wondered such things when you were alone in the silence of your rooms? So let me show you now. Let me show you. Follow me into this dark fissure, this narrow wound in the earth. Follow me down past the places where the dead are buried. See how they are laid out, arms crossed, flowers pressed to the hollows of their eyes. See how they rest in the rooms of towers that do not rise but rather travel further into the earth. See the plague pits here with their death parades. Corpses dressed in florid silk. See the coffins made of marble and brass and ivory. Then, beneath these newly dead, see the bones of the old beasts that once walked the earth when the sky was dim and black stars hung closer than the moon. Listen to the sounds the old stars made as they turned. Follow me down, deeper still. See the buried pyramids and ziggurats, mastabas and painted caves. Here there are circles drawn in the earth. Here there are remnants of the first garden. Ferns pressed beneath the weight of stones. Pits of old fruit, scattered. We are deeper now. Yet we must travel further. Trailing the empty corridors of silver ships that once sailed the darkness before there was land or water or even light. We nod to the old sailors resting in their cabins, long-fingered men with odd black eyes, dressed in collars of emerald and gold. And on we travel, until it seems as if there will soon be no earth left to plumb. Perhaps, we grow tired. We lie down and close our eyes. And, as we fall asleep, our bodies slide on loose pebbles, moving us into deeper caverns. We come to rest on the floor of an old house made of neither wood nor stone. We do not see the occupants of the house because we are still asleep. And these occupants step quietly around our heads, careful not to wake us. We ask ourselves [because we have travelled so far and because we have left so much behind] are these the other gods then? Have we finally found them? We ask these questions in our dreams, even as the figures kneel down to kiss us on our mouths, to stroke our cheeks with timeworn hands, to show us we have always been loved)."

Adam McOmber is the author of three novels, *The White Forest* (Touchstone), *Jesus and John* (Lethe) and *The Ghost Finders* (JournalStone), as well as two collections of short stories: *My House Gathers Desires* (BOA) and *This New & Poisonous Air* (BOA). His new collection of flash and experimental fiction, *Fantasy Kit*, will be published by Black Lawrence Press in June 2022. His queer retelling of Arthur Conan Doyle's The Hound of the Baskervilles is forthcoming from Lethe Press in October 2022. He is a core faculty member in the Writing Program at Vermont College of Fine Arts as well as editor in chief of the literary magazine *Hunger Mountain*.

THEIR VOICES ARE IN THEIR LEGS

emily jane morris

INSTEAD OF GOING HOME after your time in jail you head to the small cabin on the back of your property. It might not be yours anymore at all. Your husband wasn't there to pick you up. You imagined it could've been your son that pulled in—he should have his learner's by now. Neither of them had been to see you in a while, so you wouldn't really know.

You thumb your way there. A lady picks you up in a Buick. There's an empty car seat in the back and she keeps tucking her hair behind her ear. She definitely thinks you're hurt or homeless. She mentions a women's shelter later in the ride and you know she's just trying to help another woman out, but she wouldn't go farther than that. She's safe in her Buick with her suncatcher swooping back and forth from her rearview mirror. She's definitely someone that keeps time.

A song you don't know is on the radio, thrumming low. You ask if you can turn it up and she nods, a little surprised, and you both reach for the dial. She backs off first. You turn it up a little higher than normal volume. You think about how your son asked to dress like a smoke detector the Halloween before you went to jail. How you'd wanted to encourage something more creative and juvenile, but your husband shook his head and said he should be whatever he wants.

The lady drops you at the edge of your property. You think about Timmy, the contractor your husband hired to fix the back porch, and how you'd fucked him in the kitchen a few times, left a chair overturned once and your underwear under the table another time so your husband would put two and two together.

The cabin looks stagnant and you try not to compare it to anything. You grab the spare key from under the lip of the porch and wonder why your husband hasn't been renting it. The inside smells frightened, and there are crayon drawings on the wall from when your son was the age you remember him as.

You also remember some dancing. How your husband would turn on the radio in the main house and spin you. One time you stubbed your toe so hard it bled in your sock. You'd dance and twirl and press your fingers into his ears, lightly, so he couldn't hear anything else, his only sensation would be holding you. You'd twirl until you knocked a lamp over, bumped a picture off the wall, dance, twirl, until it wasn't dancing anymore and both your hands knotted into fists.

You rifle through some drawers in the cabin, find a butter knife, stained coasters, some of your son's old play-doh. You lay on the floor, try to knead the dryness out of it, listen to the crickets, the birds outside. Your son's third grade science textbook said crickets have an incredible ear for music. You drum your fingers to a beat on the floor and listen for them to pick it up. You hum a few lines of a song and wish harder than you've wished for anything in a while that they could sing it back, that you could learn what a cricket's voice sounds like, but then you remember their voices are in their legs.

You also read they are high in calcium. You eat a dead one from the floor. It tastes more complicated than you would've thought, like eggshells and fingernails, the stitches in your gums after an incisor removal, maybe mulch. You think about the word incarceration, how it sounds like a tongue licking a shard of glass.

You look in the pantry and coffee mugs are in there, mouths agape at you. You shut it.

You walk out and head for the main house and pretend it's a normal night like eight years ago, that you're just checking on your hydrangeas. When you get close you hear a man's voice, but realize it's your son and that his voice has thickened even without you there. He's throwing a frisbee to the dog, that damn dog you'd let outside and it'd always come back wet. Your son still has some baby fat on his frame and he's wearing a black t-shirt. It looks like his nails are also painted black. He rubs the dog's head and flicks the frisbee. You don't care to look for your husband. He doesn't seem that important right now.

You can't see the scar on your son's forearm from this distance, nor do you look for it, but you know it's there. It was still puckered and scabby when you went away. You rarely think about the woman you t-boned. You got a good look at her face that day, but your vision was blurry because you were so blitzed. Mostly you just think about your son's forearm and the way he'd reached for you after the crash, before he was old enough to realize you'd done that to him.

To distract yourself from the stranger in the yard you walk the mile to the closest convenience store. You ask the cashier what aisle the cereal is on and she says a single number. You wish she'd said something like 349, and that her lips would've started to melt down her chin. But no, you nod as she eyes you, then head in that direction. You avoid stepping on any cracks in the tiles because you've decided you'll be superstitious with your freedom.

There's a man on that aisle and you think he looks like your husband for a second, but certainly not. He's balder, shorter, and definitely older. You ask him if he's alright and he looks at you funny. After a beat, he asks you the same thing. Instead of answering, you pick up a cereal box, give it a shake.

Emily Jane Morris received an MFA in Fiction from the University of North Carolina at Greensboro, where she served as managing editor of *The Greensboro Review*. Her work has appeared in *Mid-American Review, Elephant Journal,* and *Moon City Review.*

THE SUN'S BATTERIES HAD grown dim as my husband Russ and I drove into the deserted center of old Bisbee.

Once the most fun small town in Arizona, Bisbee now resembled an empty Hollywood set. If someone pushed over its cardboard facade, the buildings would fall into dust and cobwebs.

A cowboy played piano on the deserted sidewalk. I extended a couple of bucks, but he refused to catch my eye. "Just toss it in that box," he barked.

Nobody looked at anyone. We all had the plague. Each citizen a potential murderer.

Polly, my mother, drew her last breaths in this town. So did my brother Josh. Smoking killed Polly. At least it was a straightforward way to go.

She'd plotted her demise since I was a kid. Polly always said she wouldn't make it past seventy. I cried and said no, you gotta do better than that. She intoned, "Too late. Nothing I can do."

Josh was my half-brother. I had no full-blooded siblings. My sister and two brothers were the spawn of a violent, alcoholic Baptist. Polly's second husband killed himself when his kids were young, setting them up for failure.

My mother moved from Mexico to Arizona in 1992, after her older son was murdered by two men in Washington state. She found Bisbee on a map and bought a four-flat for $35,000. The property needed "a little work", so she hurled herself into the task.

I loved that building. Best garden in town. A goldfish pond, even. Polly lounged in her yard and drank endless cups of espresso. She hailed from a generation of women who lived on caffeine and nicotine. The best way to deal with her was to pretend she wasn't my mother.

People came from miles around to walk past her flowers. They were Polly's proudest accomplishment. The novel she never wrote. "There's another person," she said with pride, pointing as somebody came downhill towards her yard.

A year after Polly's death, Josh scored a new job as a prison guard in Douglas. Well-paying gig for southern Arizona, though depressing.

The prison was a free-for-all. Stress makes people do crazy things. Josh impregnated another guard and lived with her part-time. He always left home at the last minute and drove 20 miles over the speed limit. Less than a mile from the prison, one of his rear tires blew out. Josh never made it to work that day.

My sister Ericka erected Josh's memorial in the exact spot where he died, on Double Adobe Road. I'd never seen it. My siblings and I had long unloaded my mother's place. I shook the dust of Bisbee from my bones. If someone had told me I'd end up moving there, I would've been appalled.

But plans are fickle, and the Pacific Northwest was too expensive for a newly unemployed cancer patient and his wife. After Russ' sudden, stage four diagnosis, we scraped together enough cash to buy a house in Bisbee. It was a town I'd tried to leave many times, but kept coming back to, like an abusive boyfriend.

I couldn't blame Bisbee for killing my family. Just like I couldn't blame it for failing to remember me. During the 90s, downtown was my playground. I spent hours drinking beer at St Elmo's bar, while dancing to cover bands. Now the town stared with a blank expression, like it once met me but couldn't quite recall where.

"I've got GPS coordinates to the memorial," I told Russ. "Let's try to find it."

We climbed into our Toyota and drove into the desert. Scrub brush, cacti, yucca trees, more cacti. How would I ever get used to that landscape?

On our left, a wooden sign read, "The Thirsty Lizard." A hand-painted iguana smiled as he regarded his cocktail. The front door of an adjacent building stood ajar.

"That bar's open already," I said.

"Lockdown doesn't end for a week," Russ pointed out.

"Some places are secretly reopening."

Josh's memorial emerged from a cluster of weeds on the right-hand side of the road. I pulled over and turned on the flashers.

I'd seen photos of the structure, so I knew what to expect. A slender male body made from steel, arms reaching skyward. His posture askew. A heavy disc underneath read, "We love you, Josh. 11/24/69—6/16/01."

A metal angel figurine lay beside the memorial. Its body had eroded and fallen into the weeds. I dusted the angel's tiny face and placed it in my pocket. No one would miss a broken angel.

I wondered if I should tell Josh that Ericka was dead. She shot herself in the heart when her husband demanded a divorce. The monster remarried less than a year later.

I didn't mention Russ' illness, since the two of them never met. Russ had helped me scatter some of Josh's ashes in the hills above Bisbee. Our relationship was still new then, but I knew it would last.

We did the same with Ericka's ashes, fourteen years later. Russ and I wanted to spread them beside the memorial. We tried our best to find it, but GPS kept glitching. Finally, we gave up and drove back into town. Once there, we hiked into the hills and scattered Ericka's ashes beside a cluster of crosses and sagebrush clumps.

I turned away. Russ stood beside the car, looking worried. "Let's get a beer at the Thirsty Lizard," I said.

"You sure?"

"Yeah, he'd want us to do it." I no longer had anything to fear. Death was a sick joke. Besides, Josh would have demanded that I break the law. Odd for a prison guard, but typical for my brother.

We climbed back into the car, made a U-turn, and headed back down the dusty road. I doubted if the Thirsty Lizard was open. Still, at least we had a destination, and the possibility of quelling our thirst.

Leah Mueller is an indie writer and spoken word performer from Bisbee, Arizona. She is the author of nine prose and poetry books, published by numerous small presses. Her work appears in *Rattle, Midway Journal, Citron Review, The Spectacle, Miracle Monocle, Outlook Springs, Atticus Review, Your Impossible Voice,* and elsewhere. Visit her website at www.leahmueller.org.

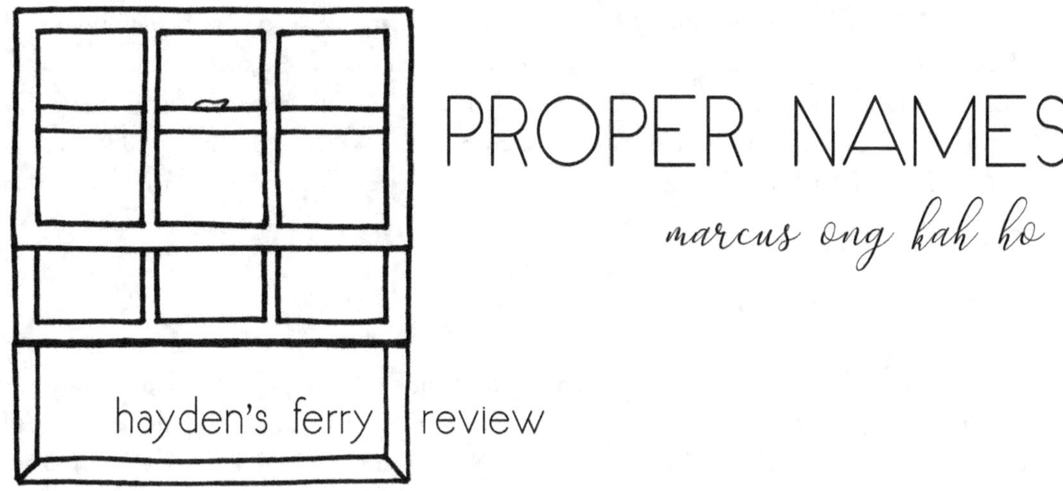

THE CHICKEN RICE seller is drinking ice-cold beer outside his chicken rice stall. Business is good, and the chicken rice seller knows it. He wears an apron around his waist and grimy rubber boots on his feet. He is relaxed, red-cheeked. He leans back in his chair, positions both hands behind his head. He stares at the long queue and studies the hungry faces and sips his beer. If mood strikes, the chicken rice seller greets customers he recognises. Exchange pleasantries.

Talk about the weather.

Meanwhile, the chicken rice seller's wife moves about the stall with quick hands and quick feet. She takes customer orders (averaging two at a time), remembers them, then, proceeds to scoop the rice, chop the chicken, drizzle the sauce, throw in the sliced cucumbers, ladle the soup, collect the money, return the change, utter the thank-yous.

After the lunchtime crowd has dispersed, the chicken rice seller gets on his feet and returns inside his stall. One regular customer of the chicken rice stall wonders why he calls the chicken rice seller the chicken rice seller and the chicken rice seller's wife the chicken rice seller's wife. The customer has never seen the chicken rice seller take orders, scoop rice, chop chicken, drizzle sauce, throw in cucumbers, ladle soup, collect money, return change, and utter thank-yous.

Within months, the chicken rice seller's skin turns yellow. There's no beer on the table. The chicken rice seller no longer smiles, no longer speaks. He sits by the table, disoriented, as if the stall doesn't exist in his life at all. He looks just like any other patron at the coffee shop, except that his skin is yellow, unlike theirs. Meanwhile, the chicken rice seller's wife continues to sell chicken rice; each plate and each packet go to the chicken rice seller's medical bills. To a new customer who has never visited this chicken rice stall, the chicken rice seller's wife is the chicken rice seller, and the chicken rice seller is simply a man who looks sickly. They might identify him as The Sick Man, and might if they knew the chicken rice seller was married to The Sick Man, call her The Sick Man's wife.

The Sick Man becomes The Dead Man.

Gathered are kinsfolk, friends, and a handful of long-time customers. Most of them will avoid the chicken rice stall for some time. Perhaps they sense an 'aura of death' surrounding the stall, the chicken rice, impossible to disregard, and feel if they consume the food, they will also ingest this aura. Others begin to talk about The Dead Man's chicken rice recipe: they wonder if it has been handed over to the chicken rice seller's wife. They wonder if the nasi lemak seller has written down his secret recipe for his wife, just in case, for he is eighty now, and one never knows when one's time is up.

Is that The Dead Man's wife over there? a child asks, her face lighting up. The child's father sticks out his finger. The correct term to use is The Widow, which means, he explains to the girl in a slow, drawn-out manner, a woman who has lost her spouse by death. The girl nods and runs along and shares with her new friends the new word. But no one actually refers to the widow as The Widow. It is, in fact, only a temporary name, useful only at funerals, and during the subsequent period of mourning. After which, not many will refer to her as The Widow, and she shall be addressed by her real name—The Widow looks up; her smiling face is tense and tremulous.

Marcus Ong Kah Ho / 王家豪 is a writer and teacher from Singapore. His stories have appeared or are forthcoming in the *Adroit Journal*, *X-R-A-Y*, *Sundog Lit*, *Guesthouse*, *Washington Square Review*, and elsewhere. Read more at www.marcusongkh.com.

THE WOMEN WATCH THE clock on the wall of the factory where they sew cotton shirts and there's an old woman over there, in the corner, bent over, and no one notices that her back is perpetually bent over like that, so much so that one day when the other women call her for lunch she doesn't answer. She's been frozen in that position for the last twenty-four hours. They thought she was working late the night before but she'd just stopped and couldn't move. They gather around her, pull at her torn red jersey, and say, What is wrong with you, May! Why don't you eat or drink or move all morning? What can we do for you? One of the women looks into May's eyes and sees a frozen lake inside each one. May's veined hands are still pressed down on the cloth. Someone gets frustrated and shakes May's shoulder, What is up with you, woman? We need to eat or the boss will take this time as our lunch! He then shows up running over as speedy as a night train and curses them. What are you silly ladies doing to May? Leave her alone, you fools! He then makes a space around May and checks her out for himself. He lifts her chin and peers into the frozen lakes. Everyone go! Now! Go to lunch, you idiots! I'll take care of this.

He watches their backs scurry out the double doors to the lunchroom, but of course a few of them are peeking through the tiny glass windows to see what it's all about. He tries to lift her arm and it's frozen just like her eyes. It makes a crackling sound like the sound of light wood breaking. He gently puts it over his shoulder and walks her across the factory floor, her feet dragging. He goes out the back door, climbs down the dusty stairs, his back aching, and reaches the first cellar where it's completely dark and moldy. He goes into the back door of this cellar and goes down another flight of stairs, and there is another door, which he goes through and goes down yet another flight of stairs. He is sweating now, his little body barely able to carry the weight of both of them. There is a fire in this third level down. He looks down at the room-sized bowl of fire and looks at May. Her weight is so much that he almost falls over with her, but he grabs her just in time. He leans in and looks at her eyes again, they are all water now and are pouring out tears into the fire. May stands up, all soft and alive, and is crying, crying, crying. He stands behind her, his hand holding onto her lower back and watches her. Several moments go by. When she clasps her hands over her eyes, he knows it's over. She looks at him, suddenly aware and awake, and they very quietly walk back up the stairs, May unaided. They go up and up until they reach the same old factory floor and he says to her, Go get some lunch, woman! I need you to be strong! and she shuffles through the door toward the other women in the lunchroom.

Cheryl Pappas is an American writer living outside Boston. Her work has appeared or is forthcoming in *Hayden's Ferry Review, Wigleaf, Juked, SmokeLong Quarterly, HAD,* and elsewhere. She is the author of the flash fiction collection *The Clarity of Hunger,* published by word west press (2021).

CONTINGENCIES

susan perabo

THIS IS WHAT YOU do if he wakes up sad. This is what you do if he comes home angry. This is what you do if he stops taking his medication. This is what you do if he stays awake until sunrise. This is what you do if he won't text you back. This is what you do if he yells at you in the driveway. This is what you do if the neighbors look over from their porch. This is what you do if he's grieving his father. This is what you do if he recoils when you touch his shoulder. This is what you do if he suddenly seems fine. This is what you do if he opens the car door while you're driving. This is what you do if he says you're a liar. This is what you do if he breaks the vase your sister made for you. This is what you do if he suddenly seems fine. This is what you do if he says his heart is racing. This is what you do if he rages while you're holding the baby. This is what you do if he rages while he's holding the baby. This is what you do if the car is gone. This is what you do if he's had three beers. This is what you do if he's had eight beers. This is what you do if he says he's a monster. This is what you do if he says you made him into a monster. This is what you do if he asks you to lie for him. This is what you do if your sister says she wants to come for a visit. This is what you do if he suddenly seems fine. This is what you do if you can't find the car keys. This is what you do if he tells you he should kill himself. This is what you do if he tells you he might kill himself. This is what you do if he locks you out of the house. This is what you do if he locks you out of the house with the baby inside. This is what you do if he says he's sorry. This is what you do. This is what you do. This is what you do.

Susan Perabo's most recent books are The Fall of Lisa Bellow (2017) and *Why They Run the Way They Do* (2016), both from Simon & Schuster. Her fiction has been anthologized in *Best American Short Stories*, *Pushcart Prize Stories*, and *New Stories from the South*, and her work has appeared in numerous publications, including *One Story*, *Glimmer Train*, *The New York Times*, and *The Sun*. She is a professor of creative writing at Dickinson College and on the staff of the Queens University low-residency MFA program..

THOUGHTS AND PRAYERS

brenda peynado

THE MORNING BEFORE THE school shooting passed like any other, all my neighbors out at dawn performing oblations to the angels on our roofs. Families clustered around the sidewalks, mist from our lawns swirling around our ankles, looking up at the angels' pale humanoid faces and downy bird bodies perched beside our chimneys. Our mothers beat their breasts, performing sorrow for the tragedies that always went on elsewhere in the world. Our parents yelled their usual "Thoughts and prayers! Thoughts and prayers!" toward the angels atop our roofs. As children, we were supposed to kneel in the moist grass and be quiet, in case the angels were ever to speak.

The angels, for the most part, barely noticed. They chewed their cud from the grasses and bugs they scavenged during the night and then shat runny white on our roofs, the shingles looking iced with snow despite the Florida heat. When I was in kindergarten, we'd thrown rocks at them to get their attention, but they'd just turned and resumed their silent watch over the neighborhood.

My parents began the ritual, already dressed in their work clothes, looking as polished as a photograph in front of our freshly painted stucco house. I was obedient in my stiff school clothes—my mother never allowed me to stumble outside in my pajamas like some of the other kids.

There was no greater argument in our house than when my mother thought I had done something unworthy of our angel.

Out of all the angels, ours was considered the most blessed of the neighborhood. When my parents came to this country after college, this house was the first one they looked at, and their immigration papers arrived miraculously within the week. While others searched for homes and jobs for months, my parents sailed into their new life, prayed gratefully to their new rooftop patron. When the economic downturn came and brought with it a plague of layoffs, my mother was able to keep her tech job, and my father flourished in a financial field that boomed in downturns ("Betting on failure," he called it). The hurricane tore apart most roofs in our Florida suburb, but not mine. Every day my mother returned to the house, pulling into our drive, she breathed a great sigh as she saw our angel perched beside our chimney: albino faced, sleek winged, dumb eyes that looked at nothing. At our basketball games the parents cheered for us, but it was known that the real game was played silently among the angels.

Across the street, my best friend Rima Patil's family kneeled in front of their ramshackle house, the embarrassment of the neighborhood: mold blooming on the stucco, brown waves along the roofline where the gutters and wooden fascia had fallen into disrepair, a bright blue tarp over the roof above Rima's room, where a hurricane had downed a tree, just barely missing their angel. The blue tarp rolled and snapped like a flag of shame.

Rima's family was known to have the worst angel on the block. Her dad was one of the first to get laid off, lose health insurance. Her older brother had developed schizophrenia and claimed that the angels gave him secret messages; the family didn't have the money for his medications. The bank had visited their house three times in the past month. When the hurricane hit, the oak tree in front of their yard not only punched a hole in the roof, but also fell onto the family car. The tarp they placed over it leaked mist and bugs and occasional angel guano. That they were the one Hindu family in a neighborhood of Latino Catholics was not lost on my mother, though the fact that they were even darker than the rest of us, my mother pretended not to notice. Rima was wild, a force of nature, and my mother was known to count this as one of Rima's mother's misfortunes. Nothing terrible had happened to Rima's sister, Shruti, yet—she was valedictorian, a national-prize cellist, who radiated beauty—but we were all waiting; there was a sense that she would not be spared. It was Shruti Rima got her strength from, though while Rima's came out in recklessness and force, all elbows and knees, her sister had merged it with a softness that came out in glory when she played music. I idolized Shruti for her ability to walk the line between strength and obedience, her ability to get away with doing what she wanted while still looking like a saint—unlike Rima, who fooled no one, and me, feeling caged and wanting desperately to do something unforgivable.

Rima winked at me and then resumed solemnity, leaning on her fists in their overgrown grass. Her long black braid flicked with the impatience of a cat's tail as she turned back, echoing how it often weaponized into a whip on the basketball court. Her sister, Shruti, inclined her head as if she were still at her cello, her own long black hair draping over one shoulder. I knew Shruti had woven Rima's braid, had raked her deft fingers through the silken mess, had crooned a Carnatic composition as she worked. For the moment, Rima's lanky brother, Rajiv, was quiet, his eyes sallow from sleeplessness, instead of having his usual energy. Their mother beat her chest with one hand and kept her other hand dug into Rajiv's elbow in case he started with one of his outbursts. Their father, still in his pajamas, gritted his teeth and barked, "Thoughts and prayers," like it was being dragged out of him. Back in Bengaluru, they'd had other words, other rituals, for the angels on their roofs.

The angels above us looked on into the distance, snapping their mouths to eat mosquitoes from the air.

How could I have known that this would be the last time I would see all of them together, that unlucky family? If I had known, what would I have done to protect them?

Sunrise bled hot over the roofs like a punctured yolk, another day given to us. Neighbors quieted and rose from kneeling on their lawns. Kids sprung up, suddenly released from piousness to get ready for school. I lunged for my backpack by the front door and dashed across the street.

Rima grinned in greeting, leaning against the crumbling stucco of their front stoop with a swagger. Behind a bush that had overgrown the half wall of their stoop, I showed Rima a tube of lipstick that I'd snatched from my mom, a cocoa pink. It wasn't Rima's style—she always went brazenly bare, glittering only with the sheen of sweat, though her parents forbade her nothing. But this small rebellion assuaged the hot throb in my chest.

"Yeah," she said. "Do it."

I painted my mouth jaggedly with the tube, my trembling excitement and the sharp line of my fear of my parents' no-makeup rule getting the best of me.

Shruti emerged from the house, backpack slung cleverly over one shoulder, her hair draped over the other. Shruti could wither anyone with a look, and her arm around your shoulder made you hum with joy. She clicked her tongue at me in pity, cupped my chin with cool fingers calloused by cello strings, dragged her fingernail along the edges of my lips to fix the colored mess.

Rajiv flung open the door, and he gave me a thumbs-up. His smile transformed his tiredness, and I noticed his bravery despite the voices that tormented him sometimes, despite what the angels told him. It was never good. The angels always said it wouldn't end well for him, but that for the rest of us there was still a chance. And yet he faced each new day with a bright smile. "Give 'em hell," he said now.

Surrounded by the bold three of them, I could pretend I was the fourth, fear of getting caught breaking the rules melting from me like candle wax.

"Stay good, kiddos," Shruti said, running a swipe of her hairbrush through her hair.

Rima rolled her eyes, any entreaties to behave sending her instead slingshotting off into trouble. "I'll race you, Paola."

Rima and I ran together to the bus stop, cutting through lawns, kicking up morning moths into a fraying cloud of white. She pulled ahead, her braid licking the air in front of me, and I followed after her, trying to close the gap. Shruti, Rajiv, and the other kids of the neighborhood streamed behind us, the daily pilgrimage. We had every reason to believe the day was bright ahead of us and we would survive it.

At school during recess, a boy on the basketball court got in front of us in a game of horse. "Wait your turn," I yelled, but that was as far as I let myself go. The boy turned around and said triumphantly as his wrist cocked and the ball swished into the net, "Go back to your country." Rage boiled in me. Rima grabbed his collar and flung him toward the back of the line. He tripped, spilled on the ground with his palms burned raw. Then Rima and the boy whirled in a fast-moving cluster as they fought on the court, him pulling her hair and her fingers around his ears, wrestling him to the floor. Police lights flailed once in the parking lot of the middle school. Two policewomen whispered to the teacher supervising recess, who turned pale and called for Rima. The boy, upset because he had always expected to have the right to call us whatever names he wanted, shook the hair out of his eyes, and stood up straight like he was innocent, and pointed at her. I thought the police were arresting Rima—for just being her fierce, untamable self. She'd been unlucky again, with her defective angel. I was afraid for her, and I knew horrible things could happen to people under police protection. I promised Rima that I would never leave her alone, that I would commit a crime just so they'd put me in jail with her, and I could be her witness if anything happened.

She laughed. "I'll be back before you know it." She squeezed my hand and let me go. She fixed her braid and walked toward the officers with a bounce. While I bucked the expectations that came with having a good angel, Rima owned that she had a bad one, wore her family's misfortunes with a grin that looked as dangerous as a lion's mouth. She made life bearable for me beyond my perfect handwriting, my straight As—life with her full of streaking across sidewalks and lawns like fireballs, secret desires whispered and let loose, the challenge in her eyes to reach for just a bit more than we were given. I knew that the only thing I ever did right was attaching myself to her, inviting her over even when my mother turned her nose up at their cursed family. When they led her away that afternoon, one of the officers putting a heavy hand on her shoulder, she didn't look back. I noticed, perplexed, that a few other kids were led away from their classrooms to the back of the patrol car.

After the end-of-school bell, my mother surprised me by being in the car line instead of having me get on the bus. I'd forgotten to wipe off the last of the lipstick from earlier, and my mother took a rough paper towel to my mouth. My lips stinging, rosaries swinging from the rearview mirror, my mother explained as she drove what had really happened:

Shruti had been in the high school music room. I imagined her curtain of hair swinging over her cello as she played. The arts magnate high school bused in musicians, painters, theater kids from across town, and Shruti was the only one from our neighborhood. It was study hall period for her, so there was no one else in the music room, and her continuous, transcendent playing must have covered the pops of gunfire, the gunman going classroom by classroom. After the boy—a white kid, someone Shruti had had no interest in going out with but who had never accepted "no" for an answer—left the music room, she was found slumped over her cello as if she'd given up on song. Fifteen other kids dead, twenty-eight injured. The boy, when he reached the end of the one long corridor, locked himself in the bathroom, looked in the mirror, and shot himself, sparing the hidden schoolmate who trembled over a toilet.

"So he's gone," my mother concluded. "And you're safe."

As we pulled into our driveway, my mother threw her eyes up to the roof where our angel was perched, as if not to anger its goodwill as she spoke. Across the street in Rima's house, their curtains were closed. Their minivan was gone. Their angel squatted between the chimney and the hurricane tarp, wings folded shut.

Brenda Peynado is a Dominican American writer of fiction, nonfiction, and screenplays. She often writes about Latina girlhood, class, race, and commodity culture through literary realism, magical realism and near-future science fiction. Her short story collection, *The Rock Eaters* was published by Penguin Books in March 2021, and listed as one of NPR.org, and the New York Public Libraries best books of 2021. Over forty short stories appear in journals such as *Tor.com*, *The Georgia Review*, *The Sun*, *Threepenny Review*, *Epoch*, *Kenyon Review online*, *Pleiades*, *Prairie Schooner*, and elsewhere. Her stories have won a Nelson Algren Award from the Chicago Tribune, an O. Henry Prize, a Pushcart Prize; inclusion in *The Best American Science Fiction and Fantasy*, *Best Small Fiction*, and *Best Microfiction* anthologies, two Vermont Studio Center Fellowships, and other awards.

BACK ON THE CHAIN GANG

meg pokrass

A charming worry

DON'T WORRY ABOUT ME, I say. I say this to people who don't. Ten thousand dreams away and lots of quick-serve Yorkshire puddings, and there's nothing to worry about. Stuck in a house with a silent human and a silent dog and nothing to fret over.

I have a friend nearby, likewise stuck in a house. Stuck in a house with a dog and no woman. She was the break in his battle, he's back on the chain gang.

If I walked over to his house, unlocked his door and freed him, would it help? Hello, I might say, I have a spare key. I might even tell him that the real him is locked inside the other him.

Today my attempts at conversation have festered. Okay. Or we're sitting on a train going nowhere, silent. These are the circumstances.

Pictures of Men Like You

There's a picture of you after you made me feel like a pigeon from hell, but I've thrown you out.

Thirty years ago means nothing to me now, I'm back on the chain gang. And there was that day, early in our marriage, when I looked in the mirror and saw my old face. Saw me old, way back then.

There are these powers that be, that bring me to my knees. This is the sad mask I live with now.

Stains and distrust

We met my mother over dinner. As if we'd been poring over a Chinese menu of potential sons-in-law until we found the one she could sample forever. How she smiled into your eyes. How she doted on you.

I owned hardly any dresses and blouses without stains, and I knew how your parents distrusted me—Jewish, funny and poor. But in bed with you I had everything, your face on mine feeling like the kind of animal no scientist has cut open and studied.

Changing pictures of you

I find these pictures of you and they keep changing. First a picture of you, and then a picture of the other you, and now it's a picture of you again but it's the one who stopped loving me.

Way back then my friends got worried: me cooking East Indian lentil stew, you saying it needed more ginger or garlic or salt, or tasted too dry or chewy. That's how it began. They stopped coming over.

The you who stopped loving me had these interesting ideas about spicing things. All I needed to do was to wake up and float through the house, descend into some frivolous outfit like a fruit fly.

Insects and Now

There's this place in the past that reminds me of why I feel sick when I see what the world did to us. I die standing here today staring at the bright leafy day, knowing that nothing I see here will bring back those days when I had the original picture of you in my life, the you that's stuck in my camera.

I'm on the train with the gang, and the living room is full of encyclopedias. I open one up, and it brings me to my knees.

Under "Control Measures" there's a description of noxious insects, but nothing about how I could never do things the way you wanted. Nothing about how you and I were an 'episode', that is, "an incident occurring before or after a previous one". You were never my break in the battle, but part of a prescribed order of events.

Meg Pokrass is the author of 8 flash fiction collections including *Spinning to Mars* (Blue Light Book Award, 2021) and *The Loss Detector* (Bamboo Dart Press, 2020). Her work has appeared in over 900 literary journals has been anthologized in 3 Norton anthologies: *Flash Fiction International* (W.W. Norton, 2015), *New Micro: Exceptionally Short Fiction* (W.W. Norton, 2018), and *Flash Fiction America* (W. W. Norton & Co., 2023). She is the Founding Series Co-Editor of *Best Microfiction*. Meg lives in Inverness Scotland.

MISS DARLING

sarah priscus

THE KIDS HUDDLE SHOULDER-TO-SHOULDER, biting their nails and eating scabs, as Mr. Morris opens the door for Miss Darling. She hops out of the car, squinting and rocking. She's as tall as a third grader, naked except for a straw hat and a thick layer of wiry hair. Her toes are orange circus peanuts on the pavement. Her teeth are cracked squares, like Chiclets.

"Look!" one of the kids yells. "She's smiling!"

"Hi, monkey!" a smaller kid yells, his tongue tangling. "Say 'hello' back, monkey! Say it back!"

Mr. Morris scolds the crowd. "Don't you know not to yell at an ape? That's what she is. An ape like you and me. A chimpanzee, to be precise."

"An ape," the kids repeat as they drift home. "An ape, like us."

At dinner, the kids ask why Mr. Morris has a funny monkey in his house. Their parents push forward plates of creamed corn. "He lost his job," they say. "And desperate men are silly."

At dessert, the kids ask if they can have pet monkeys too.

The kids kick their soccer balls into Mr. Morris's yard as an excuse to catch a glimpse of Miss Darling through the patio windows. Sometimes they hoist up a little kid to peer into the bathroom where Miss Darling number-twos in the toilet like a human being. If they slip along the fence, they can see the apricot kitchen, where Miss Darling follows the first command Mr. Morris taught her: grabbing a sippy cup, opening the fridge, and pouring a half glass of orange juice (pulped, not from frozen—the real stuff.)

Mr. Morris's house is the color of vanilla cake. The stucco is peeling. Some kids pick off paint chips and chew on them.

Mr. Morris teaches Miss Darling to shake hands. She does it right. The kids hum, impressed, until Miss Darling shakes Mr. Morris's hand so hard he yelps. The kids cover their mouths so Mr. Morris can't hear their giggles. A little kid laughs too loud. The other kids pull her into the thicket before Mr. Morris can spot them. She sucks her thumb.

The kids crawl away when it gets dark, devastated to leave.

One morning, the kids catch Mr. Morris while he's taking out a garbage bag full of diapers and juice boxes. They ask his plans for Miss Darling.

Mr. Morris puffs up. "I'm going to put her in movies."

The kids' eyes go moony.

The kid-crowd grows in the yard. Kids sit in wheelbarrows, kids squat behind firewood piles, kids put their hands over their eyes and think they've gone invisible. Mr. Morris never looks out the window.

Mr. Morris gets meaner. Miss Darling sleeps too much, he says. She's dirty and dumb. She's lazy and good-for-nothing. Some kids stick their fingers in their ears, fidgeting. Mr. Morris calls Miss Darling an idiot. She scuttles towards the TV, pointing, wanting to watch her show. Mr. Morris wipes his face with a dishrag. The kids repeat the words they learned, murmuring, "Idiot."

A heat wave sways across town.

Mr. Morris spends four hours demonstrating a jazz square for Miss Darling, but she's only interested in eating the crumbs off the carpet. Mr. Morris cracks a can of cheap beer.

"That's what my grandpa drinks!" a little kid shouts.

Mr. Morris bolts to the window. The kids disperse. He surveys the yard.

The next day, the blinds are drawn. That's fine. Little kids observe atop older kids' shoulders, peeking into the kitchen windows. "His shirt's off," one kid reports.

Mr. Morris hooks a shock collar around Miss Darling's neck. She pouts on the floor, refusing to budge. Mr. Morris does a jazz square over and over, his house shoes beating against the linoleum. He sweats until he's soaking wet. So wet he looks like he's been hosed down. He kicks Miss Darling. He shocks her. Her eyes go wide. He does the jazz square again then points to her. This is her chance. Her moment. Her performance.

She looks right into Mr. Morris's beady eyes and number-twos on the hallway carpet. She steps in it and runs in circles, then squares, tracking it across the house. Hooting. Smiling.

Mr. Morris falls. His knees land in the dirty pile. The kids gasp. His mouth moves like he's talking but he says nothing. He groans, grunting as he collapses further, panting. His chest heaves. His lips split again, his white teeth gnashing. Mr. Morris shrieks, beating his waxed chest and howling to the ceiling.

Miss Darling slips around her owner on the floor and walks to the fridge. She gets a cup and pours herself a full glass of orange juice.

Some kids scatter, and some kids stay, and some kids squirm sideways, but all of them, without understanding why, are laughing.

Sarah Priscus is the author of *Groupies* (William Morrow/HarperCollins). Her short fiction has been nominated for Best of the Net, the Pushcart Prize, and recognized on the *Wigleaf* Top 50 longlist. A graduate of the University of Ottawa, she lives in Ottawa, Canada. She is represented by Mariah Stovall of Trellis Literary. She can be found online at sarahpriscus.com, on Twitter at @sarahpriscus, or on Instagram at @sarah.priscus.

AND THE DAYS WERE made of auguries. And the cricket calls arrived disembodied from the field. And a dead mole lay on its back by the garage, gathering its thin blanket of ants. And wasps hummed outside the boy's window like primitive wraiths. And one morning, he found a dead crow in the woods and carried it back to the house, hiding it at the back of his closet like a reliquary. And sometimes he imagined the creature calling to him in the night, calling to him in his dreams, and the boy would rise, pull the string for the closet light, and open the cardboard box. And there was the crow: its dark wings motionless, its dark and lacquered eyes gazing up at him. And sometimes in the mornings, the boy stepped into the backyard and gazed at the sun with its raw, sepulchral eye. And at breakfast, now and then, he asked about his father. And his mother would cross her arms over her chest or set his plate so forcefully on the table that the boy would look away. And some afternoons, he sat in his closet and imagined the crow lifting itself on the dark oars of its wings, rowing high above the trees. Or the boy imagined a crow call fissuring the air, a crow call that was both corporeal and incorporeal at once. And the smell in the boy's closet was like something secretive congealing on the surface of a pond. And on the evening when a first light snow of the season came dropping toward the land, the boy carried the crow back into the woods and tossed it as high as he could manage into the air.

Doug Ramspeck is the author of nine poetry collections, one collection of short stories, and a novella. His story collection, *The Owl That Carries Us Away*, received the G. S. Sharat Chandra Prize for Short Fiction. Individual stories have appeared in journals that include *The Southern Review*, *Iowa Review*, *Southwest Review*, and *The Georgia Review*. His flash fiction story, "Snow Crow," received First Place in the Bath Flash Fiction 19th Award.

A MERE TWO YARDS

naima rashid

LIKE A PROLOUGE, SADNESS always preceded her. It was present when she lived in Pakistan, and I knew her as a voice at the other end of the line, a voice that made my mother's face droopy and sad. It was present in the weeks before she moved in with us when Ammi Abbu gave us a talk about how to treat her. It was present when she moved in with us, in the clean downy linen of the sheets on her bed, in the silence we all kept on the ground floor where she lived.

"They begin to feel like furniture after a while, all parents who move in with their children in the West." We were afraid of breaking her sleep with our noise and afraid of leaving her alone for too long, lest she began to feel she was turning into furniture.

Her fears were altogether strange, I thought. They were so removed from the possibilities of imagination afforded by the bustle of a day that I found them irrational. My parents did not; it seemed. Since Naana's death, they had started playing along as if they were accomplices in a game of make-belief fears she played all day long in her head.

"Nobody would have known when I died. Nobody would have been present to bury me." Every day, those words came out of her mouth, like a note in a piano that had to sound itself every day, for no reason beyond the sounding, to assure itself that melody had not left its spirit. I'm quite sure that was why they had brought her over here forever. She said the house had gone silent all of a sudden since Naana died last year. No one visited like before. Maybe all they came for was the money, of the possibility of it.

On the face of it, she was well, It felt like we were providing life support all the time, dialling up the silliest thing that pleased her, ignoring full realities that made her sad. A new version of Naani had appeared since Naana's death, a frailer one we had to tiptoe around.

We whispered among ourselves that it was Naana's picture she looked at in her diary (a long gaze of reckoning, like a rehearsal of courage) with the silky tassel where she had the phone numbers of her relatives in Pakistan. Sometimes, she called the ones who were still alive. Here in the US, she had a single niece who lived an hour's drive out. Ammi Abbu had taken her to meet them once just after she arrived.

On Eid, Ammi made us wear our shalwar kameez and made halwa early in the morning. Frail Naani was impossible to reason with. She wanted to go and give Eidi to her niece's children. It was impossible to explain to her she was most at risk. ("So important for her to feel like an elder. So important for her to have something to look forward to.")

Going through her cupboard felt like an invasion. It was the first time I was alone in her quarters. I had no choice. Ammi was too distraught to pack her clothes for the hospital when they moved her to ICU. Earlier that day, they had shown the first footage of mass graves, and Ammi hadn't stopped sobbing since. She gestured to me feebly for everything that needed to be done; I kept guessing what she meant and doing it.

Next to the lamp on Naani's bedside table was the diary. I opened it guiltily on the page with the tassel, expecting to see my Naana. Instead, on one side of the page was a glued picture. It showed an old man with death in his eyes looking into the camera. On the opposite page, in her own steady hand, was inscribed a verse in Urdu:

'Kitna hai badnaseeb Zafar dafan ke liye
Do gaz zameen bhi na mili kooay yaar main'

('How unfortunate are you, Zafar, for your last respite
A mere two yards, in the shade of kin, you could not find')

At left, below, signed in Urdu: *Bahadur Shah Zafar*

———————————————

Naima Rashid is an author, poet and literary translator. Her first book was *Defiance of the Rose* (Oxford University Press, 2019), a verse translation of selected works by late Pakistani poet, Perveen Shakir. Her forthcoming works include a translation of *Naulakhi Kothi* by Ali Akbar

Natiq (Penguin Random House India) and *Zizanies* by Clara Schulmann (Les Fugitives) as well as her own fiction and poetry. Her works and views have been widely published in journals such as *The Scores, Lunate, Asymptote, Wild Court, Poetry Birmingham, The Aleph Review* and *PEN Transmissions* among others. She was longlisted for the National Poetry Competition 2019.

THE STORY OF THE BEE

tim raymond

IT WAS SUMMER AND everything had fallen apart. But I'd not yet lost hope. It was one of those descents where you feel free almost, so long as you can sense some light somewhere to fall toward. Yoon and I had divorced on account of irreconcilable differences. It wasn't that I'd been diagnosed as autistic. It was that I was diagnosed and thought differently about everything suddenly and even quit my job because of it, which complicated our plans to start a family. As far as I could tell, no one resented anybody else, save for when it came time to file the paperwork for the divorce visa and Yoon wouldn't help me. I did it, but all the small print and uncertainty wrecked me.

I ended up in Dobong in this goshiwon, a tiny closet of a room, sharing a hallway-bathroom with people ten years younger than me who were there solely to prepare for whichever entrance-exam. Seoul National University or the Civil Service Cert, I didn't know. I had some savings and some boxes and my little side-gig designing emojis that earned me cash here and there. It was barely enough to live off of when Kakao featured my designs, which they did sometimes but not regularly.

Like I said, I was searching for some light.

I could have gone back to America, if only there'd been a place for me, or if I had some skill or other to rely on. I couldn't go back to teaching, I at least knew that. The stress of it was too much. I'd die. Not in these words, but the psychologist said my executive functioning was trash. An autistic with Level 3 support needs, which threw me because I didn't even know there were levels before getting evaluated. And here I was, the highest one. How lonely could things get, I asked myself, from my goshiwon, among the boxes I couldn't bring myself to open.

The weirdest part was that, although I was constantly on edge, I wasn't much registering any specific emotion. It was like the pressure in your ear that you can't relieve. Something there, but you don't know what, but it informs every aspect of your life, but you don't know why. The more time you spend trying to release it, the deeper it gets buried.

I had this sense, in other words, that if I felt something big, I'd know which direction had the light in it. But no, I was just walking and searching and drawing alone in this room that couldn't fit two people even if I'd wanted it to. The days pressed on.

Later, I did open a box, and did take a book out of it, and did find doing so transformative, though not in the way you might expect. I was not inspired. It was an old copy of a Hemingway translation that I never cracked open because why would I, bought years prior from Found Books in Itaewon. I opened it now and riffled through its pages, which stuck halfway through on a little bookmark I'd not known was there. It had a whale on it, below which was a handwritten note reading, *you looked and you found it, then* —R, which was my initial, too. I was not in general a person easily swayed by the signs and signals of a knowing universe, but I did find myself treating this bookmark with care and respect, as though it housed something fragile. I'd drawn that entire series of whale emojis, after all. Who, I wondered, found what, hidden by whom, and how did they or you or I know?

I couldn't sleep at all that night. I was trying to remember when I bought the book and whether I'd been with anybody else at the time. My first year in Seoul, I thought, and maybe my first time in the English bookstore. But I wasn't sure. I did like Hemingway, moreover, but what did that matter, when Nick Adams was burned out on the big two-hearted river, when I was split down the middle under a too-low ceiling. In the morning, in a daze, I got coffee and hopped on a train heading west. I was trying to plan out which questions I'd ask once I got there, but then before I knew it, I'd arrived in Itaewon and was clacking empty-minded down the sidewalk. Found Books was not only closed, I discovered, but it'd been replaced by a Pilates studio that also sold smoothies.
Just like that, my late-morning went dark.

It wasn't that I believed this message was the light-filled thing I'd been searching for, but it had been a lead and the trail was cold. I stood annoyed and bored on the sidewalk, until, minutes or hours later, a hand was on me. I looked and there was this woman there, this petite American lady, with black hair and holes in her jeans. Hi, she was saying, she was Rian.

Rian, I said.

Yeah, she said, are you Trevor?

Not by a long shot, but I was late in saying so. It'd thrown me that her name began with an R. She seemed nervous, though, and quickly asked if we should just go to the café down the street, then.

It didn't take long for me to figure out that this was a Tinder date I was on, and that I looked a lot like a person I actually was not. Rian's phone kept buzzing, but she was all courtesy and remained focused on me. It was like she and Trevor hadn't communicated at all before agreeing to meet up. I just said what was real for me, to which she nodded along and asked questions. Oh, divorced, for how long? Oh, design, what's that like? She was a voice actor, primarily for educational resources, and also a model, primarily for products that required closeups of fingers on buttons and various controls.

I wasn't sure, but she seemed lonely. We got our second coffees to go and went for a walk, her model hand enveloped clumsily by my shaky one. I asked her if she liked reading.

Sure, she said.

You don't have any interest in whales, do you?

Much interest, indeed, she laughed, and then abruptly excused herself. She thought maybe it was her agency trying to contact her. Sometimes they'd overload her like this with urgent messages about auditions and/or gigs. Sorry, she said, and scrolled through.

It was not her agency, of course, it was Trevor, who was confused and waiting. Rian made this face like I should offer her some direction or something. But me, I had none. I suggested we get lunch.

What the actual fuck? was how she put it, before turning and going.

Not a proud moment for me, but I tried to show her the bookmark before she was completely gone. She swatted at me and said she'd scream. But I thought it was going well, I said to her. Please and sorry, but I'd always been an awkward person. Confused easily and quickly rattled. Lonely. Now here, about the whales, I went on, at which point she screamed.

It was a shame, I felt, but where else was there for it to go? I, big and nameless man, had lied to her.

I got back on the train to head home, but overshot my stop because the voice announcing the stations in English sounded a whole lot like Rian's. It was intentional in its tone and robotic in that way, but I was pretty sure it was her. My brain began doing its thing where it foregoes all meaning and loses itself in timbre and texture. In taste and detail. Then the train had run its course and I was forced to get off, at this stop that was essentially the countryside. It wasn't, but compared to Seoul, it was. You could hear insects chirring from the platform, which was above ground.

Outside, I had an instant coffee and failed to find the bathroom. It was hot out. It wasn't despair I was feeling, so much as it was the usual gnawing ache ramped up slightly. Maybe it was the adrenaline of anxiety balancing me out. I missed Yoon. Or anyway, I thought I did. I missed the warmth of her and the plans we'd had fun making. The way she laughed when I paced the apartment or stared at her how I do. But she thought I was charming. She was older than me by four years. She washed the dishes quietly because she knew I hated the sound. Or she just had me do them.

I still had the book with me and so sat on a bench and leafed through it. My Korean wasn't excellent, but it was good enough to parse Hemingway, especially if I'd already read the story. In our time, every nothing was something. It wasn't in the book anywhere, but the phrase sounded pertinent and meaningful. In any case, it was stuck in my head now, among everything else. Whales were being slaughtered into extinction, for no discernible reason. Once the whales were gone, death would slowly trickle down to the rest of us, regardless of where we resided. An unlikely truth, but a truth nonetheless, only nobody cared to see it. It was all tucked away in books that we didn't read because we were too busy or too tired. A sunny day, a quiet afternoon in the country, with children laughing somewhere in the distance—yet even nothing was something. There was a stream out there, and I rose then to walk beside it.

Streams in Korea meant bikers, meant joggers, meant clearly marked bathrooms every half a kilometer or so. I saw cranes standing on rocks barely breaking the surface of the water. Fish jumped and splashed. Trees swayed. The small birds flew in the wind, and the wind hardened them.

Fish emojis, bird emojis, some other job or work, streams and wind, trees with anxiety, ear protectors, stimming hand emojis, autistic faces, blank stares and confused emotions or emotions that aren't confused at all, they just register different, and when finally I came upon the familiar white structure with the female-red and male-blue doors, I was awash with relief, because the pee in me was huge. But before I could reach the stairs leading to the structure, a biker emerging from the shade under the bridge not 20 yards away swerved and tore and flipped over his handlebars, crashing face-first and helmetless into the hard turf of the walking path. I squeezed through the heavy moment to see if he'd stand up on his own, which he did not. Like a great creature, he'd fallen.

I was frozen, because this everything was nothing, because there were mosquitoes around me and also strict rules about how to help somebody who'd collapsed. The man was older than me, but not old. But he was old enough for a heart to give out. I had my phone with me but couldn't settle on a number. Cars passed on the bridge, but beyond that, this man and I were alone. You looked and you looked and you found it, then. You were here at the exact right time to witness something no one else would. The problem with not knowing who you are for 30-plus years is that, when it comes time to be you, there's a massive pause standing in the way that you have to maneuver yourself around. It's thick and it pulls and is generally invisible. It was becoming clear to me that moving to Korea in the first place was just a ploy to make this pause that much bigger and safer, for if nothing is ever going to make sense, then at least live somewhere where the senselessness is not on you or your failures as a person. But stop ruminating and act already. I could not tell if he was breathing or convulsing. The minutes felt like hours, and then another biker was along to pound his chest and make the call and save him.

In the bathroom, I melted down. It was dark and damp in there. The pee was all blocked up inside of me, and just when I thought I couldn't get any more frustrated by it, a bee found the base of my skull and stung me. Not the transcendence I was hoping for, exactly, but it was a hole in me that allowed some measure of light in. I was burning with feeling now. Not that it taught me anything I didn't already know: I was still a garbage person, a useless and hurt one, a person laughing and crying and trying his hardest. An American person whose English was changed, whose brain was different, and whose scream-song twirled pretty in the deep. I hated bathrooms because I always thought I'd get sick in them. I hated cities because I always thought I'd get sick in them. I hated ambulances, too, but there one was, right by the stream. I could see lights flashing from where I was.

Take me away, lights, but where? Anyway, I wasn't crazy. I went home and laughed so hard that my neighbors complained. They were trying to focus, they said. I buried my face in my pillow and laughed myself exhausted. I buried my face right there in it, to ponder light not as something to glimpse, but something to taste, or smell, or enact with each new day. Something to speak and you've found it, then. The dash-letter-sound you couldn't make until you reached adulthood. The name I couldn't articulate until I was learning some Korean and it changed the way my tongue moved. It's Richard, by the way, though more and more I go by Rick.

Tim Raymond is an autie writer from Wyoming. His work has appeared recently or will appear in *Nimrod, Conjunctions,* and *Split Lip Magazine,* among others. He lives with his person and cat in Seoul, South Korea.

THE ANNIVERSARY CAME AND went. Souta glanced at the calendar with fleeting, stubborn accomplishment. Three years since he'd entered his room above the stairwell and hung his uniform. The space, once defined by his absence, smelled sour. His classmates graduated. Souta's parents surrendered after the contract with a rental sister, who ferried letters under his door.

A lacquered tray appeared twice per day. On his birthday, grilled tongue. Once, a pamphlet about a community for people like him. He wondered if he wanted his parents to continue trying, or if their failure affirmed what he believed: he was an interloper. Souta bookmarked an online article about Aokigahara, the suicide forest, for a sentence about another high schooler, so that the other boy's death served as a calculated boundary.

The day Souta sealed himself, bullies taunted him for kissing an older boy, who denied the lie without vehemence or ridicule. His calm response protected him. The story then altered. Seeing no reason why they'd been linked together, Souta, too, adopted an attitude of indifference. Copying silence proved a mistake. Because he'd skirted the edge of anyone's notice for years, he filled the shoes of those rumors with plasticity. How could two people have such different outcomes? Would it have been wiser to laugh?

What defeated Souta, at last, was the knowledge that the future unrolled with no clear direction. He couldn't stomach the idea of ordinary failure. When Souta was ten, the boundaries of his neighborhood felt safe. The grocer. The fish restaurant. The vintage record shop. Walled houses, seasonal noises, of which he liked cicadas best. Outside he could wander until dusk. But here, in the worn house, leaving was impossible. He knew what they called him. Souta grew into the sharp angles of the word until it engulfed him.

Karen Rigby is the author of *Chinoiserie* (Ahsahta Press). A 2007 National Endowment for the Arts literature fellow, her poetry appears in *Southern Humanities Review, Bennington Review, The London Magazine,* and other journals. She lives in Arizona. www.karenrigby.com.

INTERSECTION
basmah sakrani

ON THE CORNER OF Burnamthorpe and Hurontario is a traffic light. Under it stand a woman and a child, bundled in second-hand puffy jackets and slip-proof boots that fail repeatedly on icy ground. Their arms are linked, the child's hand mittened, the woman's bare.

They are waiting to cross the road, woman and child, waiting for the blinking orange hand to transform into a walking green man. It's definitely a man, that symbol, the woman thinks, because even in icon form, he stands brave and ready, already mid-step before it's time to go. No woman she knows stands like that.

The green man appears, and the woman yells, "Chalo!" and pulls the child forward with her, forward into the crossing where their boots stomp into half-formed ice puddles and piles of grey slush. Through her heavy hood, she can hear the child's hurried steps and wants, for a moment, to pause and lift him up into her arms so she can kiss some warmth into those cold apple cheeks. But she rushes onward, so brisk an onlooker might wonder what urgent matter lay on the other side of the road. But really, the woman is rushing because she knows better now, knows not to dawdle at this crossing because it is reason enough for a man in a blue car to roll down his window and yell, "Hurry up you Paki!" She knows because this happened yesterday. Thank goodness she was alone then, and not with the child. On her own, the woman can absorb any and all blows, but the child—he is sensitive. He looks at a leaf and imagines the map of a town where he is a doctor. The woman sees a leaf and imagines nothing.

They are across the road now, woman and child, and traffic rushes by behind them. They are walking slower now, the woman matching her pace to the child, who she knows now must be tired or hungry or both. They have not eaten much today, just an apple and some milk. The bus stop is a hundred feet away and the bus arrives in two minutes, and the woman wants to pull the child forward again now so she can take out her wallet and count out the exact change needed. But she hears the child sniffle and she gives his mittened hand a squeeze. It is so small, this hand, this child, she fears sometimes she will break him.

The child came to her after a decade of waiting and trying. The child came to her after the man she was married to found comfort elsewhere. The child came to her once she had already signaled defeat. He fought for space in her tired bones, made her cry every night for nine and a half months, and was the reason why she crumpled up her suicide note before even writing it. She wouldn't have gone through with it, she knows, but she wanted to try. She had no one to say goodbye to in her note, no one except the child who kicked her bladder and pressed against her spleen. My organs are his toys, she remembers thinking. I want to get him real toys. A truck and a teddy bear and a basketball and a battery-operated car. The child gave her gumption and here she was, five years later, sauntering toward a bus they would soon board. It's Saturday, and they will ride downtown together to Union Station. The woman will pay for two seats but hold the child on her lap and smile as he kicks her shins. Later she will find bruises there, brush strokes of slate grey on her skin, and she will ask herself if this is all the touch she is permitted in her life, that of a child and no other man. Together, they will look out the window and marvel at the passing cars, the rising buildings, and the sky which seems to open up as they get further and further away from home.

Basmah Sakrani is a Pakistani-Canadian writer living in Memphis TN. Her writing has appeared in *The Baltimore Review*, *High Shelf Press*, *Past Ten* and other publications. She contributes as Fiction Interviewer to *The Maine Review* and holds an MFA from Vermont College of Fine Arts. Basmah works at Wunderman Thompson.

Sky-Touched

GARY FEELS SMITED (BIBLICALLY) though he tells himself he shouldn't. That it's just a matter of being in the wrong place at the wrong time and isn't worth a rotten fig to think otherwise. The clouds after all are machines of science and those jagged volts that crackled down to ravage every cell were just that: *science in motion.*

Mourning Becomes Electric

He meets Frida at a Lightning Strike Survivor's support group, sits across from her in a hard brown folding chair. She says to the group, "Forgive me if this sounds harsh, but I don't give a rat's ass about religion." She says this after someone shares that they feel punished and blessed at the same time. "I burned a Bible soon after, at a motel," Frida says. "In the bathtub with a can of lighting fluid. You should have seen it: all those 'thees' and 'thous' going up in smoke."

They are in a semicircle with their cups of coffee, looking at her, stricken. Gary gets up to hug her. When he touches her sweater he gets a small shock of static electricity and pulls back. Only the two of them know what's happened and laugh. The only person in the group who's been struck by lightning twice gazes at her with a slightly twisted mouth and says, "Damn! Set a Bible on fire in a bathtub. You sure like playing with fire, sister."

Gary is a mattress salesman and late that night at the strip mall he lets Frida in and they bounce on each bed/mattress in a back-floor room for "firmness" and "reliability."

"I kind of liked it when they had squeaky bedsprings," Frida says. "When beds talked back."

"You like being bad, don't you?" Gary says.

"Bad is good," she says. "Goody two shoes went flying out of me as I was lying there on the ground unable to move." They are nearly naked, but when he goes to embrace her, she weeps.

After All

"Ever since, you know…it happened…things taste better," Gary tells Frida.

"I know," she says. They are in her studio eating burritos and drinking beer. "You think the electricity is like a really good spice?" she says, smiles.

He half smiles. There is a black bean pressed against his teeth. "No, I mean it. Coming that close to death. Feeling its breath on me, maybe spices things up a bit after, you know?"

"Hmm," she says. Her paintings are all around them on the walls—huge blocks and swirls of color, bold and shooting down the canvases. She tells him how after she was struck she was lost for a time, working at her uncle's music box factory. How the same ditzy tunes kept getting stuck in her head. How it nearly drove her nuts, but then she returned to an early love. She sweeps a hand demonstratively around the room.

He feels foolish when he gives her a nerdy thumps up. She goes on and on about something or other, and he stops listening but continues nodding.

The rain seems to nail him deeper to the ground, and when he comes to, he tries to move a finger, then two, and then his head, slowly. He is face down in the mud and there is a worm. A worm squirming past his vision. A watery eviction no doubt. It pauses by his face as if to catch its breath. Gary is still disoriented and wonders if he is really alive or… No, it's a fucking worm, you idiot. The thunder is everywhere at once it seems and the searing flashes highlight the worm's slow departure. He wants to scream: "Wait!" But wait for what? It's a worm after all, and not his life, as he knew it, leaving, not his faith, not his old sense of who he was, or why he is. It is just a worm is all. Just one squirmy little wet departure. Nothing more.

"Pass the hot sauce," she says.

"Oh—sure."

Robert Scotellaro's work has been included in W.W. Norton's *Flash Fiction International, Maryland Literary Review, Gargoyle, Matter Press, New World Writing, Best Small Fictions* 2016, 2017, and 2021, *Best Microfiction* 2020, 2022, and elsewhere. He is the author of seven chapbooks, several books for children, and five flash fiction collections. He has, along with

James Thomas, co-edited *New Micro: Exceptionally Short Fiction*, published by W.W. Norton & Co. Scheduled for release in 2022 are his two flash fiction collections: *Ways to Read the World* (Scantic Press) and *God in a Can* (Bamboo Dart Press). Visit him at www.robertscotellaro.com.

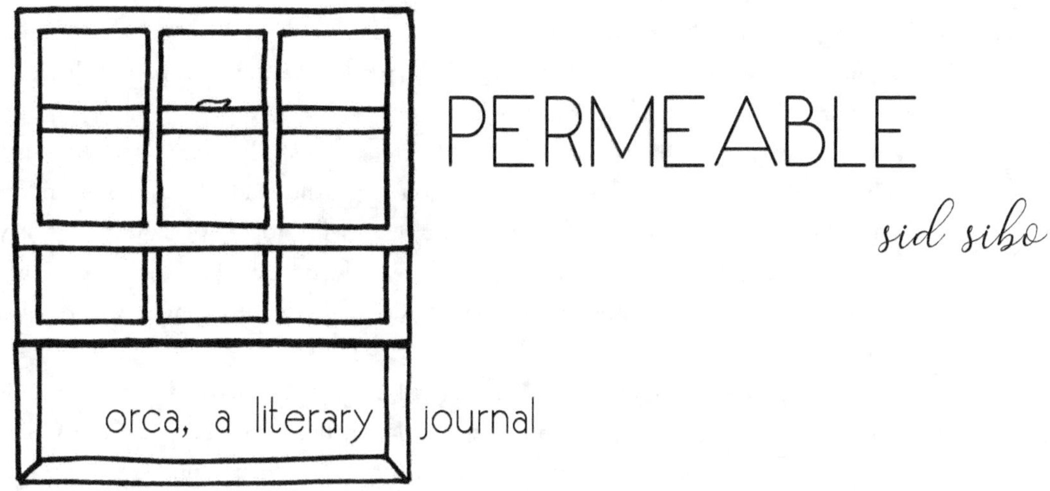

THE FOUR TO TEN p.m. watch is my favorite, even in winter when the whole time is darkness. Northern Lights keep me company then, and to stay warm, I shimmy with magnetic green or crimson curves and waves, my shadow large in their frigid glow. Now, early summer, the entire watch is a dance of changing daylight through pine needles, and basswood leaves play sultry music behind swelling mosquito hum and chant. Mostly light enough to paint while I wait, but as night climbs up from feathered moss and fragrant sweet fern, I descend our camouflaged ladder. Though I don't need to darken my bare arms, a cool mud smear keeps blood in my veins, fending off swarms of insect mothers.

"You look like a moose when you do that." Jon arrives early to spell me.

"Like my moose lips?" I pucker up to offer him a taste, wild strawberries on my tongue. We don't actually watch much. It's easy to hear anyone driving on the far side of the dense cedar grove, motors a foreign sound here on the edge of official Wilderness. The Boundary Waters, a paddler's splashy paradise, rings mostly with white-throated sparrow song and breaching walleye.

Jon can't stand gathering wild strawberries. "Like milking mice tits," he always says. His au pair raised him on out-of-season nuclear strawberries, tasting of straw. He doesn't appreciate small things, slow harvests. To him, though, these six-hour shifts are all-important, despite waiting for mostly nothing, since his mother and her corporate entourage show up almost never.

My tongue teases. I know these weightless mosquitoes will deter him from removing his clothes.

He pulls away, business on his mind. "How's the painting?"

A final black stroke of mud along my cheek before I climb again to our deer stand. He studies pages of copper-bellied fen frog—life cycles, natural history, caddis fly prey and river mink predator, jellied egg masses and leaf mulch hibernacula. Complete fiction, all of it. His idea, that I've brought to vibrant verisimilitude.

He grins. "That might slow 'em down." He slaps the sketchbook's covers closed. A single loose page drifts off the edge of our platform.

My hand strokes his sunburned face. "Not for long." In stock futures, Triplet Metals outcompetes his mother's mining conglomerate, but Jon hopes his undercover campaign will return her trust, and his inheritance. Our fellow activists will stop Triplet with this new species—last year alone, 131 rare amphibians discovered worldwide. But after Triplet leaves, the false frog dries up, and his family company accesses the lode. He had to confide in me. Stick figure frogs would never suffice.

He kisses me again, triumph near. Mud ugly I might be, but at the moment, this mansion on its remote northern lake hides only couples and a couple single straight guys. Others stay in the posh house by the wilderness a few months at most, then rotate out. I lived here long before a disowned Jon had the same idea. Occupy. And he stays occupied, secretly maneuvering, satellites at his command, unaware of being maneuvered by the muck underfoot, that protective scent I wear. The shining dark has been inside his dreams.

Tires rattle gravel in the long driveway. His eyes go wide as a screech owl's, but our drill is uncomplicated. The Humvee's path bends east around the fen, and from a waterproof cache I extract a signal flare, send it into the dusk. A parallel watcher at the house will clear the main rooms. The team will conceal all political efforts, slink away like salamanders. His mother is clueless.

"Vacation," I say. Everyone has a retreat plan, and a canoe. Some will push against the Kawishiwi's slow current, stay with friends in Ely. Jon will hide in an unused barn on high ground near a stand of jack pine, binoculars trained on the main house. Invisible as a molecule of balsam scent, I'll slip through penciled membranes, at home in Quetico waters, same as here. A mosquito grows heavy, unnoticed, on Jon's exposed neck. I leave him the sketchbook.

A few strides from the tree, I push my granddad's old birchbark canoe into a tannin-dark water trail. The loose page floats a few paddle strokes away. In it, a copper-bellied frog leaps where beakrush and fringed bogbean punctuate thick sphagnum, marking the fen's edge. I pause. The waterlogged colors run together, create movement. My hands, a silent praise hymn for past generations, for regeneration, bury the disintegrating paper beneath basswood twigs and ash leaves.

I listen to motors growing faint behind the calls of settling loons. Though fen frogs don't sing, I hear small drums. With every leap, they speak. In each beat of their padded feet, I hear the Kawishiwi's survival song.

Living just west of the Continental Divide, in the traditional homeland of Shoshone and

Bannock peoples, Sid Sibo has won the Neltje Blanchan Memorial Writing Award and an Honorable Mention in the Rick DeMarinis Short Story contest. Published stories can be found in *Fourth River (Tributaries)*, *Evocations*, *Orca*, *Cutthroat*, and *Brilliant Flash Fiction*, among others. A job in environmental analysis seeds a variety of creative efforts, including occasional blog posts at www.siboMountain.net.

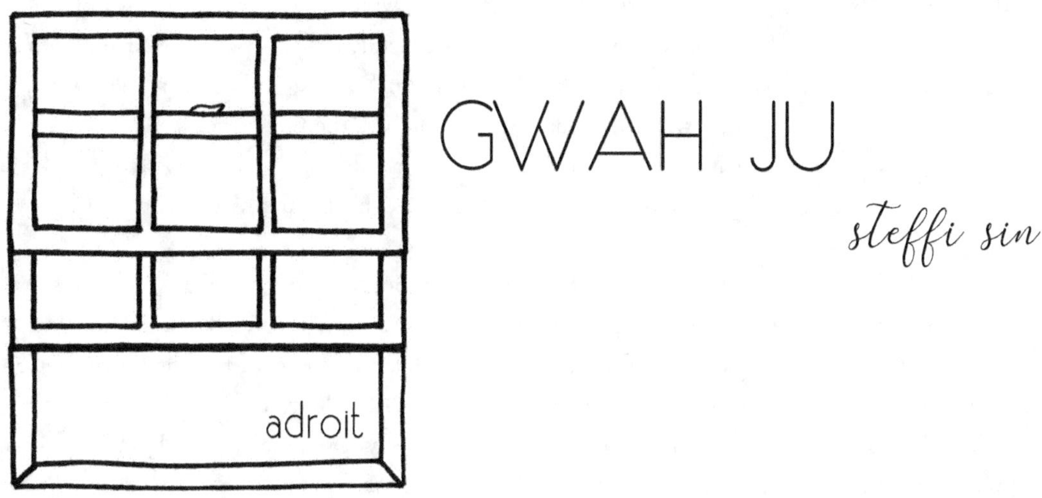

GWAH JU

steffi sin

GWAH JU: TO MISS someone or to hang something

Four Junes since my grandfather's funeral, and I still *gwah ju* Yeye around my neck like a scarf. I look right at the place I saw him last. My mother told me to give Yeye a kiss on the cheek, for luck. I thought my kisses too precious to be given away to grandfathers like charity. I *gwah ju* my arms around his stomach. Does that—

"Look Right". White-paint eyes on dusty pavement demand it of me, but the American inside me refuses. In Hong Kong, I can only look because no one fed me the right words to go with my English thoughts. I am never right, not in Hong Kong. Yeye didn't mind that about me.

Nothing in Hong Kong is right. Lines at food stands hang left. People on escalators stand to the left. At intersections, I look left before I walk.

A dump truck honks drunkenly and swerves to avoid swiping me off the low curb. The grimy metal siding exhales with the bad breath of freeways around the street corner. The pissed-off driver, sweating through his yellow-gray tank top, hurls obscenities at me. "*Lay maang-gah? Soh po. Mmm sik kay!*" Are you blind? Crazy lady. Don't know how to stand right!

Behind me, the wall of pedestrians snicker. Their left-handed country has the upper hand. Nothing in Hong Kong is right. Without Yeye, it is wrong.

I heed the directions on the pavement. I look right. I look right. I—

Look, rites. Black smoke billows into a gray-white sky. A prepubescent boy with floppy bangs rings the gong as a family in black carries their boxed-up dead down a dead-end street. They exit an ugly temple with broken air conditioning and stumble into the thick tongue of summer heat. It's bad luck to look right at them, but the kid has the same build my brother had four summers ago. When we laid Yeye to rest, my uncles wore suits that had only witnessed white and red weddings. The heavy smell of their sweat wrenched my gut as our whole family circled the block for the ritual. I'd borrowed open-toe black heels, two sizes too small, from my mother, and I lagged behind the group, watched as my uncles struggled to keep a slippery grip on the metal handles of the coffin. Never one whisper of how the body smells.

Every street corner in Hong Kong looks the same to me. The lychee stands smell of Yeye's goodbye the last time I saw him in Tai Wai, and his ghost waits with me for red lights to go green. Look.

Right there, I ate with Yeye last. We shared a boat of curry fishballs, brisket stew, a basket of lychees. Yeye's hands clutched two bottles of Coke. He handed one to me, and his words smelled of the fish market, of metal in the blood running rivers from the butcher's floor, staining my white-soled sneakers. Then he put me in a taxi headed for the airport, my two bags packed, but only with clothes I brought, no souvenirs. Flying home to San Francisco means flying with suitcases that reek of my grandmother's jasmine tea and black herbs that take two weeks to air out. I began collecting things from Yeye's Tai Wai, from Hong Kong, after Yeye died.

My father takes me to Yeye's final resting place, a columbarium, a cubbyhole on a shelf shared with thirty strangers. I look right below my eye level at Yeye. My father and my uncles paid good money so Yeye wouldn't be on the floor. I look, right at the name of the place Yeye was born, at the lines and squares carved in marble that is his name, all the characters I never learned. I do not have the right to read. I look right at the picture of Yeye, and I wish to write myself right and give Yeye a goodbye I want to remember as our last. I do not have the right to grieve.

Back on the streets, Chinese characters on signs flatten under the suffocating humidity. I do not have the right to breathe. Right-angled square figures melt to hieroglyphs of elbows and knees. On the bottom of the sign, the English only teaches me how to pronounce the Chinese. They do not tell me where I stand.

I only loved Hong Kong when Yeye waved goodbye from a street corner in Tai Wai.

Steffi Sin is a Chinese American writer from San Francisco who received her MFA in Creative Writing from Arizona State University. She is currently revising her manuscript *Bird with No Legs*. Her fiction and nonfiction have been published by *The Kenyon Review*, *The Los Angeles Review*, *Black Warrior Review*, and elsewhere. She is Nonfiction Editor of *Hayden's Ferry Review*.

WHAT THEY KNEW

eric dryer smith

MRS. PETERSEN KNEW WHAT they were doing up the road. Mr. Baum had a good idea, too. He was the town baker and although he worked a lot he still heard the rumors. Then the people who worked up the street began ordering bread from him. He resisted hearing the rumours firsthand as fact from the people who worked there, but soon realized that listening to their stories was a part of doing business with them. He had to listen to get their money and they seemed to have to tell their stories. Therefore, it was not long before Mr. Baum really knew.

The children of the town said ghosts lived up the road. In a way this was close to the truth, but children do not know everything.

Mr. Kappel prayed for the longest time that it was not true. But when enough people said it was true, at least enough for a reasonable man to wonder if it were, then he prayed even harder that it would pass soon. When rumours blossomed, he prayed as hard as possible that they would be forgiven. Kappel worked at the church and it made sense that at least some of his prayers would be answered.

Mrs. Huber was a teacher and quite educated. She believed history was repeating itself. The logical conclusion would be that revenge would be taken. She felt ashamed, but kept teaching her lessons. She knew what was going on up the road.

Mr. Schuster pretended for the longest time that he had no idea what was going on. He knew the ones in town who liked to talk about it. The ones who bragged or condemned what was happening and he avoided both groups assiduously… He never walked up the road or looked in the sky toward that direction. When the workers from there came to town, he disappeared. The whole thing, from the very beginning, had been too big for him. He was one man. He knew there was nothing he could do.

Mrs. Koch was proud of what was happening. If anyone deserved this, then it was those people. She knew they could not get away with what they had been doing. They had been doing it for centuries and now they had to pay a little. It was only fair. What else did they expect for doing what they had always done?

Mr. Farber was more practical. He figured that it was better that it was happening to them than to people like those who lived in the town. This was the logical position. After all, there was a war going on. Something had to be done to ensure internal security. Those who were not our friends could easily become friends of the enemy. The people kept up the road were never our friends.

Mrs. Vogt was horrified by what was happening. The thought of it grew in her mind daily. Why had they chosen a place just up the road to do such things? The terribleness of it was seeping into her skin. She could not sleep. Then her daughter accidently died that summer. Some combination of this and that wore down the thin wire that was left of her mind, and she snapped.

Mrs. Zimmermann would often ask rhetorically at coffee: who was she to care what happened? No one had elected her the boss. At times it did seem a little insane to her, but then again so did a lot of events. All things that happened in times such as these were bad. It did one no good to dwell too much on matters one could not control. This was wise philosophy. Besides, governments were always doing questionable activities.

Mr. Meyer thought about protesting. He made inquiries of others on the matter. No one responded favourably. He began thinking of ways he could get the place up the road closed or perhaps moved. He thought for a long time, but when he got no support, these thoughts remained thoughts and never became an idea. He never did get an idea before it was all over.

Mr. Thalberg was so old when this thing began that honestly his mind did not understand it. A few friends tried to explain it to him during conversations, but to no avail. It sounded like fantasy to Mr. Thalberg—the very little bit he understood of what they were trying to tell him. Were they talking about Hansel and Gretel? Did they think he was a child?

Mr. and Mrs. Fleischer were so stressed that this was happening so close to them that they did not have sex for seven years. They could not avoid the matter since the workers from up the road relied on their goods. Those workers insisted on telling their stories. It was profitable and maybe morally necessary to listen. Someone had to attempt to absolve the confessors. Someone had to play heaven's ear.

Mrs. Brandt was certain there were two nations within the country. It was divided between those who fostered what happened and those who would never have taken part in such business. Basically, the party system in the country justified her interpretation. It was the ones with guns who made this happen. She was part of the other group. This knowledge consoled her.

Mr. and Mrs. Henrich never favored what was happening, and especially hated those in charge. They knew justice would come. All they had to do was wait. While they waited for justice, they sneered at people who seemed to support the activities up the road. When it was over, they were proud they had kept such a low profile through it all, and they continued to sneer.

Mr. Dreher kept concentrating on the time when the rumours were merely whispers not loud enough to be truly heard. If new thoughts came, he mumbled to himself to drown them out.

Mrs. Oster knew it was all her fault. She lost seventy pounds during those times.

Miss Schreiner saw opportunity in what was happening. She made it a point to marry Mr. Burger during those times, and came up with the idea of the town specializing in new goods that the workers up the road would need. She cleverly arranged for shipments on the new trains that were arriving. She and her husband made lots of money.

Mr. Busch lived in personal horror the whole time, since he recalled a family story that some of the hated people held up the road were his ancestors. He worried that a scientific method would be developed that would discover him.

Mr. Franz ran away and joined the Resistance. Mr. Bohm wrote a book about it one day.

Mr. Weissmuller thought if he never saw the gates up the road, then no one could ever blame him.

Mrs. Ritter made herself happy by forcing herself to vomit.

Mr. Furst one night silently murdered a drunken worker from up the road.

The Barth sisters played cards so much that they had no time to think about it.

Mrs. Pabst insisted the place up the road was merely a bakery.

Mr. Gerste kept saying, "It could not be."

Mrs. Lehrer thought the workers from up the road were nice and that they must have come from good families.

Mr. Nacht tried to move away, to get far away from it, but he had so little money that he could not. He was a prisoner of those people up the road and was always angry about it.

In the end, a few people did move away. The town waited. It went on with things. Things would change since many of the old died forgetting, and the young were born before they could remember.

Eric Dreyer Smith lives in San Antonio, Texas. Currently doing studies for a PhD in research psychology. He works as a counselor at a hospital and in private setting. There are over 36 publications of short stories to his credit.

.

YOU KNOW THE ONE: the babysitter is alone in the house with the kids, it's late, the kids are in bed, and the phone rings. She (always she) hears heavy breathing on the other end. The heavy breather keeps calling. Finally, the babysitter calls the operator and asks her to trace the call. The operator rings right back, says, "Get out. Someone is in the house. *The call is coming from inside the house.*" She rushes to the kitchen to grab a knife, but before she gets there she feels the cold steel of the killer's blade against her throat.

Or some version of this. I hear it from a fifth grader on the playground when I'm six.

"How could the call come from inside the house?" one of the older kids asks.

The storyteller shrugs, having already lost interest in his own account. "Second phone line," he says.

That night and many nights after, I can't sleep.

The call is coming from inside the house.

I ask my mother to leave the hall light on and the door cracked. I imagine the killer, when he comes, to be a thin man dressed all in black, with long dark hair, his eyes wide and crazed. For years I lie awake worrying about him, listen for the sound of his step on the stairs, watch for him in every dark window.

I wake as soon as I hear the glass shattering. I'm twenty-one, I've rented this place for cheap on what several people told me is the "wrong" street. I lock my bedroom door before I'm even fully awake. Grabbing my phone, I dive into the closet, my hands trembling so hard I can barely dial the three digits.

By the time the police car arrives, I'm alone. Nothing is missing.

"He must have heard you moving about. A lot of break-ins on this street recently," the cop says. "You live alone?"

I nod. "What should I do?"

I'm worried about replacing the glass in the pane, wondering how I'm supposed to feel safe in my house until morning.

The cop appraises me. "Get a boyfriend," he says. "Or maybe a dog?"

I'm twenty-three and I have a boyfriend. Well, sort of. There's a guy who texts me sometimes in the evening: *Hey what u up to?*

We have almost nothing in common but when he touches me it lights up my whole body. He comes over and we fuck or I go to his place and we fuck. Then I don't hear from him again for days, until he texts. In between, I drink too much. One night I've been drinking alone in my apartment and I send him a text. He doesn't answer for a long time, so I keep drinking, and by the time he arrives I'm so drunk I can hardly stand. He drags me to the bed and holds me down while I protest.

"You invited me over," he says afterwards.

The next boyfriend is a real boyfriend; he takes me out to dinner and we go for walks in the park on Saturdays. I marry him. We move to the suburbs, to a two-story house with an apple tree in the backyard. The house has many windows for looking out. Our son is born a year later. I wake up often in the night, even when he isn't crying, and creep into his room to look at him, asleep on his back, his head a large moon too big for his body.

More and more often, my husband and I fight. We fight about whose turn it is to take out the trash and who was supposed to pay the utility bill and who works harder at their job and who does more housework. Sometimes I think that we must actually be arguing about something else, something more important, but then I think about the trash bag sitting on the kitchen floor and I feel rage and I think, *maybe this really is about the trash.*

One night after the baby has gone to bed we begin arguing about the credit card bill in fierce whispers, moving down the hallway. We are at the top of the stairs when I tell him, loudly, that marrying him was the biggest mistake I ever made (it's not even true—it's just a thing to say) and he slaps me across the face. I take a step back and my foot searches for the wood floor but finds only empty air, my arms windmill, grabbing for the bannister, but I miss it by a fraction of an inch. I fall. I land at the bottom of the stairs with a thud. My neck cracks.

He rushes down the stairs, saying my name, but it's too late. Cradling me in his arms, he cries. Then he reaches for his phone, thinks for a moment, and puts it away. He disappears into the garage and is gone for a long time. When he returns, he picks me up like a groom delivering a bride over the threshold and carries me into the backyard. He places me in the deep hole he has dug next to the apple tree and picks up the shovel. By next summer, when my son is toddling across the grass with his babysitter, the tree's roots are already pushing through my sternum, gently prying open my ribs.

Kat Solomon's fiction has appeared in *Wigleaf, New Orleans Review, Monkeybicyle* and elsewhere. She holds a MFA from Washington University in St. Louis and is currently at work on a novel.

THE CONFUCIUS DESCENDANTS REUNION BARBEQUE

jade song

THE CONFUCIUS GENEALOGY COMPILATION Committee has reserved the biggest pavilion in the local park for the annual Confucius Descendants Reunion Barbeque. Email invitations were sent using the committee listserv, collated from innumerable lineage confirmation appointments. Nearly all RSVP'd yes.

Hours before the descendants are set to arrive, the committee members begin setting up the barbeque. Woo Tae-ha, celebrity florist, 78th generation descendant from the Gokbu Gong clan, and Committee Executive Vice President, carries three fat watermelons from his car to the pavilion. He refuses help, cradling them as if they had burst from the loins of Confucius himself. He had worked hard to find the best watermelons, knocking thirty at the grocery store before selecting the three with the finest *boom boom boom* sound—with each step, he eagerly pictures the sweet juice that will trickle down the descendants' chins.

Kong Baocui, former Olympic gold medalist ping pong player, 77th generation descendant in the main line, and Committee Secretary Extraordinaire, brings the plastic plates and disposable chopsticks, which he places next to the stacked fifth edition volumes of the Confucius family tree. The books weigh more than half a ton, and the picnic table legs tremble under the weight of lofty lineages.

Liu BingBing, competitive eater, 79th generation descendant, and Committee President-Elect, runs through her speech in her head while absentmindedly patting smooth the red and white checkerboard tablecloths. She reminds herself to thank Confucius for bringing the masses together. Then she farts loudly, a leftover reaction from her competition the night before, where she had won first place by eating 200 dumplings in twenty minutes. In deference to their political elder, Kong Baocui and Woo Tae-ha betray no more than a wince at her flatulence. She uses a corner of a tablecloth to wave the air behind her butt cheeks—her career of smashing food into her face in front of a hollering audience has eliminated all shame related to bodily functions.

As the excrement-laced air molecules dissolve, Candy Crystal Ming, American reality TV show star, 69th descendant of the same line as Kong Baocui, and Committee Treasurer, chats with Kim Shin, top hallyu star, object of desire in Korean dramas, and Committee VIP Guest. Candy Crystal Ming is explaining how the Confucius name on her resume gives her an extra boost at auditions, but Kim Shin isn't listening to the prattling American. Instead, he observes a bumblebee crawling across a rose petal, awed at witnessing real nature after months of plastic movie set gardens. Contemplative, he crosses his arms. Distracted from their tasks, everyone moans as they watch Kim Shin's forearms flex.

After four more whispered renditions of her speech and three more loud farts, Liu BingBing claps her hands. Everyone drops their tasks to gather around her. Together they turn to the portrait of Confucius hanging neatly at the top of the pavilion. Woo Tae-ha has taken the initiative to wipe away the spiderwebs in the corners of the roof overhang.

On Liu BingBing's count of three, everyone bows to Confucius, thanking him for his strong seed.

If Confucius is the thick, strong trunk of the family tree, the Confucius Genealogy Compilation Committee members are the skinny branches, and the descendants are the papery leaves, fluttering in the wind.

They settle into their reserved picnic table. Their thighs mash as they squeeze their bodies onto the benches. One of Kong Baocui's butt cheeks hangs off the side, dangling in the air.

Liu BingBing stretches her hand into the center, and the others follow. Their palm sweat obeys gravity, mingling to create a salty swamp on the scratched wood tabletop. Liu BingBing quietly thanks them all for another year's successful barbeque planning. Without their efforts, the Confucius descendants would have drifted farther around the world than they already have. The annual barbeque is imperative to bring the descendants home.

Candy Crystal Ming nods intently at the President-Elect's words, then flips her hair over her shoulder. Kim Shin, squashed next to her, catches a mouthful—he is busy marveling at the shades of green in grass, and has forgotten to keep his mouth closed around flirty women. He accidentally swallows a few strands of Candy's hair.

Later, after the guests arrive and the Teresa Teng CD has repeated itself ten times, Kim Shin will feel high off the glorious fumes of his fellow descendants. He will swallow six shots of baijiu and seven triangles of the *boom boom boom* watermelon, so that his stomach matches the dizzying euphoria in his head.

The alcohol and the fruit and the strands of Candy Crystal Ming's hair will collect near his tailbone. His intestines will ache, and he will stumble behind the clump of rose bushes, home to the crawling bumblebee he had so carefully admired, to unbuckle his leather belt, drop his silk pants, and squat atop the grass.

He will let out a fart to rival Liu BingBing's. Then he will shit it all out.

———————————————

Jade Song is a writer, art director, and artist based in New York. Her debut novel *Chlorine* is forthcoming in 2023 from William Morrow. Her writing has been nominated for numerous "best of" year anthologies and has appeared in *Electric Literature, Hobart, The Offing, Waxwing,* and elsewhere. Find her at @jadessong and jadessong.com.

LITTLE FEET

gabriella souza

HER MOTHER USED A foot mask. The package promised that in five days, the skin on her mother's feet would molt, bubble white, and peel off in shreds, *ziiiiip*. The daughter swore her mother's eventual demise began there. You never knew what was in those foot booties with their stinking chemical aroma and lack of safety information.

"Did you feel something different, Ma?" she asked.

"Tingling," was all her mother said.

By then her mother's eyes were wide like moons, pupils dilated. She appeared the opposite of dying, instead very, very awake, but her daughter knew better. The skin all over her mother's body was shedding, as if those booties had covered her entirely and she was transforming.

The end was near; the daughter called relatives, made preparations for last rites. The priest in black, pearl collar pressing against his Adam's apple, kissed the purple sash before putting it over his head while her mother gazed heavenward, like a misplaced saint waiting for ecstasy. The priest was young, but his eyes had seen everything. Still, he balked halfway through the "Hail Mary" and dropped her mother's hand. "She's like a newborn, so smooth," he said.

"Yes, that damn foot mask," her daughter said. Now, all her mother's skin had peeled off.

Her mother's sisters arrived. They didn't cry, they never did, because tears only water feelings and make them grow. By then, her mother had begun to float, suspended in mid-air like a balloon. The aunts tied a string to her mother's ankle, and, holding the other end, reached their arms upwards to touch her little feet, interlacing their fingers through her toes. "Forgive her this once," Aunt Petula said. "Let her have her vanity."

Was that it? the daughter thought. Was she jealous because her mother's attention was elsewhere? It was true, she realized; her mother's preoccupation had ceased to be earthly.

The daughter remembered the peachy pink plastic tub where she'd been bathed as an infant, also used for her mother's pedicure baths. Emory boards and pumice stones and files and bottles of acrid polish. Her mother's toes in the ocean, red rubies nestled in the sand. Once a crab, nearly translucent, visible only through his movement, side-walked up to her mother's feet and stayed right there, unmoving, just two beautiful beings in one another's presence.

The aunts left to make a casserole. The daughter stayed by her mother, holding the string. Her mother was so high her head bumped against the plaster ceiling. She looked down, her palms lifted towards the heavens. "Those beautiful feet," her mother said, gesturing to the daughter's bare toes, naked of polish, tanned from the sun. "I made them. I made every part of you."

Her mother raised her fist and broke through the ceiling. Plaster dust, wood planks, and cloudbursts of insulation rained down. The daughter slipped onto the ground, the bottoms of her feet folded together. She wiggled her toes—her mother's toes.

Gabriella Souza's work has appeared in *North American Review, The Adroit Journal, Cleaver, New South, Lunch Ticket,* and *Litro,* among others. She has received fellowships and scholarships from The Community of Writers and the Virginia Center for the Creative Arts and won the 2020 San Miguel Writers' Conference Writing Contest. She received her MFA in creative writing from Antioch University Los Angeles, where she was the recipient off an Eloise Klein Healy Scholarship. She lives in Baltimore with her husband, a dog, and two cats.

MY GRANDMOTHER'S TATTOO

joseph tepperman

WE ALL HAD HEARD about my grandmother's racecar tattoo. I know I often wondered about it, maybe even whispered of it, and my grandmother was not the kind of person you could just ask about these things. By the time I came along, she presented as this birdlike, reticent person, smiling at us from her chair, often complaining about the cold, with an unimaginable racecar-shaped illustration hidden somewhere under her layers of wool sweaters and blankets. None of us ever set eyes on it until last year, thirty minutes before her funeral would start, someone from Simonson's Mortuary asked if we wanted to see her one more time before they sealed the coffin. My mother was the only one who said yes, and when the assistant to the funeral director brought her into the side room he told her, "I'll leave you two alone," as if speaking to two living, breathing women. "It was her," my mother told us afterward, "but it wasn't her anymore," to explain why she hesitated only a second before lifting the white burial shroud which the *chevra kadisha* had tied like a loose sack about my grandmother's little wrists and feet. There it was, the tattoo, but for a long time my mother wouldn't confirm its exact place on the body. She did describe it as more or less racecar-shaped, like we all had heard, and ever since that day all sorts of theories have emerged in the family. My mother prefers to connect the tattoo to another family legend: my grandmother may have had a foster son called Pinky who they say died as young as fourteen in a street racing accident in Queens, probably hastening the end of my grandmother's first marriage. All this would have happened in the late nineteen forties shortly before my grandmother remarried and my mother and her sisters were born. But my grandmother rarely or never spoke of this Pinky. One of my aunts claims to have talked to him on the phone once when she was a child, decades ago, and she insists he survived the street racing wreck only to run away from home and reconnect with my grandmother years later. According to this version, my grandmother's first marriage at age nineteen to a certain Lithuanian named Osip ended for reasons unrelated. As if all this was not thorny enough, my own sister, following a small contingent of our cousins, takes issue with the unspoken sexism in the tattoo story: that a racecar could only symbolize the one boy of the family, and that only the loss of the one boy would merit this secret lifelong grief from our grandmother (i.e. she'd get a tattoo for Pinky but not, for example, for her daughter Naomi who died of cancer). Personally, I keep a more skeptical tack on all this, but I don't expect my family to listen, and it's always a shock when someone outside the family cares either way. My mother confirmed the tattoo, and I have no real reason to doubt her. Why would she make it up? Even in my grandmother's lifetime, the tattoo rumor may have originated with my mother herself, so she is our best or only source for it. But, whether she can say for a fact it was supposed to be a racecar, who knows. Assuming the profile view my mother sketched for us—two racing tires, two windows, a hood, some sort of a roof—rotated ninety degrees we could take the same shape for the first letter of my grandmother's name (Bess), or for my grandfather's (Benny). Flipped one hundred and eighty degrees it becomes a heart, or an infinity sign, and on and on like this, in endless Rorschach inkblot variations. From here I'm inclined to push a more basic question: was it in fact a tattoo and not some kind of a birthmark, a liver spot? Today tattoos can mean anything and nothing, but for a woman of my grandmother's generation a mark on the skin screamed only *prostitute* or *Auschwitz survivor*, two things my grandmother wasn't. If to a certain degree I've accepted my mother's and aunt's versions, and I finally agreed to go with them—yes, we all got the same tattoo, in the same spot, from a family friend who does tattoos—then I can't justify it except to say it's only to know, to know once and for all—maybe not what the tattoo meant to my grandmother, but to find out what a racecar tattoo could mean to me, or to anyone. We all laughed and cried so hard that day, to see all of us with that little racecar blob. I know it made me think a lot about my grandmother, and about other things harder to put into words. And if the original wasn't a racecar—and if it never was a tattoo!—then let my own daughters, if I ever have daughters, puzzle over mine. But, look: the whole time we've been talking, one of the hummingbirds that lives in the hedge at the back door has sat perched, wiping clean its little beak on the sill of the window, and now it's gone.

Joseph Tepperman "works in a dreamscape and the slippery world of memory" (USA Today). His plays and opera libretti have been performed internationally, including at REDCAT in Los Angeles and the Stockholm Fringe Fest. *The Los Angeles Times* called him "a mash-up of Gertrude Stein and Lewis Carroll."

FEATHERLIGHT
pamela nakki tetteh

HERE'S THE TRUTH ABOUT Nneka:

i.

Her name isn't really Nneka. She does not know this. Not even the radio-clutching, chain-smoking grandfather who raised her knows her name. The only person who knows is a woman Nneka finds in a photograph one afternoon when she is fifteen and curious. The photograph is hidden between two encyclopedias on her grandfather's bookshelf. It feels featherlight in her hands and looks faded, soft with age. It is of a woman with Nneka's face, braids tumbling down her bare shoulders. Nneka looks at it and feels: the blurred edges of her memory sharpening, coming into focus. She *knows* who this is in the photograph, and is shocked that she has not thought to ask of her, all these years. She goes to find her grandfather and he tells her the story of a baby, abandoned on his doorstep, by a daughter he hadn't seen in years. He finds a letter, received months after the abandoning. The letter itself is unimportant to Nneka; it is the return address that draws her, a house in Accra, Ghana.

The next morning, the grandfather finds his safe open, and a fair few thousand Naira and Nneka, gone.

ii.

In Ghana, one can learn a lot by simply being, blending seamlessly into the background. No one takes much notice of a skinny girl hawking a tray of oranges. No one minds that she passes the same street everyday, asking questions about the large house with the high, pale blue walls. No one asks any questions of her, *past how much?*

She lives in a shanty with two other girls she met at the bus station the day she arrived in Ghana. She keeps her money in a purse tied around her waist and has learned to wake at the slightest sound. The girls, Adwoa and Naa, ask no questions of her and she offers nothing. She has one goal: to find the woman with her face. She finds the address on the letter easily. It is a prominent house, owned by the prominent Adjemans: retired colonel and his beautiful Nigerian wife.

So she goes, oranges on tray, tray on head, everyday, to the street, walking up and down its length, calling out *buy your sweet orange here*, making customers out of the women whose shops dot the street and the men who always seem to be around, lounging around under the shade of trees, talking about 'the good old days'. Blending in. Waiting.

iii.

And then one afternoon, the house's gates open and a car crawls out. Nneka, who is about calling it a day, stops and turns. The car passes by, slow enough for her to see the woman with her face, in the backseat, older now, colder than the woman in the photo. The woman too, looks out of the car window and sees Nneka. Shock purples the woman's face as she whispers, a single sound that is ferried from her lips to Nneka's ears alone: *Nkem.*

Pamela Naaki Tetteh is a writer and editor living and working in Accra, Ghana.

NONNA FRANCESCA OF TE WHAREPŌURI STREET

catherine trundle

HER HALLWAY IS A vein of darkened wood. It's shrouded by a plastic bead curtain. Her husband cannot pass through unless she parts it with her hair. It's intentional. How it mimics a string of fake pearls, a rosary, the sound of her undressing.

Her house is arranged to expose her up in slow succession. The front room thresholds the grandchildren like piano keys. We always knew the ghost could not live there. Glass figurines sit on glass shelves within glass-doored cabinets.

By the age of ten, her name was clipped by two letters. She gave them to me like coins. Her street is no longer wide enough for a Chief. She stakes herself against the front fence, close enough to touch twelve eggs passing, under a Greek woman's arm. Her ankles grow thick like hooves.

Her kitchen juts out into the back yard, sinking with the green smell of tomatoes. She layers the floor with linoleum and concretes over the grass. Sat at her table, we watch as she bends, holds her loose apron back, strikes the oven with a match. We all hear it: the gas pop and catch, a volcano spitting black rocks against blue fishing boats.

Slowly, her memories silt, run her aground. But her hands still move, a code of gastronomical life lessons. No amount of garlic will fix certain hearts. When she was younger, she never sat while her sons ate. Now the great grandchildren, stalky and thin-skinned, find her compressed in the armchair, fingers tapping, mouth ajar. They venture forward, peer inside her, looking for the ghost.

Catherine Trundle is a writer from Wellington New Zealand. Her poetry and flash fiction have appeared in a range of Australasian publications, including Landfall, Not Very Quiet, Flash Frontier, Takahē and Poetry New Zealand Yearbook.

I-PLY

nicole tsuno

OBAASAN ONLY WEARS JEWELRY once a year, to the Japanese Association Bingo. This time, she selects a gold-banded ring, four teeth around a black stone. As our family drives through blonde hills, she flags her jeweled hand out the window, displacing air. From the backseat, I ask if one day I can have her ring.

She turns around, locks her hands over my knees. "You won't want it," she says.

The gathering takes place in a dirt lot along a cliffside, fifteen long pine tables, sanded by paper plates and salted elbows. In the distance, waves find their shape and make their way to shore. When the water splits on the rocks, it froths, like the crackle of spit when a word takes time to speak.

Already the boys with tight stomachs have been dispatched to rearrange the tables, creating one long corridor between them. The prize table is strategically placed at the back to discourage dining and dashing, a passive-aggressive reminder of what you would be forgoing. Bulk purchases throne atop it: tubs of lavender-scented detergent, towers of off-brand ClingWrap, six-packs of disinfectant wipes. The top prize is always a giant thing of toilet paper, jumbo rolls, the kind that you find in warehouses and stingy restaurants, as thin as tracing paper. Last year, *Obaasan's* friend won and so she guards the table smugly, dimpling her chin at the rest of us who haven't been so lucky.

Before sitting, we load our plates, their bottoms flexing under the burden. I only select foods that I can find in *Obaasan's* refrigerator: triangles of *onigiri, inarizushi* that my parents call pillows because it's simpler that way. At the table, I pull off their tofu cases and let them go slippery in my palm.

At the front, bingo balls rattle around in their cage like loose teeth after the undercut. The ball collector wings his hands to catch each orb as it tumbles forth. He calls out the numbers and presents them to the woman beside him, the second set of eyes, who confirms his truth to the crowd and records it in a notebook. After that, anyone can ask to reference the notebook. If the two leaders are caught colluding, they can be ousted, banned from next year's event. Even though for many the United States is not their first country, they understand checks and balances.

Children aren't allowed to participate so we sit wedged between our parents. Next to me, a group of boys fit watermelon rinds to their teeth. I writhe free until I can see *Obaasan's* bingo card, translucent red buttons pebbling its grid. When I tug at her arm, she ignores me but in a way I respect, like it's the apocalypse and I've already been shot in the leg.

After a half hour, when their parents are no longer able to still them, the children funnel out to the beach. *Ojiisan* understands the pressures of single girlhood and hands me a kite with bent stripes like a prism. It works. I hold the kite against my body, water lapping at my feet. The boys notice and try to win my favor by throwing rocks into the ocean, their faces like fruit going soft in the heat. At last, one gives me three bottles of Yakult he stowed in his pockets before they ran out. I applaud him for his foresight and hand him the spool. As the first drink runs syruppy down my throat, the kite launches skyward. When I get back up to the bingo tables, it nosedives out of sight.

I don't realize my error until it's too late, a colony of women surrounding *Obaasan* with bright voices, my father lofting the loot of toilet paper into the car. It's so big that I have to sit on it for the whole ride, and no matter how I adjust, my butt cheeks fall into its shallows.

At home, *Obaasan* punctures the plastic with her fingernail and eases it down like a second skin. I hand her each roll and she feeds them through the frame of the cupboard, stacking them as carefully as you would CDs.

Obaasan gives me a roll of my own for my assistance, and I accept because sometimes love operates in returns. I cuff my wrist with the roll and promise to use it well. She cradles my face, ring cold against my jaw, her eyes fattening in the light. She lets her hair out of its clip and takes off the ring, nestling it in a felt-bottomed box. When I look inside, the black stone glitters like a hard body of a cockroach.

Nicole Tsuno is a chronically ill writer living near Seattle, Washington. Her work appears or is forthcoming in *HAD, No Contact, The Offing, Passages North, Wigleaf,* and elsewhere. She was a runner-up in *Salt Hill's* first annual Arthur Flowers Flash Fiction Contest and is a fiction reader for *Split Lip.*

WHEN MAMÁ'S APRON CATCHES fire, my first reaction is to grab Mamá's body and share the fire with her.

Pimientos en nogada is a dish that people eat in México at weddings and important occasions. Mamá is set on making it on our special day since she wants to prove to us, but mostly to herself, that despite her curled fingers and the ache in her knees, she can still cook. The night before the fire, she makes the nogada. She leaves the unpeeled nuts soaking with milk, mashes the nuts with fresh white cheese, a pinch of sugar, cinnamon, salt, and white wine. The mixture, after straining, is fragrant and creamy.

Mamá starts the dish with the fire, a set and steady flame that turns blue at the tips. She puts the pimientos on the stove. "How long on each side?" I ask, half looking at her and half looking at my phone. "You have to look to see," she says, her bare hands turning the pimiento to the other side. Although they must be hot, she doesn't say so.

"Mamá!" I yell, far too late, as the fabric of her hand-painted apron she had bought in México D.F. gets consumed by the flame.

Two days later, when we come back from the hospital, the nogada is still sitting on the table with the rest of the pimientos all over the floor, some blackened and some uncooked—the remnants of our kitchen incident, as Mamá would call it. Roberto, my soon-to-be husband, in the rush of paramedics and sirens, hadn't put the food back in the fridge. I touch my stomach, which is covered in bandages, and think about flies.

Mamá, who rests in bed days after the incident, predicts that rain will appear mid-ceremony and soak us all.

"Rain is a good omen," I tell her, my fingers covered in the thick white odorless matter I use for her stomach burns.

"How did it feel for you?" she says, trying to sit up after I am done with her stomach. "I didn't feel it," I lie while carefully applying the salve to my middle, which is covered in purple blisters. "My skin must have been numb from the pain."

She turns to the wall, smiling as if she were seeing it for the first time. A flash of the flames engulfing the carefully hand-painted flowers on her apron comes to my head. The same flames that traveled to my cotton shirt.

I had poured a pot of water on both of us. I can still hear the panic in her raspy smoker's voice. The way that her voice addressed me in one word: "Corre," her delirious tone convinced that we could escape the flame.

I removed the blackened apron and her shirt first, afraid that it would get stuck to her skin. My hands acted quickly as howls of pain escaped my mouth.

"The wallpaper. It's starting to crack," Mamá says.

I nod without looking. Every night after the fire, the smell of our leathering gets stuck to my nose.

Roberto, who comes to visit Mamá every day, swallowing his I-told-you-so about Mamá in the kitchen, Mamá at the stove, Mamá doing anything, is the first to be against the idea of postponing the wedding.

"I can't wear the same dress," I say, thinking about how the corsé will press against my skin.

"We will buy you another one."

"My mother will not be able to go to the beach. Her skin could get infected."

"So we marry here. Problem solved," he says, sitting on the couch and putting his feet up on the table since Mamá is in her room and can't move to tell him that he is not an animal and he is not in his own house.

I sit on his lap. Kissing his forehead, his cheeks, telling him not to press on my stomach—not now and not in the six months that it will take to heal. We start kissing, and for a while we don't check on Mamá, who after going to sleep, will miss the start of the rainy season that will stay long after the pimiento season is over and long after Roberto and I get married in the rain, my baggy wedding dress and his going out shoes soaked by the aguacero and the water that leaks from the top of the house, Mamá with her flimsy blue umbrella and with her water-resistant camera will take blurry pictures that will mark one of the first bad September storms.

When Mamá goes to sleep that night, I cover Mamá's burns in the thick mixture. In the dark room, I hear Roberto calling for me. The taxi is here, he says. I lift Mamá's shirt. My fingers get lost in her tender skin.

By next September, our stomachs will burst in a sea of scars.

María Alejandra Barrios Vélez is a Pushcart-nominated writer born in Barranquilla, Colombia. She has an MA in Creative Writing from The University of Manchester and currently lives in Brooklyn. Her stories have been published in places such as *Hobart Pulp, Reservoir Journal, Cosmonauts Avenue, Jellyfish Review, Lost Balloon, Shenandoah Literary, Vol.1 Brooklyn, El Malpensante, Moon City Review, Fractured Lit,* and *SmokeLong Quarterly.* Her work is forthcoming in *Flash Frog, Pidgeonholes* and *The Offing.* She was the 2020 *SmokeLong* Flash Fiction Fellow and her work has been supported by organizations such as Vermont Studio Center, Caldera Arts Center, and the New Orleans Writing Residency.

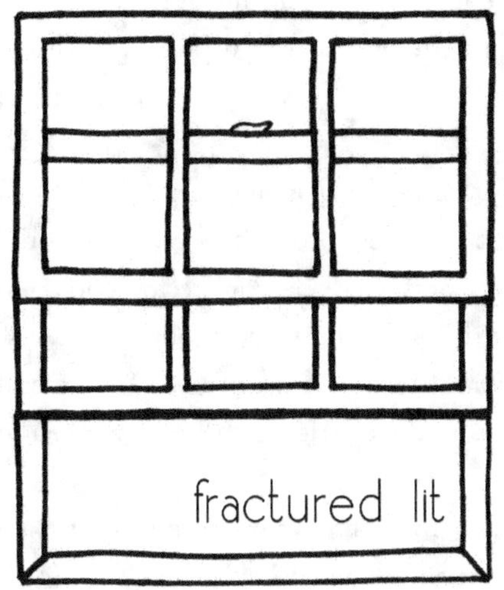

THINGS NEVER STAY WARM

maría alejandra barrios véleza

I WEAR MY DEAD sister's lipstick around the house like Grandma told me to. It leaves my lips dry and the shade doesn't suit me, it's purple and dark and velvety, against her golden-brown skin luminous and edgy. On me it looks tired. Most things do. But I wear it anyway to sit in the kitchen while I do the trick that Grandma taught me to stir the soup with my mind. Grandma was a witch. She turned the neighbour's hair red, one hair at a time. The neighbour didn't notice at first, but she started to see it around the house and she even started thinking her husband was having an affair. One, two, three red hairs in the drain. Soon, all her hair was red like the autumn leaves.

When my sister died, Grandma gave me a bag with all her clothes. She told me to wear them often and with oomph, like my sister would have. She assured me her scent of sweet candied apples and vanilla cloves would lead her back home. But I never see her. Most days, I imagine her perky voice on the phone when she was still alive and still loved me: "Sis, you are always busy. You never have time for me, your lazy sister who lives at home with Grandma." and I would laugh and tell her not to be silly. She would find her own way. But back then, all she wanted was to be with the baker's son who couldn't bake baguettes. And I, with nothing else to do when I went home to visit, would sneak out with him to throw rocks at the shore late at night, drinking mezcal and keeping the neighborhood cats company. He was the only man my sister ever loved because she liked the way he pronounced words with a vaguely French accent. And she liked how his hazel hair was always too long on the sides while sitting heavily on the top. She liked his knitted sweaters too and she liked how they always smelled musky, sparingly washed. Sis never forgave me and she never figured out a way to move out of Grandma's house, she died, and Grandma, not ready to live without her, followed.

And now it is only me, who came back home to try and sell the house when there was no one around anymore to shut my computer down and tell me, "enough, silly girl, sit here and eat some cinnamon cookies while they are still warm." Things never stay warm. Which is why, in this empty home I wear her cheap purple lipstick and sing the song that Grandma taught me to sing to turn on the heater using only my words.

The house feels warm and inviting now, and the leaves are changing. They both loved the golden light and crunchy apples, and although I don't know how to bake a pie they would like, I close my eyes like Grandma taught me and say the words that open her recipe book and flip the pages until it lands on Pumpkin Pie. The cupboards open. Flour, sugar, butter, a can of pumpkin and a whisk appear in front of me. I stand up and start to stir. I'm not in the mood for lighting a candle for them in the little altar I built with all their little keychains they liked to collect of places they would visit one day.

Not tonight. Tonight, I am in the mood for eating mediocre pumpkin pie and sitting on the couch while I hear the screaming cats and the serenade that the baker does two doors down, in the hopes I'll hear how much he's hurting. Sis, I say just in case she's listening, I never cared that much about him. I think he stinks. Like dust, cigarettes and cheap whiskey. The kitchen window opens, and the cold breeze makes my chapped, dry face burn. Grandma would know what to do for that. "Sis," I say, but the wind hits the window and closes it back.

María Alejandra Barrios Vélez is a Pushcart-nominated writer born in Barranquilla, Colombia. She has an MA in Creative Writing from The University of Manchester and currently lives in Brooklyn. Her stories have been published in places such as *Hobart Pulp*, *Reservoir Journal*, *Cosmonauts Avenue*, *Jellyfish Review*, *Lost Balloon*, *Shenandoah Literary*, *Vol.1 Brooklyn*, *El Malpensante*, *Moon City Review*, *Fractured Lit*, and *SmokeLong Quarterly*. Her work is forthcoming in *Flash Frog*, *Pidgeonholes* and *The Offing*. She was the 2020 *SmokeLong* Flash Fiction Fellow and her work has been supported by organizations such as Vermont Studio Center, Caldera Arts Center, and the New Orleans Writing Residency.

WE LEARNED THAT LIGHTNING is drawn to the homes of those who carry money too freely in their pockets, for example. A broken appliance is a sign that an important lie has been recently told. Spoiled food may indicate a promise that was never intended to be kept.

A power outage means a forgotten debt or promise. A tooth chipped on a spoon may coincide with fantasies of financial impropriety or fraud. There was no mystery to why we learned these things. Our parents told them to make the good times a little harder, or the hard times just a little bit worse. What is security but another opportunity to be creative in our fear.

My sister and I had trouble in school knowing that a child with double joints was conceived beyond the walls of the family home. A child whose rashes rise easily was conceived during business hours when work was left undone. The child who can hold their breath for unnaturally long will marry young and unhappily. A girl born with hair will only find her first love in a married man. A key whose owner has never thought darkly of a loved one will never break in a lock. Every smell a child gave off at a slumber party gave my mother some hint that misery was coming to their parents' personal business.

Our school was shaped like a big letter H and so illnesses were frequent. A small tornado formed in the dust in front of us one winter as we drank deeply from our juice boxes. It threw holly branches into the faces of the young kids in prayer group. We knew some teachers must be having an affair. The building should have been shaped like an L or an A, my father said, should have faced north, where the wind would not ruin it. It was not where everything went truly wrong but we knew it was a start.

A videotape returned un-rewound will take with it forever a minor memory or routine joy. A videotape never returned will lead robbers to a loved one's door, which is how Deborah ended up shot through the calf. Each new book never opened will keep the owner's soul trapped an extra day below the earth before Christ turned his faucet and sent the souls where they would go.

My sister almost escaped but had to drop out of nursing school when her toenails grew inwards and got too infected to walk. My first wife loved another man before me. I drove to her boyfriend's house when they were away seeing the leaves on semester break and I hid food to rot in the quiet space under his home. Under the fig tree I buried a set of plastic barbecue tongs, shining and toxic, the kind you can buy for less than a dollar.

I didn't need to do much more. If you leave the body of an animal unburied on a rival's land it will lead to luck diseases appearing in their children -- poor nightsight, hollow teeth, the bad kind of dandruff, scoliosis, mirror fear, number problems, uncooperative bowels, sleep until midday. He never got sick but after school he moved to another country whose name I remembered for years.

Businesses facing east will be the first to close during global economic lag. Businesses who offer bathroom access to the public will have poor luck in their lifetime but will be blessed in endeavours undertaken after their collapse. My father never filled his gas tank all the way and so his clients fell to unpaid debts and other unscrupulous ways. He used to cut his hair and beard with scissors meant for heavy fabrics, dreaming darkly, sleepwalking.

The day my sister told our mother that loving a man she didn't marry was not the reason parking spots seemed to hide from them even on quiet grey days, my mother missed the brake pedal and put the car through a sunglasses stall. From then I was the only one my sister ever called, another escapee. Not long ago her son died in childbirth. See his ghost still tangled in the cell phone towers by the women's hospital, the ones they built too close.

Jack Vening is a writer of short fiction and comedy from Ngunnawal country, Australia. His writing has appeared in *Hobart*, *The Lifted Brow*, *The Nervous Breakdown* and many places elsewhere, and his fiction newsletter *Small Town Grievances* goes out to about a thousand mainly European strangers every few weeks.

MY SISTERS AND I

pim wangtechawat

5. WE DRIVE AND DRIVE until we find a place where we can park and drink. We order nachos and onion rings and glasses of beer and vodka. I would prefer whiskey, but I have to drive. We are all a little jaded, a little short-changed, a little lost in the big city, in the whirlwind of early adulthood. Our twenties are more unkind than films and tv shows have promised them to be. We think we are grown ups now.

    (sort of, a little, maybe not at all.)

4. We talk about random things. Why men aren't like the men we imagine in our heads. Why we don't keep in touch anymore with the people we love. Why we need to get out of here—find new places to visit and appreciate. We mix the guacamole, the salsa, the cheese. We spin it all around and we laugh. We find nobody else funny anymore.

    (and if we do, we don't say it.)

3. We talk about love and loss. We laugh about other girls because we are bitter and we've had a couple of drinks. Yes, the dull ache is still there, we say. The dull ache which means the want, the longing, the pain, the missing something we never had. Maybe we will be alone forever. Maybe we won't find anyone else. The future does not look too bright.

    (if we think about it too much, we wouldn't be here.)

2. We take pictures in front of the bathroom against the brown bricked walls, and we walk outside with our arms wrapped around each other back to the car. At least we have us. Us—far away, close together, always orbiting around each other, always crying about one thing or

another. We stroll through the aisles in the supermarket and share stories that we don't tell ourselves when we are happy.

(maybe we'll forget them if we tell them enough.)

I. We blast music as loud as we can in the car on the way home. Sing the songs at the top of our lungs. Who cares if they are sad songs—the ones we listen to when we want a good cry? Music tastes different when it is shared by more than one person. We don't say it out loud, but we know that we are all missing people who do not exist anymore.

Are we in love? Yes. Maybe a little. With ghosts and shadows and the notes that have disappeared into the warm, soft night.

(it is better to be broken together than not to be broken at all.)

Pim Wangtechawat's short stories, poems, and articles have been published in various websites, literary magazines and journals, including the *Mekong Review, the Nikkei Asian Review, Den of Geek,* and *YesPoetry.* She has performed her poetry at events in Edinburgh hosted by Shoreline of Infinity and the Scottish BAME Writers Network, and has given talks about her writing at Chulalongkorn University and Ruamrudee International School. Her debut novel, *The Moon Represents My Heart,* will be published by OneWorld Publications in the UK in Spring 2023, with Italian rights bought by Keller Editore.

IT IS MORNING, EARLY. Sunk on a mattress. The tube isn't running or she'd feel the joists shaking. If she was home.

She's not home.

She opens her eyes. Furrowed mattress, damp with cold. Fag-scarred carpet. An ashtray, half empty, a bottle, rolling. Smirnoff. How did she get here? Swam through the usual damn portal. Her body blushes. Would she recognise him? Nope.

She thinks she can make it in to work today. She ought to try. There is no sign of her clothes or her travel card or keys. She pulls the duvet around herself and crawls to the window, peers under the blinds. Streetlights still lit. She can't remember the journey.

The glass mists. It is that cold.

A old man below is walking his dog, slow steps on glittering tarmac. She watches him tug the little white dog behind him. He doesn't look up.

The streetlights blink off.

She has to pee.

All she can hear is the drub of bass from an upstairs flat.

'Hello?' she calls, shivering, wondering where she flung her clothes. Whoever she came home with must have gone for a pint of milk. They never have milk.

On the left, a bathroom. Washbasin. Loo. No toothbrush, no towels. A cracked and gnarled carcass of soap.

She shivers as the alcohol makes its apologies. The skin in her mouth sticks to itself. She doesn't fancy drinking from the tap but she cups her hands anyway. When he gets back he'll ask for her number. She'll make something up. Perhaps give him Paul's. The thought of some nightclubber calling her boss makes her giggle, and then she shivers again.

An alcove with microwave, kettle and sink. Fat smelly bin-bag. She prods it with her toe, thinking of a steaming polystyrene mug of tea in her hands with longing.

She pulls the duvet around her shoulders like a fat pashmina, returns to the lounge. Bare. Floorboards. Books, dusty old volumes you can't imagine anyone reading, propped between house-bricks. She opens one. *Trial of so-and-so*, by some Frenchman. Words dance a gibberish jig. She shuts its thin pages before she's sick.

Front door with letterbox. Deadlocked.

From the bedroom window she can still see the footprints of the old man and his dog picked out in the frost but as she watches they blur and fade.

She pulls on the sash with gym-toned arms. The frame is clogged with gloss-paint but finally she heaves it an inch and yells.
>*Hey!*
>Nothing.
>She'd think herself dead and in limbo except for the beat of the music.

Thump thump.

When Persephone went to the Underworld she ate six seeds.

She tries to remember when she last ate anything. Maybe he'll bring back a Big Mac with the milk. It's the kind of thing they do. They can usually cook one signature meal, but to sample it you have to go through all the rigmarole. *What's your name, what do you do, are you single, what music do you like, what are your fucking HOBBIES*. Only *then* are you presented with a spag bol, a glass of merlot and a sweaty hand on the thigh. She could cry, really, thinking about it.

Why couldn't this freak leave a note like everyone else?

She walks to the front door and kneels, wedges open the letter box with her fists and yells through the gap

'I'm locked in!'

Silence.

The music has clicked off.

Footsteps, pounding the walkway.

Through the letterbox, she sees thighs in a baggy tracksuit and high-tops, their fat tongues poking out at her.

'Help,' she whispers.

A waft of caries, skunk and lager.

Eyes, red-rimmed, glacial.

'I'm listening to my fucking music.'

Man's voice, London accent, chewing gum.

'We mind our own here. Shut it.'

A dirt rimmed thumb, close, almost poking her in the eye. He's holding a lighter and he flashes it in front of her, on/off, so close she imagines hair sizzling.

She pulls away. Her stomach spasms. She hopes it's not her period. Imagine that!

She should go back to sleep and wait.

It will come out right in the end.

It always does.

———————————————

Cate West graduated with an MA in Creative Writing from Manchester Metropolitan University in 2019. She lives and works in the Midlands, UK, teaching Creative Writing, and was selected for Writing West Midlands' Room 204 development scheme in 2021. Recent publications include short stories with *Nightjar Press, Lunate, A Coup of Owls, Last Girls Club* and *The Amphibian*, as well as *Janus Literary*. Cate is editing her debut novel. @c8west.

I REMEMBER ONCE BEING sat on the sofa at home. It was early-ish in the morning in summer, maybe 8 or 9am, and the sun was streaming in through the south-facing window onto the big mahogany table we had in the living room. Must have been 200 years old that table. Joined in so many many meals with so many generations of people. Imagine.

Anyway, we had had a party around that very same table about four days before. Someone's birthday, and there was this big glass cake stand with a glass lid on it. Really nice way to present cakes and stuff you know, makes any crap old two-pound cake from the shop look grand and ornate. We had long understood the power of presentation, of context I suppose. Meals can look so depressing when you're poor, especially celebration meals you know? Some damp biscuits and a sad deflated cake on a paper plate. Happy birthday.

Anyway, there was a slice or two of this cake left over, and it had been left in the glass cake stand in the sun for four days. The inside of the glass lid was drenched, dripping with condensation. All the water from inside that cheap cake, drawn out by the heat of the sun coming through the window. The slices were all melted inside though you could barely see them because, like I say, the whole lid was covered with droplets. We kept those slices there for weeks. Couldn't bear to throw them away. It was like a terrarium or something in there, every day we would gather around to observe how the landscape was changing inside. To see what would grow there and which tribes of green and red fluff would take over and spread, making bets about how long it would take for the two different camps of mould on opposite sides of the slice to meet in the middle.

After a few weeks it really was getting quite extreme I guess, in terms of what most people would care to have as a centrepiece for their dining table, and someone put it in the bin. I never found out who, I just came in one day and it was gone and the cake stand was sparkling clean back in the cupboard. I was surprised by the force of my anger and feelings of loss. It reminded me that other people get to decide what we can find beautiful or fascinating, and how long we can enjoy our fringe pleasures for.

I thought about going straight back out the door to buy another rubbish cake to restart the whole process again but it wouldn't be the same would it. Like when you break up with someone and get back together, or you lose your phone and try to recreate all of your favourite photos that you lost: "no look a bit more over your shoulder, yeah like that, now give me a carefree laugh whilst you raise your glass. No, you're not relaxed enough. Your hair is too short now it's not going to work." So I convinced myself that there was dignity in loss, told myself that there was something poetic about resigning myself to it, not fighting back or recreating or resisting in any way. That tells you a lot doesn't it. So, I guess that's why I'm here really. In a way.

"Right," said the job centre representative. "So, redundancy then was it?"

"Yeah." She said, and shifted uncomfortably in her seat.

Alice Wilson is a PhD researcher at the University of York. Her thesis looks at women who build their own tiny houses. Wilson is also the co-director of social enterprise OpHouse, a community-led housing developer. Her nonfiction writing has appeared in *The Conversation*, *The Egalitarian*, and *The Women's Budget Group*. Her fiction has also been published in *Ruminate Magazine*.

I.

A MAN, WHOM I call sir, is trying to decide which necklace to get his wife: a teardrop amethyst on a thin silver chain or a gold lariat with an open circle. To help him make a choice, I've laid both necklaces side by side on a black velvet pad.

"I still don't know," he says, pressing his fingers down on the bright display case that separates us. After he leaves the store, I'll Windex away the smudges he's left on the glass, but for now, I pretend to not notice.

"Could you try it on?" he asks, pointing to the amethyst.

This is the part I dread, the part where I feel as though I, too, am for sale, but I hide it.

"Absolutely!" I say, picking up the necklace.

Once I fasten it in place, I stretch my neck and look him in the eyes, searching for his approval. I move slightly left, then slightly right so he can see the necklace from different angles. He squints as he imagines what it will look like on his wife.

"I'll take it," he finally says.

Although my coworkers and I joke about the awkwardness of trying on jewelry for the men who shop at the store, we always oblige because we know it means we'll make the sale. Once a man has you try on the item, he's already decided he's going to buy the piece.

2.

A man in his late 20s wearing a suit that hangs on him wants to get a sense of what the pearl drop earrings will look like on his newlywed wife.

I hold one earring up to my ear, but he tells me that won't work. I'm too dark.

"She's very pale," he says, "with light blue eyes."

I'm both relieved and offended that I'm not the right model for the job, but I don't let on.

"Alice," I call out gently to my white coworker, "would you mind assisting us?"

She looks up from the cash register and smiles. "I'd be happy to," she says.

After she puts the earrings on, she shakes her head so they dangle and says "ahhh" as if she's just performed a magic trick. Her joy looks so genuine that I can't tell if it's real or not.

The man buys not only the earrings but a matching pearl bracelet as well. I put them in a single box and finish it with a silk bow as he and Alice chat about restaurants in the neighborhood.

"I know she'll love it," Alice says when she hands him the bag. She says it with a touch of longing, as though she wishes she had a husband like him. This part I can tell is fake.

3.

A boy—technically he's a man, but to me, he is a boy—has brought his buddies with him to buy an engagement ring. I want to tell him he's too young to get married, but instead, I help him pick out something that fits within his budget—a knife-edge solitaire with an imitation diamond.

"Thank you, ma'am," he says as I ring him up.

"You're very welcome," I say.

Congratulations is on the tip of my tongue, but I can't bring myself to say it.

4.

The only piece of jewelry my husband ever gave me was the garnet ring he presented when he proposed. He said it was his grandmother's. I thought it looked plain and cheap, but I kept this to myself. I didn't want to seem ungrateful.

Eventually, the ring grew on me. I liked the deep wine color, and that it looked so delicate on my hand. I preferred it to my thick silver wedding band, which at first I thought looked sophisticated, but over time looked cold.

I wore the garnet ring every day for over a decade, not for my husband, or as a symbol of marriage. I wore it for my delight.

5.

Twice a year, a scientist comes to town for a conference and each time he stops by the store to pick out something for his wife. He doesn't need a model. He likes to hold the piece of jewelry close to his face and rub it between his thumb and index finger. Sometimes he asks if he can take it to the window to see what it looks like under natural light.

When I first started working at the store, I thought his gift-giving tradition was so romantic. I'd imagine his wife holding her hair up with one hand as he helped her put on a necklace—his warm breath against her skin. But now, five years later, I'm suspicious that his gifts are motivated by guilt—an affair—not faithful desire.

Experience and time have cooled and hardened me.

6.

On the steps outside the courthouse, on the day we finalize the divorce, I try to give the garnet ring back to my now ex-husband. It seems like the right thing to do since it belonged to his grandmother.

"That's OK," he says. "You keep it."

I don't know if he's being kind or cruel. Maybe both: he wants me to have a memento, but also know that the ring isn't valuable to him. Giving the ring back was supposed to give me closure. I assumed he would thank me. I slip it back into my purse and feel sorry for it, as though it were a living thing—an unwanted child.

I feel the urge to hug him one last time, but stop myself because it feels inappropriate to touch. In a few weeks, he'll propose to another woman with a ring I'll never see.

———

Naira Wilson is a writer and editor based in the Washington, D.C., metro area. Her writing has appeared in places such as *Wigleaf, Typehouse Literary Magazine, Nymphs, Dynamis Journal,* and *Scribble.* She is currently working on her first novel.

THIS ISN'T ANYTHING

francine witte

WHEN BURLEY COMES HOME late every night, I tell myself he's busy. He tells me that, too, but I believe it more when I say it.

Now, I do understand. He's been busy before, but this is a busy with a smell on it.

This particular night, it's 9 p.m. exactly. He comes in all fed even though I made pot roast. The pot roast that burned while I waited for him, the flat char of it still coating the air. Burley whooshes himself into the shower. Careful to take off his jeans and shirt and ball them into a wad. "Best to leave those," he says. "I stopped for gas, and some jerk spilled coffee all over me."

I wait till the shower is running to give his shirt a good sniff. Not a hint of coffee anywhere. Nothing is wet. And then I go for his jeans—in the pocket, a matchbook. Red with the black outline of two lovers, two cocktail glasses about to clink.

After the shower and him toweling himself off. "Whatta day," and "I shoulda called."

I hold up the matchbook. "Oh this," he says. "This isn't anything. Guy at work was passing them out. New place opened up down the street."

Burley says, work's gonna be a bear this week, just so I know. He likes to compare everything to animals. Guys at work are a bunch of donkeys. Me, I'm a cute little cat.

And I am. Curled up and patient, like my mother taught me to be. This is what men like, she said. And really, I don't mind. Although Burley forgets sometimes that a cat needs attention. A tickle on the back of its neck, a rake of fingers through the hair. Later, in bed, I nuzzle up, kitten-like. He turns on his side. "Tired," is all he says.

I whisper, "hey I'd love to go to that matchbook place with you. Have drinks like we used to." I say this as his breath becomes even with sleep. I wobble his shoulder, and say it again, but he doesn't move. He is a lost mountain to me now.

Something that isn't hunger exactly gets me up on my feet and into the fridge. I pull out the leftover pot roast, burnt as it is. I kitten my face into it. Nuzzle and nibble and suck. Soon I go from tame little cat to feral. I crouch down to the floor and start gnawing like a lion on one of the nature shows I watch when Burley isn't home. And then, without a sound, Burley just like that in the doorway. The swell of the fluorescent light overhead, sudden and sharp.

Burley leans over and struggles the pot roast away from my mouth. A look on his face like he caught me kissing another man. He lifts me to my feet. He flinches as my fingernails dig into his shoulders. Any harder and there would be blood. "What's wrong with you," he says with a look on his face like one of those animal trainers who realize they've gone too far. "I told you," he says, "none of this is anything," He grabs a dishtowel, wipes the grease off my chin and kisses me down to the floor.

Next morning, the mess from last night all over the kitchen and Burley humming from the bathroom. The pot roast, the dishtowel, the spot on the floor with naked us rubbed into it. I think about asking Burley now to tell me about the gas station. *What was the feel of it, I want to say. Who was this guy? Was he bigger than you? Was the coffee hot? Why weren't you burned?* I clean everything up and put on a pot of coffee, the smell of it filling the room. The same smell that wasn't anywhere on Burley's shirt, and when Burley comes in and kisses me on the cheek, pulls back and winks at me, I feel a million questions on my tongue, a lion's growl forming in my throat…

Francine Witte is the author of the flash fiction collection, *Dressed All Wrong for This* (Blue Light Press), three flash fiction chapbooks, *The Wind Twirls Everything* (Musclehead Press) *Cold June* (Ropewalk Press) *The Cake, The Smoke, The Moon* (ELJ Editions), and a novella-in-flash, *The Way of the Wind* (Ad Hoc Press). Her flash fiction is included in numerous journals and anthologies, including *Best Small Fictions* 2020, the W.W. Norton anthologies *New Micro* and *Flash Fiction America*. She is the flash fiction editor for *FLASH BOULEVARD* and *The South Florida Poetry Journal*. She lives in New York City.

SYNONYM FOR TREE ON FIRE

becca yenser

LATELY YOU FIND FEATHERS in the snow: downy, juvenile. You find bones in your salmon, and hair in your mouth.

The last time you touched another human being was five months ago, unless you count the gynecologist who warned you the gel would be warm. *Warm,* you said, *warm?* You didn't quite cry but looked off into the distance while Garth Brooks nearly cried, too.

Underneath the snow, a sad garden of pill bug exoskeletons and the tomato plant who tried all summer to produce, despite the light-socket heat every day, who finally, in August, grew one tiny misshapen tomato with scars and a glossy green bottom. Everyone is trying.

The blood that comes out of you is a black web, and you are almost impressed by its intuitive precision for horror; this isn't the Barbie-pink spotting of pregnancy. There's nothing cute about it.

Your ex brings kimchi that explodes in your fridge. You eat it anyway, later finding the hole in the glass where the acid ate it away. Everyone is eating.

When you see your uterus on the computer screen, you think, *That's it?* You once felt so full of life you would explode, the baby opening and closing its fists until it didn't.

You hold the bones of your grief against snow against blood against feathers against glass against scars against heat. You are alone on a golf course in the snow, and a single tree is on fire.

Becca Yenser is author of *Bang the Dream* (Selcouth Station Press, 2021), *The Grief Lottery* (ELJ Editions, 2022) and *A Constellation of Wounds* (Bone and Ink Press, 2022). Their semi-autobiographical novella, *The Ms. Pac Man Chronicles,* won the *Daily Drunk Mag's* 2021 novella chapbook contest. Recent fiction, poetry, and nonfiction appear in *Hobart, Bending Genres, Tiny Molecules, Heavy Feather Review, Susan, Ink Node, Fanzine, Superfroot Magazine,* and *X-Ray Literary Journal.* Yenser was born in Iowa, raised in Oregon, and currently resides in New Mexico.

GROCERIES

anne-marie yerks

MY BOYFRIEND'S A BIKER who likes the beach. We walk up the ridge overlooking Union Lake, sliding through the mud to the canoe rented from the park office, leaving our shoes onshore. He looks at me and says you are a box of Rice-A-Roni, a bottle of baby aspirin, a bundle of asparagus from the clearance rack in the produce section. He says you are a discounted ham bone, a bag of frozen strawberries, a damaged box of oyster crackers.

The canoe is wobbly, dented on the sides. It's a beautiful day.

I don't come to the lake often because I work fifty hours a week. Just about every hour of the fifty, I'm parked in station twelve by the automatic doors. And I'm a can of peas, a half-pound of hazelnuts, a plastic tray of cauliflower and carrots and peppers arranged around a plastic soufflé cup filled with ranch dressing.

There are three boys looking down from the ledge, staring and pointing at me. My boyfriend bristles because no one looks at his woman. I tell him I am not his property. I am a box of powdered dishwasher detergent, a Lean Cuisine, a bag of Meow Mix, three cantaloupes on special, a bundle of beets.

"Take a picture, it'll last longer," my man calls up to the boys.

They give him the bird.

When I was young, I had braces but after they were off I never wore the retainer and now my two front teeth overlap. I wear purple-tinted eyeglasses and my hair is long red frizz. I don't look like anyone but myself.

"It's her," one of the boys shouts. "It's that lady who works at Price Chopper!" Their laughter stirs a flock of blackbirds sitting on an electric line.

Our canoe hits a wave, rocks and spins.

"They know you," my boyfriend says like a question.

Fifty hours a week.

I am three ears of corn, husked, in a plastic bag. A box of diapers, a bottle of Pepto Bismol. I am without shoes floating in an aluminum can, torn apart like a slab of baby back ribs. I am not surprised.

Anne-Marie Yerks is a writer and writing teacher from metro Detroit, MI, where she lives with her husband and cat. A graduate of George Mason's MFA program, her work has appeared in *Juked*, *The Penn Review*, and in several anthologies. She is the author of *Dream Junkies* (New Rivers Press, 2016) and *LUSH* (Odyssey Books, 2020). She's also a certified seamstress (but prefers the word "sewist"), a fiber artist, and a beginning gardener. Contact her on Twitter @Amy1620.

SHE GIVES ME A pocketknife. It has an ergonomic handle with smartly placed finger notches, a nice stainless-steel blade that folds up, a sturdy, low-riding pocket clip—perfect for those inconvenient moments you need to cut something loose. I think about all the stupid women in horror movies, their knitted sweaters tangled with tree branches, their fates at the hands of a serial killer. How many lives could be saved with this folding knife? How many grandma-eating wolves maimed, brambles and thorns cut down, ugly stepsisters decapacitated? *You can use this to carve out your thighs*, she tells me. She draws a wide arch in the air with the flimsy stick she calls a wand. *Like this*, she says. *One uniform curve, from start to finish*. But I know it'll take more than one cut. That night, in my room, I shake off my sweatpants. I start the knife at my knee and angle it just slightly inward. I don't want to cut off my leg. I maneuver the curve in and then out, ending a breath away from my labia. The severed skin is almost crescent-like. I face the mirror, placing my feet together so that my accessory navicular bones touch. Through my thighs, I can see the bedpost, the corner of a women-in-leadership book I've never read, the sleeve of a hoodie too thin for this weather. The carpet begins to get soggy beneath me. Tiny red foam bubbles form near the balls of my feet, as I shift my weight from one side to the other, and blood trickles down like a heavy period. From my window, I can see the patio, the iron table, the cardboard box on the table containing slabs of pork belly dangling from twine. The pork belly has shrunk to less than half its size, condensing the soy-sauce and Shaoxing wine flavor. It had so much to lose, I marvel. I slice up my other leg, my hand now more practiced, the cut more linear, more precise. I look through the gap between my legs again. This time, through the hole, I can see parts of my mattress, the entire spine of the book, the dented metal zipper of the hoodie. I withdraw the blade and slip it into my cabinet. The ballerina music box sitting on top sputters out a note. The gap seems to be getting bigger as blood trickles out. *What percent of the body is fluid? What if I cut too close to my femur?* I want to ask. But she has already left, as she always does, right after providing a solution and idiot-proof instructions, in a dusting of twinkles and glitter. *Is this about right?* I bend over and carefully fit my fist between my thighs. Neither my knuckles nor my fingernails touch the wounds. The gap isn't even that wide, but I feel like I could be swallowed into the opening, spit out the other end, and I'd turn around, look back through the opening, find it no different from where I had begun.

Lucy Zhang writes, codes and watches anime. Her work has appeared in *American Literary Review, The Rupture, The Offing* and elsewhere. Her chapbook *Hollowed* is forthcoming from Thirty West Publishing, and her micro-chapbook *Absorption* is forthcoming from Harbor Review in 2022. Find her at https://kowaretasekai.wordpress.com/ or on Twitter @Dango_Ramen.

FAITH

xueyi zhou

THE FIRST TIME MOTHER tasted religion was when she was seventeen, dissatisfied with the men her father arranged for her. She prayed under a tree that Yue Lao would lasso her an adequate husband with a red string. The Yue Lao she talked to was not the real Matchmaker God, but an old village man who claimed that he had sacrificed his eyes for desperate people, for the service of hunting their missing halves. His fingers slipped from mother's palm to her wrist like an eel on an oily floor, his nail-lines black as his teeth. When he had swum mother's hands, he glossed his lips with the scent frozen on his forefinger and said, "A pretty bird like you would fly out from the mountains and find home in a rich house." Mother paid him and used that to shield against the butcher's son, the tailor's son, the fisherman's son, and the farmer's son. At thirty-one, pregnant, she married a factory owner who thought his wealth justified his temper.

The second time mother picked up religion, she was kneeling inside a temple, smoky with incense, tearing red candles with golden engravings. Three kowtows, in the proper way of her forehead kissing the cushion violently. She wore long relaxed-fit pants and long-sleeves: the former to hide the maternity fat, the latter to cover her bracelet of bruises. She requested a remake of her drunk husband, who, by that time, was constantly absent, who was harder to put up with when present. Sitting in front of the monk, an authentic one this time, she waited for the explanation of the stick she drew from the bamboo cup. She left before the monk could find the page in the book of fortune. Mother was scared that Guan Yin couldn't hear her among the Namo-Amitabhas, more scared that Guan Yin might have heard her. After all, what she had asked for was her husband's death.

The third time mother tested religion, her own mother was shrinking on the hospital bed, tubed and unconscious, a barely breathing lump. The doctor tried to lay out the math of the experimental treatment for her: a couple painful months, at best; decades of debt, for sure.

Mother had stepped into every temple she could reach for the god of longevity, and returned with two silver Guan Yin statues and five tortoise-shaped talismans. That night, after she prayed to every god in our home, she opened the only bottle in the cabinet, Nu Er Hong, the rice wine that parents keep intact until their daughters' weddings. The flashing kaleidoscope aurora from the Buddha chanting player failed to color her face. The liquor she swallowed down flooded back out from her eyes. "What's the good of living long, Bao Bei? What's the good of living long?" She was jealous of her late husband, her sick mother, her young daughter. When I moved her to her bed, I heard her mumbling, "Sorry, Mama, I'm so sorry." The plot she splurged on was approved by a master of Feng Shui, in a cemetery cradled by green hills and unnamed lakes. The master said that it was a good place: the mountains were palming it by forming a bowl, and as water meant money, no drop of fortune could escape.

The fourth time mother wielded religion, she begged to have the man competing with her hit by a loaded truck, so she could secure the promotion. The fifth time, she tried to use religion to do what legislation failed: free her new boyfriend who was arrested for a pyramid scam. Two years later, she wanted him to stay and rot in prison like a forgotten fruit. No successful woman would carry a fifty-year-old ex-con, though she would love to keep the Cadillac he left in our garage. She prayed when she felt the fever on my forehead; she prayed when she saw depression gushing out from my wrist. She always prayed for what she needed. I asked her what she told Guan Yin last night. She said, "Bao Bei, I wished us a long, happy life."

Xueyi Zhou was born and raised in Foshan, a city of manufacturing in Guangdong, China. After she earned a BA in Translation and Interpreting in Shanghai, she returned home and worked in a stainless-steel company. English writing pulled her out again and dropped her into the US deserts, where she is currently pursuing her MFA at UNLV. Her fiction has appeared or is forthcoming in *X-R-A-Y, Waxwing, Passages North, Chestnut Review, Pithead Chapel, JMWW, Atticus Review, Tahoma Lit Review, AAWW* and *Guernica*. She tweets @xueyizhou.

FATHER WAS FOLDING A pile of Polo imitations, emerald with electric yellow logos yelling POST OFFICE. These were not real Polos, but nylon uniforms he stole from the factory's warehouse, whose guard would feign amnesia for a loosie. He folded them into blocks, sized as the one-yuan tofu we bought from the market for dinner, and put them into the freezer. Allegedly, the coldness would peel off the prints, then I could wear them outside without fear. *No proof no crime* was his logic; just a small convenience for a textile man. Hours later, he reopened the T-shirts and found the prints stubborn, so he flipped out his penknife and started scraping. He sat hunched on the stool, his cigarette and sweat glowing, and the plastisol rained down like fluorescent fish scales.

He always smelt like smoked mackerel, a hard sell that took me years to get used to, and that night I thought to myself: if he could quit and cleanse and wear fancy colognes, maybe mother would have stayed. When I woke up the next morning, father was already in the factory for his morning shift, loading clothes into industrial washers and dryers. The skin of the emerald T-shirts had been cleaned up, all seven of them. I put one on. He had marked them with stitches, Monday to Sunday, and a faint smell of tobacco.

I grew in oversized male T-shirts, wearing them as nightgowns, grew out of them, then in fake Nike hoodies, Levi's sweaters, Tommy Hilfiger dresses. For a summer I only wore tie-dyed T-shirts of explosive color clashes, like neon green with bright blue or pink with purple—it was the fad overseas and father was tying white tees day and night. The following two years I wore jeans ripped open manually with electric spinning wheels. One day a worker fell asleep and the wheels ate three of his fingers. The jeans became history. If that textile man saw the punk jeans in the stores, would he stroke his deboned wounds and be surprised by how soft they were? One of the nameless hidden prices behind the mass production of machine washables, the clothes my mother despised.

Her body wanted something delicate enough that transcended machine washing, so she left us to keep her aspiration alive. But the machine washables warmed me. They stayed rough and tired but stayed.

By the time I got to the real Polos, the ones with carefully embroidered emblems, the factory owner suddenly laid off everyone. Diagnosed with heart disease, the owner decided to close for good. At the dismissal meeting, the owner stressed that he was sorry, but he was old and tired, and he wanted to rest. Father and the other workers, all middle-aged or above, listened with sadness, not for the owner's health but for their absence of a future. After the owner drove away in his imported Maserati, the textile men scattered into the corners of other factories sniffing for jobs. Father grabbed a bulky bag of Polo shirts to take with him; a fair compensation.

He waited for me to come home with a cupful of cigarette butts and the needle with the biggest eye.

I threaded it, and his needle swam up and down, sewing the buttons on. "Aren't you bored with these old man's T-shirts anyway?" he asked as he burned the loose threads with his lighter. "I know a factory that makes linens for chain hotels. Do you prefer florals or solid colors?" He forced a smile when he looked up, but the needle bit his thumb. He put it in his mouth and ducked my gaze, his shoulders slightly trembling. I hugged him from the back and said that linen sounded great; we would get much more fabric than T-shirts and jeans. Then I took over the needle, wiped off the blood, and carried on sewing.

Xueyi Zhou was born and raised in Foshan, a city of manufacturing in Guangdong, China. After she earned a BA in Translation and Interpreting in Shanghai, she returned home and worked in a stainless-steel company. English writing pulled her out again and dropped her into the US deserts, where she is currently pursuing her MFA at UNLV. Her fiction has appeared or is forthcoming in *X-R-A-Y*, *Waxwing*, *Passages North*, *Chestnut Review*, *Pithead Chapel*, *JMWW*, *Atticus Review*, *Tahoma Lit Review*, *AAWW* and *Guernica*. She tweets @xueyizhou.

SPOTLIGHTED

JOURNALS

The Best Small Fictions (**Michelle Elvy**): Congratulations! We are thrilled to see the three selections from *Fairy Tale Review* in this year's volume: Lauren Groff's "The Maiden Without Hands," Ilana Masad's "The Frog Prince," Sarah Shun-Lien Bynum's "The Twelve Dancing Princesses." They are from the 2021 issue of *FTR*, The Gold Issue. Can you tell us more about the idea of 'gold' as a fairy tale thematic in your journal's 2021 volume?

Fairy Tale Review (**Kate Bernheimer**): The Gold Issue of *Fairy Tale Review* is a tribute issue to *Transformations* by Anne Sexton on the occasion of the 50th anniversary of its publication. Gold is the ritual color associated with 50th anniversaries, so it was an easy choice. Gold also invokes alchemy, a kind of magical transformation. The issue was shaped around the contents of Sexton's yearning and angular volume, which is one of my favorite, crushingly overlooked fairy tale books by a misunderstood poet. I hoped that inviting works in direct conversation with Sexton's poems would inspire writers to engage with fairy tales in their own way—as she did, well before many others—and invite scholars to take a look anew at *transformations* and a generation of new fairy tale thinkers. We curated this issue in direct correlation with her table of contents.

BSF: You started in 2005 with The Blue Issue. Tell us how it all got started, and how blue was the first colour to explore.

FTR: When I started the journal, the first thing I did was get a Post Office Box in the small town where I lived, got some stationery printed, and wrote some letters telling people I had begun a fairy tale journal. I chose blue as the first color because it was the first color in Andrew

Lang's rainbow fairy book series, and because it called forth the Andre Breton epigraph to the journal's mission: "There are fairy tales for adults yet to be written, fairy tales almost blue." I founded *Fairy Tale Review* after publishing four literary books about (and based on) fairy tales, and finding myself invited to speak about fairy tales and read my fairy tale fiction at museums and universities. The diverse audiences were across the board flabbergasted and delighted that fairy tales could be considered through a deeply aesthetic, artistic lens and very lit up by this notion. At the time, literary works based on fairy tales were depressingly marginalized by the literary editors and critics in my orbit. And I knew first hand that a whole lot of imaginative works were being turned down in mainstream literary journals. I also knew that a lot of emerging writers were simply not being offered opportunities in mainstream workshops to engage deeply with this ancient art form—a radical form technically and in its content. As an author of fairy tales, I knew that I had centuries of editors and folklorists to thank for fairy tales being among us, so I I wanted to know more about the art of editorship, which shaped fairy tales as we know them. I was on a mission to change how fairy tales were received. I feel it is safe to say that the mission has been accomplished.

BSF: You publish prose and poetry, also art and graphic art. How does each form lend itself to the exploration of myths and realities in your journal?

FTR: Fairy tales as an art form respond to stories via the telling. Just as memories and dreams are breathed into existence by telling—which is a *retelling of something experienced*—so too are fairy tales. Fairy tales thus can take any form. They can exist in a series of photographs by Cindy Sherman, prints by Kiki Smith, silhouettes by Kara Walker. As an editor I am less interested in distinctions between genres like fiction, nonfiction, and poetry than I am interested in looking for the strands of fairy tale techniques that entwine disparate works in a tradition, that bring starkly different forms together that feel like a collective somehow. My theory, since beginning to edit books—and later the journal—has been that a collection absolutely needs a range of forms and modes of expression in order to create a hospitable environment for 'the reader' and 'many readers.' It sounds counter-intuitive but I absolutely rely on this theory to ethically shape every work that I curate, for the sake of my reader.

BSF: In the three stories selected this year for *Best Small Fictions*, we notice themes around safety and danger, of belonging and being cast out—of the thin line between existing and not existing, perhaps. Today we live in a world dominated by war and plague—in some ways, the same themes across time. Do you think the works you are reading today are asking even more questions and pushing on more boundaries, or do you think the fairy tale has always been a place where this can occur?

FTR: Fairy tales have for hundreds of years enacted confrontations with the threat of non-existence, the lines between inside and outside, the often dangerous question of self and other. The themes you cite are classical themes from fairy tales over the centuries. Safety has always been elusive in fairy tales, as in real life. The works I am reading today do not push boundaries any more than old fairy tales—I don't require them to, but mainly because it would be fairly impossible to push boundaries more than old fairy tales, which often times were radical works, and no stranger to violence, war, plague, abuses of just about every kind you could imagine. So I haven't seen new themes being introduced in new fairy tales, but that truly isn't a concern of mine—I'm more interested in how each artist makes her own work—through what shapes, images, idioms, drives she makes it—and how that work enters the fairy tale collective of past, present, and future, from her own moment. Fairy tales have since the beginning confronted questions of isolation, existence and non-existence, the threat of obliteration (of self, body, family, place). And something readers don't often consider is that fairy tales have always been contemporary to someone. So our new fairy tales are no newer than old fairy tales were—to their authors.

BSF: Is there more continuity or break in fairy tale writing and reading? Does writing modern fairy tales allow us to make connections to our past, or to break away in ways that allow for new explorations?

FTR: These are good questions, and the answer through a fairy tale lens is definitely "both/and" in most cases. Fairy tales are very much a non-binary, both/and art form. That is part of their beauty.

BSF: *FTR* is a journal dedicated to diversity and innovation—and your contents and contributors reflect this. Can you tell us how these central goals are reflected in the way you make selections for an issue, and also address how each of the pieces featured here demonstrate these central tenets of your journal?

FTR: The short answer is that fairy tales have always been both a refuge for "diversity" and representation of how "diversity" is perceived in systems of unequal power. *Fairy Tale Review,* since its founding, has been dedicated to celebrating the diversity of and in fairy tales and among fairy tale makers (whether artists, authors, editors, translators, filmmakers, playwrights). It hasn't needed to be particularly central to how we make selections for the issue, because it would be almost impossible not to be inclusive based on the wild array of submissions we receive—thousands to each issue—none quite like the other, as is the fairy tale way. By way of metaphor, I can share that I teach a class to hundreds of students each year where they gather oral literary histories of Little Red Riding Hood from friends, relatives, and others. Not a single one replicates another; it would be impossible. And, not to sidestep the chance to sing the praises of the contributions featured so kindly and generously in *Best Small Fictions*, I would prefer to let your readers encounter the works without my words as a rubric for their experiences. Each of these pieces invites the reader into a whole world that can only exist because they brought it to life in their words.

BSF: And your own work? You teach creative writing at the University of Arizona in Tucson. How has your own teaching and writing changed as a result of editing *Fairy Tale Review* since 2005?

FTR: My teaching has flourished, because I get to teach the work that I live and breathe as an author and editor, which is fairy tale ethics and aesthetics. When I began teaching, it was hugely unusual for fairy tales to be in the classroom, and I taught only graduate classes. Over time, and as the conversation about fairy tales has made its way into the undergraduate classroom (nationally, sometimes through students of mine, sometimes through students of Maria Tatar and others), I have had the chance to develop a popular, very large fairy tale class that is sometimes a little too popular—last year I taught over a thousand students, with the kind assistance of graduate teaching assistants. But I would not change a thing and I'd teach more students if I humanly could: through that class, I get to share what I love with a new generation of readers who will carry the form forward for us, and who need fairy tales and their radical techniques as they confront some really serious problems on earth. At the same time, I get to learn from my students what excites them in art and culture and what political and philosophical questions haunt them the most, which makes me a better person and hopefully better writer as well. As an author of fiction, my work has not changed as a result of editing the journal, apart from the fact that I know I am not alone in my love of fairy tales. My nonfiction has definitely developed in harmony with editorship. It all goes together, and I'm very lucky it worked out this way.

BSF: In 2023 you will publish The Rainbow Issue. Tell us more!

FTR: The Rainbow Issue of *Fairy Tale Review* will be dedicated to queer fairy tales written by queer writers. Long-time volunteer Prose Editor Benjamin Schaefer will serve as Editor for the issue. (Our entire editorial team—including myself—is a fully volunteer staff.) To inspire potential contributors, Benjamin chose this quotation, which I love: "We gays cast our nets out into the mythic sea, searching for our own lost archetypes…those symbols of the human psyche which we may claim as emblematic of our own particular way of being." It's from Stanley Johnson, "On the Banks of the River Time Looking Inland."

The Best Small Fictions (**Nathan Leslie**): Aaron, I have been following *Hobart* for a long time. When I think of *Hobart* I really think back to the beginnings of online literary magazines (you also had a print mag for years). Tell me about the origins of *Hobart* and how it has grown. And now there is also *HAD!*

Hobart (**Aaron Burch**): It's funny, when I started Hobart in 2001/02, I thought *another* literary journal was probably unnecessary. There were already so many journals doing really great, fun, interesting stuff—*Pindeldyboz, Eyeshot, Opium, Sweet Fancy Moses*… Who was I to start a journal? (I was nobody; I had no editorial experience, hadn't published anything myself, knew no writers, hadn't even been an English major…) I think about Tony, in the first episode of *The Sopranos*, saying, "It's good to be in something from the ground floor. I came too late for that and I know. But lately, I'm getting the feeling that I came in at the end. The best is over." But I had just graduated college and didn't know what else to do with my life and it seemed fun and mostly was a way to entertain myself and a few friends…and then I just kept doing it. After a year or so of just the website, we started doing print issues, and then a few years later grew into books, too, and then a few years later the website moved from monthly issues to daily, and then another few years later, we stopped doing the print issues and focused that energy back to the website. I think the two biggest reasons it is still going, much less has grown into what it's become, is because I got better at delegating work and now have a whole team of editors, and, rather than follow or even pay much attention to larger trends or what seems popular, we've always pretty much just followed ideas that excited and interested us in the moment.

BSF: It also strikes me that *Hobart* has a certain aesthetic that is difficult for me to put my finger upon. There is a bit of a punk vibe going on, but also a the long-running baseball focus and the "fucked up modern love" essays. Is there such as thing as a *Hobart* piece?

Hobart (AB): It's hard for me to define or put my finger on, too! I've mostly taken to thinking and calling that aesthetic *"Hobart-y,"* a kind of Justice Stewart on pornography like, "I know it when I see it."

Building on the above, I think starting the website without any connections or even having any idea of what I was doing, other than wanting to have fun with it, kind of embed a bit of that punk vibe in its DNA, and then just trying things that seem fun and interesting and following through on ideas that excite us lead to an annual baseball issue (because I love baseball) or "fucked up modern love" essays (because Elizabeth Ellen knew there were all these great essays getting rejected by, and/or were just too "fucked up" for, the *New York Times* "Modern Love" column and wanted to publish them) or growing into publishing comics or ongoing columns or serializing longer stories, etc.

And, finally, that team of editors (plus occasional guest editors) each brings to *Hobart* their own blend of their take on *"Hobart-y"* and their own tastes and aesthetic. In fact, the editors that selected the stories chosen for inclusion here in this year's *BSF* will speak about them a bit below.

BSF: How have you seen flash fiction evolve over the past couple of decades?

Hobart (AB): I'm not sure I could put a finger on it. It seems more…established? Some of that is the form, some is online journals and publishing. Twenty years ago, you'd pretty rarely see such short fiction included in collections, and there was this real stigma hanging over online journals that they were lesser than print journals and just much less well respected? As time passed and with some more experience behind them, and with it a longer history of publishing really great stuff, credibility seemed to grow, and then also the funding and economics of print publishing has gone all sideways, highlighting some of the pros of online publishing. The form has always been really great, but it seems like, especially in the last decade or so and probably more and more every year, there's just…*more.*

BSF: *Hobart* (and now *HAD*, also) has had a continual presence in *Best Small Fictions* over the past few years. Do you see more flash in the submission queue? Stronger work coming in?

Hobart (AB): We do. The number of submissions per month just grows every year. And between more people writing it, more submissions, and our own history giving us some cred and recognizability, the quality of submissions is pretty high. Ten years ago this September, we redesigned and relaunched the website, moving from monthly issues (of 4-6 pieces/month) to something every weekday (so, at least 20 pieces/month, minimum). My worry at that point was finding and getting enough good stuff to suddenly be publishing 5x as much. That meant a little more hustling and soliciting at the outset…but now so much great stuff comes in, we often publish a couple of pieces every day and have grown to weekends too!

BSF: On to the pieces from this year, Jack Vening's piece "Local Curses" is almost built out of little truisms, maxims of modern life. At least that is what struck me about it from the get-go. What jumped off the page for you?

Hobart (**Lauren Lauterhahn**): What drew me into "Local Curses" was the way the story builds on conventional emotional and narrative satisfaction. Each sentence offers an anecdote or observational topics that accumulates into a mosaic that is gratifying in its aesthetic wholeness.

BSF: Lucy Zhang's piece "Thigh Gap" is vividly severe, to say the least. It provides a commentary on the inanity of expectation, perhaps. What's your take on this flash?

Hobart (**Kimberly Bliss**): "Thigh Gap" takes the female (Asian) gaze and literally slaughters it piece by piece, synchronizing this visceral physical violence with a POV that is as emotionally detached as any other celebration of gratuitous violence. While you are mesmerized with the blade and all it cuts, the severance is the lens itself and we see what she sees. The contemplation is the story.

BSF: The *HAD* story "The Summer Before the Glitter Fell Out of My Eyes" has the feel of a classic growing up story. Yet with a twenty first century twist. What about this piece appealed to you?

Hobart (AB): I think exactly what you said—that it has this classic growing up feel, while also feeling new. Nostalgia and coming of age are two of my own personal biggest themes, while acknowledging how easy it can be to fall into the trap of indulging in that without any complication. On top of that, I'm especially a sucker for lists and/or stories that work via accumulation of pieces, and *also* negation in stories. So, not only did the writing itself immediately grab me, but the childhood sleepover party + pileup of Brunette Brittany's house…Maggie's house…Kelsey's house…+ "I didn't know"s at the end was almost as if the story was just for me.

BSF: What is next for *Hobart*, *HAD* and your literary doings?

Hobart (AB): No specific plans for what's next right now…but we rarely have plans. More often than not, what happens next and anything new is an outgrowth of an idea that I or we get excited about and then try out to see how it goes. This last year we published the first two *HAD* chapbooks, and it was fun doing hard copies of something again but with a more simple, black and white, stapled, DIY style and energy.

The Best Small Fictions (**Michelle Elvy**): Congratulations! *Litro* is one of this year's spotlighted journals, which is a testament to the strength of your work in flash fiction. Could you tell us about your view on flash fiction and its place in the literary landscape?

Litro (**Catherine McNamara**): I think that flash fiction has earned its place in today's literary landscape. It speaks to us of brevity and nuance, and holds the grand scope of story in a bold, breathless embrace. A difficult form to master, and a brilliant training ground for writers in the essence of language and intent, it is rapidly gaining ground, as we see in the number of new magazines and competitions, published flash fiction collections and flash-in-a-novel books. Flash fiction, while still a slightly enigmatic form, is more mainstream than ever.

BSF: Litro publishes works by first time authors and Nobel laureates. Tell us about the magazine's early days—how it all began.

Litro (**Eric Akoto**): The magazine began 20 years ago from my bedroom in Nottinghill, fuelled by a passion for bringing together diverse stories and creators. Initially a freebie handed out in London streets and bookshops, *Litro* is now published in the UK and the USA, with regular online content and themed print editions, and our World Series Festivals which take place across the globe. When Covid hit us hard we were forced to pull back from live festivals and have developed a Masterclass Series, with an international team of teachers providing classes that range from poetry to resilience to sensuality in writing.

BSF: When—and why—did you add Flash Friday?

Litro (EA): Flash Friday was added early on as I felt it is a perfect vehicle to express the dynamism and diversity of our world. Flash fiction is as broad as it is meaningful, and as our attention spans are reduced by our dependence on smart phones and rapid communication, it is a powerful form that resonates with readers.

BSF: Catherine, you came on as Fiction Editor in 2016. Have you seen any trends in flash fiction over the time you've been editing flash fiction at *Litro*?

Litro (CM): My submission list is always wildly diverse although there are quite a few recurring themes which I'm sure other editors notice too. With Covid I've noticed a lot of fear and physical uncertainty, a real sense of constriction with regard to time and movement, and quite a lot of depression! But on the other hand I feel there has been a return to nature and a beholding of miniature things, a slowness. I think writers have slowed down and are maybe looking through the lens of the past, or that of their immediate surroundings. I think many writers—as all of us—have had their confidence in the outside world shaken, so a certain bravery is gone; people are tentative and looking for new rules, new logic, new refrains.

BSF: And what of your own writing? (Catherine, you are known to us for your own flash fiction as well, with your work also included in this year's volume). How does your writing help you as readers and editors as you are making selections for your magazine?

Litro (EA): Running *Litro* allows me the ability keep in touch with the real issue of the survival of the arts in a fast and edgy world. I'm affected by contemporary events and am keen to see them represented in our content. As a publisher, editor & writer I want to show the truths of our world, but also the beauty of art and creation, and how we must continue to provide a platform for both of these.

(CM): I started out as a short story writer with a deep love of language, and moved into flash fiction around the time I began as an editor with *Litro*. I've published two short story collections and one flash fiction collection. The challenge of flash fiction is immense. When I read my selections I'm aware of how difficult it is to find an idea, a meaningful story to tell, and how to use compelling language to convey this. There is always great joy in the discovery of a stirring piece, and I am so happy to see my writers get ahead in their careers.

BSF: Let's look at the two pieces from *Litro* in this year's *Best Small Fictions*: 'A Folktale of Follicles' by Victoria Buitron and 'Shoes' by Mustapha Enesi. Both take up a kind of dreamstate quality in the way they are written, with fierce undercurrents in realities. Both hold a fluency and an urgency, with clear style, message and voice. Both are by international writers, too: Buitron from Ecuador, Enesi from Nigeria. Can you tell us why these stories stand out, for you?

Litro (CM): Both of these stories swept me into their worlds with fearless and lyrical language, real and tangible characters. For me they are human, universal and unforgettable. Both were entries for our Summer *Nature* Flash Fiction Competition and as such were thrilling takes on the theme. This year we received a 200-strong crop of stories, many brilliant works.

BSF: With each reading of these stories, the reader finds new exploratory avenues. The reader thinks: *Here there is something new to discover.* Is this something that you think guides the overall expectations and goals of *Litro*, across all its contents, whether essay, interview or fiction?

Litro (EA): *Litro* is committed to both the established and less experienced writers everywhere. We have a specific interest in the under-represented, and are proud when our writers do well. We view *Litro* as a hotspot for talent and growth, where writers such as Victoria and Mustapha show their talents and gain a footing in the literary world.

(CM): As an editor, I think one of my aims is to select stories that will engage our readers, stimulate them and make them come back for more. In this way, our stories must follow the shape and concerns of *Litro*. So yes, I'm always on the lookout for something new, but I appreciate it when authors who submit are also readers of our magazine, who understand our aims and express these in some way through story.

BSF: We know, too, that both of you have spent time living in different places around the globe. And at *Litro*, we see that your pages emphasise diversity in both content and form. Is that a central goal of the magazine, and do you think it springs from your own experience in the world?

Litro (EA): I established *Litro* with the intention of producing a pocket-sized magazine for a city as diverse and dynamic as London, so my outlook has always been grounded in appealing to a broad range of readers on these terms. As we have expanded, I have had the chance to put that into practice in the hiring diverse staff members for the team, and involving writers and contributors from all over the world. We are proud to say that our online readers come from nearly every country.

(CM): I think it is apparent to readers that our content reflects a genuine interest in stories and voices from all over the globe. We receive submissions from many different countries, high-quality work that is hugely satisfying to read. While I grew up in Australia, I have lived non-English-speaking countries ever since, so my outlook is international and I can't imagine working for a review that did not have these tenets.

BSF: And connected to all of the above, what's next for *Litro*?

Litro (EA): Our next print issue will be about experimental writing & art published in May 2022 and we look forward to resuming live festivals in the near future. In the meantime we feel that our Masterclasses offer a wealth of skill, knowledge and literary experience for *Litro* followers.

The Best Small Fictions (**Amy Barnes**): Please share a brief history of the *Portland Review*, the journal's journey and the path you and the university envision going forward.

Portland Review (**Kynna Lovin**): *Portland Review* launched in 1956, making us Oregon's oldest literary journal. In our first issue, from Fall 1956, we called ourselves "Portland State Review of Student Writing". Initially, we were a student-led magazine, intended for the students of what was then called Portland State College. Ten years later, we were known as *The Review*. By the mid '70s, we'd become *Portland Review*, and were clear about making a shift in our magazine's goals, which included giving space to marginalized voices. Our Spring 1974 issue opened with a promise: "Shortly following this issue of the *Portland Review* will be a special double issue featuring poetry from Indians in the North West, works from Portland Black writers, works for, by, and about, women, as well as reviews and art work." We began as a literary magazine created by Portland students, for Portland students.

For many years we were part of the Student Media department, along with the student newspaper, the *Vanguard*, and other student-led publications. In 2016, *Portland Review* joined with Portland State University's English Department. We've found a supportive home there. The move gave us greater faculty support, funding, and cemented a longtime change for the magazine: our audience had expanded beyond PSU students, or even Portland's literary scene. We had become part the global literary and art communities.

Welcoming new creative voices to the ongoing artistic conversation has always been the journal's goal. In the records that remain to us, we can see the editors outlining their concerns in their reading guides—"Realism or [the] concrete is not as important as form or function… Ask yourself: Does it work on the writer's terms?" "We are reading to find the art of writing, which includes experimentation and descriptive definitions of language use rather than prescriptive… Respect those choices and assume they are intentional." These kinds of ideals are the backbone of *Portland Review,* and continue to influence our publication.

In 2020, we made the switch to fully digital publishing. We were already publishing online, but between pandemic print-logistics and the changing landscape of publishing in general, the timing was right. We used to manage 2-3 volumes per year, with issues being between 50 and 200 pages. Now, we are publishing a new piece of prose, poetry, or creative nonfiction each week. Our audience doesn't have to wait months between issues, and our staff doesn't have to work through the grueling crunch-time of pre-publication.

Going forward, we hope to continue putting great work, from fresh voices, out into the world. We are also considering expanding our publication schedule to year-round—so stay tuned for that!

BSF: "Prose, poetry and Art since 1956" on your website stands out for its longevity and variety. In nearly 70 years, what changes have you heard about and what have you watched in the last decade or since you were the editor? While prose and poetry may be expected, what role does art play in the journal? Do you choose artwork mainly from submissions, match existing art with stories or commission as well?

PR: First, I should make clear that while I am the current Editor-in-Chief, I have only been with the magazine for two years, and served in the EIC position just this year. Staff turnover, however, has always been part of *Portland Review.* New editors join each year. Some stay on for multiple years, some for as short a time as a few months. This keeps the magazine from being "stale" or getting entrenched in certain styles, practices, or preferences.

The downside of this is, I can't speak to trends over the last decade. But I can say during my time with the *Review,* I think one thing we are exploring more are pieces that cross genre. We're interested in art that expands our conceptions of prose, poetry, (or both) and in so doing, creates something new. Can a nonfiction piece be written entirely as a one-sided conversation? Why not? Is it a poem if it takes the form of an index? Of course. What about a fiction story compartmentalized into chat-room logs, narrative vignettes, and footnotes? We've got that too. Just this year, we published our first foray into comics. We hope it won't be the last.

As far as the role of art in our current, digital format, that is something we are still figuring out. When we published print issues, each issue included pieces of artwork received as submissions. In our current format, all publications are paired with art. We simply require more art pieces than we used to receive. The images we currently use are created for a specific piece, typically by the Editor-in-Chief, or other editors. The benefit of this method is the artwork is tailor-made for the prose or poetry it accompanies. The downside is, fewer artists get their work out there. All this to say, we are looking into ways to bring art submissions back.

BSF: The recent change from print to digital? Was that accelerated by the pandemic or had it been a change in the works for a while? What have you learned with the change from print to digital? Are you able to publish more? Does the journal feel more accessible?

PR: The change to digital publishing was certainly accelerated by the pandemic, but to an extent, felt inevitable. We are far from the only literary magazine that has switched to digital in recent years. We had already been publishing some work as online exclusives, so making the swap was a fairly easy process. While we are not publishing more, in terms of strict number of authors per year, we are able to publish more frequently, which is rewarding for audience and author alike. Our move to digital also allows us to publish work that previously would not have met the limits of a physical issue.

It is also a change we have embraced due to the benefits it offers our audience—the largest of which is accessibility. Whereas before, you would need to purchase an issue of *Portland Review* through our website, or a retail distributor; now, our published content is available online, free of charge.

BSF: The recent "Labor," the title and image are memorable and also a great play on words offering writers the opportunity to write to a theme, but also broadly or narrowly interpret it. How do you choose titles and images for each issue?

PR: You pretty much nailed it with your description—we try to choose themes that gesture in more than one direction, feel wonderfully open to interpretation. Last spring, we put out a call for a series titled "Transit / Transition / Translation". We wanted work that fit under any of those labels, and possibly more than one.

The task of deciding on how many series we'll publish each year, and their respective themes, falls to the Editor-in-Chief. In that way, I think the EIC gets to have a greater impact on the magazine than they might otherwise. We have a new person in the role each year, but during their tenure, they get a chance to add their own shade to *Portland Review's* palette.

BSF: In that same vein, the *Portland Review* is now publishing one piece each week. How does that change your approach from a print journal publication? Are you able to publish more voices? Does each piece then get a more singular impact? Are you having to find/accept more submissions?

PR: When you're publishing a single issue, you have to consider how the various parts bend toward the whole: how each piece of prose, poetry, or artwork fits or chafes against the issue's theme, how they transition into and out of each other, whether they function together and separately.

There is less pressure on these factors when you publish in a digital series, as we do now. When you're dealing with a space of 100 pages, there isn't room for two equally well-written pieces that share certain similarities. They will feel too close to each other. When you're publishing those same pieces digitally, ten weeks apart, their similarities aren't so noticeable. Our current publication style lets us consider pieces on more of an individual basis.

I also believe our digital format has allowed us to grow our audience, considerably. In our first year as a digital publication, we received enough submissions to keep us reading at our usual pace. After announcing our series theme this past fall, we received many more submissions than is typical; in fact, our reading teams had to read through 1.5 times the usual number of submissions each week. When I put out our spring call, I had to implement submission caps for the first time ever! We were floored when we hit those limits within hours of submissions being opened. We're excited by the interest in *Portland Review,* and are considering whether we can expand our publication schedule, to allow us to accept more pieces for each series.

BSF: What is the make-up of your masthead? Does it change at regular intervals as students graduate and enter the program? I read for The MacGuffin and we do first reads and then discuss together as a group over Zoom every two weeks and also help with formatting the issues. What is your reading/editing process? Do readers participate in the process from start to finish if they want to take on those roles?

PR: Just as when we started in 1956, *Portland Review* remains a student-run publication. All of our editors and readers are students. Most are graduate students, and writers, themselves. Returning editors advise the new hands. If we run into trouble, our faculty advisors are available to assist us. Reading teams (which include all staff editors) are given a set number of submissions to read through each week, based on the total volume of submissions received. Notable pieces are flagged for the genre editors, and with their approval, are brought to the weekly editorial meeting on zoom.

With the exception of our undergraduate reading teams (who read as part of the coursework for a separate class) all readers are invited to participate at every level of the decision-making process. By the time the meeting starts, editors have read and cast a preliminary vote on the pieces up for discussion. Not everyone can make it to the editorial meeting, so we rely on thorough comments from readers and editors to assess what a piece is doing, how effective it is, and whether we think the piece is ready for publication. For poetry submissions, we read each out loud during the meeting, to be sure we get a chance to hear the piece, as well. Those who are present discuss the merits of a given work. We look to the comments to provide a voice to those who could not attend the meeting. After discussion, we take a final vote on whether or not to accept the piece, and move forward with publication.

BSF: The Portland Review has been in *BSF* many times over its history. The site mentions publishing a "wide spectrum of aesthetic staples and voices." What do you feel like within that space lends itself to short fiction? How have those aesthetics and voices changed over seven decades?

PR: The demands we place in our minds for short fiction allow for more unexpected choices. What I mean is, when we know a story can only have, say, a maximum of 1,000 words, we don't put the same pressures on it, don't hold the same expectations of what it must include, or how the story could, or should, play out. We enter short fiction with a sense of curiosity, to see what can be accomplished—aesthetically, thematically, plot-wise—in fewer words.

It's hard for me to say how the aesthetics of *Portland Review* have changed over the past seventy years. Paper degrades, offices move, files get lost—our record of the magazine is incomplete. We continue to feature local established authors, such as Ursula K. Le Guin, Primus St. John, and Lidia Yuknavich. But I think we give greater attention to the task of elevating fresh voices. We strive to be an inclusive publisher who welcomes the new and experimental.

BSF: Because the journal has been publishing for so long, it would seem like there are interesting stories about the team, the journal or the processes? Are there stories and/or legends associated with the journal that you can share with the *Best Small Fictions* readers? Funny events? Issues that were delayed?

PR: I wish I did have those sorts of stories! My time with the magazine has been too brief to truly accumulate that kind of knowledge.

BSF: On your website, you speak to equity, experimentation, exploration, making space for different approaches and vantage points, a regional connection but also one with the environment, a focus on Portland and the Pacific Northwest. In the 2022 issue of *BSF,* you have two pieces included. "The Story of the Bee" and "Bon Appetit." What did you find outstanding or interesting to include these two pieces? Did you work with these writers to publish their short fiction? Do you think that the two pieces are a representation of the journal's focus? How do you go about increasing diversity at the journal?

PR: "Bon Appetit" was a blistering read. The story sticks with you. It is unafraid to let the main character's silence reverberate through every scene. It raises questions about our notions of the meaning of the word *custody,* of religious freedom, and how far authority's reach makes a practice of extending itself—past the borders of the body, down the throat. It makes a point about the way white America finds it easier to choke out what it refuses to understand. We knew we wanted to publish Matan Gold's story, exactly as it was written.

"The Story of the Bee" led us into a different world: the world of its neurodivergent protagonist. He is a man coming to terms with not only his diagnosis, but reconciling how to exist in the world, with this knowledge. He's discovering who he is, a journey that's relatable to pretty much everyone, though this character's particulars are not. On the sentence level, the language of the story manages to be eloquent, yet defamiliarizing. Because this story is told through the autistic protagonist's perspective, we worked directly with Tim Raymond to make a few small edits on the line level. We felt these changes were necessary to keep the story's defamiliarizing energy, while maintaining narrative clarity.

I do see each of these as representative of *Portland Review's* focus. We look for work that is unafraid to shows us something we haven't seen, or just haven't seen often enough. We seek fresh perspectives, styles, and voices. Increased diversity in the voices we publish is a natural side-effect of these practices, but it is also an intentional choice.

BSF: In "The Story of the Bee," it opens with a reference to summer but was published in December.

"It was summer and everything had fallen apart."

That opening line carries so much weight beyond setting the scene—both setting and personally. The reader knows instantly when this story will take place but also the mental state of the narrator, all without exposition. The line "You don't have any interest in whales, do you?" Later on in the story feels like a conversation with the opening and yet, the story itself goes so much further with the movement into exploring nature in other ways with the Korean streams and the closing line that feels like a natural ending without wrapping things up too much.

"The name I couldn't articulate until I was learning some Korean and it changed the way my tongue moved."

Are you drawn to opening sentences and closings that frame stories with such a position of clarity? More spare in description but still powerful?

PR: I'm not necessarily drawn to that, though clarity at both ends of the story certainly doesn't hurt. I would say I'm drawn to a beginning that demands to be read past, to the point where I get to page ten before I realize how long the story has held me. And I love a messy ending. How many things in life end without at least a little mess? As authors, we often feel compelled to land the story in a place that feels *right*. Yet a phrase I've heard countless times during our editorial discussions is, "I wish this one ended a few sentences sooner."

BSF: In a similar way, the second story "Bon Appetit," opens with an instantly immersive paragraph. The reader knows this takes place in a prison of some kind. The descriptions are more physical in nature—"slamming against a cement wall," "peer in as if into the mouth of a cave," "steps are difficult for old knees" and "it is easy to become winded." The reader is immersed right along with the prisoners into a painful situation. While the title "Bon Appetit" implies this might be about food, it is nearly half-way through the story before we get "at meal times" and a clearer view that this in such a unique POV: "Trust me, we take no pleasure in seeing you strapped up like this."

What elements made the second story a pick for the journal as well as for *BSF*? The more visceral nature? The unique POV? The immersive read?

PR: Yes, the visceral feelings the story brings up, and leaves you with, were definitely part of our decision to publish. The silence of the main character was unique, as well. It's a testament to Matan Gold's brilliant writing that the story makes you genuinely feel discomfort. And refuses to shy away from that, or apologize for it.

BSF: What is the next path forward for the *Portland Review*? Are there new projects planned for 2022-23, specifically in the digital space as you move further away from print issues? Events? Classes?

PR: Naturally, we want to continue to publish great work, every week. To continue bringing new artistic voices to the literary conversation.

We're hoping that as things continue to open back up, we'll be able to hold more in-person events, such as readings. And we haven't ruled out doing a print issue at some point in the future. My time with *Portland Review* is almost done, so I'll be looking forward to seeing what comes next just us much as everyone else.

The Best Small Fictions (**Myna Chang**): How & when did *Wigleaf* get started? What were your original goals, and have they changed over the years? What things have stayed the same?

Wigleaf (**Scott Garson**): In the spring of 2007, my wife and I got jobs at the University of Missouri and were getting ready to move cross-country with our then-babies. I'd been teaching at Santa Clara University, and I remember talking with the poet Rebecca Black, who also worked in SCU English, about the move, and her saying that I should introduce myself to Speer Morgan and see about getting involved with *The Missouri Review.* I couldn't see introducing myself to a lit-famous person, but it's possible to trace the idea for *Wigleaf* to that time. In '07, believe or it not, I think there was only one online journal devoted exclusively to very short fiction (*SmokeLong Quarterly*). My favorite journal was *Quick Fiction*, a print mag run by Jennifer and Adam Pieroni. With *Wigleaf*, I wanted to have the kind of fun I imagined Jen and Adam were having. (Things are more complicated now, but that's still a main goal!)

BSF: Tell us about your masthead. Why did you choose to bring student interns onto your staff? What advantage does this bring to the journal? To the students? How does this mesh with the rest of the *Wigleaf* staff?

Wigleaf: So, aside from the *Wigleaf* Top 50, our student interns are the staff, pretty much. With the internship program, which started in our tenth-anniversary year, 2018, MU English got to add to a distinctive strength (i.e. existing editorial internship opportunities with *The Missouri Review* and Persea Books); students got direct and consequential experience with running an independent journal; and *Wigleaf* got younger. We've always been about newing it up—and the interns bring freshness and openness and energy. That's been so valuable.

BSF: How do you *describe* Wigleaf's personality? What essential elements do you seek in each story you publish? What's the story behind the *"Dear Wigleaf"* postcards?

Wigleaf: Our personality, that's a complicated question! Today's answer: we're not big on convention. What that means, in terms of the stories we run: they tend to each go their own way. I don't know what would characterize a typical *Wigleaf* story beyond its (hopefully!) being hard to quit reading. (That's actually something we talk about a lot, at the editorial table—the reading experience.)

Re: *Dear Wigleaf*: the lengthy author bio is one particular convention I'm not a fan of. I wanted to keep bios to one or two lines. And I thought, If authors feel like saying more, how about postcards?

BSF: This year's featured stories include "Men Buying Jewelry for Their Wives" by Naira Wilson, "The Babysitter" by Kat Solomon, and "Live Maine Lobsters" by David K. Gibson. What drew you to these stories? How do they fit into the *Wigleaf* aesthetic?

Wigleaf: Sometimes, when I know of the writer and admire their work, I'll give a submission a 'priority' tag, which lets the first reader know they should maybe get to that one sooner rather than later. In the case of these three stories, I wasn't familiar with the writers beforehand. So all three stories were discoveries: each, on first read, got an omg response, and each was bumped up to the editorial table for immediate discussion. You can probably guess by this point that I won't have a very satisfying response to the question of how they fit into our aesthetic, but may I tell you one thing I love about each?

I. Naira's story: the human dynamic she's looking at is so interesting, so particular. I feel like: as a writer, she wants to get that right. She wants to tell the truth about that. And love how naturally the story itself seems to flow from that impulse.

2. Kat's story: do you see how this story does not mess around? I read somewhere a bit of writing advice that at first seemed so obvious as to be useless: *be interested.* Be interested? Of course writers are interested. But no: be interested *first.* Kat seems to know exactly what interests her in this story, and she doesn't try to bury that or disguise that; she goes right for it. Does she know from the start where her interest will lead? I can't say. But my guess would be no. To me, as a reader, it feels revelatory.

3. David's story: I mean, what an ending. Just wow. When we discussed the story, I sensed how we wanted to take a second and feel the power of that moment together. That's when I knew: our readers, we had to give them this. They had to have this experience.

BSF: Everyone looks forward to The *Wigleaf* Top 50 (Very) Short Fictions of the year. Can you tell us how the list came about? What is the process of selecting the stories and presenting the final list?

Wigleaf: In 2007, I was keeping a list of great new shorts. I had a fantasy about this list somehow finding its way to Houghton Mifflin and turning into a Best American Flash Fiction annual. Maybe that's still a fantasy! But in the meantime, I developed *Wigleaf* and eventually put two and two together.

Shome Dasgupta is our Series Editor for the *Wigleaf* Top 50. He does a great job of running things there, coordinating the team of readers and ultimately coming up with the longlist. He also fixes us up with Selecting Editors (the Selecting Editor for the *Wigleaf* Top 50 2022 will be Kathy Fish!).

BSF: Has editing *Wigleaf* influenced your own writing?

Wigleaf: I imagine so!

Just in terms of process: with the best of my own stuff, I feel, simultaneously, like I don't know what I'm doing, and like I'm really confident. Maybe my experience with *Wigleaf* helps me bridge that logical divide.

BSF: What question do you wish I'd asked?

Wigleaf: I wish you'd asked me what the secret password to the *Wigleaf* tree fort is, so I could say NOT TELLING

EDITOR BIOGRAPHIES

Elaine Chiew is a writer and visual arts researcher. Her short story collection *The Heartsick Diaspora* (Penguin SEA 2019 & Myriad Editions UK 2020) explores the Malaysian and Singaporean Chinese diaspora living primarily in London, New York, and Singapore; it has been mentioned as a recommended read in *The Guardian, The Straits Times Singapore, BookRiot* and *Esquire SG,* been featured in literary festivals in Singapore, Malaysia and Kerala, received a Special Mention in the UK Saboteur Awards and reviewed favourably in Malaysia, Singapore, UK and US. She is also the compiler/editor of *Cooked Up: Food Fiction From Around the World* (New Internationalist, 2015). Twice winner of the Bridport Short Story Competition in the UK, she has had numerous stories published in Singapore, US and UK anthologies, most recently with BBC Radio Four and in *A View of Stars* (Marshall Cavendish, 2020), and shortlisted most recently for The Manchester Short Story Prize. Her articles on arts and culture have appeared in *ArtReview Asia, Ocula* and *ArtsEquator,* and she has made guest appearances on BBC Radio London, Open Book for BBC Radio 4 as well as BBC Cultural Frontline.

Nathan Leslie's ten books of fiction include *Three Men, Root and Shoot* and *The Tall Tale of Tommy Twice.* Nathan's poetry, fiction, essays and reviews have appeared in hundreds of literary magazines including *Boulevard, Shenandoah* and *North American Review.* Previously Nathan was series editor for *Best of the Web* anthology 2008 and 2009 and he edited fiction for *Pedestal Magazine.* He was also interviews editor at *Prick of the Spindle.* Nathan's latest work of fiction, *Hurry Up and Relax,* was just published by Washington Writer's Publishing House after winning its 2019 prize for fiction. He is the founder and host of the monthly Reston Readings Series and he teaches in Northern Virginia. Find Nathan on Facebook and Twitter as well as at Nathanleslie.net.

Michelle Elvy is a writer, editor and manuscript assessor. Her online editing work includes *52|250: A Year of Flash*, *Blue Five Notebook* and *Flash Frontier: An Adventure in Short Fiction*. In 2018, she co-edited *Bonsai: Best small stories from Aotearoa New Zealand*. She was also an associate editor for *Flash Fiction International*. Her poetry, fiction, travel writing, creative nonfiction and reviews have been widely published and anthologized. Her new collection, *the everrumble*, is a small novel in small forms, launched by Ad Hoc Fiction at the UK Flash Fiction Festival in June 2019. Find Michelle at michelleelvy.com.